Praise for *Race the Sands*

"Durst imbues a thrill-filled story about monster racing with impressive thematic depth and a refreshing spectrum of female characters. . . . Durst consistently defies expectations in both plot and characterization while exploring sophisticated themes of found family, integrity, and morality. This excellent epic fantasy will appeal to adult fans of Tamora Pierce and Megan Whalen Turner."

—*Publishers Weekly* (starred review)

"*National Velvet* with monsters and a big helping of palace intrigue, *Race the Sands* is monstrous (literally), heartwarming, and empowering in equal measure. An incredibly fun and inspiring read."

—Katherine Arden, *New York Times* bestselling author of *The Bear and the Nightingale*

"Sarah Beth Durst is one of the most prolific authors I know, yet each of her beautiful stories is infused with exciting action and fully rounded characters whose struggles are both relatable and fantastical. *Race the Sands* is a fast-paced adventure that will have you falling in love with its heroines and the monsters they ride."

—Peter V. Brett, *New York Times* bestselling author of The Demon Cycle

"*Race the Sands* is not only a blistering rush through a brilliantly credible and original fantasy landscape, it's the story of resolve, family, and personal destiny we all need. Highly recommended."

—Julie E. Czerneda, author of *The Gossamer Mage*

"*Race the Sands* is a rousing stand-alone fantasy adventure. . . . If you're in the mood for monsters or racing or a primarily female cast surviving against all odds, *Race the Sands* delivers on all counts, in one delightful package that doesn't require a series commitment!"

—Fantasy Book Critic

"Durst's latest delivers the same sweeping prose and lush world-building as her 'Renthia' series, with strong female protagonists and lively supporting characters. This compelling fantasy will please fans and engage new readers."

—*Library Journal*

"This stand-alone fantasy blends classic horse racing tropes with political fantasy and even a dash of Pokémon."

—*Kirkus Reviews*

"*Race the Sands* is told with Durst's usual flair for deep emotional connections intermingled with people getting gnawed apart by ravenous mystical creatures. Read if: you like some karma in your fantasy; you're not afraid of change; you would absolutely watch monster NASCAR on ESPN the Ocho."

—Lightspeed

Praise for *The Deepest Blue*

"Fans will be eager to reenter Renthia and discover another queen."

—*Booklist* (starred review)

"This intriguing dive into the powers that attempt to control Renthia yields an action-packed fantasy."

—*Library Journal*

"Engaging characters, both good and evil, and magical menaces of all sizes make this a highly enjoyable read. Mayara is every possible trait to root for and deservedly so. What she has to best, be they inner or outer demons, makes this a page-turner."

—SciFi Pulse

"*The Deepest Blue* by Sarah Beth Durst is a beautiful story featuring strong and compassionate characters, a rich setting, and a plot with nonstop action. The writing grabs readers on the first page and doesn't let go until the very end."

—Bookreporter.com

"*The Deepest Blue* is an excellent stand-alone story that will have you looking at the ocean in a whole new light, and one I highly recommend. Read if: you like inspirational female protagonists; you thought *Island of the Blue Dolphins* could do with a lot more violent deaths; you want to unleash the kraken."

—Lightspeed

Praise for *The Queen of Sorrow*

"Durst brings her lavish saga to an emotional and breathtaking end, as this epic tale continues to thrill and enchant until the very last page."

—RT Book Reviews

"The thrilling and sometimes melancholy finale of Durst's Queens of Renthia trilogy. . . . The well-crafted denouement wraps up the entire adventure perfectly."

—*Publishers Weekly* (starred review)

"The Queens of Renthia series . . . concludes with an earth-shattering conflict between three determined queens, two countries, and a multitude of bloodthirsty spirits."

—*Booklist* (starred review)

"Ms. Durst has given us a refreshing, provocative and ultimately convincing remake of modern fantasy conventions. The wonder is that we ever saw things the other way around."

—*Wall Street Journal*

"*The Queen of Sorrow* is . . . filled with intricate battles, a lot of action, intriguing strategies, and an entertaining story. The amazing fantasy characters remain true to themselves."

—Washington BookReview

"With a story focused on powerful women and worldbuilding worthy of Guy Gavriel Kay, this series has been a dark delight."

—B&N Sci-Fi & Fantasy Blog

"*The Queen of Sorrow* is an excellent finale to the trilogy. . . . The Queens of Renthia is a must-read of the genre. Highly Recommended."

—SFFWorld

Praise for *The Reluctant Queen*

"In Durst's excellent second Queens of Renthia fantasy, the world of Renthia remains a dangerous place where the spirits of the elements want to kill humans, and only powerful queens . . . can control them. . . . Durst throws a lot of balls in the air but manages to juggle them deftly. . . . New readers will benefit from starting with the first book, but they'll want to get to this one as soon as they can."

—*Publishers Weekly* (starred review)

"Durst's Renthia continues to fascinate with its very incongruity, juxtaposing idyllic villages and cities built among the trees and the personal journey of the female protagonists with the relentless brutality of the spirits and the ruthless machinations of humans."

—*Kirkus Reviews*

"This sequel to *The Queen of Blood* introduces new protagonists while bringing back familiar characters. Durst's strongly woven story supported by solid worldbuilding will please epic fantasy readers."

—*Library Journal*

"Series fans will be captivated and eager for more of the Queens of Renthia."

—*Booklist*

"This brutal tale continues with an intensity equal to that of the first title in this series, with an immediately emotional and violent opening that will keep readers enthralled to the last page, where a captivating new development will leave them fascinated and ready for more."

—RT Book Reviews

"It is a pleasure to visit Renthia again. Durst paints a gorgeous, leaf-strewn horror house setting that makes it easy to immerse yourself in her world, and stay there (I read it in a single afternoon). It is very much a sequel that amplifies everything the first book did right—your favorite characters are back, in a plot that is in many ways a more intense, mature variation of the first, with higher stakes clearly leading somewhere bigger."

—B&N Sci-Fi & Fantasy Blog

"*The Reluctant Queen* was a fantastic next installment for this trilogy."

—Girls in Capes

Praise for *The Queen of Blood*

American Library Association Alex Award Winner

"What a great story! A truly wonderful fantasy novel which doubles as an allegory for our own earthly struggle between Man and Nature. Filled with fresh ideas and excitement, told with verve and heart. This book deserves a wide readership, and I think it will find one."

—Terry Brooks, *New York Times* bestselling author of the Shannara series

"Thrilling—heartrending—enchanting—absolutely un-put-down-able!"

—Tamora Pierce, *New York Times* bestselling author of the Tortall series

"Mythopoeic Award–winner Durst launches her Queens of Renthia series with a stellar and imaginative tale. . . . In addition to a solid cast of characters and great political intrigue, Durst delivers some fascinating worldbuilding, and the spirits are malevolent, cunning, wild, and mysterious antagonists."

—*Publishers Weekly* (starred review)

"Durst presents a thrilling beginning to a sweeping series about searching for sovereignty and truth in order to save one's land."

—*Library Journal* (starred review)

"Durst dives into adult fantasy with thrilling results."

—*Shelf Awareness* (starred review)

"Durst is an expert world-builder and has crafted an enthralling tale filled with an intriguing ensemble of characters."

—*Washington Post*

"*The Queen of Blood* is full of rich tension from the opening scene to the nail-biting finale."

—Jeff Wheeler, *Wall Street Journal* bestselling author of
the Kingfountain and Muirwood series

"I was up late finishing this book because I just could not stop. This book has been my happy place for the past several days. The world-building and unique system of magic are just brilliantly put together, and this is a good example of a first book in a series that ends with a definite conclusion—no cliffhanger—but still leaves you desperate to find out what happens next. . . . Massively recommended."

—Charlie Jane Anders, award-winning author of
The City in the Middle of the Night

THE
Bone
Maker

THE

Bone
Maker

A NOVEL

SARAH BETH
DURST

HARPER Voyager
An Imprint of HarperCollinsPublishers

THE BONE MAKER. Copyright © 2021 by Sarah Beth Durst. All rights reserved. Printed in the United States of America. No part of this book may be used or reproduced in any manner whatsoever without written permission except in the case of brief quotations embodied in critical articles and reviews. For information, address HarperCollins Publishers, 195 Broadway, New York, NY 10007.

HarperCollins books may be purchased for educational, business, or sales promotional use. For information, please email the Special Markets Department at SPsales@harpercollins.com.

Harper Voyager and design are trademarks of HarperCollins Publishers LLC.

FIRST EDITION

Designed by Paula Russell Szafranski

Frontispiece © Lemberg Vector studio / Shutterstock

Library of Congress Cataloging-in-Publication Data has been applied for.

ISBN 978-0-06-288863-1

21 22 23 24 25   LSC   10 9 8 7 6 5 4 3 2 1

For Deborah Fisher

THE
Bone
Maker

Kreya always wore her coat with many pockets when she went out to steal bones. As she pulled it on, she inhaled the familiar dusty smell. The leather had faded from brilliant blue to indistinct gray, and the hems were frayed, but then, after all this time, she felt faded and frayed too.

She checked the pockets:

Empty.

Empty.

Empty.

Bear claw, with knuckle bone.

She drew it out and examined it. A fracture ran from the knuckle to the tip of the claw. Worse, the carving for strength was cracked and the inlaid gold had fallen out. "Useless," she muttered at it. She tucked it back in its pocket anyway. In another pocket, she found a talisman carved from the femur of a mountain sheep, bearing the symbols for steadiness. The grooves were worn but intact. *Can't weather an avalanche with this*, she thought, *but okay for a climb.* "You'll do," she told it.

She patted more pockets, stopping when she found a third talisman, marked for stealth, and a fourth for strength. She found a few others, mostly drained or damaged from overuse.

She used to have hundreds of them—high-quality ones, not the cheap, ten-minutes-then-done variety—but over the years, her supplies had dwindled. She'd have to replace them soon.

But that required gold she didn't have. A *problem for later,* she told herself. Right now, she had a task. She'd heard whispers of a death in the village of Eren, a child who had slipped off the edge of a cliff while chasing a stray goat and fallen on her neck. The body would be burned at dusk, which meant Kreya had four hours to cross the mountain, sneak into Eren, and position herself to liberate the beautiful bones before they were destroyed.

She raised her voice. "Weather?"

Gears whirred as one of her constructs—a birdlike part-metal-and-part-bone creation—hopped onto a windowsill. As wind whipped inside, it wobbled but didn't fall. Papers on Kreya's desk fluttered, and a quill was blown onto the floor. Reaching out a bony appendage, the construct snagged the weather monitor from the hook on the outside of the tower. As it turned to deliver its prize to Kreya, another burst of wind puffed into the room, and the skeletal bird tumbled off the sill. Kreya lunged forward to catch it, felt a muscle in her back twang, and missed. The construct crashed onto the stone, and a bone in its arm snapped.

Squatting, Kreya scooped it up and cradled it. "You aren't as spry as you used to be either, are you?" It whirred as it tried to right itself in her arms, but she cooed to it. "Calm, little one. Let's see what we can do to fix you up."

Ignoring the fresh ache in her back, she carried the unnatural bird to her workbench, cleared a space with a sweep of one arm, and laid the construct down. It twisted its skull head to look at her with its empty eye sockets. She'd forgotten how long ago she'd made this one, but it had served her well.

It whirred at her, the gears within its rib cage rotating. She'd added them to help its mobility—when she'd first created this construct, it had tried so hard to fly, but without flesh and feathers, it couldn't. Once she added the gears, though, it could propel itself around the tower as fast as it pleased. Deftly, Kreya wrapped the snapped bone in a strip of bark and secured it with resin, smearing it liberally. The resin would harden after a day or so. "You be more careful."

It spun its gears as if it were agreeing with her.

Kreya was never quite certain how much her constructs understood—not much, her old teachers would have said—but that didn't stop her from talking to them. She set the skeleton bird back onto the floor, and it hopped over to the fallen quill. It pecked at the feather, while she examined the weather monitor it had retrieved.

Moisture, normal.

Wind speed, normal.

Stability, high.

There hadn't been a tremor on the mountain in weeks, which boded well for her journey. She left the monitor on the workbench, picked up the fallen quill, and sidestepped around the bird construct. It continued to peck at the carpet where the quill had been, adding yet another hole to the threadbare fabric.

As she descended the spiral stairs, she paused on the third level to check on her husband. He lay, as always, carefully wrapped in white linens. "Tomorrow, we'll watch the sun rise together," she told him. "You'll say something that will make me laugh, and I'll make willow tea that you'll ruin with too much honey. And then we can do whatever you want. Walk in the woods. Mend that step you're forever tripping over. We'll have time."

A construct made from a rag doll and animated with dog bones trotted over to his bed. It patted the linen sheets, smoothing them with its floppy hands.

"Keep an eye on him, please," Kreya told it.

She continued down the stairs, sidestepping another construct. She'd made this one to clean the tower, but it had malfunctioned months—was it years?—ago, and it scrubbed only a single step. Smooth and concave, that one stone gleamed like polished silver. Kreya hadn't had the heart to remove the bones that animated the dutiful, broken creature, and it could be several more years before the last of its power finally wound down. "Beautiful work," she told it.

It made a noise like a purr.

On the ground floor, she lifted the three iron bars that locked the door. She then stepped over the broken step that Jentt liked to complain about. Calling over her shoulder, she said, "Lock!"

It took an extra minute for the bars, powered by bones, to lock back in place. She'd have to examine the mechanism when she had more time. *It's always about time*, Kreya thought. *How much you use, how much you waste, and how much you waste regretting the time you already wasted.*

She'd eaten up precious minutes in preparation, but there was still plenty of time left before dusk. She estimated the hike would take her three and a half hours. If she left now, she should arrive exactly on time. The sun was high between the peaks, casting a golden light on the gray rocks. Picking up her walking stick from beside the door to her tower, Kreya started on the path.

Made by mountain goats, the path wound its way across the rocky face of the mountain before plunging into the pine forest that clung to the slope. Birds chirped cheerfully to one another, unconcerned with the lone hiker who was picking her way through their territory. They startled more when a cable car rattled across the open void between two of the nearest peaks. Kreya halted where she was, hidden within the pines, until the contraption was safely out of sight. Of course it wasn't forbidden to walk at such an altitude, but it was unusual enough to be memorable, and it was safer if Kreya's passage wasn't memorable.

She knew Jentt would have been surprised at how cautious she'd become, but she'd learned her lesson. A cautious bone worker was one who got to see another day.

The last bits of fall were clinging to everything: the aspen leaves were as golden as candle flames, the fallen leaves crunched under her feet, and the berry bushes were heavy with the final fruit of the season. Squirrels and rock mice skittered everywhere, stocking up for winter. Up on the rock faces, wildflowers clung to the crevasses, not yet blanched by frost, and the wild goats nibbled at them, their legs splayed for balance. As she hiked, Kreya tried to enjoy all the beauty around her, but her thoughts kept drifting back to her goal: the village of Eren.

She hadn't set foot in Eren in five years, and she hoped the villagers had forgotten her, or assumed she'd died in the wilderness. It would be best if she didn't have to use the stealth talisman until absolutely necessary. She wasn't certain how much power was left in it. Talismans always burned out far more quickly than her constructs did—the former powered living flesh, while the latter were made from inanimate objects, which made the difference.

Exactly three and a half hours later, as the sun danced lower across the cliffs and crags, Kreya halted at the edge of the forest and looked down on her destination. Charmingly picturesque, the village was nestled on a meadowed slope, framed by pine forest. A mix of stone and wood, the buildings were brightly painted reds, blues, and yellows, with brilliant white trim—as if in defiance of the gray stone mountains all around them.

Once, when she and Jentt had first talked about being together forever, they'd discussed living in a place like this. Jentt had liked how the neighbors all seemed to look out for one another, making sure even the weakest made it through the winter storms and the avalanches and the earthquakes, and Kreya had liked how even the vivid paint color seemed to be saying fuck you to the gray mountains. Later, though, after the war, Kreya couldn't bear to live so close to other people. It reminded her too much of everything she couldn't have.

She lurked within the pine trees now, watching the village for a few moments. All the inhabitants would be gathering by their Cliff of the Dead for the ceremony, but she saw no movement on the streets or between the houses. *They must already be there. Am I too late?*

She didn't smell or see smoke, and the sun had only just touched the edge of the western mountains. The ridgeline glowed orange. As she skirted around the village, she heard pipes playing: at least six or seven musicians of varying skill playing slow and sweet melodies that wove together in a gentle lament. Her fingers moved in the pattern of the notes. She hadn't played since childhood, but she remembered the feel of it, or at least her fingers did. Her heart was beating as fast as the heart of a bird, and she tried to let the familiar music soothe her. So far, no one had seen her, and she'd done nothing to alarm anyone even if they had.

A flock of mountain sheep barely budged from their grazing as she passed them. Ahead she heard murmured voices, like a soft breath of wind beneath the music of the pipes. As she rounded the corner of a bright red barn, she saw the Cliff of the Dead before her: an exposed rock face stained by decades of smoke and ash, with the names of the dead carved into the rock.

As she'd suspected, all the villagers were gathered at the base of the cliff, pressed tightly together. Kreya identified the relatives of the dead girl by their white scarves—the color of winter, the color of death.

Seeing the white, Kreya wanted to flee. *I shouldn't be here.*

These people had lost a loved one. A child. And she was about to intrude on their grief. Granted, if the stealth talisman worked as it should, they'd never even know. But that didn't change the fact that what she was about to do was morally reprehensible.

And illegal. Don't forget that.

There was a reason that the dead were always burned: so that no bone worker would ever be able to desecrate their legacy by using their bones for magic, as she planned to do.

I can't do this.

Flattening against the barn, Kreya tried to calm her racing heart. She breathed in. Out. Methodically, she seized each of her thoughts:

It's wrong.

Yes, it was. Both by the laws of Vos and by basic decency.

It's unfair. A child died! So much life unlived, dreams unfulfilled!

Yes, it was unfair. But so was what had happened to her and Jentt.

It's not what Jentt would want.

That stopped her for a moment. "The child's already dead," Kreya whispered, as if Jentt could hear her. "I didn't cause it, and I can't change it." All she could change was whether the child's end was merely an end, or whether it led to someone else's beginning.

It was an undeniable tragedy. But if she could create good from it, wrestle joy out of sorrow, then that was forgivable, wasn't it? Or at least understandable? Kreya pulled on her fire-resistant gloves, and then, reaching into two of her pockets, she withdrew the talismans for stealth and strength. She held one in each gloved hand.

She felt calmer now. Ready.

The pipe music stopped. A murmured voice, loud enough for the mourners to hear, but not loud enough to carry to where she hid, began to speak.

She peeked around the corner of the barn. They were unwrapping the linen sheets from the body—it would be burned without the wrappings so all would see that the body was whole and intact. Until this moment, it would have stayed wrapped tightly and been guarded as if it were a treasure, which meant that this was her only opportunity.

Smoke curled through the air. She tasted it as she inhaled, and she swallowed back a cough. Through the gaps between the villagers, she glimpsed the fire, growing at the base of the cliff.

She'd have to time it right: strike after the body had begun to burn, when it was dry to the point of being fragile, but before the bones had time to succumb to the heat. She'd use stealth to slip through the crowd and then use strength to remove the limbs.

If all went well, the family would never even know what she'd done. They'd see a blur that they'd mistake for smoke, and then it would be over. She'd steal as much as she could, and the flames would devour what remained, eliminating all evidence that she was ever there.

Her death will give life, Kreya thought, trying to convince herself.

One pipe began to play again, a mournful melody.

She saw the flames leap higher and sparks fly up against the rock face as the body was placed on the pyre. The mourners embraced one another, and Kreya counted silently. One minute, two, three . . .

She kept counting, the pipes kept playing, the mourners cried, and the body burned.

Now.

Breathing a word onto the stealth talisman, Kreya shot out of her hiding place, no more visible than a shadow. Her coat flapped around her, but she weaved through the crowd, moving with them as they spoke softly, words of sympathy and words of comfort—all words that Kreya had heard before, the kind of words that didn't help anyone but had to be said because the silence was worse. A few mourners startled, feeling an unexpected breeze as she passed them, but their eyes darted all around, unable to see her.

Zera always did make the best talismans, Kreya thought. She wished she could thank her old friend, but that would have required explaining what she'd been doing with the power. Also, it meant actually speaking with Zera, which she hadn't done in twenty-five years.

At the pyre, Kreya didn't look at the girl's face. She tried not to think of the corpse as a person at all. Just a collection of ingredients she needed to obtain. Whispering to the strength talisman to activate it as well, she shoved both into her pockets and then grasped the limbs she needed.

The strength of a bear flooded through her, allowing her to yank.

Snap!

One arm bone broke, and she pulled a knife from one of her pockets—

And the magic failed.

She felt it sap out of her, the strength and the stealth simultaneously abandoning her. Around her, she heard the cries of the villagers:

"Thief!"

"Desecrator!"

"Bone worker!"

"Stop her!"

"Grab her!"

"Burn her!"

She hacked at the shoulder, but without the bear strength, she didn't have the force to slice through the burnt flesh. A hand grabbed her arm, and she pulled away, kicking behind her. She felt her foot make impact.

She thought she heard Jentt shouting at her, inside her head: "Run, Kreya! Run!"

Not without you! she cried back.

Abandoning the shoulder, she hacked at the fingers. One snapped off under her blade. She shoved it in a pocket, and then she ran—not into the crowd, but instead around the pyre toward the Cliff of the Dead. As she ran, she yanked out the talisman for steadiness.

Please, work!

She whispered its word.

Kreya didn't slow as she ran straight toward the rock face.

Fueled by the talisman, her feet stuck into the crags and nooks. She climbed as fast as she could. Glancing down, she saw the villagers below her. It was sacrilege to climb a Cliff of the Dead—none would risk angering their beloved lost ones.

But that did not stop them from throwing rocks.

The first hit the stone beside her and shattered. She felt her grip slip. *Don't fail me!* Continuing to climb, she pushed herself up higher and higher. Her arms began to shake, and her palms were sweating within the gloves. She didn't know how long the talisman would last. It had been weak to begin with, and she was draining it fast.

Another rock hit. Even closer.

She kept climbing. She could see the top—

The third rock hit between her shoulder blades. She cried out, but she made herself keep climbing. Another rock hit beside her. One grazed her ankle.

Her fingers reached up and touched grass. Clawing at the soil, she kept pushing until she heaved herself over the edge. Panting, she lay there. Her arm muscles were screaming.

Cheek pressed into the dirt and grass, she felt the ground vibrate. Quake? Or people—running up a path, toward the top of the cliff, toward her. She scrambled shakily to her feet. Reaching into her pockets, she felt for another talisman. Strength. Speed. Anything.

Her fingers closed over the carved bear knuckle and claw, and she activated it with a whispered word. She felt cool relief flood through her body, and she had the strength to run.

She fled into the pine forest, fueled by magic. Branches whipped against her, and Kreya felt a sting on her cheek as one bit into her. She reached up and touched wetness—blood. But she didn't slow. She heard crashing behind her, the villagers chasing her, and she knew she couldn't lead them straight to her tower, where Jentt waited for her. Her constructs couldn't defend against a mob. Or, really, anything more dangerous than an errant cobweb—she hadn't designed them for that. She'd counted on stone walls and isolation to protect her, but that wouldn't hold against angry and determined mourners.

I'm sorry, she wanted to tell them. *But I need her bones more than she did.*

She didn't know if she'd even been able to salvage enough to make a difference, and she couldn't check now. Her lungs burned, her legs ached, and the spot between her shoulder blades throbbed. Some of her pursuers were quite a bit younger, and they had rage to urge them on. Most of her rage had burned out years ago.

But the bit she had left wasn't going to fade.

Kreya weighed her options. She knew the mountain as well as or better than these villagers who never ventured beyond their sheep pastures. If she had the right talismans—*I should've been more prepared.* She thought of the waste of all those beautiful bones, rich with power, burned to ash by now.

What's done is done. Now, focus!

She heard the rattle of the cable car. For an instant, she imagined herself leaping from a cliff onto the top of it and riding it away from her pursuers. Maybe Jentt could have done that, years ago. He'd been capable of manipulating talismans to pull off amazing feats. She knew her limitations, though, and part of that was the lack of any usable talismans. Instead, she used the rattle of the cable car to hide the sound of her switching direction—she veered left, between the trees, crashing through branches without fear of being heard.

Ahead she knew the path turned right, but instead she went straight toward a collection of rocks. Her lungs were screaming, and she was sure she'd pay for this tomorrow. Of course, that depended on whether or not she lived to see tomorrow. She knew what the people of Vos did to bone workers caught stealing human bones.

She had no doubt the villagers had left the fire burning for her.

Kreya saw the outcropping ahead of her. She forced herself to run faster, as the cable car rattled louder overhead. She spurted across a meadow and then ducked between the rocks.

Shaking, she leaned flat against one rock. Her breath raked across her throat, and her vision became speckled with black dots. The world tilted, and she squeezed her eyes shut.

Don't faint. Not now.

She heard her pursuers shout to one another as they crashed out of the woods. They'd reached the meadow. She didn't know if any of them were good enough trackers to spot the direction in which she'd run. She knew she couldn't count on incompetence to save her, though in her experience the incompetence of people was surprisingly reliable.

Move, she told herself.

She peeled herself off the rock where she'd been leaning, and she plunged deeper between the rocks, into the caves she knew were there. She'd discovered them several years ago, after being caught in a thunderstorm. She'd returned a few times to map them. It had kept her occupied one summer while she waited for news of a fresh corpse.

Keeping her hand on one wall, Kreya hurried into the cave. As the evening light disappeared behind her, she slowed, picking her way deeper into the mountain.

Shouts came from behind her, at the cave entrance.

Kreya didn't slow. The odds that the villagers knew these

caves, that they'd risk entering without knowing if there were crevasses that could swallow them or unstable rocks that could fall and crush them, were low. She hadn't seen anyone holding a lantern or torch. *Their smartest bet would be to seal the cave entrance*, she thought.

If they caused a rockfall, then they'd either crush her or trap her. A sensible option. She didn't know, though, if any of the villagers were thinking sensibly after the death of one of their children. But she couldn't control what other people thought; she could only control what she did, and what she did was not stop.

Left.

Right.

Right.

Pressing against the rock wall, she skirted around a drop she knew was there. She slowed even more as the cave dipped downward, careful to keep her footing on the loose pebbles.

Behind her, she heard a rumble and a crash.

The villagers had collapsed the entrance after all.

Smart, she thought. *Just not smart enough.*

She followed the caves unerringly through the dark, until she saw a sliver of graying light ahead of her. Moonlight. Climbing over fallen rocks, she emerged into the night, many miles from the village.

Standing, Kreya looked up at the moon, three-quarters full and heavy over the mountains, and the stars, splattered across the sky. She reached into her pocket and drew out the dead girl's finger. It was only a sliver. Even less bone than she'd hoped.

At best, it would give them a day.

Ash flaked away and was caught by the wind and carried off the side of the mountain. Far below, the deadly valley that ran throughout Vos between the mountains was invisible, shrouded in shadowy mist. It would swallow the ash, eventually. Her hand closed around the tiny bit of charred flesh and bone.

All this—the wasted magic, the painful chase, the villagers' rage, the ruined cave entrance. All of it for a single day.

I'll take a day, she thought.

CHAPTER TWO

Kreya cleaned the sliver of bone. She laid it in a box that had been made for jewels, closed the lid, and locked it. She then sank into a chair with a half sigh, half moan.

As if concerned about her, the bird skeleton hopped around her feet.

Peeling off her shirt, she twisted to view her back in the cloudy mirror on the table beside her. During the night, while she'd slept fitfully and uncomfortably, a vicious flower of purple had blossomed between her shoulder blades where the rock had hit. "Jentt will have questions about that," she muttered.

She eased her shirt back on, after checking to be sure the rock hadn't broken skin. *Or my ribs. Or lungs.* Lifting her foot, she examined her ankle next. Another developing bruise, plus it had been skinned. Dots of blood had dried along the scrape. On the plus side, she felt whole, if achy. Her muscles would probably throb for days.

If Jentt saw her like this . . .

He's seen me worse. Of course, that had been during a war, and he hadn't exactly been sanguine whenever she'd been injured then.

She should wait until the bruises faded and her muscles

felt less like quivery goo. But it had been months since she'd spoken with her husband and had him answer, months since she'd been able to look into his eyes, months since she'd seen his smile. She didn't want to wait any longer.

"And they say the young are impatient," Kreya said to the bird construct.

Patience, she decided, is for people unaware of their own mortality.

She permitted herself a few more minutes of rest before propelling herself out of the chair. Shuffling across the room, she pulled several books from the shelf and piled them on her makeshift bed.

After a few years of failing to sleep near Jentt's body, she'd taken to sleeping in the library and had built a bed out of quilts and blankets that looked more like a nest than a proper piece of furniture. It was nestled in the corner of two bookshelves. In another corner was the stove where she prepared the bulk of her meals. Despite the size of the tower, this one room was where she spent most of her time. It was comforting to be surrounded by so many books, as if the past experience of all the authors could protect her from the unknown future. She loved the smell of the room, with that distinctive old paper and old binding-glue scent, mixed with dust. She'd spent years collecting these volumes. Many of them were one-of-a-kind. A few shouldn't even have existed.

Kreya reached to the back of the shelf, unlatched the hidden door, and pulled out a black metal box. Running her fingers over the lid, she couldn't suppress a shudder. When she'd stolen these books, she'd planned to destroy them. Their author had poured everything he knew into his journals—knowledge he'd used to inflict horrors. No one knew she hadn't burned them, though.

Certainly no one knew she'd read them. Studied them. Found a way to use them.

Knowledge itself isn't evil. It's how you use it. And she had a very good use for it. Opening the box, she lifted out the top book.

Given the atrocities committed by the author, the book should have been bound in human skin, for the sake of the appropriate level of melodrama. But it was ordinary cloth, as threadbare as the carpet, with scorch marks on the spine. The pages were stained and brittle, and Kreya turned them carefully. She'd pored over them so much that she had most of it memorized, but this was too important to trust to that. A mistake would be unforgivable, and she wasn't taking any chances when it came to Jentt, especially when she had so small a bit of bone to work with.

She read the words silently, mouthing each syllable. It was more complex than anything she'd learned through the Bone Workers Guild—"A perversion of our purpose," the master teachers there would have said.

"They're not wrong," Kreya told the skeleton bird, who was pecking at the carpet again, pulling stray threads as if prompted by a memory of worms. She let it continue, her focus back on the book. The techniques in it were not approved by any guild.

In fact, the guild didn't know they existed.

As far as the guild was concerned, there were only three types of bone workers: bone readers, who used animal bones to reveal the future, understand the present, and glimpse the past; bone wizards, who created talismans out of animal bones that imbued their users with strength, speed, stealth, and other attributes; and bone makers, like Kreya, who used animal bones to animate the inanimate. Ships, weaving machines, cable cars . . . all the advances of the past few centuries had been fueled by bone makers. She could have had her pick of commissions after the war. Instead, she'd turned them all down, shut herself away in this tower, and devoted herself to studying these books.

Now she mouthed the words she'd need and then carefully closed the book, placed it back in the metal box, and returned it to its hiding place at the back of the bookshelf. While all knowledge could be dangerous in the wrong hands, Kreya considered it simple practicality to be extra careful with books written by genocidal maniacs. Especially books you'd sworn to destroy. It was just common sense.

"Want to watch?" she asked the bird construct.

It whirred its gears, confused by the question.

"Come on."

It followed her down the stairs and into the bedroom where Jentt lay. Startled, three rag doll constructs climbed the curtains and scrambled onto the beams that crisscrossed the ceiling. They peered down with button eyes.

"Such bravery," Kreya said. "What would you have done if I were an intruder?"

The three dolls stared down at her, chittering to one another in a language that, near as Kreya could determine, wasn't a language at all. They were simply imitating sounds they heard, mashed in their cloth mouths.

"Never mind. Stay there, if you like." She pulled a tray next to the bed and set the jewelry box with the bone on it, beside her favorite knife.

Only then did she let her eyes fall on her husband.

He was clothed in linen sheets from head to toe. Gently, she unpinned them and pushed them back from his arms, his torso, his legs, and his face. It had been three months since she'd last woken him, and it showed. His cheeks were sunken, his skin gray, and his chest had collapsed so every rib was visible. She'd tucked sachets of lavender beneath the mattress to mask the stench, and she'd instructed her rag doll constructs to bathe him daily to keep him free of maggots and other indignities of death, but that only did so much.

"You look terrible," she told him. "Never wear gray."

She reached for the knife and realized her hand was trembling. Glaring at it, she held her wrist steady until it stopped. She'd overused her muscles climbing that rock face, even with the talisman helping her.

I really should wait, she thought.

But looking at her husband's gray-toned face, she knew she wouldn't.

Closing her hand over the knife's handle, she lifted it up and, in one swift movement, sliced her palm. She winced at the sting but didn't take her eyes off her husband's face. Squeezing her hand, she made blood well into her fist, then she laid down the knife and opened the jewelry box with her uncut hand. She smeared her blood onto the bit of bone.

"Take my day, take my night, take my sunrise, take my life." She lifted the bit of bone, stained with her blood, and then took the knife again and sliced over her husband's heart.

It didn't bleed.

She pressed the bit of bone into his flesh and then covered the wound with her bloody hand. "Take my breath, take my blood. *Iri nascre, murro sai enri. Iri prian, murro ken fa. Iri sangra sheeva lai. Ancre murro sai enzal. Iri, iri, nascre ray.*"

The bit of bone dissolved with her words, melting into his flesh like sugar in water.

Outside, the wind hit the tower, and the windows shivered. The rag doll constructs crooned to one another in their senseless language. Kreya felt a shudder run through her body. It was hard to breathe, but she made herself hold still, her hand pressed to Jentt's chest as the bone magic spread through him. Her muscles began to shake.

See, I was right, she thought. *I should have waited.* One night's sleep wasn't enough recovery time for this drain. The drain of a magic that she wasn't supposed to use, that wasn't even supposed to be possible . . .

But she locked her knees and didn't sag.

Beneath her hand, his body began to change. It plumped as the flesh was restored. She felt his heart—a stutter and then a steady beat. Blood began to flow through his veins, and the gray faded from his skin.

She'd never been able to grant life to any of her constructs. That wasn't how it worked. A bone maker's magic only animated them. But this . . . this was different. She wasn't giving him the power of the bone like she did with constructs. Here she was using the bone to give him what was inside her. That was the key, and the secret, of the resurrection spell.

For each day he lived again, she would live one day less.

Worth it, she thought. *A thousand times worth it.*

His face was his own again, with flesh thick and healthy over his bones. It wasn't the illusion of life. It was life itself. Restored. She waited, barely breathing, for his eyes to open. At last, they did. He blinked them open, looked at her, and then looked beyond her.

"Fuck, those things are creepy," Jentt said.

She twisted to look up at the rafters, where now five of her rag doll constructs peered down at them. "Useful, though. Especially when you're indisposed."

"Oh? Is that what we're calling it now? 'Indisposed'? Like I ate a bad fish?"

"You looked like a bad fish."

"Nice." He pushed himself, slowly, gingerly, up to sitting, and looked down at his chest, which was streaked with a thin smear of blood. He wrinkled his nose. "And I assume the smell of rotting fish is me, too. Sorry. Is there time for a bath?"

Kreya's heart gave a little lurch. She knew what that question really meant: *How long will I live this time?* She wished she didn't have to answer. Her mouth felt dry as she tried to formulate the words to tell him as gently as she could.

She didn't have to tell him. He read it in her face. He guessed, "An hour?"

"A day. If we're lucky."

"A day," he repeated, then he smiled at her and covered her hand with his. "I'll take a day." The look in his eyes made her feel more alive than she'd felt in months. She smiled back, and all the lonely hours and days fell away. He added, "And I'll take a bath."

She helped him stand. His balance wasn't the best after he first woke, but the spell had returned all his muscles—he'd be able to walk on his own in minutes.

"What time is it?" he asked.

"Nearly dawn."

"Excellent. So we can watch the sunrise together. Unless it's raining. Or snowing. What time of year is it?"

Again, he wasn't asking the key question, which was, *How long was I dead?*

"It's fall," she said. "Same year." He leaned on her as they hobbled across the room, and she hissed as his hand touched the bruise on her back.

He stopped. "You're hurt."

"I had some challenges."

"Do I want to know?"

"You really don't." She hoped that would be the end of it. She didn't want to spend his one day of life arguing about whether she took too many risks for him. "I used up most of the remaining talismans—"

"I told you their power diminishes with use—"

"Are you seriously saying 'I told you so'? Because I did not wake you in order to listen to a sanctimonious lecture about how you were so much more careful than I am when you're the one who got himself killed."

He fake-staggered as if her words had wounded him. She sagged as his weight shifted and then shrugged him off. He was strong enough to stand on his own. Arms crossed, an exaggerated frown on her face, she waited while he righted himself. "You know it's only that I worry about you," he said. "Or I would worry, if I weren't so busy decomposing."

"Very funny."

"You're smiling."

She was. She couldn't help it. He was alive again! Following him down the stairs, she watched him pause when he reached the cleaning construct.

"Good work," he told it.

It purred.

She smiled again. *My Jentt.*

Sidestepping the construct, he let himself into the bathroom. She washed her hands and bound her cut with clean cotton—

she'd have another scar to add to her collection, a spiderweb-like array on her palm—while he filled the bath. The water came from a tank of rainwater collected at the top of the tower and traveled through pipes, warming as they passed the stove. If you wanted a hot bath, you could boil individual pots of water, but this worked well enough for a lukewarm soak. She'd stolen the idea from the guild headquarters in Cerre. They'd had far larger stoves, furnaces, that heated the water more effectively, but she was still proud of her contraption. Jentt had helped her install it a few years ago, when he'd lived for a full month.

He undressed and submerged himself in the bath. She watched him bathe, drinking in the sight of him, which, she thought, was probably as creepy as the rag doll constructs watching him come back to life. Stopping her ogling, Kreya crossed to the window and opened the bathroom shutters.

Outside, it was predawn gray. Lemon yellow teased at the ridges of the mountains.

"You know I'm naked, don't you?" Jentt asked. "What will the neighbors think?"

"You know we have no neighbors." She loved how easily she slipped back into saying "we." She rolled the word around in her mind: *We, we, we.* Leaning out the window, she inhaled. It was perfect crisp fall air, smelling of pine.

"The birds might be scandalized."

She heard water splash and knew he was climbing out of the tub. He padded across the floor, and she felt his arms wrap around her waist. "Should we scandalize them properly?" she asked.

He laughed softly and kissed her neck.

They made love on the bathroom floor. He didn't say a word

about the bruise on her back, but he was gentle. She loved him all the more for that.

Outside, the sun rose.

AT SUNSET, THEY CLIMBED TO THE TOP OF THE tower and leaned side by side against the water tank to watch the sun kiss the western mountains. Golden light spread over the slopes, while half the mountains were already in shadows.

"You can't keep doing this," Jentt said, "especially without working talismans."

"I'll get more talismans."

"How? You haven't taken a commission in . . . Years? It must be years. Have you even been asked? Does anyone know you're here, or do they all assume you've joined me in the great silence?"

Kreya didn't answer that. Instead, she leaned her head against his shoulder. The sun was staining the sky a burnt amber, and the rocks were glowing rose. "I'll find a way."

"You'll get yourself killed."

"Not if I'm careful."

"You need someone to watch your back. When I'm dead, do you speak to anyone? Anyone at all? Because I feel a hermit vibe from this tower that wasn't there a decade ago."

"I haven't hosted a dinner party in a while, if that's what you're asking. Last time I invited all the woodland creatures, but the squirrels trashed the library. I won't even describe what the raccoons did." She kept her voice light but couldn't bring herself to look at him. It was going to happen any time now. She'd seen the weakness in him as they'd climbed the last set of stairs. His arm was limp around her.

"Please tell me you're joking."

"Half the guests left in a huff because I served venison."

"You need to let me go." He kissed her silver hair, and she felt his breath warm on her scalp. "Leave this place. Be around living people again."

"You're living."

"You know this can't last forever."

She knew far better than he did. But she wasn't going to say that out loud. "All I need are enough bones, and it can last. Not forever. But enough." She wondered if it would ever be enough, or if everyone, when they died, felt their life was too short, too fast, too unfair. Turning her head, she studied his profile. He was watching the sun spill onto the mountain ridge.

"So we're hoping for a natural disaster? Earthquake? Avalanche?" His voice was light, and she knew he was joking. Her Jentt would never want any harm to befall anyone.

"Body recovery would be difficult. How about a plague?"

He nixed that. "Chance of contagion. How about a war?"

"Already did that." Kreya touched his cheek. "I didn't like what it cost me."

"But if we're noncombatants this time . . ." His voice failed him as the joke ceased being funny to either of them. He swallowed. She felt his breath shudder against her.

Gently, she said, "It's time to go downstairs."

"I'd hoped—" He stopped. Tried again. "To see. The sun. Set."

"When you wake again, we'll watch sunset after sunset until you're sick of them." She helped him to his feet. *We waited too long*, she thought. They stumbled toward the stairs. He fell against the doorway.

"Open windows. Please. I want. To see it. Tonight. In case, last time."

Haltingly, they stumble-walked down the stairs. She guided him into the bedroom. His jaw opened and closed as if he wanted to say more, but speech had left him. With her assistance, he lay down on the bed, on top of the linen sheets. She kissed his forehead, his nose, his lips.

She then crossed to the window and opened it.

A drop of sun remained. Blood red on the ridgeline. Above, the sky was a fierce orange, and the rocks gleamed like bronze. "See? We didn't miss it." Kreya turned back to Jentt as she spoke those words.

He lay lifeless on the bed.

CHAPTER THREE

Kreya stood by the window, her back to the bed, while the rag dolls wrapped her husband in the linen sheets. The night breeze smelled sweet. Closing her eyes, she breathed it in and tried not to choke on the loneliness that burned in her throat. Her hands curled into fists.

Behind her, the dolls murmured to one another, and Kreya wanted to scream with every cell in her body. But she didn't. She merely stood, eyes shut, facing the window, as her constructs finished covering his body.

Every time he died again it was harder to take. *This can't go on*, she thought. Not emotionally. And not practically, since she was out of talismans. She couldn't steal more bones without them.

Jentt had joked, but he was right: they needed a natural disaster. Nothing else would provide both the quantity of bones she needed and enough chaos to steal them. But it was too terrible to hope for the deaths of many to save the life of one, and as badly as she missed Jentt, she couldn't wish that fate on anyone.

I don't want anyone to have to feel like this.

There had been so much loss already. She'd seen it first-hand twenty-five years ago. In the Bone War. Hundreds had died at the hands of Eklor's grotesque army before Kreya and Jentt's team began their final attack. *We've already had a war in my lifetime. I'd never wish for another.*

So much death.

So many bones, she thought.

"Don't think about that," Kreya warned herself.

It wasn't a new idea, but it was a bad one. When she'd first started down this path to save Jentt, she'd promised herself to never consider it. She'd bring him back with bits of stolen bone from nearby villages instead—which was exactly what she'd been doing ever since she'd cracked the secret.

But that was before she'd used up all her talismans. And before she'd nearly been caught.

Before those bones were no longer available to her.

She opened her eyes. The stars speckled the sky, and the mountains were full of shadows. In the war, hundreds had died, and their bodies had rotted on the plains beyond the mountains. Due to the severity of Eklor's infraction, it was ruled illegal to venture onto the plains, even to burn the dead. The guild master supported this, both in words and in action—by funding the construction of a vast wall and assisting in supplying it with armed guards, in perpetuity. Eklor had been one of their own, before "the unfortunate incident" (as the guild phrased it), or before he became a homicidal maniac (as Kreya would have put it), and Kreya suspected the guild had donated a lot of gold in the aftermath to deflect blame and assuage guilt. Also, to keep ordinary people from realizing the depths to which he'd sunk— and the full extent of the horrors that an immoral bone maker with enough skill could commit.

They figured it out anyway, Kreya thought.

Regardless, the law remained: it was punishable by death to cross into the so-called "forbidden zone."

"A bit of an on-the-nose name," she said out loud.

The rag dolls crooned as if they'd understood her.

"Do you think Guild Master Lorn drops his voice an octave when he mentions it? 'My friends, we need to guard'"—Kreya lowered her voice—"'the forbidden zone!' 'Be afeared of'"—low voice again—"'the forbidden zone!' He absolutely says 'afeared.' And all his sycophants nod along and then send more soldiers to guard the dead. Asshole. Those people deserved for their ashes to rest in their own Cliffs of the Dead. Their families should have gotten proper goodbyes." It was the guild master's cowardice that had prevented them from having the peace they deserved.

Which meant that the bones were still there, even after twenty-five years, waiting for her.

She knew Jentt would agree with her about the guild master. She also knew he would hate what she was thinking about doing. He never wanted her to risk herself.

One of the rag dolls let out a trill, to signify they'd finished rewrapping her husband. And as if the finality of that act signaled the start of a new one, Kreya made the decision to cross yet another line she'd sworn never to cross. "Sorry, Jentt. But that asshole's cowardice might save your life. And besides, if I get myself killed, you won't ever know."

Pivoting, Kreya strode past her husband's linen-wrapped body without looking at him.

A little voice inside whispered, *This is a stupid idea.* That same little voice had told her not to keep the books that let her save Jentt. It had told her not to study them, not to steal her first bone, not to pervert nature by violating the permanence of death. By now, she was an expert at ignoring it.

What she couldn't ignore was the fact that if she was going to cross the mountains and sneak past the guild's soldiers over the barrier wall, she'd need power. Lots of it.

Her first step had to be to acquire more talismans. In truth, that had to be the first step in any plan. Even if she wanted to continue stealing shards of bone from nearby villages, she'd need new talismans. *If I get to the wall and chicken out, they'll still be useful*, she thought, climbing the stairs to the library.

Crossing to her desk, she checked her stash of gold: pathetic.

"Can't buy them." Besides, even if she had enough to buy from the traveling merchants that crisscrossed the mountains, the quality wouldn't be as high as the ones she'd had—the ones made by her old friend Zera. The majority of bone wizards created talismans that only lasted for short spurts, but Zera . . . Her talismans could weather multiple uses and be used for sustained lengths of time before they cracked. She was an artist.

Years ago, Zera had been their team's own bone wizard, supplying them with a steady stream of talismans, culled from nearly every animal imaginable and carved with elaborate spells of her invention. She'd also been Kreya's closest friend.

Had been. Past tense.

"Maybe it's time for a reunion."

The bird construct whirred behind her.

"You'll have to keep watch over the tower while I'm gone. Keep watch over Jentt. It'll take me a few days to reach Cerre." Zera lived on the fifth tier of the city. Or she had. It was possible that Zera had moved. Or died. But Kreya didn't think that was likely. "I'd have heard. Zera's a famous hero, after all. People love to gossip about famous heroes."

She cringed, remembering some of the gossip from back in

the day. A few of the "songs" about Kreya and Jentt had been appalling.

Kreya hauled out her travel pack. She began to stuff it with the essentials for travel: leather-reinforced pants, underthings, climbing gear . . . only to pause, once more second-guessing herself. Visiting the city wasn't the same as hiking across the mountains. Kneeling in front of a chest, she opened it and rifled through until she found a silken shirt and embroidered slippers, the only fancy clothes she still owned. She pulled them out and laid them on her desk, on top of the strewn papers.

Touching the fabric, she remembered the last time she'd worn this: on a visit to the Tririan Waterfall. She and Jentt dined in the glass-globe restaurant, suspended in the middle of the falls itself, with the water cascading all around the glass. The spots that discolored the shirt were from drops of water sprayed by the falls when they'd crossed the bridge into the globe. She remembered the waiter had apologized, but she hadn't cared. She'd been too transfixed by the way the curve of the glass and the spray of the falls caught the sunlight. It felt like being encased in a million rainbows.

She couldn't wear it again, not without Jentt. She put it back in the chest, along with the embroidered slippers. She'd worn those on their first wedding anniversary, before the war.

Zera would have to take her as she was.

If she takes me at all, Kreya thought.

THE TRIP TO CERRE STARTED WITH A TREK DOWN the mountain by switchback trails, followed by a cable car ride across the crevasse of Triault and another up the slope of Androus. She then hiked the highway of Renntak, which had been cut into the rocky side of the massive Mount Eirr. She could have hitched a ride, but that would have required talking to people, and she was in no mood for that. Better to have the company of her own mind and memories than to bear the weight of others with all their curiosity, indifference, and expectations for her behavior. She kept her coat with many pockets tight around her, acutely aware of how empty those pockets were and how useless they'd be if she ran into trouble. But the journey went smoothly, and she arrived in Cerre without incident five days after she'd left.

The famous city was carved into the stone, with its renowned aqueducts creating its shape: arch after arch in multiple tiers, like an elaborate cake. Its people lived in houses that jutted out of the mountain, with more rooms carved into the rock—the richest in vast palaces that put the word "cave" to shame. Diamonds, rubies, and emeralds adorned nearly every building, though Kreya had heard rumors that most of the gems had been replaced with glass to fund the hobbies of the aristocrats. Regardless, it still glittered, dripping with the illusion of wealth, in the morning light.

"Hate this place," Kreya muttered.

She adjusted the pack on her shoulders and trudged toward the first gate.

Every tier had its own gate, to separate the wealthy from the riffraff. The first gate, which led to the lowest level, was only loosely guarded. Farmers, goatherders, travelers, and visitors flowed beneath the blue-painted arch while three red-clad guards watched for anyone who looked suspicious—or, more accurately, anyone who irritated the guards enough for them to stir from their cushioned benches. Kreya kept her head down and lips pressed shut.

The number of people in the first tier made her skin crawl.

It felt as if everyone were chattering at the same time, oblivious to the fact that it meant no one was listening. Shopkeepers were hawking their wares to passersby. Passersby were gabbing to one another, or else shouting at one another to move out of the way. Kids were running through the streets and splashing through the fountains without any heed for, well, anything.

She used to love coming to the city with Zera and Jentt and watching all the people. Now she couldn't help but look at everyone and wonder what loss they were hiding. All of it— all the rushing, all the shouting—felt tinged with frenetic desperation.

Or maybe it's just me, Kreya thought.

She passed by the second gate using a false name, one of several she'd used before. The guards found it in their records and let her pass. The second tier was for the middle class: merchants, academics, and artisans, for the most part. The bulk of the people of Cerre lived split between the first and second tiers.

In the third tier were the headquarters of the guilds who ruled Vos, as well as all the institutions of higher learning. The University of Cerre and the Great Library were both in the third tier, sheathed in their gold (i.e., painted yellow) walls and diamond (i.e., studded with glass) décor, as well as the teaching hospital and the official guild headquarters of the bone workers, the glassworkers, the mechanics, the merchants, and so forth. It was calmer than the first two tiers, with fewer people clogging the streets and fewer shops for anyone to linger over. People came to the third tier purely to study and work.

She'd spent over a year of her training in that library, reading up on the great bone makers of the past. Passing by its doors, she was tempted to go inside. She wondered if any of the librarians she remembered were still there and if they'd remember her—and if they'd remember her as the student she'd been or as the mythic (and missing) hero she had become.

Afraid it would be the latter, she didn't stop.

At the fourth gate, her belongings were searched, including every pocket of her coat. She waited while they compared her face to a sketchbook that held the likeness of everyone approved for entry into the fourth tier.

The sketch was old, but it passed, under a different false name.

The wealthy lived in the fourth tier, and it showed.

Kreya was able to ride a moving platform, powered by bones, to the fifth gate. The fifth and final tier held the true elites: Those with unfathomable wealth, fame, and power. The masters of the various guilds. The owners of the theaters. The heads of the financial powerhouses. And several of Vos's most valued and beloved bone workers, such as Zera.

This gate wasn't a vast arch like the others. It was a single door of thick iron, with guards on either side and above it. She suspected there were other guards, archers, positioned out of sight, awaiting the signal of the gatekeepers.

She couldn't give any of the names she'd used for the prior gates. There was only one name that would grant her access here: Her own.

But once she gave it, word would spread. It would be known that Kreya Odi Altriana, the legendary bone maker who had disappeared over a decade ago, was alive and back. Whispers would spread. Rumors would start. And she'd have to find a way to vanish from the public imagination all over again, if she wanted any peace.

"It will be worth it," she told herself.

Hopefully.

"Ma'am?" one of the guards said. He eyed her threadbare coat, hiker's boots, and leather-reinforced pants. "You are aware this area is restricted?"

"No area is restricted to me," Kreya said.

And she gave him her name.

The expression on the guard's face almost made it worth it.

They consulted their books, and each other, but it wasn't long before she passed through the gate into the fifth tier.

If the fourth tier was known to be decadent as sugar cake, then the fifth tier was like sugar cake drizzled with honey and soaked in chocolate sauce. Kreya stepped onto a disc of white stone carved to resemble a cloud, and it lifted her up the slope of the street. "No one told them this was absurd?"

Men and women, traveling on their own ridiculous "cloud" lifts, stared at her. She met their gazes until they blushed and looked away. She knew how she appeared to them: ragged, travel-worn. *I probably smell.* Subtly, she raised her arm and sniffed. *Definitely smell.*

In contrast, they were swathed in layers of Liyan silk, undoubtedly imported from the lake islands beyond Vos and woven by elite weavers who created their magnificent fabric in absolute silence. From the shimmer, the thread looked to be spun gold. Kreya had worn such a garment exactly once. It had ended up spattered in blood, the day Eklor had announced his intention to wage his war against the Bone Workers Guild and anyone who supported them. She had lost interest in wearing silk wraps after her favorite mentor had bled to death at her feet and she'd been unable to save him.

She did not enjoy the memories that the fifth tier brought back.

Switching onto a new cloud lift, Kreya traveled in a spiral up to the palatial home of her friend. She remembered the location perfectly, but as she was carried to the arched entrance, she didn't recognize anything else about it. Years ago, Zera's palace had been an elegant apartment, expensive but tasteful, with a spectacular view.

"The view is still nice," Kreya said.

The word "tasteful," though, did not apply.

Murals of either gems or colored glass covered the exterior, which would have been fine if the gems weren't in the shape of animal, bird, and fish skeletons. Worse were the statues that clogged the gardens. Dozens of them. Each was a white stone carving of an animal, with its skeleton outlined in gold inlay.

Subtlety had never been Zera's strength, but this was impressive in its hit-you-over-the-head way of announcing a bone wizard lived here. *Couldn't she have just invested in a sign?* she thought.

Sidestepping between the statues, Kreya approached the entrance. Before she could knock, the door, which was flanked with more skeleton-themed statues, flew open. A woman with shockingly bright multicolored hair in a gold silk robe beamed at her.

"Kreya!" Zera cried.

"Hello, Zera."

Zera looked her up and down. "You look terrible."

"And you look ridiculous."

Maybe this is going to be all right, she thought. She didn't let go of the ball of worry in the pit of her stomach, though.

"Just so we're clear, I'm not embracing you until you've had a bath." Zera wrinkled her nose, which caused her makeup to crinkle. She'd painted her cheeks in streaks of gold, and her eyelids were ruby red. "But I think it's fantastic you're not dead."

"I'm not dead," Kreya agreed. "Glad you're not either."

Zera flashed a smile that reminded Kreya of all the jewels in the city winking in the sun. And suddenly Kreya knew everything was *not* going to be all right. It was a false smile, the kind Zera used to use on potential buyers or on bandits to distract them before Jentt and Stran, the warriors of their team, attacked. She'd never, ever used that smile on Kreya.

Shit, Kreya thought.

"A hundred curious eyes are watching us," Zera said gaily. "Come inside where only half that many will stare at us, and you can tell me what you've been doing the past twenty-five years, why you've never contacted me in all that time, and what brings you here now."

Kreya heard the edge in her voice, beneath the bubbles.

Definitely not happy.

She let Zera guide her inside anyway.

Half-naked men and women of varying ages lounged around the salon, reclining on couches between pillars shaped like animal skeletons—when Zera liked a theme, she apparently went for it. A shirtless man played a harp by a pond with one of the fake waterfalls that cascaded from a vaulted ceiling into a koi pond. Two women played a child's game with grape-size balls and circles drawn on a marble table. It smelled like cloying flowers and reminded Kreya of the unforgettable taste of poisoned wine. With all the tiny waterfalls (pouring out of vases, out of sculptures, and out of mosaic walls), it sounded as if two dozen people were simultaneously peeing on the floor.

"You live like this?" Kreya asked before she stopped herself.

"*You* are judging *me*," Zera said in a singsong voice. Her diamond smile hadn't faded, which was not a good sign. "How delightfully droll from someone who looks as if she climbed the aqueduct pipes to get here. You do realize you're wearing the same coat you wore twenty-five years ago? Your hair hasn't been cut or combed in that long either. And you left without a word, without a goodbye, and never once reached out to see if I was all right."

"It all—well, I'll be blunt—*stinks*."

She's not wrong. Except about the hair. Kreya recalled instructing a construct to hack half of it off a few years ago, after she noticed silver strands sticking to her shirts. "You look like you've done all right." She waved at her golden silk scarflike clothes, the multiple waterfalls, and the random assortment of lounging partially dressed people. "But I am sorry for leaving without a goodbye. It was just too painful—"

"And you're the only one whose pain matters, of course. Tell me, Kreya: did you come after all this time because you missed me, or did you come because you need me?"

She waited for an answer. Kreya opened her mouth, then shut it.

"What a pity."

"Zera—"

"No," Zera said, her face hard, her smile chipped out of granite. "Whatever it is you've come to ask me for, whyever you decided that now was the time to crawl out of whatever hole you've been living in, however much you think I care about our past friendship . . . The answer is no."

"I haven't asked anything yet," Kreya protested. She'd known there was a high probability that Zera would be dramatic about their reunion, but this was extreme. "You can't say no before I even ask. That's absurd."

"I prefer 'eccentric,' not 'absurd,' thank you." Zera spread her arms wide and beckoned to her . . . friends? Followers? Sycophants? Lovers? Kreya didn't know who they were and didn't much care, except they were all watching Zera. Even the ones who acted absorbed in their own selves, such as the shirtless man with the harp, had their bodies twisted toward Zera, as if they were flowers and she was their sun. It made Kreya's skin crawl. "Aren't I delightfully eccentric, my darlings?"

The harp stopped. "You're the pinnacle," the musician said, and then beamed at her.

"The pinnacle of what, my love?"

That flummoxed him.

"Come now, I can't be the pinnacle of nothing. A pinnacle is the highest point, by definition, so who am I crushing beneath the glory of me?"

His face brightened. "Everyone!"

Zera laughed, as if delighted. "And do you know *how* I became so glorious?"

She hasn't changed, Kreya realized. Underneath the ridiculous face paint and the gold silk, Zera was still the girl who chose to fight her battles with dramatic flair. She'd provided the distraction, as well as the firepower, when they'd gone after Eklor. Quietly, Kreya said, "You don't need to perform for me. I'm not your enemy."

"Of course you're not! You're my dearest friend!"

It was worse than Kreya had thought. Zera not only wanted an argument, she wanted a spectacle. Exactly what Kreya didn't need. She checked the distance to the exit. She wasn't convinced she could make it there faster than Zera's sycophants could, especially if they had any of their leader's talismans tucked into their virtually nonexistent outfits. Plus it was likely that Zera had locked it behind her anyway. She wondered precisely how angry Zera was beneath the drama and what sort of control she had over her temper.

Zera settled onto a couch that was plump with cushions. Sinking in, she positioned herself as if posing for a portrait, artfully arranging her many silk scarves. Her followers flocked closer, sitting at her feet. She patted a cushion next to her, inviting Kreya to sit with her, but Kreya crossed her arms and leaned against a column that was carved to resemble a croco-raptor skeleton. Undeterred, Zera beamed at her audience. "You've all heard the legends. There were five of us, tasked by the guild master to eliminate the threat posed by the rogue bone maker Eklor." She held up one finger. "Kreya, our bone maker, a rising star in the guild, chosen for possessing a power that could rival Eklor's—if she lived long enough to hone it." A second finger. "Zera . . . that's me, my loves." Her audience cooed appreciatively, and Kreya rolled her eyes. "Bone wizard. Unknown until then, but soon to be unrivaled." Third. "Marso, a bone reader, with a unique gift of seeing the truth of the past, present, and future that far exceeded the skills of other bone readers." Four. "Stran, a warrior with experience in using bone talismans to enhance his already prodigious strength." And five. "Jentt, a reformed thief, who specialized in using talismans of speed and stealth to win his battles."

Kreya felt a pang at his name. She didn't know what Zera was playing at, acting like a storyteller. "Everyone knows this."

"Ahh, but what not everyone knows is this: the legend says that the guild master tasked five, but he did not. He tasked only one. Kreya. *She* chose the rest of us. All that befell us is her fault. All the glory, and all the pain."

Ouch.

Of course it wasn't anything that Kreya hadn't thought a million times before. She'd insisted Jentt was perfect for the job. She'd pushed Marso to read the bones again and again, until his eyes were sunken and he murmured in his sleep. *I pushed all of them. Zera, too.*

"Plucked from obscurity, we were chosen to become the best of the best," Zera continued. "Kreya insisted upon it. She pushed us to train and train and train until I thought my fingers would erode to only bone themselves." She twisted her hands in the air, and jeweled rings flashed. Each ring was linked by gold chains that braided themselves into bracelets that wound up her arms to her elbows.

Kreya remembered how they'd trained: holed up in an abandoned farmhouse. Jentt and Stran had hunted together, practicing with speed and strength talismans, bringing home ferrets, rabbits, even a bear once. They'd skin them, process the carcasses, and harvest the bones. The wood floors in the kitchen had been soaked with blood by the time they were done, and the house stank of death, but she remembered how much they'd laughed, how long they'd talked, and most of all, how alive they'd felt.

It had been among the happiest times in Kreya's life. Even though they were preparing for war. She'd never been much good at making friends, and these people . . . they'd been more than friends. *We were family,* she thought.

Zera was studying her, her eyes glittering like a cat's. "I hated her sometimes, for her unswerving faith in my abilities. And loved her for it. I didn't know she was right, that I was destined for greatness. She believed in me more than I believed in myself. Until she didn't. Until she betrayed me."

"I didn't mean to steal your moment. I only wanted to avenge Jentt." She'd *told* Zera this twenty-five years ago, and she'd thought she understood. But apparently she'd just had twenty-five years to brood.

"She'd laid all the plans," Zera told her sycophants. "We'd all agreed to them."

Kreya cut in. "But reality had other ideas. It was never in the plan for Jentt to die. And that changed everything."

"She went in alone, to face Eklor," Zera continued for her audience. "Despite our plans. Left us behind to face an army, while she went after Eklor without us. Oh, it was very dramatic. Death all around. Hopelessness. Despair. He'd even condemned children to serve in his army of horrors, both before and after death, and our heroine Kreya marched through it all, buoyed by self-righteous grief and rage."

Kreya peeled herself off the pillar. "Enough. There's no need to relive it. I stopped him. You stopped his army. World saved. Everyone went their separate ways. The end."

"You went your separate way first," Zera said. "Or did you miss the part when I said you went in alone, leaving us to face an army of nightmares?"

One of the girls at Zera's feet, starry-eyed, sighed and said, "You were so brave, Master Zera. A few against an army. Saving us all."

Smiling, Zera patted her on the head as if she were a well-behaved puppy. "That's right. We were victorious, even though our friend and leader, our *sister*, abandoned us. And then she walked off into the sunset, still without us, to grieve a loss we should have shared."

Kreya snorted. "Seriously? You're angry at me for grieving my husband. That's it?"

"Yes. And for all the years since then."

"Sorry for saving the world at great personal cost and needing time to recover."

"Twenty-five years, Kreya. A quarter century! Maybe, just maybe, I needed you too! Ever think of that?" Zera shot to her feet, and her sycophants, who had been leaning in closer and closer, fell backward.

"I was in pain."

"So was I! My heart hurt!" Zera grabbed the fabric of her shirt over her heart and yanked. Pearls and beads and jewels popped off. They sprinkled onto the marble floor, and Kreya watched them roll, scattering in every direction.

Zera's chest was heaving, as if she'd run a race, and her curves were visible through the torn fabric, which Kreya had no doubt was intentional. She wore an expression of pure martyrdom, holding the pose, while her sycophants looked from her to Kreya and back again, waiting with bated breath.

Slowly, sarcastically, Kreya applauded.

Zera quit panting and closed the front of her shirt. "Go," she said to her followers.

They scrambled up and out of the salon. A few of them slid on the pearls that littered the marble floor, then caught themselves on the pillars carved like skeletons. In seconds, all of them had tumbled out of the room. All that remained was the sound of waterfalls, trickling.

"You left me," Zera repeated, but this time there were no theatrics.

"I'm sorry," Kreya said quietly. She meant it. She'd never intended for any of it to happen—or yes, she had. They had defeated Eklor and become heroes, exactly as they'd wanted to.

She had just never anticipated that doing so would destroy her. "Have you been all right?"

"Do you even care?"

Kreya considered that. It was an honest question; it deserved an honest answer. "Yes."

Zera sank again onto her couch. "I told myself you'd come back. For a long time, I made excuses. 'She just has to grieve.' 'She needs to be alone now.' 'She cares, but she doesn't know how to express it.' I waited for you. Kept my heart open for you. And then, when you didn't come, all that hope switched to anger. I succeeded here, built all of this, in part to spite you, to show that I could be fine without you."

Kreya didn't know what to say, but she didn't need to, because Zera wasn't finished.

"And you know what I discovered? I *am* fine. Without you. Now that you've come back, I look at you, and I know I should feel all that old anger and hate. I know that's what they"—she gestured to where her sycophants had disappeared—"expect. But you know what I feel?"

Kreya shook her head.

"Nothing." Zera scooped up a few of the fallen pearls, spread her fingers, and then let them fall again in her lap. "I feel nothing for you, Kreya, because you are nothing to me now. You are the past, and I've let go of the past."

Kreya felt as if her ribs had tightened around her heart. She deserved that. And more. She hadn't expected forgiveness. Still, a piece of her had hoped for it all the same. After all this time, she did still care what Zera thought and felt. "Very well. I understand. But the talismans—"

"What will you use them for?"

"I . . . I can't tell you that." She had intended to tell Zera the truth. She'd thought she owed her that much. But now . . . There was too great a risk that she'd be overheard, or that Zera would disapprove and try to stop her.

Zera laughed, an empty sound. "You came here, after all this time, to ask a favor and won't tell me why? You have not lost your nerve."

"It is for a good cause."

"Is it? That's nice. I charge for good causes. And for bad. My power bones are among the most coveted, and therefore most expensive, in Vos. How much gold did you bring with you, Kreya dear?"

"None. I had hoped our past friendship would be enough—"

"Friendship means connection. And for that, you need to actually stay connected. You are nothing to me now, Kreya. I don't think you understand that. *Nothing.* And so I will give you nothing." She rose and crossed the room. Holding open the front door, she waited. Her expression looked, more than anything else, tired. And a little sad.

Kreya tried again. "It's important."

"To you. Not to me."

"If you knew why . . ."

"Will you tell me?"

"I . . ." Kreya wanted to say the words: *I can bring Jentt back! He can live again!* But the words stuck in her throat. Could she trust Zera? Years ago, she would have said, *Yes, no question, I trust her with my life.* This wasn't Kreya's life, though; it was Jentt's. Given Zera's flair for theatrics, combined with the prohibition against using human bone for magic, she couldn't guarantee that Zera wouldn't immediately rush to the guild and kill any chance that Kreya ever had of restoring her husband. Or rush to her tower and destroy Jentt's body. "I . . . can't. I ask you . . . I beg you, in memory of the friendship we once had, to please help me."

She couldn't trust her with the truth, but Kreya would happily sacrifice her pride.

Gripping a skeletal pillar for support, Kreya lowered herself to the floor and knelt. "Please, Zera. I wouldn't ask if it weren't important. I would have left you in peace—"

"You left me in war. That was worse."

"I apologize. On my knees."

Zera wrinkled her nose. "Yes, I see that. It's pathetic. Stand up."

Wincing as her back twinged, Kreya stood. "Zera. Please give me another chance." Another chance at happiness. At hope. At the life she was supposed to have.

"You had your chance. We all did. And now it's time for you to leave."

Quick thoughts flashed through her head: she could beg more, explain more, try to overpower her, try to blackmail her, try to steal from her, but looking at Zera's painted face, Kreya knew she'd do none of that. She'd find another way that didn't involve her old friend. *I've hurt her enough*, Kreya thought.

She walked past her without a word and kept walking out of the fifth tier, out of Cerre, and did not stop until night fell on the mountains. Only then, in the darkness, did she stop and cry. Not for herself. Not for Jentt. But for Zera.

She had not realized until now that the war had also broken her best friend.

CHAPTER FOUR

Zera had her old nightmare, the one she'd banished many years ago, for the next three nights: She was back on the plain, facing Eklor's army. Jentt was dead. Kreya was gone. Stran was using his talisman-fueled fists to pound soldier after soldier made of armor and bone. Marso was whimpering as he stabbed and slashed the smaller bone critters with his knife. And she was searching through the pockets of a coat she'd trashed long ago, the twin to the one Kreya still wore.

In reality, twenty-five years ago, Zera had drawn on her entire arsenal of talismans, supplying Stran and Marso as fast as they could use them, and all three of them had fought with the strength of a thousand bears and mountain lions combined. But in her dream, she could not find a single one. She searched, and her friends died beside her—sometimes Stran would be impaled by the antlers of a skeletal deer, sometimes Marso would be sliced across the sternum by a sword, more often he'd be cut to ribbons by one of Eklor's bone-powered metal monstrosities. Sometimes Kreya would be there, bleeding at her feet and trying to form words that Zera could never quite make out. And sometimes Jentt would be just beyond reach, dying again and again as the army overwhelmed him.

It was, to say the least, an unpleasant dream.

She woke after each one drenched in sweat and screaming.

"Fuck me," Zera said the third night.

"Gladly," the naked man beside her said sleepily.

She ignored him, stood, and stretched her neck. She felt stiff and sore, as if she'd been fighting in her sleep. An odd feeling, since she hadn't thrown a punch or held a knife in years. She'd seen no point in keeping up with the training that Kreya had insisted they all get.

She heard a harp strum. "Perhaps some music will relax you?" her lover offered.

"Make it appropriately melancholy."

He played an arpeggio in a minor key and then shifted to an old tune, one about a goatherd who pined for the miller's son. Or was this the one about the weaver who lost thirteen sons and six daughters in a series of implausible tragedies? She liked that one. Very gory. A death in each verse, followed by a lament. Sometimes it was refreshing to hear about someone who had suffered worse than you. He sang softly, his voice still a bit rough from sleep but pretty.

She listened for a while as she looked out her window at the stars over the mountain. On the sixth verse, she spoke. "Guine, what do you think Kreya needed my talismans for?"

The harp didn't cease. Guine knew better than that. "She did not say?"

"She did not."

"Curious."

"Not for Kreya," Zera said. "She always delighted in being cryptic as she ordered us around." The nightmare, in contrast, had been remarkably unsubtle: her failing to give talismans to her friends and, as a consequence, her friends' dying horrifically.

She didn't need a dream reader to tell her she felt guilty for not helping Kreya.

"She doesn't deserve my help," Zera said.

"She does not," Guine agreed.

"You weren't there. You don't know."

"I cannot possibly understand," he agreed again.

Zera shot him a glare across the shadow-laden room. "By the bones, it's irritating when you do that. You're allowed to have a mind and produce your own thoughts. You'll still have those lovely muscles even if you express an opinion."

His fingertips danced over the harp strings. "And if my opinion differs from yours?"

"I'll toss you off an aqueduct." She held up a finger. "No. I will have someone toss you off an aqueduct for me. Perhaps I should hire a servant who specializes in convenient murders. Is that a thing?"

Politely, Guine said, "I believe that's called an assassin."

"I am teasing you, you know," she told him. "In case it's not clear. When I tire of you, you'll be set up with your own house on the fourth tier, with servants of your own. No murder servants, though."

"I hope you'll never tire of me."

"That's unlikely." Zera patted his bare shoulder. "But it's good to have hope. Makes for a sunnier disposition." She resumed staring out at the dark mountains, made darker by the glare of torchlight from the city tiers below. At night, the city glowed brighter than the moon. She couldn't see the mist-covered valley beyond and below; it was sunken in shadows. "She could be in trouble. Must be, if she needs my talismans."

"Ask her."

"She left." *After I kicked her out.*

"Then follow her." He played an arpeggio in a major key.

"Kreya is in hiding."

"You must know where she is."

And the truth was, she did.

She was, perhaps, the only one in Vos who knew. A few years after the war, she'd locked herself in her workroom and created tracking talismans, made from the bones of an elite hunting dog. She'd sold most of them for a fortune, but she'd used one herself, to locate Kreya. She had tracked her scent out of Cerre, across several mountains, beyond villages too remote to have ever heard of running water, to a lonely tower, picturesquely perched on a cliff. Zera didn't know whether Kreya had built the tower herself or inherited it from a hermit who liked clichés and nice views. Zera had stared at that tower for a solid hour, watching Kreya read an old, weathered book by a window. Kreya never saw her, and eventually Zera left. If Kreya was still living in that same tower, then yes, Zera knew where to find her.

"What do I say to her?"

"What do you want to say?"

Zera thought she might tire of Guine sooner rather than later.

Guine continued to play, the harp music wafting around the room like a pervasive perfume. "What would give you peace?"

That was at least a more helpful question.

She considered it a moment. "To know Kreya is safe. I wasn't able to protect her in the war. She chose to face Eklor alone. If I can be certain she's safe now . . ."

"Go then. Give yourself that peace. And then come home to sleep the night through. Or"—he smiled prettily—"do things other than sleep."

She liked that idea. Very much. Drawing him into her bed,

she amused herself and him until dawn spread its lemon fingers through her bedchamber.

ZERA'S NEW COAT WAS THE ENVY OF EVERY BONE worker in Cerre, or so she believed. Made of the softest lamb-swool and trimmed with the finest leather, it was embroidered with gold thread that depicted the skeletons of the birds, fish, and animals of Vos. Each gold skeleton had rubies sewn in for eyes. Before leaving to visit Kreya, she filled the pockets with talismans, unsure of what she'd need. She didn't intend to simply give Kreya unlimited talismans, obviously, but if the situation was dire enough . . . She wanted to be prepared for whatever she'd find.

She gave Guine specific instructions to lie about where she'd gone: to source new material for her talismans, he'd say, and he'd blame her famed eccentricities for the suddenness of her departure.

Walking out onto the balcony, Zera let the glow of the morning sun wash over her. She had no railing on her balcony, despite the fact that the city fell away beneath it. She knew some of the servants would dare one another to venture out onto it, and her guests avoided it completely, but she loved it. There was nothing between her and the sky, between life and death.

Plus it looked so delightfully dramatic when she stood on it.

Stepping to the edge, she spread her arms. The sleeves of her coat draped down like wings. Catching the sunlight, the gold and rubies sparkled. In her left hand, she held a talisman made from a bird bone. She imagined the men and women on the lower tiers watching her, silhouetted against the sky.

She called out the activation word: *"Renari!"*

And then she leaped from the balcony.

Wind rushed against her, and the talisman of flight lifted her. Zera felt the current buoy her up, and she laughed out loud. There was no rush like flying! *I should get out more often,* she thought.

Arms spread wide, she breathed in the air: fresh, clean, empty of all the scents that clung to her palace. She felt the sun warm her back, even as the wind chilled her skin. Her sleeves were puffed with air, and the fabric of her pants fluttered around her legs. Below her, the city of Cerre glistened in the early morning sun, and she saw people beginning to bustle in the streets. From this high, they looked like dolls.

She flew, with swallows swooping around her. "Hello, fellow citizens of the sky!"

Her words were lost in the wind, but that didn't matter since birds couldn't speak.

Angling herself, Zera soared over the gap between mountains. She aimed for a cable car that was trundling up the next mountain. Wind pushed her from side to side, but she steadied out. Using her sleeves to slow herself, she landed on top of the cable car.

She hit hard, and the car rocked beneath her from the impact. Inside, the passengers screamed. "Apologies!" she called to them. "But if you could have seen that from outside, you'd have been impressed."

Lounging against the mechanism that held the cable car to the wire, she tossed the flight bones over the edge. They were spent. The talismans could handle decent jaunts, but they had limitations, such as durability and lift. Technically, they were more "glide" than "flight"—she hadn't succeeded in creating talismans that could fully overcome the density of a human body—but so far, none of her customers had reported any fatal splats, so she counted them as a success.

From another pocket, she withdrew a sticky cinnamon pastry, wrapped in paper. She ate, licking her fingers and enjoying the ride up the mountain. She even had a nice view of the valley mist below, swirling ominously as usual. Luckily, her path wouldn't take her anywhere near that morass.

At the docking station, Zera climbed down the ladder and was helped off by a nice-looking young man in a sleeveless shirt. She thanked him and then signed autographs for the passengers as they disembarked. One little girl wanted to touch Zera's cheek, which was charming. She requested soap and water after the girl and her family had departed.

Her duty to the public complete, Zera waltzed back to the sleeveless handsome boy, dropped a pouch of coins into his hand, and bought his mountain horse.

It was named Rock, the boy told her.

She renamed it Merridia, because it sounded nicer.

Only distantly related to the horses who raced through pastures at lower altitudes, mountain horses were stocky, with thick, fluffy fur to protect them from the wind and snow, and surprisingly nimble. She didn't even have to use a talisman for steadiness on Merridia. "You're a good girl. Or boy." Twisting in the saddle, Zera tried to check, but the horse's fur blocked her view.

The horse snorted until she pulled herself back up.

"You're a fussy one." She decided that meant it was a boy.

Using a bit of a speed talisman, Zera urged the horse to move faster. Unlike bones carved by a bone maker, a bone wizard's creations couldn't animate any kind of inanimate transportation, but her talismans could imbue living things with particular properties. Her enhanced mount galloped over the road that wound around the mountain. Soon, she passed the passengers from the cable car. She sat up straighter as they gasped and pointed, amazed at her speed. She was glad she'd left her multicolored hair loose so it could stream dramatically behind her. They'd return home with a tale to tell.

Soon, though, she had to slow, as her route took her away from the civilized, stone-lined road and into the thick pine forest. Birds sang out from the trees, and Zera whistled back at them. She wasn't meant to be out on her own, with no one to talk to or to entertain her. She wished she'd brought along Guine or one of the others.

The problem with being alone was that it gave you time to think.

And worry. And regret. And experience all those other inconvenient emotions.

But she muddled through, and thanks to a judicious use of talismans on Merridia, Zera reached the tower by late afternoon. She hitched the horse to a tree, dismounted, and rubbed her thighs, which were unaccustomed to this much travel. Perhaps she should have taken a more leisurely approach. "Enjoy the grass," she told Merridia. "I'll ask Kreya for a bucket of water. She might even have grain or oats, but I wouldn't hold your breath for that. Looks like she's embraced a more austere aesthetic."

Looking up at the tower, Zera realized it was decidedly more shabby than the last time she'd checked on her old friend. Moss grew over the stones, and grasses were knee-high around the path to the door. Inside it was dark, though that could have been only because it was so sunny outside. She hoped Kreya was home.

Scooping up the hem of her coat so it didn't drag in the dirt, Zera climbed the steps to the door. She searched for a bell or a door knocker or anything to signal her arrival. *Has Kreya ever had a visitor?*

Making a fist, she knocked.

It barely made a sound on the massive door.

"Kreya? Oh, Krrrreyaaaaa?" She sang the name. "Darling, I've traveled a long way to see you, and I would like some tea for me and some water for my horse. Or vice versa."

The tower was silent.

"I know our last conversation didn't go as either of us imagined a reunion would go," Zera said. "For my part, I apologize. I could have come visit you sooner as well."

Still, nothing.

"Are you here?"

Perhaps she'd moved.

Or Zera could have beaten her home. She *had* taken a rather direct route.

She tried the door. It creaked and clanked, and, to Zera's surprise, swung open. Stepping forward, she peered in. The lock mechanism swung free, barely held by one screw. Whatever Kreya had been up to, it hadn't been home repair projects. Or security. "Helloooo? Kreya?"

Her voice echoed up the dank stairwell. It was a toss-up which was thicker: the shadows or the cobwebs. As Zera stepped inside, she tried not to touch anything. She noticed a hatchlike door, presumably to a cellar, as well as a door to a shadow-laden bathroom. She was distinctly disinterested in viewing how clean or unclean it was. Lifting the hem of her coat, she climbed up the stairs.

One turn up, she shrieked.

A spiderlike creature made of metal, cloth, and bone was scrubbing one of the steps. She stopped shrieking when she realized it wasn't attacking or even trying to move off its beloved step. She wondered if it *could* move. It had worn through the stone so badly that the step was more bowl than stair.

As Zera carefully stepped around, it paused and "looked" up at her. It had no eyes, but it twisted its body so its empty metal eye sockets pointed toward her.

"You're doing a fabulous job," she told it.

It purred and kept scrubbing.

Exhaling, she tiptoed past it. All right, so Kreya had made a cleaning construct that had malfunctioned and had just left it there for possibly a decade. That didn't mean her friend—*Ex-friend*, Zera corrected herself—was in mortal danger.

That construct was a prime example of why she preferred being a bone wizard to being a bone maker. The power in her talismans was temporary, burning itself out in a few beautiful and pure minutes of glory or, if she was bragging about her skills, hours of use. But a construct made by a bone maker could linger creepily for years before it eventually wore down. Unnatural things.

She was huffing by the time she reached the next level. It was stifling inside the stairwell, and it stank like three-day-old fish left out on the table. She felt the stench and the dust and grime seeping into her skin. *When I get back home, I'm taking a bath that lasts for three days*, she promised herself.

Which better be sooner rather than later.

"Kreya?" she called as she pushed against the door and poked her head in.

Zera expected more darkness and grime, but this room was light and airy and surprisingly clean. It had high rafters, plus several windows with open shutters that let the sunlight stream in. A canopied bed in the center was piled with linens.

"Are you asleep?"

Tiptoeing in, Zera crossed to the bed—

She halted as three shadowy shapes lurched away from the walls. They were murmuring wordlessly. Out of the corner of her eye, she saw movement on the rafters above: more of them, doll-like monstrosities made of scraps of fabric scuttling over the beams.

Sucking in air, she let out a proper bloodcurdling scream, while her hands jabbed into her pockets to find talismans. The dolls shrieked back and rushed toward her, and she heard footsteps on the stairs.

A doll latched onto her leg.

Still screaming heartily, Zera activated a strength talisman and flung the doll across the room. It smashed into the wall just as Kreya rushed through the door.

The dolls halted as soon as they saw Kreya. Clustering around the foot of the bed, they chittered at her. Kreya's face contorted in horror as if Zera had slaughtered a child. "Did you hurt him?"

Zera glanced at the doll she'd chucked across the room. It was collapsed, motionless, on the floor. "Um . . . is self-defense an excuse? Because it attacked me first."

But Kreya didn't rush to the doll. Instead she ran to the bed. She examined the linens from top to bottom, feeling along them, and Zera drifted closer, keeping an eye on the freaky dolls. They hung back for now, clustered together.

The linens looked . . .

"Kreya, what's that?"

It looked as if the linens were covering a body.

Oh no, she didn't. "You're making a human-size doll? Aren't your other horrors bad enough? Are you planning on giving all your visitors heart attacks?"

"He's no doll." Kreya blocked Zera's view. "And visitors aren't welcome. Why are you here? And how did you find me?"

If it wasn't a doll, then what? "Please tell me that's not a dead body in your bed. Because I cannot look the other way if you've become a murderer." Zera may have retired from the official hero business, but she still honored the laws of Vos. She palmed the strength talisman, readying it if she needed it again. The freaky rag dolls were still staring at her, while murmuring in their whispery voices. She'd counted at least seven.

"You shouldn't be here," Kreya said as she finished her examination. Apparently satisfied, she exhaled.

"I was concerned about you," Zera said loftily. "And now I'm even more concerned. What are these atrocities, and who is that in your bed?"

"None of your concern. And I did not hear so much 'concern' in your voice when I came to beg, on my knees, for your help." Kreya sucked in air as if she was about to escalate to shouting, but then she seemed to deflate. "Unless you came because you reconsidered? I still need the talismans."

"Why?"

"I told you I can't tell you."

"What *can* you tell me? Can you answer other questions? Like why this tower? Why are you alone? Why make these horrors? Why the corpse? I have questions, Kreya, and I'm not leaving until I have answers." She thought she would have sounded more authoritative if her voice hadn't crept up an octave by the end of her little speech. She was hot beneath her coat, and her palm was sweating squeezing the talisman.

With a significant glance at Zera's hand, Kreya asked, "Do you plan to fight me?"

"If necessary. But that's not why I came. Out of consideration for our past relationship, I came to make sure you're safe, and I will do what it takes to ensure that."

"You'd attack me to keep me safe?"

"Okay, yes, that didn't make sense. But you have creepy dolls! And a corpse!"

Kreya sighed. "Put the bone away, Zera."

Zera slid the talisman back into her pocket before she even considered why—she was still in the habit of obeying Kreya's orders, even after all this time. That was almost more unnerving than the dolls themselves, and she nearly pulled the talisman back out just to prove that she wasn't so pliable. But the dolls hadn't moved any closer, and she couldn't imagine Kreya as a threat to her. She left the talisman in her pocket.

Kreya was studying her, so Zera studied her back. Her old friend had many more lines around her eyes than she'd used to, as if her skin had been crumpled like a tissue, then inexpertly smoothed—far more lines than she should have had, at her age. *Hard living,* she thought. Off the top of her head, Zera knew of at least three creams that could help with that.

At last, Kreya said, "If you promise not to overreact, I will show you who this is, and you will understand why I need your talismans."

Zera drew herself up. "I never overreact."

"You are the definition of 'overreacting.'"

"I react the exact appropriate amount to a given situation." Yes, she had screamed at the animated dolls, but look at them! "You must admit, we have been in some unsettling situations."

"Like the mountain lion? Remember that?"

Of course she did. She wasn't about to be drawn into reminiscing, though. This wasn't a reunion. This was . . . a check-in visit, to assuage Zera's guilt over refusing to help. *I won't let it become anything more.* She was done with giving her friendship and trust to someone who was willing to disappear from her life without a backward glance.

"I never understood why it targeted Marso," Kreya continued. "He had zero meat on his bones. If he stood still, you'd have mistaken him for another skeleton. I never saw him eat."

Zera kept her eyes on the rag dolls. "You didn't know? He used to carry dried venison in his pockets, instead of talismans. He nibbled as we traveled."

"Truly? I thought he just absorbed nutrients from the air, or whatever bone readers do."

"He couldn't eat if he thought anyone was watching him."

"Huh. Wonder if he ever got over that."

"I . . ." Zera shut her mouth. She truly didn't know. She'd kept in touch with him and Stran for the first few years after the war, but they'd drifted apart, each consumed by their own life. She'd had her business, which needed to be tended and grown. Stran had had his new family, which also needed tending and growing. And Marso . . . She didn't know.

"You aren't having regular lunches with them?" Kreya asked. "Then why am I the target of so much of your anger? When did you last see Stran or Marso?"

"That's different," Zera said. "You left!"

"I had a good reason."

"You always have a good reason! But did you ever once consult the rest of us, to see what we thought or what we felt?" Zera was shouting again, and it felt good. The rag dolls, though, became more agitated as her voice grew louder.

She stopped herself.

All the dolls and Kreya were watching her, and she felt shivers run over her skin. She drew herself taller and wrapped her coat closer around her.

In a tight, quiet voice, Zera said, "You had to grieve—fine, I can understand that. But you *abandoned* us to do it. After abandoning us on the battlefield." She hadn't intended on unearthing the same argument they'd had in Cerre—*This isn't why I came*, she thought—but Kreya still didn't seem to understand. Or maybe she did, and didn't know *how* to change. In truth, Zera wasn't certain what she wanted Kreya to do or say to fix the way she felt. All in all, it was a very unsatisfactory way to feel. She usually knew exactly what she wanted and then got it.

"I did abandon you then, and I'm sorry. But I wasn't grieving," Kreya said softly.

"Of course you were. Your husband died!"

Kreya moved to the bed. Slowly, she unpinned the linen and began unwrapping the fabric from the corpse's head. Zera inched closer, unable to help herself. The cloying scent of dried flowers only partially masked the aroma of decay. It was an unmistakable scent. Even though she hired people to process animal carcasses for her now, she had never forgotten the odor. It crept through all other scents, souring them.

Shifting in front of Zera to remove the fabric, Kreya blocked her view. And then she stepped back. She'd only unwrapped the linen from around his head, but it was enough. Zera would have known that face anywhere. Even in death.

"Jentt."

"Yes. I wasn't grieving because I hadn't yet said goodbye."

Zera stared at him, his face ashen but oddly . . .

"He's not very dead."

"Oh, right now he's very dead."

"I mean, he looks as if he died a few days ago. Not twenty-five years ago." She knew death, as much as she tried to surround herself with life. All the guests she encouraged, all her servants, lovers like Guine—they were to balance out the death that dominated her work, her memory, and her dreams. "Kreya, dearest, tell me: why does he look as though he just died last week? It doesn't make sense. I *saw* him fall on the plains twenty-five years ago. We all did. *You* did."

Kreya didn't answer for a while. She stared at her late husband's face. With one finger, she stroked his sunken cheek, and then she began lovingly rewrapping the linen.

"Did he or did he not die on the plains?" Zera demanded. She'd mourned him for years. Missed him. Reviewed every last second that led to his death. If he'd survived and Kreya had hidden it from her . . . from all of them . . . from the world! All of Vos had mourned the fallen hero, who had sacrificed himself for everyone. If she'd kept him secret—

"He did die that day."

Zera exhaled. At least that bit of the past was preserved. Speaking of preservation, though . . . "How did you do it? Keep him so . . . fresh?" It was a terrible way to refer to someone they all had loved. But it was a valid question. His body wasn't chilled, and he wasn't submerged in formaldehyde. He should have decayed much, much more.

"I know how to bring him back."

For once, Zera had no words.

"It took me many years to learn how. And it's not an easy process. It requires . . . an ingredient that is not easy to come by, and so far, I have not been able to obtain it in enough quantities to sustain his life for long. But if I could, then I could bring him back permanently!" Crossing to Zera, Kreya took her hand. "That's why I need the talismans. So I can use them to obtain what I need."

Zera felt . . . She didn't know how she felt. As if the world had tilted, sliding everything to the side. Such a thing shouldn't have been possible. She'd never heard of it. A bone maker's power was to animate the inanimate. It created a false semblance of life. Never life itself. But here was Jentt, with a face only a few days dead, as proof. "What do you need? What ingredient could possibly work such a miracle?"

Kreya took so long to answer that Zera thought she wasn't going to. But then she did.

"Human bone."

"Excuse me."

Zera made it as far as the stairwell before she vomited. Hand against the grimy wall, she knelt and emptied her stomach. When she finished, she wiped her lips with the back of her hand. She rose shakily.

She sensed Kreya hovering behind her. "Tea?"

Her mouth tasted as vile as what Kreya had done. It was unthinkable, a crime against man and nature, a perversion of the natural order. Everything they'd been taught, everything they'd believed, everything they'd fought for . . .

"You've become a monster," Zera spat.

"I know," Kreya said calmly. "Come upstairs and have some tea."

Looking at Kreya, she saw Eklor's army of atrocities and the plain littered with the dead and the dying . . . It was Eklor's arrogance and his willingness to violate the laws of both nature and Vos that had led to the Bone War. "*He* used human bone."

"I'm not him."

"But you've crossed the same line he did. You've become the very horror we all fought against. The very horror that Jentt died to defeat."

"For very different reasons."

"You'll be burned to death," Zera said.

"Someday, yes. But not today. Unless you wield the torch."

Zera wondered if it was going to come to that and wished wholeheartedly that she'd stayed cocooned in her lovely human-corpse-free palace in Cerre. Casually putting her hand back in the pocket with the strength talisman, she said, "Explain to me why I shouldn't."

CHAPTER FIVE

Kreya guided Zera upstairs. She kept her voice soft and calm, even though the fear of what Zera was going to do or say was enough to choke her. "A nice cup of tea will help."

"Will it really?" Her voice had a note of hysteria. "Because it won't erase the sight of your not-so-recently-deceased husband. Or the knowledge that you've done what's forbidden."

She had a point. "It will settle your stomach and clean your mouth." Lightly, Kreya added, "Your breath right now is worse than a wild boar's."

When Zera didn't even display a flicker of annoyance at that insult, Kreya felt her nerves ramp up. She didn't let it show, though. Entering the library, she led Zera around the stacks of books and across the threadbare carpet. She knocked a pile of blankets off the one cushioned chair.

Zera sat, which Kreya thought was at least better than her running out of the tower screaming. Or burning it all down.

Kreya crossed the library to the fireplace. She'd had a low fire going already, and the kettle had water. She hung the kettle over the fire, just above the flame. Her hands were shaking, and she tried to hide it as she busied herself searching for a clean cup.

She located one without chips, but it wasn't entirely clean. She contemplated taking it down to the sink, but that would require leaving Zera alone. *Not going to risk that,* she thought. Instead, Kreya wiped the cup with a stray towel that smelled of mildew and hoped Zera was too distraught to notice.

"It's my duty to stop you," Zera said.

Locating a canister of tea leaves, Kreya opened the top and sniffed it. "It isn't."

"Decency demands it."

"It doesn't." She scooped dried leaves into the cup.

"The law demands it."

She located a spoon and checked it for cleanliness. *Close enough.*

"There are lines we do not cross, Kreya, and for good reason. Bone readers—if they try to twist the truth of what they see, it drives them mad. Bone wizards—if we carve talismans that affect the mind, it's a straight path to prison. And bone makers . . . You saw what Eklor made, how he twisted your art. Using human bone. There's a reason it's forbidden."

At least Zera was still sitting. Kreya tried to formulate the correct arguments. It had been a long time since she'd spoken to anyone but Jentt, and even longer since she'd had to explain herself to anyone. "When I first realized what was required for the spell to work, I reacted the same way you did."

"I'm so glad. At what point did you change from a reasonable reaction to 'I'm going to commit an atrocity'?"

"When I realized that the spell worked."

The kettle whistled, and Kreya removed it from the heat,

poured the boiling water into the teacup, and carried it to Zera. She couldn't hide her shaking hands as she gave it to her. Zera studied her. "I see fear, Kreya. You know what you're doing is wrong."

"I know what I'm doing is dangerous. So yes, I am afraid."

"Afraid of me?"

"Afraid of failure."

Zera sipped the tea and grimaced.

Kreya retrieved a small pot of honey from a dusty table, beside a pile of scrolls. She added a dollop of honey to Zera's cup and then took a breath and said, "Would you like it if I said I'm afraid of you? You could save me or destroy me."

So far, Zera hadn't moved from her chair, but Kreya was aware of how much power her old friend had tucked into her coat. Without talismans of her own, Kreya had little defense. Her run-down contraptions were no match for a bone wizard at the height of her strength.

Zera stirred her tea. "Have you been murdering people? For their bones?"

"What? No!"

"It's not so shocking a question, Kreya, considering what you're doing. So you're stealing them, then."

"I never had any involvement in their deaths." What kind of person did Zera take her for? She still had a moral compass, though she was aware she had fudged certain boundaries. Still . . . she was no murderer!

For one thing, Jentt never would have stood for it.

"I swear, I haven't changed that much," Kreya insisted.

"Except for the fact you're a thief now," Zera said. "That's a new hobby for you. Or should I say 'profession'?"

"And what about you? You've taken up a career as a decadent

profligate. What happened to the Zera who wanted to make the world a better place for all? Do you ever even leave the fifth tier?" Kreya remembered Zera used to talk derisively about bone wizards only interested in amassing wealth. She'd said she wanted power and wealth so she could use her influence for good. How much good was she doing, surrounded by her fake waterfalls and fake lovers?

"I'm here, aren't I? Though that was an obvious mistake."

"Clearly a mistake," Kreya agreed. "I didn't invite you to come and judge me. I asked you to help me."

"Help you break the law?"

"Help me save a friend."

They glared at each other.

Kreya broke the stare first. "I don't enjoy stealing bones. That's why I wanted . . . I have a plan. One that will hurt no one. And one that will bring Jentt back for good. But I can't do it without enough talismans."

"What plan?"

Kreya hesitated again, just as she had in Cerre, weighing the risks. Zera had already seen Jentt. How much worse if she knew it all? Perhaps more damning, it wasn't as if Kreya had a chance of executing her plan without Zera's help. She looked her friend in the eyes and hoped the term "friend" still applied.

"There are human bones unburied and unburned beyond the mountains. On the plain."

Zera shot to her feet, dropping her teacup.

The cup shattered. Tea splashed onto the carpet, Zera's hem, and a stack of books. Kreya didn't move. By the window, her bone-bird construct whirred anxiously. She knew her dolls would be in the stairwell, listening, ready if she needed them.

She also knew they wouldn't be enough if this went sour. Zera's coat had many pockets.

Keeping her voice calm, Kreya said, "The bones rot. Unclaimed. Unmourned. If I were to take enough of them, I'd only need to cast the spell one more time. No more thefts. No more atrocities."

"Until the next time a bone maker figures out this spell of yours."

"I plan to destroy all record of it. The knowledge of the spell will die with me, when it's my time. All I ask is for enough talismans to get me safely into and out of the forbidden zone. And then this ends." She managed to keep her eyes from sliding to the shelf where Eklor's journals were hidden.

Zera laughed, shrill. "All you ask? You want to go back to the place where . . ." Her voice faded, and her eyes looked haunted. Kreya knew she was remembering. Because she was doing the same.

It was the smell that Kreya remembered the most. A stench of rot that filled your nose and mouth until it was all you breathed. It was so strong it seeped into your eyes and made them tear. It felt like it was permeating your skin and you'd never be clean again. You felt coated in it. Even when the memory of the screams faded, she'd still remember that smell.

It was the same smell that lingered on Jentt now.

"I have to."

Fetching a towel, Kreya mopped up the spilled tea. She gathered the shards of the cup and deposited them against a wall where she wouldn't step on them. Out of the corner of her eye, she watched Zera finger a pocket.

What would she grab? Strength? Speed?

She could reach Jentt's body faster than Kreya could stop

her. She could set him ablaze. Or tear him apart. Or take him away. All before Kreya could react.

Yet she didn't move—not yet. "It's called the 'forbidden zone' for a reason."

"Yes, because Guild Master Lorn is terrible at naming things," Kreya said. "With stealth and speed, I can bypass the guards and cross the wall. With strength, I can carry what I need."

"And if I don't give you the talismans? What will you do then?"

"Continue to steal from the recently dead. Until I'm caught and killed." Which would be soon without any talismans to help her, especially with the near-disaster at Eren. Word would have spread, and the villages would be alert now.

"Or you could stop this. You *must* stop this," Zera said, more serious than Kreya had ever heard her. "Jentt is dead. You must admit the truth, burn his body, and grieve, like everyone else in Vos. It's not healthy or right to defy nature in such a way. Life ends, and you have to let it end with respect and—"

Kreya cut in. "He died for you."

Zera sat down again, hard.

"That arrow would have hit you. He took it to save you."

Faintly, Zera said, "He sacrificed himself for all of Vos."

"Generally, yes. But specifically?"

"Low blow, Kreya."

"Yet true."

"I'm burning him." Zera's fingers closed around a talisman, and Kreya leaped forward, clapping her hand over Zera's mouth before she could say a word.

"I can burn them all," Kreya pleaded. "Let me have the talismans I need, let me save Jentt, and I will burn all the bones on the plain. Give them the peace they deserve. Once I cross the wall, there's no one who will stop me. I can do what should have been done decades ago, and then live out the rest of my life with Jentt, in peace, the way we were supposed to." She stared into Zera's eyes, her hand still pressed against her mouth. She heard her bird-bone creature near her ankles, its gears whirring. "Then after, I'll destroy the spell. Dismantle the dolls. Whatever you want. Name your price, and I'll pay it. Just let me do this. Please." She hated having to beg. But it was far better than wishing for an avalanche or a plague. This hurt no one but herself. And clinging to pride was for the young, or at least those who didn't have their priorities straight.

Zera opened her hand, the one holding the talisman.

Slowly, Kreya lowered her hand from Zera's mouth.

"One condition," Zera said.

"Anything." *With exceptions*, Kreya amended silently.

"I come with you."

THIRTY MINUTES LATER, AFTER THEY'D TAKEN care of Zera's horse's needs, Kreya cleared off a table in her library and spread out a map of Vos. She'd bought it off a traveler years ago, and it was one of the most accurate maps she'd ever seen—exact elevations of all the mountains, bridges and paths marked according to accessibility, and zones rated by avalanche danger. Vos stretched across multiple mountains, and they'd have to traverse six of them, as well as skirt the broadest stretch of inhospitable valley, to reach the plains. She began to trace out a route with her fingers.

Poking her head over Kreya's shoulder, Zera pointed to a peak. "We climb here, use a flight talisman to cross to here, repeat here and here, and we'll be there in less than two days.

Spend the night in between in"—she checked the distances by spreading her fingers—"Avioc. Oh, yes, they have a darling inn that is supposed to have delectable wildberry pie."

"No flying," Kreya said. "It's far too visible, and memorable. And certainly no inns."

"My overland trekking days are over, my pet. And I swore off sleeping on the ground years ago. We can afford to do this civilized." She tapped the map with her fingernail. "I require pie before I desecrate a mass grave."

"Don't be absurd."

She now remembered why she'd never let Zera plan their adventures.

Obviously, this would have to be a stealth mission. Both of them were recognizable, even more so now than when they'd first made the trek to the plains, and they didn't need any curious fans figuring out their destination. No flying. No inns. They'd bypass all towns, stick to the less traveled trails, and climb where they needed to. "I estimate two weeks—"

Parroting her, Zera said, "Don't be absurd. If you want to go overland, then I am summoning my servants to carry supplies, because I am not subjecting myself to the kind of situations I tolerated in my youth."

"Tell me you're joking."

"I am not. You need me, so I set the conditions. This time, I will journey comfortably." She paused. "I am joking about the servants, yes, but I'm not traveling by foot or even by horse, as charming as Merridia is. And I'm absolutely not sleeping on the ground. Those days are long over. I swore to myself that I would never again suffer like that."

"Think of it as a recreational camping trip, with hiking."

"You know I hate camping."

Yes, Kreya knew that—she remembered how much Zera had whined last time about every burnt dinner, every rock under her bedroll, every truncated night of sleep due to bugs or snakes or bears—but . . . "You're the one who wants to come."

Zera smiled gaily at her. "And you're the one who needs me."

"I only need your talismans. Give them to me, and you don't have to endure any of this."

"This isn't me being spoiled," Zera said.

Kreya snorted.

"I'm serious. This is me being practical. If we wear ourselves out on the journey, we'll be diminished when we arrive at the wall. I know myself well enough to know I don't have the stamina I used to, and I would venture to guess you don't either. You want us at our best for the difficult part? Then we do it my way."

That . . . actually made sense. "So what do you suggest?"

She spread her arms theatrically. "Like I said. We fly."

"Huh."

"I have talismans."

"And will they keep us from being seen as we soar majestically through the air? You know there are towns and villages and farms between here and the forbidden zone. All it would take is for someone to look up." Only a handful of people in Vos had the kind of wealth to purchase a flight talisman, and combined with the gossip undoubtedly caused by Zera's absence from Cerre, it wouldn't take a genius to guess their identities if they were spotted as they flew.

"So we fly at night."

"You have experience with that? Controlling your trajectory at night? What's to keep us from crashing into a mountainside we can't see?"

"Lights?"

"Again, someone could look up, especially if we're using the lights from the houses to navigate." It was too risky. There was, however, an alternative to flight that didn't involve either walking or horseback riding and would allow them to keep a low profile, both literally and figuratively. "Come with me."

Scooping up a lantern and lighting it, she led Zera downstairs, past the bedroom where Jentt lay, over the broken cleaning construct, and then down farther into the cellar. She hung the lantern on a hook on the wall and surveyed the mess.

Beside her, Zera surveyed it too. "You live alone. You have nothing but time on your hands. And yet you live in squalor."

Stepping over a broken cart, Kreya tried to remember where she'd stored the old crawler. It shouldn't be hard to find—the thing was enormous. "I have other priorities."

Zera picked up a shield and blew dust into the air. "This is the Shield of Lothmenan, worn in battle by the legendary . . . what's-her-name. You know, historical legend woman. It's priceless, and you have it leaning against a barrel of undoubtedly sour wine." She laid the shield down and waded into the room. Opening a trunk, she peered in. "You let moths and moisture destroy masterpieces—"

"Possessions don't matter to me as much as they do to some people." Maybe she should have taken better care of her belongings, but after Jentt's death, she just hadn't been able to bring herself to care. *Later,* she'd always said. Later, when she didn't have to worry about finding more bones. Later, when Jentt was with her every day and she wasn't consumed with fear of a permanent goodbye. After she brought him back, then she'd tackle all the tasks she'd postponed.

"You're trying to insult me to deflect from yourself, but I see you. This is how you express your pain, through a lack of care for yourself and your belongings." Zera picked up a rusted scythe. Cobwebs clung to its handle.

"Cleaning just isn't important to me."

"Obviously."

Aha, there it was! Kreya climbed over an on-its-side wardrobe and pulled aside a carpet to reveal her prize: a crawler. Made of metal and wood, the crawler was—like everything else in the cellar—not in the best of shape. The carriage, an orb large enough to hold two passengers, was disconnected from the eight spiderlike metal legs. *Seven*, she corrected. One leg was missing. She began searching for it. If she could get the contraption operational again, they could take a much more direct route across the cliffs, rather than needing to follow roads. That could cut their travel time in half.

Given the choice, Kreya would take a construct over a talisman any day. Constructs didn't run out of power anywhere near as fast as a body could burn through a talisman. Just look at her little friend still scrubbing her stairs.

Zera was still complaining. "I detected an odor in the tower, but I assumed it was from Jentt. If it's you, we're going to fix that before we travel togeth—whoa, is that a crawler? Neat. You know those are considered old-fashioned now. The bone makers in Cerre have been working with the mechanics' guild on new cable cars that—"

"It's fast, it can climb, and it can conceal us—if I get it working again." Crawlers, especially old ones, were common enough to be unremarkable. Or, at least, untraceable.

"What are the odds of that?" Zera asked.

Undeterred, Kreya scanned the basement until she spotted the missing leg: wedged between two crates. She freed it and held it up triumphantly as she climbed back to the crawler.

"Wonderful."

Despite her sarcasm, Zera—with the use of a strength talisman—carried the pieces of the crawler outside and spread them out on the grass between the pine trees. Removing her coat, Zera cleaned the inside of the carriage, while Kreya worked on the mechanics.

Forgetting that Zera was there, Kreya sang to herself as she worked. She was on her third ballad when she realized that a voice was singing along with her, softly. She broke off and looked over at Zera, who then stopped singing.

"We had a nice harmony going," Zera complained.

"I don't . . ." She didn't know how to explain that she'd never sung where anyone could overhear. She must have gotten even more used to being alone than she'd thought, if she'd so quickly forgotten that anyone else could hear her.

"I had no idea you could sing. You shouldn't do the soprano bits, but your alto register is quite lovely." Zera demonstrated a high trill, then a lower warble. "I'm a soprano. Guine has been helping teach me to harmonize better—I have a tendency to steal the stage."

"I'd never have guessed," Kreya muttered.

"Are we going to try to get along on this journey, or are you going to keep sniping at me? I recognize that you don't approve of who I've become, but it will be tedious cooped up inside the crawler with you if you don't try to hide your opinions."

Kreya raised her eyebrows pointedly. "Like you do?"

"My opinions are truths."

She almost laughed. Zera was still so . . . Zera. "Just help me attach the undercarriage."

Working together, they lifted the orb onto the base, and

Kreya scurried around, connecting it. Finishing, she stepped back and surveyed their work.

"Much better than hiking," Zera said, satisfied.

Kreya wondered if she'd still feel that way when the crawler was inching up a near-vertical slope and they were dependent on their handiwork for their lives. She hoped so.

IT TOOK A FEW MORE HOURS TO LOAD THE CRAWLER with supplies: dried venison, nuts, berries, jars of water, a cache of weapons, extra unused animal bones in case of repairs. Kreya said no to additional cushions, as well as no to Zera's request to "just hop on home for a few items."

She didn't say no, though, when Zera insisted on anonymously gifting her horse Merridia to a local farmer, even though "local" was many miles away. There were too many wolves, bears, and other predators to safely leave the horse here untended. Zera promised she'd use a bit of a speed talisman to both deliver Merridia and return.

At least Zera isn't so self-absorbed she fails to care for her horse, Kreya thought.

Climbing the stairs to the bedroom, Kreya retrieved the rag doll construct that Zera had tossed across the room. While she waited for Zera to return, she sat on the bed beside Jentt's body and repaired the construct—the problem was the bone that animated it had been knocked out of alignment. She reset it, placed her fingertips on it, and closed her eyes. "*Insa anira. Ori ranna. Insa anira-lee, anira-ra, anira-nee.*"

It shuddered under her fingers and then sat up. Opening her eyes, Kreya noticed that the other rag dolls were clustered around, some on the bed and some by her feet. She gathered them into her arms, and they swarmed all over her, patting her hair and stroking her back. "I'll be gone for longer than usual, little ones. You'll keep him safe, won't you? And yourselves?"

After she patted each of them, they dispersed, up into the rafters and back into the shadowy corners of the room. She turned to Jentt, still wrapped in linen, still motionless, still dead. "I know you won't approve of this, but you don't get a vote. Not until you live again. And then you can fuss at me all you want, and I'll love it."

She checked all the locks on the window shutters and repaired the locking mechanism on the front door, the one that had allowed Zera inside without any effort. After she was certain it was functional, she exited the tower.

Zera returned shortly after, and they were ready to embark.

"Go on," Zera said, wiggling her fingers. "Do your thing."

Getting down on the ground, Kreya lay on her back under the contraption. It was fueled by three bones: one from a goat, another from a mountain lion, and the last from a horse. The lion bone was cracked, and the horse bone had tiny fractures running through it, but they still had power vibrating through them. She wished she'd been able to afford a fresh river lizard bone—that would have really given the crawler a jolt. These would do the job, though.

"Do you have one more adventure in you?" she whispered to the crawler. *Do I?* she wondered.

She laid her hands on the bones, fingers spread to touch all of them, and said the spell to animate it. Through her fingertips, she felt it begin to shake. It hummed, vibrating, as its eight metal legs began to click and twitch.

"Watch out!" Zera shouted.

Kreya rolled to the left as one leg slammed down. Its point pierced the dirt where she'd been. Reaching under, Zera held out her hand, and Kreya grabbed it and scrambled up toward the tower, out of the way, as the crawler lurched side to side on its spider legs.

"What did you do?" Zera cried as she shoved Kreya back behind her. She pressed a talisman into Kreya's hand, and Kreya glanced at the markings—speed.

"Give it a minute."

"Oh? Is that how long it'll take to crush us?"

The crawler careened closer to them, as if drawn by their voices. It tipped, unbalanced, as it strained to walk on only two of its legs, then the other legs seemed to remember what their purpose was. It scuttled backward toward the cliff.

Zera squeaked and clutched Kreya's arm.

Kreya shook her off. "It'll be fine."

It tottered back even closer to the cliff.

"Probably," Kreya added.

Then it lurched forward again, before settling in a squat, motionless except for a purring kind of vibration. The hatch popped open.

Kreya started for it. "All right, let's go."

"Are you mad? Didn't you just see that?"

"It was just getting its bearings. Think how discombobulated you'd be if you were asleep for twenty-five years." Crossing the clearing, Kreya climbed into the carriage. It gave a shake as it absorbed her weight. Looking over her shoulder, she beckoned Zera. "Perfectly safe! Until it breaks, and we plummet to our deaths."

She sat back in one of the benchlike seats. The windows were slits, making the view of the opposite mountain look like a framed painting. A few seconds later, Zera climbed in with her and shut the hatch. "I hate this, and I hate you."

"Beats walking, doesn't it?"

"Doesn't beat flying," she snapped.

Then the crawler lurched, and Zera clutched the walls, arms spread wide.

Leaning her head back, Kreya closed her eyes.

"You're going to nap?" Zera's voice crept up an octave.

Eyes still shut, Kreya smiled as the crawler began to climb across the mountain.

CHAPTER SIX

The crawler clung to the side of the cliff.

"Kreya? Sweetheart?"

Her eyes closed, Kreya contemplated pretending she was still asleep. Or dead. It had been blessedly lovely not having to listen to Zera prattle on for the last few hours.

She felt a tickle on her cheek.

Then a shake.

"Dearest, the crawler isn't moving."

She knew that.

Okay, no, she hadn't noticed. *Maybe I really did fall asleep,* she thought. Kreya opened her eyes to see Zera's concerned face two inches from hers. She scrambled back, hit her head against one of the supply packs, and glared at Zera. "How long have we been stopped?"

"A few minutes. It let out a pathetic whimper, and that was it. Good news is it hasn't lost its grip, so hooray for that. Bad news is—"

Kreya stuck her head out the hatch and saw the bad news. They'd been traversing the near-vertical cliff face of Mount Dorian and were about halfway across. She looked up and squinted into the sun. It was a thousand feet to the top of the cliff. And down . . . down were the deadly monster-ridden mists.

"I'll fix this." She rooted through her supply of spare bones. She didn't have any perfect replacements, which was why she hadn't replaced them before their journey, but so long as she could get herself and Zera off this cliff . . . Opening another pack, she located her climbing gear.

"You can't climb out there. That's an idiotic idea."

"You used to like my ideas."

"Of course. Back when your ideas were 'let's save the world,' not 'let's take unnecessary risks' or 'let's violate the laws of nature for personal reasons.' I question your judgment these days."

Fair enough, Kreya thought. *So do I.* She pulled on her climbing harness and then clipped the tether to a metal beam above the entrance hatch. "Get your flight talismans ready."

"Sad as I am to admit it, they don't have enough oomph to fly the two of us *and* the crawler *and* our supplies to safety." She scooted closer to the door as Kreya opened it.

"Noted." Wind hit Kreya's face, and she braced herself. Holding on to the side of the crawler, she stuck her foot out until her toes touched one of the crawler's legs. Taking a deep breath, she shifted her weight and pushed off the crawler's body. She clung to the leg.

Zera was still squawking her objections, but Kreya couldn't hear her over the wind, which was a plus. She affixed another clip to the leg. Bracing herself between the cliff face and the crawler, she positioned herself so she was standing on two legs at once, with her back against the cliff. Her muscles shrieked in protest against the awkward position, but it was the only way to reach the underside of the crawler.

Her heart thudded fast and hard, and she was aware of the amount of nothingness beneath her. *Don't think about it,* she ordered herself. *Focus on the task.*

She studied the bones. One of them, as she'd expected from the lack of motion, was shattered. She could replace that. But the larger problem was the bone that *hadn't* failed, the mountain goat femur that was responsible for steadiness . . . and the sole reason they hadn't fallen yet.

It had fractures running through it.

Her heart thumped faster.

One problem at a time, she told herself. If she let herself imagine everything she knew could go wrong, she'd be too paralyzed to do anything. Right now, she had to fix the bone that controlled motion. *Get to the top, and worry about the next catastrophe then.*

"Be ready!" Kreya called to Zera.

Zera called back, "What's wrong?"

Focused on the task, she ignored Zera. Her thigh muscles began to shake with the strain of holding her position, but she stayed steady. First, she dislodged the broken bone. She let it fall, tumbling through empty air, as she swept out the remaining shards. She fit the replacement bone into its slot. She drew a knife from her belt and shaved it down so it fit snugly in position. Quickly, she carved the markings that would allow her to access its power. It was a bone from an old sheep, which wasn't ideal due to the age, but it should last . . . fifteen minutes? Twenty? Less?

She checked her work once more, making sure the bone was secure, and then glanced down. Very, very far down. Between the mountains, the valley was drowned in swirling mist. She'd never been down there, even at the height of her adventuring days. There was nothing at the base of the mountains of Vos but death.

That seemed doubly true from this position.

She spoke the word to animate the bone, and the crawler shuddered beneath her touch.

Her muscles screaming at her, Kreya climbed back up inside. She shut the door and stole a second to lean against it, catching her breath. Everything ached, and she knew she'd pay for it later.

"You did it!" Zera cheered.

Kreya didn't answer as the crawler restarted its climb across the cliff face. She scanned their supplies. They'd need the essentials. Her coat, of course. A canteen of fresh water. Knives, for both defense and carving. Quickly, she added the key items to her pack and secured two of the knives to her belt. "Gather what you can carry. If we don't make it, we'll need to fly out of here."

"You said no flight, remember? Because secrecy."

She *had* said that, but it was better than falling. "I can't replace the steadiness bone while we're on the cliff—the crawler will lose its grip if I remove it. If we're lucky, it'll last until we're on flat ground, and I can fix it. If we're not lucky, we need an escape plan."

"Still the same Kreya, always with a plan."

"Wanting to avoid dying is not a personality quirk."

The crawler lurched across the rock, and Kreya tensed as it faltered. But then it shuddered again and kept going. Zera handed her a flight talisman, and Kreya examined it. The markings had been inlaid with a matte silverlike metal that Kreya didn't recognize, which probably meant it cost more than a small village. "The activation word is '*renari.*'"

"How far will these fly us?" Kreya asked.

Zera hesitated.

Kreya narrowed her eyes. "I'm not one of your customers. Tell me the truth."

"It's more 'glide' than 'fly.' And the trajectory will be downward." Zera mimed their descent with wiggling fingers. "They're designed for travel between closer-together, less sheer peaks. You know, places where civilized people *want* to go."

Kreya looked out the window at the mist below, too wide a span to cross without lift to keep them airborne. Swirling, the mist looked as if it wanted to swallow them whole. "Can we climb? How many steadiness talismans do you have?"

"Plenty at home. Not enough here."

"That was stupid."

"You're lucky I brought any at all! I'd planned to save you from danger; I wasn't anticipating a cross-country quest to defile remains."

Kreya wasted no more time. Gathering up what she'd need, she secured it all in her pack. Beside her, Zera did the same. After that, it was a matter of waiting. And hoping.

"Come on," Kreya whispered to the crawler as it lurched along. "Just a little farther."

"Does talking to it help?"

"It doesn't hurt."

Leaning until her lips were almost pressed against the metal, Zera crooned, "That's a good crawler. You can do it. I believe in you!"

She looked and sounded so ridiculous that Kreya laughed.

Zera broke off talking to the crawler. "You started it."

"True. But I've been living like a hermit for the last twenty-five years, with only brief respites. I'm supposed to talk to all sorts of inanimate objects by now. You just look absurd."

Spasming, the crawler jerked backward, and Zera shrieked.

Her heart pounding, Kreya squeezed the talisman harder. The bone dug into her palm. *Please, hold on a little longer,* Kreya thought. She could see the end of the cliff in sight: trees and a walkable slope. If they could just reach it, then she could fix—

She heard the bone crack.

Such a little sound.

And then a cascade of pebbles down the rock face as the first leg broke away from the cliff. "Get outside," Kreya said. "Now. If we're separated, three sharp whistles."

"Like the old days. Yay. You know, I didn't miss the mortal danger part of knowing you." Zera shoveled several more items into her pack and then tied it shut. She hoisted her pack onto her back.

Outside, a louder cascade, as the second leg lost its grip.

"Go," Kreya ordered as she pushed Zera toward the door.

Zera climbed outside. The crawler shook as the weight shifted inside—and the third leg snapped off. Kreya grabbed the wall as the crawler jerked downward. She heard Zera scream.

"Status!" Kreya barked as she got her balance back. She gingerly inched toward the hatch, trying to avoid any sudden shifts that could dislodge the crawler.

"Not dead!"

"Then fly!"

"Not without you!" Zera shouted. "Get your ass out here!"

Kreya launched herself out the door as the fourth leg peeled off the cliff. She grabbed Zera's extended hand as the crawler lost its grip—the other legs snapped off the rock, and the spider began to tumble. Kreya's hand slipped out of Zera's.

Out of instinct, she clutched one of the legs. The crawler somersaulted. She clung to the leg and saw the cliff, sky, mountain peaks, and mist all flash by as she spun. Her stomach lurched into her throat. But she steeled herself and brought the flight talisman to her lips. She held it tight in her hand as the crawler rolled. *Not yet . . .* If she released at the wrong time, she risked hitting her head on one of the many legs. *One minute more . . .* Sky, cliff, mist . . .

Now!

"Renari!"

She felt a lightness flood through her, as if the wind were within her, raising her up, and she released the crawler. It tumbled down the cliff below her as she glided above.

Ahead of her, Zera was already soaring. She circled in the air, lower than Kreya—she'd lost altitude and was losing more. Angling herself downward, Kreya aimed toward her as the crawler was swallowed by the mist.

She heard it crash, echoing up from the valley. From the area where it hit, she heard cries and shrieks as it scared the birds and animals and, yes, deadly monsters in the region . . . which gave her an idea. A terrible idea, but still an idea.

"We can travel through the mist!" she called to Zera.

"Are you crazy?"

"It will hide our approach to the wall!"

"Yeah, because we'll be too *dead* to approach anything!"

Must Zera always *argue?* It wasn't as if they had many choices. Up and down were their only options, and she knew they didn't have enough talismans for up. "It's that or scale the cliff by hand," Kreya called to her. "Your choice!"

"I want an option C!"

"Aim for the crash site!" At least it would be momentarily predator-free. With luck, they'd be able to retrieve more of their supplies. And maybe, just maybe, the crawler would still be functional.

Certain it was the better of two bad choices, Kreya spread her arms as she glided down toward the murky whiteness. It enveloped her gradually, erasing the mountains and the sky, until she was swaddled in the misty fog. She heard the sounds of birds, the calls of monkeys, and the roar of the river monsters, but all felt muffled and distant.

And then all of a sudden, the ground was there, racing toward her. Flinging her arms and legs out, she tried to slow, and she crashed into a thick mat of greenery. Branches cracked beneath her, but the leaves cradled her. Air whooshed out of her as she hit.

Ow, she thought.

Regaining her breath, she took stock. She hadn't felt anything snap, thankfully. She'd be bruised, but she wasn't broken. Sitting up, she looked around and saw murky greenness. She did not see the crashed crawler.

Damn it, we missed.

She judged they were south of the crash site. Or else the crawler could have bounced or rolled. They had to find it. Fast. And they had to find each other. And not find any monsters— that would be nice too.

Within the valley, the trees were thick, their branches weaving together, their trunks wreathed in vines, and the vegetation between them was hip-deep with ferns and bushes. She stood, pursed her lips, and whistled three times.

She heard an answering three-note whistle back.

Wading through the ferns, Kreya headed in the direction of the whistle. Ahead, she heard the roaring whoosh of water from the river that ran between the mountains. Zera better not have landed in it.

Kreya spotted her through the trees: Zera's coat and hair

were vibrant against the relentless green. She was standing motionless, her back toward Kreya, looking at . . .

Closer, Kreya saw what had caused her friend to freeze.

The stone fish dominated the river. Easily twice the size of the crawler, it looked and acted as a boulder, shaping the river around it. Betraying its camouflage, its venomous spines poked out of the churning water, and its black glassy eyes were trained on the shore, watching for movement. She'd never seen one in person before and wished she could still say that.

"Stealth," Kreya whispered.

Moving slower, Zera withdrew a talisman from her pocket and whispered to it. She passed one to Kreya. Together, they backed away from the river and the deadly fish monster.

It shifted, and water sloshed onto the muddy shore.

Kreya and Zera froze.

She wondered how good its eyesight was. Did it hunt based on sight? Smell? Luck? Its glassy eyes swept over the thick greenery.

Instinctively, she closed her eyes, as if that would keep it from seeing her.

Wind brushed her cheeks, and the stench of fish filled her nostrils. Kreya opened her eyes, and the stone fish had shifted out of the water. On bulbous legs, it prowled the shore only a few yards from where they stood in the greenery.

Her heart thudded against her rib cage so hard that she felt as if she were rattling. The fish stench invaded her skull, making her head throb, her eyes water, and her vision swim. This close, she could see the viscous fluid that coated its body.

She felt pressure in her palm—Zera had given her a talisman. *Speed*, Kreya guessed. With as small a movement as possible, she shook her head. Here, the forest was woven too tightly, with vines, ferns, and underbrush. She couldn't guarantee those first essential steps, even with the best talisman. The stone fish was too close. All it would take was one brush against its venomous scales.

"Patience," Kreya breathed.

She'd learned to wait over the years. Hated it. Always hated it.

But she could do it, when she had to, listening to her heart beat, the river gurgle, the birds call out a warning from above. The glass eyes swept over them again, and she saw her and Zera's reflection, distorted in the curve of its pupils.

At last, the stone fish slipped back into the water and submerged itself up to its eyeballs.

Clamping her hand onto Zera's wrist, Kreya retreated slowly back through the trees until she could no longer see the river or its deadly inhabitant. Only then did she allow herself to take a full breath.

"You know, a few decades ago," Zera said, "you would have handled that differently."

"A few decades ago, I got Jentt killed."

"Yeah, and now you freeze at danger. Are you sure you're up for this?"

Kreya checked her compass. "North. This way."

"Not that I'm not having fun. Really, this is fabulous. Love the scenery."

They picked their way through the forest, keeping the sounds of the river to their right. Every so often, the underbrush would clear, and they'd make faster progress, but then they'd soon be back to climbing over logs and wading through ferns.

"Still sure this is a good idea?" Zera asked.

"Still sure neither of us has a better one."

Catching her breath, she scanned the greenery up ahead.

As the mist moved between the trunks, Kreya thought she saw a hint of openness. She led the way toward it, and Zera followed, muttering under her breath.

She spilled out onto a trail. All the greenery had been trampled, the soggy ground churned up, and the nearest branches broken. A shiver of unease crept up her spine.

Zera strode ahead, walking in large strides. "Much better."

"Be ready with a speed talisman."

"You want to jog through the valley?"

Kreya continued to scan the trees. "I want to run from whatever made this trail, once it notices us." If it hadn't noticed already. With this much thick foliage, it was possible they were already being hunted, and they wouldn't know until it was too late.

Zera displayed her talisman. "Ready."

Alert, they continued on. Kreya wasn't sure what was more draining—the hike itself or the constant state of wariness. She wondered how long they'd be able to maintain this pace, and how long they had until the sun set. She didn't relish the idea of being in the valley after dark.

Ahead of her, Zera halted.

Kreya stopped. She rose onto her toes, trying to see beyond her. She listened, but the sound of the river drowned all other noises.

Zera continued, and Kreya crept after her, emerging into a clearing. Lying across the mossy rocks was the body of a river lizard. If she'd thought the stone fish was large, this could have eaten that monstrosity for lunch. It was roughly the size of Kreya's tower, supine, with jaws that could have broken her home in half.

Luckily, it was dead.

Its torso had been ripped open, and it had been stripped of half its flesh, but that didn't make it any less alarming to behold. *In fact, it makes it worse. Because it begs the question: what killed it?*

They crept around it.

The kill looked recent, which meant it was possible that its foe was still nearby. The last thing they wanted to do was be that predator's dessert.

As they passed by its rib cage, Zera paused.

Kreya saw her eye the exposed ribs. It was tempting. Such bones were rare, due to the difficulty of collecting them, and the strength they held . . . "We can't linger," she whispered. But she stopped beside Zera, staring at the exposed bones.

"Think of the possibilities."

And she did. "I can use a strength talisman to break it off," Kreya finally said. "Speed to get us out of here before anything notices us."

Eyes glued to the beautiful bones, Zera passed her the necessary talismans, while Kreya drew out her sharpest knife. She felt the weight of the blade in her hand and readied herself. Bringing the talisman up to her lips, she whispered to it. She felt the strength fill her arms. Climbing up to the dead beast, she swung the knife and hacked through a rib.

Close by, much too close, a creature roared.

Kreya yanked the rib free. It was heavy, but she was still imbued with strength. She positioned it over her shoulder and then activated the speed talisman. They both fled down the trail as another river lizard, larger than the slain one, crashed through the trees behind them.

"Shit!" Kreya swore.

"Pass it to me!" Zera said.

Kreya handed the rib to her. "Peel off," she ordered. "Five hundred paces, whistle."

They separated, each plunging into the forest, forcing their pursuer to choose. Kreya ran toward the river, hoping her speed talisman would last until they rejoined each other. Alone, she felt the forest close in on her, but she kept her pace up, scrambling over the underbrush.

At three hundred paces, she veered in the direction in which she knew Zera had run. *Please be okay*, she thought. *Please don't be caught. Don't be dead.* She listened as she ran, knowing that any second she could hear the sound of a river lizard making a kill. She could hear her friend's last scream. And it would all be her fault. Again.

I shouldn't have let her come. I shouldn't have—

She heard three short whistles. When she found the trail again, Zera was only a few yards ahead of her. Giving herself a burst of speed from the talisman, she caught up with her. Her sides were heaving hard, sweat shone on her face, and blood dotted her forehead.

Not dead. Very much not dead.

But there was no time to feel more than a flash of relief. Just because they'd survived a few minutes apart was no guarantee they'd survive for longer together.

Wordlessly, Zera handed her the rib, and Kreya shouldered it.

They kept running, side by side, until the talismans' power wore off, and then they slowed, stopped, and panted, listening for any sound of pursuit. Kreya tossed her drained talisman into the bushes.

Lowering the rib bone to the ground, Kreya looked at it, then at Zera.

Zera grinned at her, and Kreya grinned back.

"I missed this," Zera said. "Never thought I would." She then eyed the lizard bone. "Hello, my pretty. You were worth it."

Kreya imagined if she'd had *this* kind of bone to fuel the crawler, it could have scrambled across that cliff in minutes. *She's probably calculating how much she can sell lizard talismans for*, Kreya thought.

But Zera said, "I spotted the crash site, not far from here. The crawler is pretty banged up, but if you could use the lizard bone with it . . ."

Kreya was startled. "You want me to use it?" It was worth a fortune, and Zera was a businesswoman now first and foremost. She'd made that clear enough with her life choices.

"Of course."

"Then we are still a team?" She hadn't thought that, after so many years, after Zera's disapproval of what she'd done and what she planned to do with Jentt, they were still . . . well, anything to one another but reminders of the past. She'd thought Zera had accompanied her out of some kind of leftover sense of responsibility or guilt or . . . *I don't really know why she came.*

Zera rolled her eyes. "Obviously. You don't flee from a river lizard with just a casual acquaintance. Come on, hermit girl. That busted-up spider won't walk by itself, you know. And we still have a long way to go."

THEY SLEPT NEAR THE CRAWLER CRASH SITE, BE-neath the shell of a dead giant tortoise, which was cramped for two and stank of swampy rot but was at least relatively safe. Kreya woke to the cry of a bird she didn't recognize and listened for a while before crawling out from beneath the shell. *We're not dead*, she thought.

Nothing had killed them during the night. She marveled at that.

She checked for any sign of nearby predators before relieving herself and attending to her teeth. She was still sucking on a mint leaf to rid herself of the last taste of morning breath when Zera emerged from the shell.

"I will never not smell of dead tortoise," Zera announced. "It's seeped into my skin. It's a part of me now. Henceforth, all tales and ballads about me will speak of my reptilian aroma."

"Mint leaf?" Kreya offered.

"I packed my own, thanks." Hands on her hips, Zera surveyed the remnants of the crawler. "Any thoughts on how we do this?"

The crawler had cracked open like an egg, and the passenger compartment was unfixable. But the underside was intact, even though a few of the legs had snapped off. *I could reattach them,* Kreya thought. *But we'd have to ride exposed.* It wouldn't be pretty, but it was possible she could get it moving again. "Plenty. I need you to be lookout while I work."

"And if something comes to eat us before we finish?"

Kreya shrugged. "Eat it first. I could use some breakfast."

She got to work, hauling the snapped-off legs back to the crawler body and lashing them together with vines. There was no shortage of materials in the sunken forest, which was a nice change from the mountain forest—she had access to an abundance of timber around her tower from the pines and spruce, but the myriad vines in the river valley made for excellent ropes. She also had her full array of tools. No respectable bone worker would ever be without them.

Or unrespectable, she conceded.

As she worked, she abandoned hope of manufacturing any

kind of compartment for them to ride in and instead devoted all her attention to the floor and legs. It required her to use a bit of a strength talisman to rebend the metal back into the right shape, but in the end, it all fit.

"Almost done?" Zera asked.

"It won't be comfortable," Kreya warned. "We'll feel every bump and bounce."

"But will it go fast?"

Kreya eyed the fresh lizard bone with glee. "Let's find out." Measuring, she decided half would do. They could save the other half for later. With Zera's help, she sawed the bone in half and installed one piece on the crawler's underside, between its many legs. As she carved the markings, she felt it begin to hum beneath her finger. This bone, even halved, had a *lot* of power.

Poking her head under the crawler, Zera asked again, "How about now? Almost done?"

"It'll be done when it's done."

"Sooner would be better, dear one."

Kreya paused, listening. "How many are coming?"

"Let's just say it's more than even Stran could fight with one of my best talismans."

She carved faster. Spreading her palms across the bones, touching each of the marks, she said the words that would infuse the crawler with the power of the monster's rib. "Get on," Kreya ordered.

She could hear the predators coming: croco-raptors, from their cries. Smaller than river lizards, but known to be just as deadly. They hunted in packs. *Shit, we're going to cut it close.* Their luck had run out. It was time to go.

Zera climbed on top of the crawler, and Kreya joined her. There weren't seats—those had been smashed beyond fixing—

but Kreya had lashed on a log for them to use as a bench. She wished now she hadn't wasted the time on that.

"Come on, bone, show us what you've got."

As the cries grew closer, echoing on both sides of them as the croco-raptors surged to surround them, Kreya ordered, "*Na-cri-ze.*"

The lizard bone hummed, the legs clicked, and the crawler moved forward. It crashed over bushes and rocks, and Kreya steered for the river lizard trail, using it as if it were a road.

Behind them, the croco-raptors gave chase.

"Faster," Zera murmured in her ear.

"*Raca!*" Kreya commanded the bone. It threw more power into the legs, and the crawler raced forward. She clutched the steering rod, keeping it steady.

"One to our left!" Zera cried.

Gritting her teeth, Kreya concentrated on steering. She headed for a tree with a massive trunk, gauged the speed . . . "*Raca!*" And then veered at the last second.

They heard the cry of the croco-raptor as it hit the tree.

Branches crackled as they smashed through them. Ducking, Kreya steered the crawler along the path. It rattled so hard that she felt as if her bones were clacking against one another.

"Hold together, baby," she said to the crawler.

"Kreya, I think we— *Fuck!*" A croco-raptor leaped onto the side of the crawler. Its jaw clamped onto Zera's coat, and it yanked her off the seat.

"Zera!"

Kreya lunged across the side of the crawler, but her hands closed over air. Her friend sailed backward, pulled by the monster, between the trees. Swearing, Kreya leaned hard on the steering, forcing the crawler to pivot fast. Its legs shrieked in protest.

Behind, she heard the other croco-raptors gaining on her.

"Go, Kreya!" Zera shouted. She let out a cry of pain as she was dragged over rocks. "Get out of here!"

Not happening. She hunched down beneath the branches. "*Raca! Raca!*" The trees blurred around her as she focused exclusively on the river lizard dragging Zera. "Use strength! Break free of it!"

Ahead, she heard branches breaking.

And then suddenly silence.

"Zera!"

Behind her, they were still coming. She didn't know how many. But where was the one who'd taken Zera? *No, no, no,* Kreya thought. She was *not* losing her friend. Not like this!

The crawler burst into a clearing, and suddenly Kreya saw them:

Suspended above the clearing were webs, thick vinelike ropes that crisscrossed between tree trunks on either side of the opening. Caught in the middle of the web was the croco-raptor. Zera was prone on the ground beneath it.

She wasn't moving.

"Get up, Zera!" Kreya called.

She lay staring up.

What's wrong with her? Kreya wondered. "Zera! Snap out of it!" *Please, stand up. Run!* Every bit of her felt as if it were vibrating with the need to scream at her friend to move *now*. A web in the valley—

Lifting her arm, Zera pointed. "Pretty as the sun."

Kreya ordered the crawler to stop as she looked up. She

expected to see one of the wolf spiders, known for their size and their webs—this was obviously a wolf spider's web. But what she saw was far worse.

Rare, very rare, the mindcloud jaguar was perched on a branch above a tear in the web, a dead wolf spider beneath one of its paws. She'd only heard descriptions of the elusive predator: shadow-gray fur, onyx-black teeth, and eyes . . . they were said to be golden.

You didn't ever look in its eyes.

The mindcloud jaguar hypnotized its prey, before it killed them.

Only three feet in length, the cat had been known to take down river lizards many, many times its size, subduing them with the power of its mind before ripping them apart with its teeth. Behind her, Kreya heard the other croco-raptors burst into the clearing, see the mindcloud jaguar, and then retreat. They prowled just beyond the clearing, ready to catch her when she ran, unwilling to risk the stare of their enemy.

"Listen to me, Zera. I am your commander. Not that cat." Squeezing her eyes shut, she kept her voice even and firm. "And I need you to get up and run. Run toward my voice."

"I'm sorry, Kreya. I can't move. It doesn't want me to move. I can't . . . I can't stop looking at it. You have to go. You have to leave me. Or it'll take you too."

Not an option. "You're looking at it right now, yes?"

"Yes. Said that."

"Then you guide my aim." Kreya drew one of her knives. She adjusted her grip on the hilt. Her palms were sweaty from clinging so hard to the controls of the crawler. Lifting the knife, she said, "Give me a position."

"Raise it higher."

She did.

"Left, twenty degrees. Less."

Kreya breathed in, steadying her arm. She'd never had Stran's strength with a sword or Jentt's speed and efficiency with daggers, but she knew how to throw a knife. She'd practiced for hours each day, at Jentt's insistence, and she'd continued having the occasional practice even after she'd exiled herself to her tower. No matter how many constructs she created, he wanted her to be able to defend herself. It had been a while, but her muscles remembered the grip, the angle.

"Lower," Zera said. "Only a—yes, there. There."

As soon as she moved, it would see her and switch its attention to her. She'd have only a brief second between throwing and when it could seize her mind.

She didn't hesitate.

Snapping her eyes open, she gauged the distance, adjusted the angle, and threw. As her arm completed the throw, she felt a warmth spread through her body. Her thoughts slowed, as if they were swimming through mud, and she dropped to her knees.

Distantly, she heard a wet thunk.

The blade buried itself in the jaguar's neck. It screamed, and in that instant, it lost control of its prey's minds. The croco-raptor thrashed in the web. Zera sprang from the rock and ran. Kreya grabbed the controls of the crawler. Reaching out an arm, she pulled Zera up onto the crawler with her and shouted, "Na-cri-ze! Raca!"

The crawler shot back into the forest.

Beside her, Zera activated a strength talisman. As one of the waiting croco-raptors hurled itself at them, Zera kicked it back. It slammed into a tree. A second raptor leaped for the crawler, and Kreya turned hard right toward the river.

Closer to the river, the forest was less dense. She urged the crawler faster, beyond the speed of the croco-raptors. At last, the cries of their pursuers faded. Soon, they were gone entirely, off to hunt easier prey.

"I fucking hate this place," Zera said.

Kreya agreed. "*Sinna*," she said soothingly to the bone.

They slowed to a less breakneck speed, and they continued along the river, northward, between the mountains and toward the forbidden plains.

CHAPTER SEVEN

After stashing the crawler beneath an overhang of vines, Kreya crept out of the mist to emerge just beyond the mountains. Zera was behind her, peering over her shoulder. Ahead of them was the border wall. Beyond it was the forbidden zone, an uninhabited land that stretched so far that it exceeded the horizon.

We made it, Kreya thought.

Getting here was supposed to have been the easy part. Instead, she felt as if she'd been shoved through a cheese grater. Zera looked in even worse shape, with a bruise across her left cheek and a slash through her left eyebrow. One arm was wrapped in bandages, though thankfully not broken. Kreya felt an ache through her whole body, plus a pain in her lower back that felt as if someone were drilling between her vertebrae. Still, they were at the wall.

"Should I distract the guards?" Zera offered.

Kreya snorted. "Not enough of them to be worth the effort."

She counted—three guards visible on this stretch of wall, which was far too few for the size of the area. Just bowmen, mostly clustered by the guardhouse. Catapults had been set up at intervals, but no one manned them.

It looked like no one cared.

Last time Kreya had been here, the guards had very much cared. When Grand Master Lorn had sealed the forbidden zone, he'd done it with an army. Where was that army now? Maybe there was something she was missing. A trap.

"Stealth and speed then, and they'll never know we were here." Zera started forward.

But Kreya grabbed her wrist. "It's too easy."

"*You're* too worried. Eklor's dead. There are no traps. Just a few barely-out-of-diapers guards to keep up appearances and keep out ordinary bone thieves. Darling, it's been a good long while since we've been ordinary. No one's expecting anyone like us."

Kreya loosened her grip. *She's right*, she thought. No matter how fresh the memories felt to her, it had been many years since the end of the war. This guard duty . . . It looked as if it was considered mostly ceremonial at this point, a light duty for those in training before they took on more important assignments. In fact, the nearest guard looked barely older than a boy. She couldn't see his face from this distance, but his body was lanky, the stretched-out look of a just-grown child. *Still a baby*, she thought. He hadn't even been born yet when the war happened. Besides, no one was expecting any thieves to try to cross the wall, especially here. Thanks to their crash into the valley, they were approaching from a completely unexpected direction.

She wondered if people had forgotten what had happened here. Had it been long enough for it to fade into legend? Luckily or unluckily, she didn't have to rely on half-forgotten legends. She had memories.

And she remembered there were culverts with drainage

grates along the wall, every quarter mile, to allow rainwater to flow from the plains and funnel into the valley. When the wall had first been built, they'd been secured with fine ironwork, the thick kind—impenetrable. "How long does it take iron to rust?"

"Depends if it's been exposed to water."

"Remember the grates? Think twenty-five years is long enough?"

Zera grinned.

Keeping to the trees, they crept parallel to the wall until they spotted a culvert. Sure enough, the grate that had been welded so proudly into position was riddled with rust. Even from here, Kreya could see the red-brown flakes on broken bars.

"Not one single guard is watching their weak point," Zera said. "I'm embarrassed for them. Honestly, how do they look themselves in the eye as their take their pay when they're doing this shoddy a job? If it weren't utterly against my interests to do so, I'd report them."

"We still proceed carefully. Stupid to survive the monsters and get taken out by a kid with an itchy bow-finger. Come on."

Together, they used stealth talismans to slip across the open stretch to the grate. Kreya didn't hesitate to wade into the river. Here, it was knee deep, and the chill bit her skin. River water swirled around her shins. The low arch shielded them from view.

Carefully keeping the hem of her coat out of the water, Zera picked her way over the rocks. She squatted on one rock and peered at the grate.

"Definitely rusted," Zera whispered. "Break it?"

Kreya shook her head. Breaking it would be too loud. Even the most inattentive guard would hear that. She mimed swimming under it, as an alternative to bashing through it.

"Fine. We do it the boring, careful, *wet* way. You know, you used to be fun."

"No, I wasn't."

"Yeah, you're right. You weren't."

Zera shed her coat and handed it to Kreya, along with an empty pack. She then swam under the grate. Pushing the coats and packs through the holes in the grate, Kreya then swam under it as well. On the other side, Kreya shivered.

Checking the wall—the sparsely posted guards were still unaware—they shared speed talismans and sped away from the wall across the plains. As she ran, wind whipped against her, chilling her wet skin and flinging droplets of water behind her. She was like horizontal rain, defying gravity as she sped over the plains.

Kreya felt a burst of joy. *We're here! Jentt, we did it!*

Three miles from the wall, beyond the limit of how far anyone could see across a flat surface and therefore safely out of sight of any guards, they slowed.

Zera whooped. "Loved that! Want to do that again. So refreshing to run without fear of crashing into a tree or falling off a cliff or being chased by a monster." She shook her sleeves. "Hey, I think we ran ourselves dry. Mostly. Perhaps I should add that to my sales pitch as a benefit of the speed talisman." She pulled her coat back on and executed a spin. Her coat flared out around her.

Pulling on her own coat, Kreya was only half listening to her. Yes, they'd made it, and that was wonderful. But as the adrenaline faded, she began to look at where they were: the place she'd sworn to never return to, and the place she returned to every night in her nightmares. She'd been so focused on saving Jentt, she hadn't fully anticipated what this moment would feel like.

Standing on the plains, she felt as if a hundred memories were crashing into her, threatening to drown her. Here, they'd come to fight Eklor. Here, he'd unleashed his army of atrocities. Here, they'd been outnumbered and, for the first time, she'd tasted fear and doubt. Until then, she'd believed wholeheartedly that the righteousness of their cause would lead to triumph. She'd been naïve and focused only on their goal, and this earth had soaked up Jentt's blood, as well as the blood of the hundreds of soldiers who had fought and died with them.

Yet twenty-five years later, the plains looked peaceful, with hip-high verdant green grasses blanketing them for miles. Lace-like white flowers swayed in the breeze, as well as stalks flush with lavender blossoms. Shining gently, the sun made it all shimmer for miles and miles.

In the distance, she saw the silhouette of a tower, broken. It was as jagged as the scar on her thigh, and she remembered how, at the height of the fighting, the tower had burned. Today, though, it was only silent stone. A tomb.

Beside her, Zera surveyed it all as well with her hands on her hips. "I can't decide if it's pretty or creepy, which, come to think of it, is about the same way I feel about you."

"The worst of the battle was closer to the tower." Kreya pointed. They should find the highest concentration of bones there.

They walked eastward, toward the ruined tower. A few birds were singing, perched in a nearby tree. Unlike the narrow pines of the mountains that strained toward the sun or the twisted trees of the valley, this young tree looked fat and free, with its arms spread wide and flush with leaves.

"Looks like nature found a way to bury the lost without any human help," Zera said. "Maybe we don't need to burn anything after all." Her voice was subdued, and Kreya wondered if the memories were flooding into her as well.

A few minutes later, they found the first skeleton.

Stripped of flesh, the bones lay curled within tattered fabric, all that remained of a soldier's uniform. Kreya knelt beside it, laying her fingers on an arm bone. She felt its power: weak but still there. "I'll need several, to match the potency of the freshly dead."

Zera sighed. "I suppose this is my last moment to stop you."

Kreya tried to keep the flash of fear off her face. She knew Zera's coat pockets were full of talismans. If Zera wanted to, she *could* stop her, and it needn't be right here. She could raise the alarm with the guards on the wall on their return if she didn't want to dirty her own hands, and there was very little Kreya could do to prevent it. She fingered the speed talisman they'd used to get here. If necessary, she could use it to flee, with as many bones as she could grab. Maybe it would be enough. "Well?"

"We came all this way together, and you still don't trust me. Thanks, Kreya. Love you too." Zera turned her back on Kreya and walked a few paces off, then stopped. "There are more remains here." She stood there, quietly, and Kreya didn't push her. Zera looked at the bones. "If Jentt hadn't done what he did, I'd be lying with them. Along with the rest of the guild's army. We bring Jentt back, and then you destroy any trace of the spell." She looked up at Kreya. "That's the deal."

"Sorry. I—"

Zera waved off her apology. "That's the deal, right?"

"That's the deal."

Zera nodded and started loading bones into her pack.

Moving methodically through the grasses, Kreya selected

the best bones and added them to her pack, cushioning them as best she could. It took only a few minutes for both of them to fill their packs with more than enough to ensure the resurrection spell would work. Far less time than Kreya had imagined. She'd been picturing this moment on the journey here, how she'd feel, desecrating the bodies of those who had sacrificed themselves— men and women whom she couldn't bring back, whom she hadn't come here to try to revive.

It hit her, then, that the magic—and bones—could do exactly that.

I can't, though, she thought. *I don't have the life to spare.*

Because even if their bodies had been whole, she had to save every bit of herself for Jentt.

Maybe it was selfish. Others lost loved ones every day. Why should she have a second chance when others didn't? *Because I sacrificed for it,* she thought. *I suffered. I worked and studied and did what had to be done, forbidden or not.* Still . . . "I wish I could save them all."

"I wish they'd never needed saving," Zera said. "Shame Eklor isn't here, and we can't skewer him again for what he did. The worst part is that he'd enjoy his status as most hated man in history. He wanted fame as much as he wanted revenge."

Surrounded by grasses that hid the dead, Kreya said quietly, "That's not the worst part."

Zera sighed. "I know."

The two of them looked at the broken tower, lost in memory, guilt, and regret.

They were still standing, wrapped in their own thoughts, when the abomination attacked.

Man-shaped but cloaked in a lizard skin, it sprang out of the grasses where it had been lurking and charged at them. Its head was a skull, with eyeless sockets, and it wielded a soldier's rusted sword. Its jaws opened as if it were screaming, but it made no sound.

"Watch out!" Zera cried.

Kreya drew a knife as the abomination swung the sword. Kneeling, she blocked it with her blade. The force of the stroke reverberated through her arms. Zera charged toward them, her knife drawn, and the inhuman soldier pivoted to knock her knife back.

It struck at Zera, with a slice aimed at her neck.

She ducked and swung up, as Kreya pressed her attack with slashes at his sword arm. He blocked her with a rusted shield. Brown-red flakes sprayed into the air, and the clash of metal on metal rang across the plains. But that was the only sound— the inhuman soldier was silent. It could not call out. It had no throat. Just bare vertebrae.

She heard the heavy huff of Zera's breath as she pounded at the soldier, and she felt her own heart hammering in her chest. The soldier fought back, its strokes practiced, fast, and hard.

Kreya signaled to Zera.

A nod back.

Quickly, Kreya lunged in, aiming for its shield arm. She sliced through the joint of metal and decayed flesh. It faced her, parrying her next stroke to its head—

Zera plunged her knife between the soldier's shoulder blades.

The abomination toppled forward.

And Kreya remembered the true horror of the Bone War: Eklor's soldiers were near impossible to kill, because they weren't truly alive. They just kept coming.

As if to remind her, the soldier rose again. Sword ready.

Grabbing Zera's arm, Kreya activated the speed talisman.

She didn't dare run toward the wall, not while they were being chased. The guards on the wall would spot them. So instead she ran north, sprinting through the grasses.

They slowed as soon as they'd put enough distance between them and it. The inhuman soldier lacked any talismans—it couldn't catch them. Still, it lumbered after them, a tiny figure in the distance. Her heart was pounding hard. That had been much too close.

"Where," Zera panted, "did that come from?"

"It shouldn't exist," Kreya said.

"Tell that to *it*."

She stared back at the impossibility. There was no doubt in her mind that it was one of Eklor's creations. The skull, the lizard skin, plus the vestiges of clothes and the sword, built on a humanoid frame made of animal bones . . . his signature style. He'd mixed dead matter with the inanimate in an unmistakable way.

But none of Eklor's creations should have lasted this long. A well-made construct could outlast its creator's death, as demonstrated by the cable cars that had been running for decades throughout Vos. Its life span, if one could call it that, was determined by the skill of the bone maker and the quality of the bone used. But no construct could last forever. Not without new bones to fuel it.

And someone to activate those bones.

Zera tugged on her arm. "Shit. There are more of them."

"Down," Kreya ordered, and then both flattened on their stomachs in the grasses as six of the unnatural soldiers moved in a V-formation not far away. They looked, Kreya thought, like a patrol. Their skull heads swiveled, as if sniffing the air, and they moved soundlessly as a unit.

Leftovers, gone feral?

Except . . . she knew what happened to a bone maker's creations if left unattended and unmaintained. Look at her cleaning construct. It would polish the same stone until eventually it quieted and stopped as it drained the last of the living essence captured in its bones. The key was that eventually it *would* stop.

But these hadn't slowed. And they certainly hadn't stopped.

They're new, she thought. She was sure of it.

Almost sure of it.

Or at least she thought it was a very real possibility. And if they were new constructs, or even freshly maintained constructs . . .

"Ready the talismans," Kreya said. "We need to get closer."

THE TRUTH WAS THAT ZERA HAD MISSED THE AD-venture.

She'd never have admitted that where Guine or anyone else could hear her. After all, she was at the pinnacle of success—how could she miss crawling through bug-infested grasses while inhuman soldiers hunted them? But there was something about how it made your heart race, skin tingle, and breath speed. *I feel alive*, she thought.

And she wanted to keep that whole "alive" feeling. Preferably elsewhere, while soaking in a hot spring and reveling in how very brave she'd been on the plains of the forbidden zone.

But now Kreya wanted to get closer?

"Closer? To what?"

"To the tower." Kreya began creeping through the grasses, in the direction of the ruins.

"I think you mean the opposite. *Farther.* You definitely mean *farther* from the tower."

"We need to see who created them," Kreya whispered. "We need to know . . ." Her voice trailed off, and Zera didn't need her to finish to guess what she didn't want to say, because saying it would invite both absurdity and horror.

"We *do* know. He's dead, Kreya. Very, very dead, the no-doubt-about-it and no-way-anyone-could-have-survived-*that* kind of dead. You know it's true. You witnessed it." Zera could not believe they were having this absurd conversation. She knew Kreya had been on her own for a while and that could unhinge anyone, but this was a new level of paranoia.

Still, Kreya was continuing to creep toward the tower.

Scurrying forward, she caught up with her. "Say it with me: 'He died.'"

"I know he died," Kreya said.

"Even his apprentice was executed. Publicly, remember? Oh, what was his name? Anyway, there was a festival in Cerre to celebrate his execution. It was a grotesque display of the basest of human instincts, reveling in revenge." The war had ended and the dying should have been over, but the public had been thirsty for revenge. They called it justice, but a different label didn't change what they meant. So Eklor's apprentice, a mere boy misled by the master manipulator, had had his blood spilled on the steps of the Bone Workers Guild headquarters. The red had stained the marble. Zera had excused herself to vomit behind one of Grand Master Lorn's favorite statues.

Kreya had left Cerre for good.

"I remember. Yet here are Eklor's constructs."

"The dead are dead." Zera stopped. Then she considered what they were carrying in their packs, and why. "I see your point. Let's check the tower."

Using the stealth talisman, they bypassed the patrol. It was a blessing that the grass was so long, though Zera tried not to think about how many ticks must have latched onto her coat by now. She'd need a thorough cleansing when she was back in Cerre.

The important thing was that she squash the tendril of doubt that made her worry whether she'd make it back to Cerre. Of course she'd be fine. Eklor wasn't still alive, or again alive, or whatever. The unnatural soldiers were remnants whose power simply hadn't expired yet. Right? Of course, right.

Of course . . .

Closer to the tower, Zera could see scorch marks on the stones, as well as black stains that she didn't want to consider. She saw the heavy iron door was bent, as if bashed by a battering ram—but she knew it had been hit with Stran's fist.

"Just like we left it. Except with a landscaping problem." Zera couldn't hide the relief she felt. She didn't know how she'd been sucked in by Kreya's ridiculous suspicions. Of course Eklor wasn't resurrected. How could he be? He didn't have anyone like Kreya, willing to bring him back. That was one of the flaws with being reviled. Even his apprentice had fled the battlefield, to be caught a mile away by the guild's unforgiving soldiers.

"No weeds by the door."

Yes, that was true. While weeds choked the cracks in the rocks, all the ground around the tower was matted down. Probably by the undead soldiers. It made sense they'd take shelter in the only semi-standing structure on the plains. That didn't mean anyone was living here—anyone living, that is.

"If I prove no one's home, can we leave?" Zera whispered.

"Don't do anything—"

But Zera was already moving.

"—stupid."

Clutching the stealth talisman, Zera darted to the tower and knocked on the door. "Hello? Eklor? You home?" Before anything could answer, she darted back into the grasses.

"You're an idiot," Kreya told her.

"I'm bait. That's always been my job."

"Which would be fine if we had Stran and Jentt to fight, but we don't."

Her heart was racing, and Zera had the inappropriate urge to giggle, but she kept control and watched the door. It was absurd to think a few leftover contraptions meant anything. After all, she'd seen the rag dolls and neglected constructs in Kreya's tower. Eklor had been an extraordinary bone maker, his skill unparalleled both before him and after. He could easily have created a few hardy constructs that had lasted and were simply continuing the tasks he'd given them before his demise.

And no one opened the door.

Nothing in the tower moved at all.

"See?" Zera began to say, turning to Kreya. She stopped as the grasses beyond her old friend bent in the opposite direction from the wind, and she felt her skin go cold.

"You're right," Kreya said. "My fears got the better of—"

Zera gripped her wrist. Made a slow circle motion with her finger. *Surrounded.*

The patrol, or another patrol, of unnatural soldiers had crept up on them through the grasses. So far, Zera had spotted ten of them.

No—eleven.

Shit.

Her heart began to thump faster, and sweat prickled her skin. She hoped Kreya had a plan. *Of course she does. Kreya always has a plan.* It was one of the things that Zera loved most about her. And hated. But mostly loved. "Tell me what to do, Commander."

"Run."

Zera started to sprint away, but Kreya hauled her back and they ran *toward* the tower. *Why always* toward *the tower?* Behind them, the unnatural soldiers burst out of the grasses.

"Strength," Kreya ordered.

Zera passed her the talisman, and Kreya didn't slow—she bashed shoulder-first into the bent door. It held for an instant and then popped open. They raced in, with the soldiers close behind.

Pivoting, Zera and Kreya slammed the door shut.

"Up," Kreya said as the soldiers piled against it. The hinges strained and creaked.

"It won't hold them long." *We're going to die,* Zera thought. *And unlike before, if we die here now, no one will know. They won't know how. They won't know why. We'll just be gone, and that's it.* She wished she'd never followed Kreya here. No, she wished she'd never gone to her tower; then she wouldn't have been facing her nightmares.

"Up *quickly,*" Kreya said.

They ran up the spiral stairs.

Zera tried not to think about the similarities of this tower to Kreya's hermit tower and what it could mean. Grime on the walls. Stifling air. Cobwebs. She tried not to touch anything as they ran up, past closed doors.

Behind them, an enormous crash shook the tower—the soldiers had bashed the door down. She heard their claws scrambling on the steps behind them. *We're trapped!* This was it. And she hadn't said goodbye to Guine and . . . No other names came to her mind, but there were plenty in her life she hadn't said goodbye to.

She'd always planned to die in her bed, with music and wine, with the chatter of people who adored her. She'd planned to be so old that makeup couldn't fill her wrinkles and so famous that random children would burst into tears at her demise.

With a burst of speed, Kreya and Zera pounded up the remaining steps until they stood at the top of the tower. It had been a library—half the walls still stood, with charred and empty shelves. A tree grew, gnarled, in one corner.

"Kreya?" Zera hated how her voice squeaked. She was supposed to be a professional! *Get a grip, Zera,* she told herself firmly. They'd been in worse spots than this, hadn't they? *Have we?*

Either way, she'd been much younger and much more in shape then.

"Flight," Kreya ordered.

Yes! Brilliant. The atrocities wouldn't expect that. Such a power bone hadn't existed twenty-five years ago. She drew out the talisman and brought it to her lips. But Kreya stopped her.

"On my count. Three . . ."

The soldiers were halfway up.

"Two."

"Kreya? Now?"

The first of the soldiers burst into the room.

"One!"

Hand in hand, they leaped from the tower, shouted the activation word, and soared over the grasses. All of the soldiers who had poured themselves into the tower and stuffed themselves into the stairs now had to shove their way back out. But those outside sprinted across the grasses.

Soaring above them, Zera thought she heard a familiar sound ringing out.

A laugh that she'd last heard twenty-five years ago. It crept inside her ear, nestled in her brain, and echoed there, the horror of it building inside her. *My imagination,* Zera thought. But she couldn't shake it.

Landing, they raced toward the wall, with the inhuman soldiers close behind them. Gaining on them. Her breath scraped her throat as she gasped in air, and she shoved her hand into a pocket, searching for the next speed talisman—and felt nothing.

"We're out!"

"Keep running," Kreya panted.

Zera glanced back. Swords out, the soldiers were closing the distance between them. A few had fanned out, to prevent their prey from switching directions. Ahead, she saw the wall—still a mile away, maybe two miles, though now she could make out the outline of the catapults and the guard towers. Her leg muscles burned, and her side seized, but she kept moving.

"Got anything?" Kreya asked.

"Stealth. Steadiness." They'd used up their speed and strength talismans.

"Got anything *useful*?"

"No." She wished she'd brought every talisman she'd ever made. She thought of her storeroom back in her palace at Cerre. She'd intended to bring enough for whatever crisis Kreya faced, but she'd underestimated their enemy.

Or overestimated herself and Kreya.

We're not going to make it, she thought.

But then—"They're falling back!" Kreya cried.

She glanced again and saw she was right: the soldiers had slowed. But why? Zera allowed herself to slow, catching her breath, and Kreya caught her arm. "Stealth to pass the wall," Kreya said. "We don't rest until we're on the other side."

"Right. No rest until we're safely with the deadly monsters."

"Exactly," Kreya said, but there was hope in her voice now, and Zera felt hope course through her too. Maybe they would get out of here alive.

Still, she kept hearing Eklor's laugh, mocking impossibly in her mind.

CHAPTER EIGHT

Keeping the pack of human bones close beside her, Kreya bore down on a chunk of river lizard bone with her knife, carving as fast as she could, as the crawler carried them into the valley. She heard the deer scatter in between the trees and the birds take to the sky, and she hoped the monsters hadn't noticed them yet.

At least the unnatural soldiers hadn't followed them to the wall.

He wouldn't have risked allowing the guards on the wall to see his creations. They'd halted a few miles from the border, to protect the secret of their existence. *That's why we were able to escape them*, Kreya thought. The only reason.

"You know I am right," Kreya said, not looking up from her work. Any second, the river lizards and other predators would begin hunting them. She had to carve quickly.

"I know no such thing."

"He lives."

"How? Who would bring him back? Even if someone else miraculously discovered the same secret you did, who would do it? Why would any bone maker want him to live again? He tried to destroy them all, remember?"

Kreya had no idea. And Zera didn't even know the cost of the resurrection spell. If she did, Kreya was sure she'd agree there was no bone maker who would pay that price—the years of their own life—for Eklor. Blowing on the bone, Kreya cleared bone dust from a groove and continued carving.

"It's not as if he could have resurrected himself," Zera continued. "That would be technically difficult, I'd think."

"If he somehow cast the spell on himself before he expired . . ." Theoretically, she supposed the spell could be adapted to heal oneself using one's own future, or to be precise, the future one would have had if one's life hadn't been shortened by violence . . . but even if such a thing could be done, she'd witnessed his death; he'd been choked by a construct she'd made. There had been no time for him to save himself. He'd had no breath to utter the words.

Could his apprentice have done it? No, she couldn't believe that explanation either. Even if Eklor had shared his most secret knowledge, which would have been highly uncharacteristic of him, the boy hadn't been anywhere near the tower at the time of Eklor's defeat. When he'd been captured, the boy had said Eklor had ordered him away the night before the battle. And he couldn't have come back to do it later.

Not after what the people of Cerre did to him.

"Marso confirmed Eklor's death both to us and to Grand Master Lorn," Zera said. "He never misreads the bones."

She knew that. But she knew what she'd seen on the plain: fully functional constructs, made in Eklor's signature style, patrolling his former home.

"Eklor is dead and never coming back," Zera said. "Those atrocities were remnants, that's all. He was the most powerful bone maker who's ever lived. Surely, his creations could have outlasted him."

You have to admit it's possible, she told herself. *And much more likely than the alternative.*

As badly as she hated him, she knew Eklor had been a genius. He could have found a way to extend the lives of his monstrosities. He could have intended for his soldiers to outlast him, to torment his enemies, for decades.

Yes, that had to be the explanation. Eklor was of course dead. She'd let paranoia get the better of her. "You're right. Of course you're right." Finishing the carving, she began installing it in the floor of the crawler, between their feet.

"Obviously."

"His creations still need to be destroyed," Kreya said. Such dangerous abominations couldn't be allowed to roam the plains. They dishonored the dead by their very existence. They should have been purged from the world after Eklor's death—the guild should have seen to it. "And I swore to you I'd burn those bones."

"Exactly what do you want to do? Take them on just the two of us? Or, ooh, visit Guild Master Lorn and say, hey, we were just out for a picnic in the forbidden zone and noticed—" She broke off as a river lizard roared.

Nearby, another answered.

Glancing up, Kreya saw the canopy of trees quiver above them as a hundred tiny birds and tree mice fled. "*Raca,*" she ordered the crawler, and then tightened the bolts holding the bone in position.

"Or were you thinking more of an anonymous note?" Zera

continued. "Because those are always well received." She shook her head. "No, we should just forget about what we saw."

"You can't be serious."

"I'm the only one being serious. They're doing no harm." Zera held up one hand while clinging to the crawler with the other. "Hear me out: They're beyond the wall and obviously haven't even come close enough for the guards to notice them. They're not going near any populated area. All they're doing is roaming an area inhabited purely by the dead. Let them roam. Eventually, in a year or a decade or whenever, their power will fade, and that will be it. No one will even know they outlived their maker."

The idea of leaving those monstrosities free . . . "They're designed to kill. They should be destroyed. An innocent person could—"

"Literally no one innocent will ever be in the forbidden zone. Honestly, those atrocities are a better deterrent than the guards on the wall. In fact, I wouldn't be surprised if Grand Master Lorn knew about them and left them alone to take care of trespassers."

Kreya opened her mouth and shut it. Knowing Lorn, it wasn't impossible. He could have decided it was an effective deterrent. "So we tell no one?"

"Well, you can tell Jentt when we get there." Patting the pack of human bones, Zera beamed at her with a sparkling smile, and then she waved airily behind them. "You know, assuming we outrun whatever herd of river lizards wants us for breakfast."

Shooting her a look, Kreya allowed herself to smile. She gestured at the newly installed lizard bone, now carved with steadiness symbols. "How about we just outclimb them?"

"Ooh, you finished! Will it work?"

Valid question. This wasn't the traditional use of the animal, but Kreya had a few tricks up her sleeve for adapting bones. She hadn't just been pining over Jentt for the past twenty-five years. "Do you trust me?"

"I know you want me to say 'with my life,' but in the interest of complete honesty, I'm going to have to go with 'sometimes.'"

Leaning over, Kreya activated it.

The crawler pivoted sharply and made its way toward the cliff that hemmed in the valley. They tilted backward as it began to climb.

"Yikes, that's unsettling," Zera said. It jerked as it slipped, then caught itself. "Or terrifying. Your choice." She braced herself, clinging to the log bench.

"Hold on," Kreya said.

"Really? That's the extent of your advice?"

"Hold on tightly." But she passed Zera a rope before tying herself to the crawler, a makeshift seat belt. Muttering to herself, Zera looped the rope around a bar and knotted it around her waist. The crawler continued to climb steadily upward.

As they left the valley behind, Kreya heard the river lizards below them howl their dismay. She didn't look back. "It works."

"I love you."

"You know my heart belongs to a dead man." But Kreya couldn't stop smiling. Soon, she'd be with Jentt again, and they'd have another chance at the future they were supposed to have. And it was thanks to Zera and her talismans and a friendship regained.

"That is both sweet and deeply disturbing," Zera said.

KREYA FELT AS GIDDY AS A TEN-YEAR-OLD WHO knew she was about to be given the present she'd desperately wanted—in her case, at age ten, that dream gift had been a collection of marmot bones. Unusual, yes, but it was what any budding bone worker would have wanted. And the gift had meant even more than that: when her aunts gave her that skeleton, she knew they were saying they approved of her dream.

Becoming a bone worker was one of the only choices available for a smart kid from a mining village. Her mother had been adamant that Kreya wouldn't waste her life within the heart of the mountains, and when her mother was killed in a cave-in, Kreya swore she wouldn't disappoint her. So she'd asked for a marmot skeleton, and her aunts had delivered. Aunt Lirra had trapped the marmot, prepared the bones, and gifted them to Kreya on her birthday, wrapped in leaves Aunt Neen had painted with pictures of woodland creatures. Later, they'd pooled every bit of gold they had to buy her an apprenticeship in the Bone Workers Guild. But it was that first moment—that gift—that she was most grateful for.

This felt like that day.

It even involves a skeleton, she thought.

She was grinning as she and Zera rode the crawler out of the pine forest into the clearing of her tower. And then she felt as if her face, her blood, her every thought had frozen inside her as she looked at her ruined home.

Charred and blackened, the broken door lay strewn in pieces on the moss. The window shutters had been burned away, and the windows were shrouded in shadows. The roof was gone, also burned.

"Fuck," Zera whispered.

"Jentt!" Kreya flung herself off the crawler and half-ran, half-stumbled toward the tower. All she saw was the window of the bedroom, dark above her.

"Kreya, come back! Whoever did this could still be here!"

But she already knew who had done this. The villagers of Eren. They must have been searching for her ever since that girl's funeral. She should have known they wouldn't have given up. She should have moved Jentt into one of the caves. She should have left stronger constructs to protect him. She should have taken him with her, or been here with him, or . . .

"Jentt!"

She knew he couldn't hear her, but she couldn't help screaming his name.

Racing into the tower, she ran up the steps. The stone was cold to the touch—the flames must have died down hours, even days, ago. Only the stench of smoke still lingered in the air. She tasted the bitter tang as it coated the tongue.

A few steps up, she found the cleaning construct. Its bones and gears had been broken, as if it had been stomped on, and it too had burned. It lay on its smooth step, motionless. "I'm sorry." She was crying now, hard enough that it was difficult to see, and she slowed so she wouldn't trip and fall.

Zera's voice drifted up from the base of the tower. "Kreya?"

Kreya stopped in front of the door to the bedroom, or what was left of the door. It had been hacked with an ax, either before or after the fire. She touched the splinters, lightly, as if they were hallucinations that would, she hoped, vanish when they encountered reality.

But it was real. And she didn't want to see it.

She felt as if she'd been hollowed out with a spoon. It was difficult to breathe; every breath she took rattled around inside of her.

Footsteps behind her.

And then Zera's hand was on her shoulder. "I'll go in with you. Or for you. Do you want me to go in first? I can do that."

It was a kind offer, especially since Kreya knew how badly Zera did not want to enter that room. She tried to smile, to show she appreciated the words, but her face felt brittle.

"Are we positive our friendly neighborhood arsonists are gone?" Zera asked. "If I were them, I would have kept an eye on the tower, in case you returned."

"If they're here, they'll wish they weren't." Kreya pushed the door open. It stuck, creaking, and she shoved harder. Ash rained down on her shoulders. She blinked it out of her eyes.

Sunlight streamed in through the unshuttered window in a way that Jentt would have loved. She made her eyes shift from the window to the burnt bed—

The burnt, *empty* bed.

"They took him."

Kreya pivoted, striding back to the stairs, but before she could take more than a step out of the bedroom, Zera caught her arm. "Who took him? Where are you going? You can't go rushing off—"

"The villagers. The last ones I stole from. It must have been them." They'd taken him, presumably to burn him on a pyre and hoist his ashes onto their cliff. "I need a speed talisman."

"A, we don't have any left. And B, I'm not going to let you race off and get yourself killed because you—"

"They'll destroy him! I can't bring him back from ashes! Give me a talisman!"

"I don't have a talisman! Kreya—stop. Think."

Sucking in air, she prepared to yell, and then she deflated.

With the amount of time that had passed, Jentt had to be already gone. It was a lost cause. She'd returned too late.

"I'm not saying don't go after them and kick their asses, but plan first. Please. Or you'll be on the pyre too." Zera unloaded several talismans, shifting them from her pockets to Kreya's. She didn't know how useful they'd be—one for steadiness, another for flight. "Take these. Use whatever you need. I'll be right behind you. Just . . . please, one second to think, okay?"

Kreya heard a whirring from the stairwell. Faint. Familiar. She pushed past Zera, homing in on it. She stepped past the crushed cleaning construct and down to the entrance.

Her bird construct was there. Unharmed.

She didn't know how it had survived the destruction. Kneeling, she touched its skull lightly. "Hey, little one, I am so glad to see you."

It whirred at her, and then it pivoted and hopped toward the cellar.

"You hid down there? Clever." She wondered if any of her other creations had had the chance to escape the fire. She hadn't seen any of the rag dolls, though she hadn't expected to—they would have burned like tinder.

The bird led the way down the stairs, and she joined it, descending into the darkness.

Behind her, Zera said, "You're just . . . following that *thing* into the dark. See, this is what I'm talking about when I say *plan*. You could ask me if I have any cat-eye talismans. I do. Want one? Offers better night vision. Or if you want to preserve my talismans for emergencies, we could use a lantern. Nice, simple solution. How about a lantern? You don't even have to do or say anything to use one." When Kreya didn't answer, she said,

"Okay then. I am going to grab a lantern. Don't . . . Just . . . I'll be right back."

The darkness folded around her like a coat. She stepped carefully, knowing how much trash had been shoved down here, knowing it was all wrecked and burnt and nothing would be where she'd left it. Her toes collided with an object, and she felt ahead of her, climbing over it.

Ahead of her, the bird whirred, and she followed the noise.

"So very clever," she said, praising it.

The villagers wouldn't know the cellar led into the caves, but her construct had remembered. Kreya hadn't known it was that bright.

Listening hard, she heard the murmuring, nonsense words tumbling over one another, and she smiled in the darkness, as much as her heart ached. "My little ones."

She felt fabric brush against her as the rag dolls surrounded her. Stopping, she knelt, and they clambered over her. She stroked them as if they were living pets in need of reassurance. "I'm sorry I wasn't here. You must have been so scared. But I'm here now. I'll take care of you. I wish . . ." Her voice broke. She swallowed and continued. "I wish you could tell me what they did with Jentt. Did they destroy him? Did they take him with them? How long ago were they here, and what direction did they go?"

She knew they couldn't answer, and she wasn't certain whether they could understand any of what she said. They continued to crawl over her, nestling against her neck, circling around her waist, pressing against her as if her closeness comforted them.

And then they shrieked and scattered as light flickered against the wall.

"Come back, it's okay," Kreya called.

Zera carried the lantern into the cellar. "Oh, look at that, the Shield of Lothmenan—or what's left of it." She poked at the shield with her foot. The heat from the fire had melted the designs, though the shape was still intact. "Where's your little atrocity?"

Kreya took the lantern from Zera and climbed over the rubble in the cellar. She pulled aside a crumbling barrel and squeezed behind it.

Gently, Zera said behind her, "You shouldn't get your hopes up. One little bird can't have been strong enough to carry Jentt's body to safety."

Kreya hadn't let herself hope that, even to form the thought in her mind, but now that Zera had said it out loud, it suddenly *did* seem possible. She rushed into the caves. Behind her, she heard Zera swear and hurry after her.

The bird construct was waiting for her inside, as were the rag dolls.

"Oh, they survived," Zera said. "Yay."

"On their own, they're weak," Kreya said, her heart pounding so hard it hurt. *Please, please . . .* She couldn't even articulate the hope. It was too delicate. "Together, they're strong."

"Like us. Except not. Because I'm badass on my own, thank you."

They followed the rag dolls and the bird deeper into the cave. Kreya thrust the lantern before her, hoping with every fiber in her body that its light would fall across the one shape in the world she wanted to see.

How deep did they flee? And had they really carried Jentt this far? Could they have? Why would they? Maybe she'd misunderstood. Maybe she was wasting time, when she could have been chasing the villagers. After all, the constructs weren't—

She halted as the cave widened. Here, natural light filtered through a slit in the cavern. It shimmered as dust from the cave lingered in the air, so that the beam seemed solid, as if she could touch it. It fell on a slab of granite, and lying on the stone . . .

"I'd asked them to give him sunlight," she heard her own voice say as she stared at the linen-wrapped body on the stone. "He always wanted to see the sunrise and sunset, every time I woke him. They remembered that."

"I don't believe it," Zera said. "Your little monsters did it!"

Kreya knelt. "So clever, my little ones."

They swarmed her like happy puppies.

"Okay then," Zera said. "I'll get the bones. You do the spell. Before a torch-wielding villager comes back to check on his handiwork, because I've had enough of this shit day."

Kreya laughed. "As always, you elevate a meaningful moment to pure poetry."

Zera grunted at her. "I'm taking the lantern. You keep the atrocities."

As Zera disappeared back into the tunnel, toward the tower, Kreya moved to the granite slab. She sat beside Jentt's body, while the rag dolls huddled around her. She had nearly lost him, for a second time. "Never again," she swore.

CHAPTER NINE

Kreya did not need the book.

She would have burned it herself after this final spell anyway, or so she told herself. It was best it was gone, though she'd mourn the rest of her library. Later.

Carefully, she unwrapped Jentt's body. The sun was shifting from the slice in the cave ceiling, and she didn't want to lose the light before this was complete. Not that she needed the sun for the spell. She just wanted Jentt to wake with sun caressing his face.

All she truly needed was the words, the bones, and a knife.

As she unwrapped him, the rag dolls rolled the linen strips into balls. They hadn't strayed more than a few feet from her ankles since the bird construct had brought her into the caves. She didn't mind. She hadn't known constructs were capable of feeling things like fear or loyalty, but she supposed these were different—they'd been with her for so long.

She wondered again at the soldiers on the field, lasting despite having no one to maintain them. Unless they did. But she shoved that worry away. Now was the time to focus.

"Yep, still dead," Zera said, peering over her shoulder.

"I need to concentrate."

"You know, he might be enjoying the extra sleep."

Kreya leveled a look at her.

"Just eliminating some of the tension," Zera said. "It helps."

"It actually doesn't." She made a shooing motion with her fingers, and a few of the rag dolls clustered around Zera's feet, chattering at her. Zera backed up rapidly after that, and Kreya suppressed a smile.

Maybe it helped a little.

She turned back to Jentt. He didn't look as if he were resting peacefully. There was a motionlessness to death that wasn't the same as rest. If it was peaceful, it was the serenity of stone. A lack of breath, not a breath suspended.

She wondered what kind of nightmares he'd have after this was over.

It's time, she thought.

She inhaled. Steadied herself. Picked up the knife.

Opening her hand, she sliced her palm and spread her blood over the first of the human bones. "Take my day, take my night, take my sunrise, take my life." She then sliced Jentt's sternum over his heart. She pressed the bone against the blood-less wound. "Take my breath, take my blood. *Iri nascre, murro sai enri. Iri prian, murro ken fa. Iri sangra sheeva lai. Ancre murro sai enzal. Iri, iri, nascre ray.*"

She repeated this, bone after bone.

As the spell spread, the flesh of his chest absorbed the bones, and the bloodied bones dissolved within him, becoming a part of him. She spilled more and more of her own blood, until her vision began to swim.

Dimly, she heard Zera's voice cautioning her. She was being too reckless with her cuts. She shouldn't slice so deep. She couldn't maintain this pace.

The rag dolls clustered around her, supporting her.

Even with them, she began to sway. *Not done yet. Must hold on.*

She felt hands on her elbows.

"You need to stop," Zera said in her ear. "You're losing too much blood."

"Help me," Kreya murmured.

Zera began to draw her back, away from Jentt, but Kreya struggled, shaking her head. "Help me finish," Kreya said.

Zera swore at her, but then Kreya felt Zera's hands on her wrist. She helped her squeeze more blood to spread on the bones. Kreya said the words as Zera guided her hand, pressing the bone into Jentt's body.

At last, Kreya staggered back. "Enough."

Half her life, drained into Jentt, so that he would live.

They'd live and they'd die together this time. Barring accident. Barring murder. Barring disaster. *And barring my getting any of the words wrong.* However many years were left of her natural life span, they now each had half that. But they'd have it together.

Sagging against Zera, Kreya felt faint. A giggle bubbled out of her lips.

"Okay, that was way too much blood to lose with not enough food," Zera said, wrapping a strip of linen around Kreya's hand, tight to cut off the loss of any more blood. "You need juice and—whoa, that was fast." Her eyes wide, she gawked over Kreya's shoulder. "Hey, Jentt."

Calm and warm, Jentt's voice filled the cave. "Hey, Zera."

She lifted her head to see her husband, sitting up in a pool of sunlight in the moments before the light slipped beyond the slit in the ceiling. He looked as if he were glowing in gold, or perhaps that was just her vision blurring from blood loss. She didn't care which it was. He was awake and alive, and he'd stay that way. "I did it. Wheee." She lacked the strength for a proper cheer. Her head felt as if it were swimming through murk.

"Blood loss?" Jentt asked.

"Yes, she failed to warn me about that," Zera said. "Any minute now she's going to faint dramatically so we'll make a fuss and worry over her." She was still pressing steadily on Kreya's palm, stanching the blood. Kreya was fairly certain it had stopped flowing a while ago. She hadn't cut an artery, after all. She'd been careful. Just the right amount of blood for the right amount of bones. It was only that she'd used a lot of bones, to buy the necessary years. "How do *you* feel, dead boy?" Zera asked Jentt. "Any dramatic side effects for you that Kreya conveniently forgot to tell me?"

"Right as rain," he said.

He tilted his head back to feel the last of the sun as it slipped beyond the slit in the stone ceiling and the cave fell into shadows. She saw him breathe deeply, then hoist himself off the slab of granite. She opened her mouth to tell him to recover more first, but somehow the words wouldn't form in her mouth. Her tongue felt thick.

Suddenly, Jentt was beside her, lifting her onto the granite slab. "She needs sugar, to replace what she lost."

"We're lacking access to the larder right now," Zera said. "Hang on, though. I might have . . ."

Kreya didn't hear the rest of what Zera said or Jentt's response. She felt as if she were floating in an ocean, with the night sky overhead. *I've never seen an ocean*, she thought. *I'd like to, someday.* She felt liquid drops touch her lips. She licked and then swallowed.

A few minutes later, her eyes fluttered open. She thought it was minutes. It could have been hours, weeks, years, but no, Jentt was here, with Zera. Her rag dolls and the bird construct were pressed all around her. She petted them, reassuring them, as she sat up.

"She's awake!" Zera said. "Good to see you back in the land of the living, love." Then she snorted at her own joke.

Jentt caressed her cheek and then checked her pulse in her neck. "You scared us."

Kreya smiled at him. "Promise I won't do it again." Still feeling weak, she didn't try to stand yet, but sitting was fine. She couldn't stop staring and smiling goofily at him. *We did it. It worked!* "I'm retired now. No more bone work. I think we should travel. See beyond the mountains. Swim in the ocean."

"Or," Zera said, "you could come live with me in Cerre."

She liked that Zera had offered—that was a very good sign that Zera had forgiven her for involving her in all this. But it wasn't practical. "Too many questions to answer."

Jentt agreed. "I don't relish three thousand iterations of the 'why aren't you dead' conversation. A quiet life in Kreya's tower is fine for me. And we can travel, when you're strong enough."

"You didn't tell him why we're in the caves?" Kreya asked Zera.

"Kind of busy here with you fainting and almost dying and all."

Jentt looked from one to the other of them. "You didn't choose this location for its ambiance? What happened?"

"Someone—multiple someones, most likely—burned the tower down." It hurt more to say than she'd expected. She'd felt such relief when she saw the rag dolls had saved Jentt. But still, that tower had been her home for twenty-five years. She

thought of the books in her library, so many of them irreplace-
able, collected over a lifetime of study. Her notes, taken pains-
takingly. Maps of Vos. Histories. Poetry. Journals of past bone
makers. She had meant it, about destroying Eklor's book after
she'd brought Jentt back, even though it held other knowledge,
such as theories on how to adapt the resurrection spell to heal
illnesses and purge poison. But the rest? It was painful.

It also reminded her of something urgent.

"But there is a more serious problem: Eklor's soldiers."

"What about them? They're dead, right? Twenty-five years
dead?"

"So were you, Jentt," Zera said.

He looked at her, then Kreya, who explained, "Remnants
from Eklor's army are still functioning in the forbidden zone."
Succinctly, she told Jentt where they'd gone, what they'd done,
and what they'd seen on the plains.

Predictably, he freaked out. "You went *where* and did *what*?"

She ignored him and said to Zera, "We have to tell Grand
Master Lorn. What he chooses to do about them is beyond our
control, but he needs to be told so he can make an informed
decision based on all the facts."

Zera objected. "I told you before: we don't have to tell him
anything. Let the remnants decay on their own. They're separated from all of humanity. What harm can they do?"

"You don't like that the job's unfinished," Jentt said to Kreya.
He was still scowling at her as if he had a hundred more things
he wanted to say, most of them critical of her choices.

"I wish I still believed it was finished," Kreya said. It didn't
make sense that they could be functioning so well without
any maintenance whatsoever. But it couldn't be Eklor—Zera
was right about that—so she was content to let someone else

investigate. "If we warn the grand master, he'll be obligated to look into it."

Jentt covered her hands with his.

"There are zero ways you can explain without answering questions," Zera said. "None. Zip. Zilch. You remember Lorn, right? He'll jail you if you don't tell him how you know. He'll burn you if you do. Leave it be and forget what you saw and heard."

Kreya felt herself still.

What she'd *seen* was inhuman soldiers.

What she'd *heard* . . .

She'd thought she'd imagined hearing Eklor's laugh. After all, she'd had hallucinations so often in the past, living alone for so long, that she didn't trust her own psyche. "What did *you* hear? When we were leaving."

"I heard nothing," Zera said too quickly, twisting her hands. "The wind."

"Zera."

"He had a fucked-up laugh. I remember it. And I thought I heard it, okay? Is that what you want me to say? You want me to admit that I'm still damaged. I look put together, I look like I have it all, I look like I've moved on. But no. As badly as I tried to leave it all behind. Eklor. Jentt's death. You, abandoning all of us. And the aftermath, when everyone wanted to celebrate and I felt like I'd died. Guess it's still implanted in my subconscious, tearing at me, no matter how much I've achieved, and when we were back there at his tower with his atrocities around us again, I hallucinated his laugh. Happy now?" Zera sucked in air but didn't allow Kreya to speak. "That's why I don't want to reopen this wound. It's over. The war ended. We won. And now we even have Jentt back! Yay! Let the atrocities have the plain, and let me have a future free of those horrors."

Kreya felt Jentt watching her. He knew her better than anyone, even with the secrets she'd kept from him. He was squeezing her hand as if he knew what she was going to say. Carefully, she said, "I heard his laugh, too."

"Shared hallucination," Zera said dismissively.

Kreya shook her head.

"Why not? We shared the trauma. Makes sense we'd share the nightmares."

"I heard it as we flew from the tower. When did you hear it?"

Zera paced through the cave, and the rag dolls skittered out of her way. "He's *dead*."

Mildly, Jentt twisted her earlier comment back at her. "So was I."

Zera glared at him. "Kreya and I had this argument before, and she agreed that he's definitely dead."

"Before I knew you heard him too!" This changed everything! Couldn't Zera see that? It was one thing if Kreya had hallucinated his laugh, but if they both—

"I *imagined* hearing him too," Zera corrected. "Very important difference. He died, his apprentice was caught, and there was no one left to revive him."

"I don't know how he did it, but he could have found a way," Kreya said. He'd done the impossible before. By the bones, she'd done the impossible just now! Jentt was living proof that bone magic could be stretched and bent. "If he wasn't fully dead when we left him—"

"This is bullshit!" Zera yelled. "You killed him! You were there! And after, Marso confirmed it. He swore he was dead! Even if you flaked out after, Marso didn't."

Kreya was about to respond when they heard a sound: voices echoing through the caves.

The villagers, she thought.

And they were close. Much too close. Intent on their own conversation, Kreya, Zera, and Jentt hadn't been paying enough attention to the sounds in the tower above. She swore silently to herself.

She was too weak to fight, and Jentt was too newly revived to risk. They'd have to flee.

Quickly, without a word, they gathered everything—the linen strips, the knife, the lantern. She scanned the cave. There wasn't much they could do about the bloodstains on the stone except hope whoever followed didn't notice them. Without the direct sunlight, the stains faded into the granite.

Kreya opened her coat, and the rag dolls climbed up to the pockets and squeezed themselves inside. She lifted the bird construct onto her shoulder. Catching the attention of Zera and Jentt, she nodded toward one of the tunnels.

They fled through the caves, with Kreya in the lead. She couldn't move fast. She felt as if her muscles had been sapped of their strength.

Glancing back, she saw light splash across the rock. Harsh whispers ricocheted through the tunnel. She signaled Zera to douse the lantern.

Zera obeyed, and the tunnel fell into darkness. Kreya felt Jentt's hand on her shoulder. On her opposite side, Zera pressed a talisman into her palm. "*Cartini,*" Zera whispered.

"*Cartini,*" Kreya and Jentt whispered.

Blackness lightened to overlapping shadows as the talisman adjusted her eyesight. She hurried forward, stepping as quietly as she could. Behind them, the voices were growing louder.

She didn't think they'd left any clues to which direction they'd gone.

Their dumb luck, Kreya thought. *Our bad luck.*

She moved faster, pushing her body to obey, never mind how bone-deep weary she was from the spell. Beneath her feet, loose pebbles rattled.

Behind them: "Up ahead! I hear her! She's here!"

Jentt whispered, "Give me a knife."

"You can't—" Kreya began.

Zera withdrew a spare knife from one of her pockets and handed it to him. He tested the weight and adjusted his grip on the hilt. "Go," he said. "I'll hold them off."

"No," Kreya said. "We all escape." She thought fast. From the sound of the footfalls and voices, she estimated a dozen villagers, undoubtedly armed with either blades or farm equipment. She thought of her cellar—they could have helped themselves to weapons there, albeit rusty ones. Enough to do damage. "Scare them. We're not killers."

"They are," Zera muttered.

"Only because they're scared. Because I committed an atrocity, remember?"

"Oh, I remember this is all your fault."

"Maybe this isn't the time . . . ," Jentt said.

"Zera," Kreya said, "you must have at least one speed talisman that isn't drained. Check your coat."

Zera dug into each of her pockets and withdrew a talisman. She passed it to Jentt. "It's already been used, but it *might* have a few seconds of juice left. No more. One burst. Use it wisely."

"Get their lights," Kreya told him.

He nodded once and then darted backward through the tunnel.

Abruptly, the lantern light that had been dancing on the walls vanished, and she heard men and women cry out in alarm.

Jentt was suddenly back with them.

To her rag dolls, she whispered, "Fast and silent. Go for their ankles, then return to me." To Jentt and Zera, she whispered, "Keep moving."

She felt the rag dolls swarm out of her pockets and saw with her enhanced vision as they scurried back through the tunnel. She wanted to tell them go for the throats. For all her speech-ifying about not wanting to kill, the villagers had burned her home, and they would have burned Jentt if they'd found him. *They definitely want to burn me.*

But escape was more important than revenge.

Kreya, Jentt, and Zera kept moving, as silently as possible. She heard cries behind them and the thud of flesh on rock. Soon, the rag dolls tumbled back down the tunnel. Bending, she scooped them into her arms. They crawled over her and back into her pockets.

She counted them—all here.

Her heart was thudding fast, worse than it should have been—these were villagers, not undead soldiers. They'd faced far worse. So why was fear clawing at her throat?

Because now I know what I could lose.

They kept going.

Kreya felt her muscles begin to shake. The spell had drained her. She wasn't certain how much energy she had to draw on. She needed to rest, but had to—

Her knees gave out.

Jentt caught her.

Lifting her by the armpit, he braced her against him. She tried to make her legs walk forward, but they felt as limp as cooked noodles.

She heard him whisper to a strength talisman, and she felt

him lift her into his arms. Her head swam. It was hard to make sense of the shadows. But she was the one who knew the way—

"Give us orders," Zera whispered.

"Left three hundred feet," Kreya told them. "Then third tunnel on the right." She listed the rest of the directions, picturing the caves in her mind.

"Got it, Commander," Jentt said. "Now rest."

WHEN KREYA OPENED HER EYES, THEY WERE OUT-side the tunnels and it was sundown. The mountains were bathed in amber and rose. "Put me down."

Jentt lowered her to the ground.

"Everyone okay?" she asked.

"Are you?" Zera asked her.

"Fine." She took a deep breath, taking stock of her body— all the old, familiar aches were there, and she still felt drained, but she could survive all that. "I'm fine," she repeated. "Thanks."

"Anytime." Jentt grinned at her.

"Rather not repeat that, thanks," Zera said.

Looking around, Kreya took a minute to orient herself. She knew exactly where they were—they'd followed her directions, and they were now far from both her tower and the village of Eren.

There was a traveler's hut nearby, stocked for hunters and usually empty this time of year. She led them there and was relieved to see it was vacant.

The mountains of Vos were riddled with huts like these, maintained by travelers for other travelers. Kreya had used this one herself a few times.

At the hut, they fell into tasks: Kreya hauled wood from outside into the hearth and lit the fire, while Jentt aired out the musty blankets on the cots and pulled water from the well out-side. Zera discovered a dead mouse in the corner of the hut and liberated its bones, using them to carve a speed talisman—the kind that would give a five-minute burst. She offered it to Jentt, and he returned with a rabbit, which Kreya skinned and Jentt cooked.

They ate before Jentt said, "Do you truly believe he's alive?"

She knew exactly who he meant. "Yes."

"Maybe," Zera said.

Kreya admitted, "Maybe."

"We have to warn people," Jentt said.

"Absolutely not," Zera said. "Didn't you hear me say 'maybe'? We don't know Eklor is really there. Imagine how it will look if we claim he lives and he doesn't. I have a legacy to protect, you know. I'm not tarnishing that with unfounded accusations that will make me the laughingstock of Vos. You guys too."

"So we make sure he's dead ourselves," Kreya said. "No one else needs to know. If he is, no harm done. If he's not . . . we handle it."

"How?" Zera crossed her arms. "I'm not going back."

"Marso. He saw the body. And he can read bones to confirm it." Once she said it, Kreya liked her idea more and more. There was no other bone reader with the range, clarity, and accuracy of Marso. He was unique and extraordinary. If he saw what Kreya believed he'd see, it would be evidence that neither Jentt nor Zera could ignore.

"Love it," Jentt said. "Love you." He kissed her.

Zera sighed heavily. "Yes, you're adorable. And smart. It's a perfect solution. How's this: if Marso says Eklor's dead, then we never speak of this again, and we send a nice anonymous note to Lorn about the remaining constructs. Agreed?"

"Agreed," both Kreya and Jentt said.

Staring into the fireplace, Kreya watched the flames dance from log to log. The crinkle of the fire was soothing, and she allowed herself to enjoy being here with Jentt and Zera. It would be nice to see Marso again too, even if he laughed at their paranoia. He should be told that Jentt lived. He'd mourned his friend as they all had, and he could be trusted with the truth.

I shouldn't have distanced myself so much, Kreya thought. She'd missed this, being with friends without fear of losing them. She felt at peace, for the first time in . . . well, she couldn't remember the last time she'd felt this.

Zera speared another piece of rabbit. "So what's death like?"

Jentt considered it.

That was a question Kreya had never asked him, and he'd never spoken about it. It had always felt better to focus on the living moments while he was alive. They were so few and precious. Still, she didn't try to stop Jentt from answering. She found herself wanting to hear what he'd say.

"Dying was painful, until it wasn't," he said.

Zera whistled. "Yeah, figured that. At least the way you went."

Kreya wanted to glare at her but couldn't help but laugh. "I don't know how you functioned in high society and still never learned tact."

Zera wiggled her finger. "Power. And wealth, which is the same as power. You can get away with outrageous behavior if you have what others want."

Jentt offered her more rabbit. "You didn't used to be so cynical."

"Hard living. Or soft living. One of the two." She waved her jeweled hand. "But you didn't answer my question. Death. Is it endless dreaming? Or timeless nothingness as you're suspended in the eternal now? Were you in the great silence, and was it truly that quiet? Tell me which of the philosophers is right."

"Can't." He shrugged. "Every time I wake, all I remember is life."

Disappointed at that answer, she tried a different tack. "How does the math work? Are you younger than us now, since you've been alive for technically much less time? Kreya, how often did you bring him back? Are you married to a younger man now?"

"Does it matter?" Kreya asked. She'd never considered any of this. It wasn't as if temporary death were a valid way to preserve one's youth.

"Curiosity, my dearest. Never talked to a formerly dead guy before."

Jentt laughed. "I want to hear what you've been doing since I died."

"Oh, little of this, little of that." But she was being modest. As they ate, Zera regaled them with tales of life on the fifth tier in Cerre, the galas and the banquets and the excesses. She shared gossip about the debaucheries of her tier-five neighbors, and they laughed as the fire dwindled late into the night.

Only when they each lay in a cot, Zera by the hearth and Jentt and Kreya side by side, did Zera's voice shift to serious. "Many call me frivolous," Zera said. "They say I have wasted the life you gave me with your sacrifice."

"Nonsense," Jentt told her. "You made a success out of your-self. A farmer's daughter, living with the elite of Vos, the toast of the town. Your parents would have been proud."

Kreya agreed with him. "You can return to Cerre, if you want. Jentt and I can find Marso, reassure ourselves that we heard nothing, and send word to you. You've done more than anyone ever could have asked of you." Especially given how

Kreya had distanced herself, never reaching out, never considering Zera's pain as equivalent to her own. "You made this possible. Thank you."

Zera was quiet for a few minutes, and Kreya wondered if she'd offended her.

"We're not trying to get rid of you," Jentt said.

"Yes—please. I didn't mean to make it sound like you should go. Come with us if you want," Kreya said. "Visit Marso with us. It will be like a reunion. All we'll be missing is Stran." She couldn't read Zera's reaction to tell what she thought, which was a switch. Years ago, she'd been able to read Zera better than she could read Jentt. "I can't tell what you're thinking."

The fire in the hearth burned low, its embers smoldering. It shed a soft light throughout the hut. Outside, the mountain forest was black, alive with the chirp of crickets, the cry of night swallows, and, far away, the howl of a wolf.

At last, Zera said, "I'm thinking I heard a laugh. And I want to hear Marso say that's impossible."

CHAPTER TEN

The mountains of Vos boasted three cities: The gleaming city of Cerre, renowned for its wealth and beauty and as the central headquarters of the country's most important guilds. Tevvan, the holy city, famous for its philosophers, its flute music, and the serenity and wisdom of its mostly elderly citizens.

And then there was Ocrae.

The city of Ocrae was significantly less dignified than either of its two sisters. Like the others, it was still run by the guilds, but here, they were less concerned with decorum. Known for being loud and garish, Ocrae was, as Jentt had once described it, the rebellious younger sibling who didn't like to wear pants. Full of the hopeless and the hopeful, it was the city you went to when you *wanted* so desperately that it ate at you until you were willing to risk it all.

Wanted what? Well, that was up to you.

What is Marso doing here? Kreya wondered.

She rode the cable car up to the city center, squashed between Zera and Jentt. Twice the number of people were crammed into the cable car than was considered safe, and she kept her eye on the roof, as if she'd be able to do anything if it suddenly separated from the wire.

Beside her, Zera was unfazed. She'd already befriended ninety percent of the passengers and was regaling them with tales of half-tested talismans failing in spectacular ways and of wild parties where the revelers all used speed talismans to make love to as many people as possible. *I don't even want to know if that's true*, Kreya thought.

Catching Kreya's eye, Zera winked, which meant either that she was making the whole thing up or that not only had Zera done it, but it had been her idea. With Zera, it was hard to tell.

Jentt murmured in her ear, "At least she's distracting them from us."

True.

No one had noticed that Kreya and Jentt were traveling with Zera. It helped that both of them kept the hoods of their coats up, and that no one expected them—a known hermit and a dead man—to be here. She hoped their anonymity would last.

With a jolt, the cable car reached its destination. The passengers lurched forward from the impact, and a woman who stank of cheap wine smashed up against Kreya. Untangling herself, Kreya squeezed out the door and checked the contents of her pockets.

Already she felt filthier than she'd ever felt in her dilapidated tower.

"I hate this place." Out on the landing, Kreya was jostled as the other passengers flowed around her. She squinted up at the buildings, all of them with multiple spires, each painted a more garish color than the last. It gave her a headache.

Zera breezed past her. "I love it. Next time I send instructions to Guine, remind me to tell him I want to buy a second home here. Expand my business." She waved at a few strangers who were staring at her and blew a kiss at another.

"You're going to need to stop drawing attention to yourself or we'll never get anywhere," Kreya complained.

"Your wife is a spoilsport," Zera told Jentt. "I don't know how you tolerate her."

With an absolutely straight face, Jentt said, "Because she's excellent in bed."

"Ah, that explains it. I've been baffled for years. Can't be her personality."

Jentt gave a fake shudder as they pushed their way through the crowds. "Definitely not. She's much too bossy."

"Mmm," Zera agreed. "Always thinks she's right."

"And far too serious. So a guy dies. So what? She overreacts to everything." Wrapping an arm around Kreya, he casually elbowed a few pedestrians out of the way.

"I hate you both," Kreya said.

"Aw, I'm wounded." Zera mimed a knife wound to the heart. "We mock because we love. You know that." She skirted a clump of acrobats who had halted in the middle of the sidewalk to practice flips.

One of the acrobats tumbled in front of them, straight into a lamppost. He lay there upside-down, puckering his lips and flopping his hands like fins in an imitation of a beached fish.

"Sorry to disappoint, sweetie, but you are not a trout," Zera informed the acrobat.

Kreya stepped around him.

Leaning down, Jentt pressed a coin into the acrobat's hand. He then put his arms around both Kreya and Zera, and they plowed on through the crowded street.

"Where did you get that money?" Kreya asked when they were a block from the acrobats. "You didn't have any coins."

"Zera did."

Yelping, Zera whacked his arm. "You picked my pockets."

"Technically, one of the passengers on the cable car picked your pockets, and I rectified the situation. You'll find that most of your coin has been returned to you."

"Most?"

"Finder's fee."

Kreya grinned. Death hadn't slowed him or changed him one bit. Dying may have had an impact—she knew he had nightmares—but all the important parts of Jentt were there. No matter how much time had passed or how much they'd gone through, his essence remained. He was so full of life, even in his second life. "Remember how we met?"

"I stole your necklace, and you stole my heart."

He smiled as he looked at her, and she felt as if she were melted goo inside.

Zera rolled her eyes. "Seriously? You know it didn't happen that way. I introduced you, and you talked to each other every day for, like, a month. The ballads had to spice it up because you two were so damned boring."

"He made me laugh," Kreya said.

"*I* made you laugh," Zera said. "He made you feel smart."

"She's brilliant," Jentt said as if it were a fact as immutable as sunrise. She loved that about him. He believed in her. Even after her plans had gotten him killed.

"Are you two even aware of how nauseating you are?"

"Oh, yes," Jentt told her. "It's one hundred percent intentional."

Kreya agreed. "You make hilarious faces when we're lovey-dovey."

Arm around her, Jentt squeezed her closer and kissed her, and Kreya kissed him back, running her fingers through his hair.

She'd need to cut it again, now that he was going to be alive for a while. Zera huffed and walked faster, ahead of them, and from the way her shoulders twitched, Kreya knew it was so that they wouldn't see her laughing.

She'd missed teasing Zera as much as she'd missed kissing Jentt.

She remembered those early days when they'd both been unsure of their feelings, when every little word was so fraught with the weight of meaning. The popular love ballads went on and on about new love as something so amazing with all its firework-newness, but Kreya vastly preferred this: the absolute certainty that Jentt had her back.

Ahead, Zera paused to check the street signs. "Only a few blocks," she reported. "If he hasn't moved." She pointed toward the twisty streets, as if they shaped the buildings into anything like "blocks." It was more triangles or trapezoids. No city planning had gone into Ocrae. It had sprung up naturally, with buildings erected on a whim and streets laid out where they could fit. In fact, the whole city looked like a childlike god had dribbled mud into towers. *And then a drunk god vomited rainbows on it,* Kreya thought.

She didn't know what Marso was doing here. This was the worst kind of place for a sensitive bone reader, especially one of Marso's unparalleled range. He should have been someplace quiet and peaceful, like a forest glade. He couldn't possibly read any bones in this cacophony.

They turned onto Marso's supposed street and were confronted with an open-air market with dozens of fruit, clothing, and trinket vendors clogging the sidewalks. Each had spread a colorful blanket across the paving stones to display their wares. A few beggars were positioned between them, as well as performers. On opposite corners, horn players were belting out tunes that clashed into one another, while a bell ringer focused on her windchime-like cascade of notes. A few girls with braided hair were dancing around a boy with a tambourine.

All three of them halted.

"Marso can't live here," Zera said.

"You're the one who said he did," Kreya reminded her. Zera had claimed the info was only a few years old, though, so maybe the market was a new addition and Marso had moved to a quieter area of the city. Or out of the city entirely. "He can't have changed so much that he'd *like* this. He used to stuff his ears with cotton so he could block out the sound of crickets in the forest."

"In his defense, crickets can be loud," Jentt said.

Crickets were soothing. *This* was an assault on her eardrums. And eyes. She felt as if she were being bombarded with too much activity, and belatedly she realized why she hated it so much. It wasn't that she was used to her quiet tower. It was that it reminded her too much of being in the middle of a battle, where there was too much motion, too many screams, too much danger, too much death. *If it feels this way to me*, she thought, *what must it be like for Marso?*

Jentt snagged a boy with ribbons tied to his back as he ran past. "We're looking for a bone reader named Marso. Silver coin for you if you can help us."

"Don't know any bone readers. Thought they were all dead long time ago. Killed and stuff." The boy squirmed out of Jentt's grip. "But do know a Marso. Everyone does. He's the guy who sleeps in the fountain until the city guards make him stop. Back there the next day, though, and then the guards give up for a while until someone complains they don't want to wash their laundry with a naked guy snoring and drooling on their skivvies."

"That can't be our beloved Marso," Zera said.

But the boy dragged Jentt forward, through the market, and Kreya and Zera followed along. "You said a silver coin?" the boy prompted. Halting, he pointed at a fountain of three horn players. Water spouted out of the horns and into a murky pool, tiled with either green tiles or algae-coated tiles. Sure enough, a man lay on top of the fountain.

Jentt tossed him a silver coin, and the boy scampered away.

"Seriously, how much was your 'finder's fee'?" Zera asked Jentt.

Both Kreya and Jentt ignored her, instead staring at the man on the fountain. Stretched across the trumpets, he was naked except for a tattered loincloth. His body was so sun soaked that his skin looked like leather, and you could see every one of his ribs. He was waving his arms in the air as if he were dancing.

It was undoubtedly Marso—except the Marso they remembered never would have acted like this.

"Huh," Zera said. "I think he has a new tattoo."

Kreya and Jentt stared at her.

"Just because he's made different life choices than you two does not mean this is a cry for help." Zera waved her hand to indicate his nearly nude body.

Hearing her, Marso giggled. "Help." He then twisted over and licked at the water flowing from the horns, as if he were a feral cat.

"That's arguably more of a cry for help," Zera said.

"In fairness, it's not as if the two of us have done so stellar since the war," Jentt said. "Of all of us, Zera is the only success story."

Kreya opened her mouth to refute that, but it was a valid point. While she'd been poring over forbidden texts in search of a way to defy nature, Zera had been excelling as a highly successful businesswoman at the top of her craft. Maybe her taste was tacky and her spending habits frivolous, but that didn't change the fact that she had done what she'd set out to do.

Marso, on the other hand, most likely had never planned on becoming an accessory to a water fountain. *So much for his "unassailable reputation,"* she thought. "We should help him down."

"Agreed," Zera said.

Jentt waded into the fountain. "Come on, buddy."

Leaning over, Marso reached out a hand and touched the tip of Jentt's nose. "I know you. You are nice." He tapped his nose three times.

"That's right," Jentt said. "I'm your friend, and I'm here to help you." He wrapped an arm around Marso's waist, but Marso giggled and pushed off him. Using the momentum, he swung around the horns, holding on to their undersides.

"It drowns them," Marso said, as if he were explaining.

"Yes, water can drown," Jentt said patiently. "Release the fountain, and let's find someplace nice and quiet we can talk instead of drown."

"There's no quiet here. No quiet anywhere. That's why I drown them!"

This is going nowhere, Kreya thought. She stepped forward, checked to make sure no one was paying attention to them, and pushed back the hood on her coat. "Marso, it's me, Kreya, your commander. Get off that fountain right now and come with us."

Marso smiled happily at her, released the fountain statue, and fell into the water. He splashed down, spraying Jentt. Kreya put her hood back up as Jentt helped Marso out of the fountain water. She noticed there were chicken bones in the water, left by people wishing for good luck.

In a singsong voice, Zera said, "We're drawing attention."

Surrounding Marso, they hustled him through the market. A few of the vendors called out after them, and Kreya thought she saw the boy who'd helped them and a few of his friends following along, but the boy lost interest once they were beyond the market.

They checked into an inn, with Zera paying, and ordered soup and meat rolls to be sent to the room. Zera also slipped the innkeeper an extra coin for private access to the bathing facilities, which, despite spending his days in water, Marso definitely needed, and another extra coin for a set of new clothes for him, also definitely needed.

Aided by his friends, Marso was bathed and dressed in fresh clothes. Sitting cross-legged on one of the beds, he ate soup with a shaking hand while Kreya, Zera, and Jentt all stared at him.

Zera finally broke the silence. "So . . . did you take something that messed with your head, or did your head mess with your head all on its own?"

"He wouldn't need chemicals to do this," Jentt said. "A place like this, stirring up his magic—it would be bad enough to stir up his mind."

Marso took a sip of soup, lifted his spoon, and stared at it as if it had spoken.

"Then we have to un-stir it," Kreya said.

"It'll take time," Jentt said. "And quiet."

Kreya shut the window as revelers outside decided to sing three different songs simultaneously. "We need to take him out of the city." But where? Her tower was gone. Zera's mansion wasn't private enough—even if she dismissed all her sycophants, word would spread from that act alone. Plus Cerre was too many miles away. A close, quiet place . . .

She had it.

"The farmhouse."

The abandoned farmhouse where they'd trained wasn't far from Ocrae. She didn't know if it would be still standing after twenty-five years, or if it had been claimed by new owners, but if it still existed, it would be ideal.

"It's not abandoned," Zera said.

"Oh. Maybe we can buy it?"

"You mean maybe *I* can buy it?"

"Well—"

"No need. Stran lives there," Zera said. "With his family."

Kreya felt her jaw drop open.

"What?" Zera asked. "I told you I kept tabs on everyone. Except Jentt, of course, because, you know, he was dead. And obviously I didn't keep close enough watch on Marso. But Stran is there."

"He has a family?" Jentt asked.

"He lives in the farmhouse?" Kreya asked simultaneously. "He remembers how many animals we deboned in that kitchen, right?"

"My guess is he didn't share that detail with his wife," Zera said. "Who knows, though? Never met her. She might be fine with that."

"Guess we'll find out," Kreya said. She found herself smiling at the thought of Stran with a family. If anyone deserved an ordinary happy life, it was Stran.

THE FARMHOUSE WAS NESTLED INTO THE SIDE OF A mountain between terraced fields. It had been freshly painted white, with a ruby-red roof. A chicken coop and a rabbit hutch were on one side of the yard and a vegetable garden on the other. Someone had built a long wooden table with benches under an old massive tree—Kreya remembered they'd buried the unused bits of animal carcasses under that tree, but there was no sign of that now. It was blanketed in wildflowers. All in all, it was picturesque and perfect.

"Pretty," Marso said.

"Wow, yes," Zera said. "Stran has done well."

Together they started down the well-worn path toward the farmhouse. A few deer, the tame kind, froze, watching them as they passed, before resuming grazing on the wildflowers.

"Am I dead?" Marso asked.

"No, buddy, you're not," Jentt told them.

"Are you dead?"

"Not anymore."

Marso smiled. "That's nice."

Closer to the farmhouse, though, Marso balked. He dug his heels into the dirt and sat backward so fast that none of them had a chance to catch him. His face had gone pale, and his hands were shaking.

Zera squatted next to him. "What's wrong, honey?"

He shook his head.

"Get up, Marso," Kreya told him. "We're going to see Stran."

But Marso hugged his knees to his chest and rocked back and forth. Wrapping her arm around his shoulders, Zera began talking to him in a low, soothing voice. Kreya watched them for a minute and wondered if what was wrong with Marso was anything that could be fixed. He hadn't shown any sign of the cravings or withdrawal that she would have expected if he were an addict, which made her even more certain he'd addled his brain by overloading his magic.

If I hadn't locked myself away in my tower, could I have prevented this?

She'd let Marso flounder on his own when she could have helped him. She had no idea how long he'd been like this, but it couldn't have happened overnight. If she'd checked in on him, maybe she'd have seen the signs. She could have gotten him help, even if it was beyond her to help him herself.

"We're here," Zera was telling him. "You're safe."

At least with Zera, Kreya could reassure herself that her friend had fared fine without her. Even thrived. But Marso . . . The guilt threatened to choke her. Retreating from them, she said, "I'll say hi to Stran, tell him we're here." *Make sure he hasn't fallen apart too.*

"I'll come with you," Jentt offered.

"Might want to stay back," Zera said. "Seeing Kreya is going to be a surprise on its own. Seeing you? 'Hi, Stran, long time no see. I brought you a heart attack. Enjoy!'"

Jentt took Kreya's hands. "She has a point. Can you do this?"

"It's Stran." He was an overgrown puppy dog. Of course she could handle him.

"I mean, can you try to break the news gently? About me. About Marso. About . . . well, what we suspect. Or maybe save that until later?"

"You think I can't be diplomatic?" Kreya tried to sound offended, but she knew as well as Jentt did that diplomacy had never been one of her strengths. She'd try, though. She always *tried.* "I'll be gentle."

He kissed her forehead, as if to either agree with her or encourage her.

She left them comforting Marso and continued the rest of the way down the path to the farmhouse. From inside, she heard multiple voices, a baby's cry, and a warm male laugh that boomed through the house and across the yard.

Stran, she thought.

Approaching the door, she knocked and waited.

She heard voices calling to one another, asking someone else to get the door, and then at last footsteps. The door was opened, and a petite woman in a leather apron, heavy boots, and an embroidered blouse stood in the doorway. She was smiling as bright as sunshine itself.

"May I help you?" the woman asked.

Kreya gawked at her. *This* was Stran's wife? It was clearly his house—nothing could have convinced her more than hearing that familiar laugh—but this was not the kind of person she'd expected him to marry.

Looking curiously at Kreya, the woman was, hands down, the loveliest person she'd ever seen. Luminous eyes, soft skin, fragile features. She reminded Kreya of a lily in sunshine, glowing with a delicate beauty. Except wearing work boots. "Stran married *you?*" The words were out of Kreya's mouth before she thought about how they'd sound.

The woman laughed, and even that was beautiful, like a waterfall in springtime. "Yes, Stran is my husband. Why is that a surprise?"

"Well, last time I saw him . . . He always looked like he'd been punched a few times. I can't imagine age has improved that. You, on the other hand, look like you were carved by a master artisan." She'd always pictured Stran with another warrior, a tough, battle-scarred, and sheathed-in-muscles battle-ax, not this flower. This young flower. She looked to be about twenty years younger than Stran.

Stran's wife blushed prettily, and it occurred to Kreya belatedly that she shouldn't have said that out loud. *Not exactly diplomatic. I am out of practice with people,* she thought. It was a good thing that she wasn't planning on interacting with anyone but Jentt after this was over.

Suddenly, the woman gasped. "I know you! You're his old commander! *The* Kreya of Vos! Oh my goodness, come in! Stran is going to be so excited to see you! I am so honored to meet you!" Raising her voice, she called, "Stran! Come see who's here!"

"Honey, do you know where my spare boots are?" came Stran's voice from within the house.

She frowned and even that was lovely. She had the kind of face creased with laugh lines; a frown looked like a novel expression on her. "Why not wear your regular boots?"

"Vivi has her dolls in them, and she says I shouldn't wake them." Stran came into the hallway and, seeing Kreya, halted. He looked exactly as she'd remembered: as wide as two men, with arm muscles as thick as her waist. He'd shaved his beard, and his hair had silvered. He boasted a few more wrinkles in his sun-worn face than she remembered, a few more laugh lines around his eyes. But he was unmistakably Stran. And if she hadn't been sure, his nose still looked as if it had been pounded by multiple fists, which was in fact true.

His wife waved her hands as if presenting Kreya. "Look who came to visit!"

"Kreya? By the bones! It's you!" Crossing the hall in two strides, Stran scooped her up, swung her in a circle, and set her down. Startled, she nearly missed hugging him back, but she managed a pat on his shoulders as she caught her balance again.

Stran spun with her to face his wife. "Amurra, did you arrange this? You are amazing! You didn't even hint—"

Amurra laughed. "She surprised me too!"

Stran turned his attention back to Kreya. "This is fantastic! It's amazing to see you!"

"Very glad to see you too," Kreya said, and she meant it. She hadn't been expecting such a joyful greeting. She'd braced herself for more accusations, like with Zera, or for the feeling of guilt, like with Marso, but Stran seemed honestly happy to see her.

I hope he feels the same once he knows why I'm here, Kreya thought.

Amurra poked Stran in the ribs. "Introduce me."

Releasing Kreya, Stran wrapped his arm around Amurra and pulled her tight against his side. "My wife, Amurra. Meet Kreya, my commander."

"He's told me so much about you," Amurra gushed. "Honored to have you in our house!"

"Honored to be here," Kreya said. "Actually, I didn't come alone. I have some other people with me who will be very happy to meet you. And to see you, Stran."

Amurra clapped her hands together. "Zera and Marso?"

"Fantastic!" Stran roared. "It's been my greatest regret that so many years have passed. I meant to visit everyone, but life . . . We talked about it, right, Amurra? But somehow the timing was never right. Life got busy."

"He truly thought of you often," Amurra said.

"Are they out there?" Stran asked, poking his head outside.

Kreya laid a hand on Stran's arm. "Yes, but Marso isn't well. We were hoping—"

Whooping, he barreled out the door. "Marso! Zera!" She tried not to wince. So much for breaking the news gently.

Guess he'll see for himself.

Amurra smiled fondly as she watched her husband race up the path. "He often says he became the man he is because of the adventures he had with you. I owe you thanks for that, because I love the man he is."

"You're, uh, welcome," Kreya said. Amurra was the first person who'd thanked her for anything in a while. It felt strange. After the war ended, she'd been showered with thanks, gifts, and gold. Every city had thrown parades and banquets. She would have traded it all for a few seconds more with Jentt. Now she had her Jentt, and she didn't miss the fuss. "We are here to impose on your hospitality. Our friend Marso is not himself, and we need a quiet place where he can recover."

"Of course!" Amurra said. "I can't promise quiet with the kids, but Stran's old companions are and will always be family."

"Thank you."

But she wasn't sure if that offer would stand after Stran met up with Jentt. Up on the path, Kreya saw Stran approach his old companions, and she wished she'd gotten the chance to break the news about the one who should have been dead. She saw Stran hesitate for a moment, and her breath caught—then Stran wrapped Jentt in the same kind of sweep-you-off-your-feet hug that he'd just gifted Kreya with.

From within the house came a girl's voice: "Hey, that's mine!" And then a boy's voice, muffled, which Kreya couldn't quite hear. "Two kids?" she guessed, then remembered she'd heard a baby earlier. "Three."

"A seven-year-old, five-year-old, and thirteen months. Stran is an excellent father."

"I'm sure he is." Kreya didn't doubt that. And she didn't doubt that Stran would be willing to help nurse Marso back to health. Maybe after Marso read the bones and this was over, Stran would even help Marso settle someplace that would be better for his health than an outdoor market in Ocrae.

Scooping the bone reader into his arms, Stran carried him like a baby down the slope and into the house. "Amurra, this is Marso, Zera, and Jentt. Everyone, this is my lovely wife. Love of my life. Light of my days. Cuddle-bear to my—"

Amurra smiled her sunbeam smile at him. "Enough, you. Get that poor man onto the couch." She gave him a gentle shove through the hallway. They all followed as the room widened into a light and airy living space.

Except for the layout of the house, it looked nothing like the place Kreya remembered. All the floors had been sanded and stained honey blond, seats and benches piled high with pillows filled the room, and the walls were decorated with tapestries that mirrored the embroidery on Amurra's blouse. It looked, in short, like a home, and Kreya had to push down a sudden spurt of jealousy.

If Jentt hadn't died, they might have had a place like this.

But you have him back now, Kreya reminded herself. *And our home will be wherever we are.*

There was no need to feel sorry for herself anymore or jealous of anyone. She was happy for Stran, truly she was. He'd found himself a wife who clearly adored him, and vice versa. Plus he had the family he'd always wanted.

Gently, Stran laid Marso on the couch and covered him with blankets. He was gentle and practiced, as if he'd cared for the sick many times. Even though she thought of him as a kind man, in Kreya's memories of Stran, she kept seeing him impale skeletal soldiers, rather than nurse an old friend. Twenty-five years is truly a long time.

"Is he ill?" Amurra asked. "The kids—"

"I don't believe it's anything contagious, my dear," Stran reassured her. "I suspect he did this to himself."

Kreya suspected that too. But why? Was it the pain of the memories? If so, she could understand that.

Stran continued. "I should've checked in on him. Ocrae isn't far. Just got so busy around the farm, with the kids. No excuse."

Amurra wrapped her arms around him. She was at least two feet shorter than her mammoth husband; her arms only circled around half his waist. "You can't be everything to everyone. Don't beat yourself up. You had your own life to look after."

"I should've made an effort. Not just with Marso, but with all of you. Jentt . . . Never thought I'd see you again. It's a miracle."

Releasing her husband, Amurra turned abruptly to gawk at Jentt. "Jentt! The Reformed Thief? The Martyr of the Bones? Everyone said you died!"

"It was touch-and-go for a long while," Jentt said mildly, "but I pulled through in the end. We've been keeping it hush-hush. Delighted to meet you, ma'am."

"Kids!" Stran bellowed. "Come meet my friends!"

A girl, dragging a boot by its laces, came into the room, followed by a slightly older boy hauling a pudgy baby. The baby held a fistful of the boy's hair and was attempting to shove it into his mouth. Swooping in, Stran lifted the baby into the air. He cooed with delight.

The girl stuck her hand into Kreya's, holding it tight and

looking up at her. The child's hand was moist and sticky. "I'm Vivi."

"Nice to meet you, Vivi. I'm Kreya." She extracted her hand from Vivi's by turning her grip into a nice, friendly shake. She wiped her hand on her coat.

The boy was named Jen. "After you," Stran told Jentt.

"I'm honored." Jentt knelt in front of the boy and gravely shook his hand. "It's a warrior's name."

"Papa said you were a thief."

"On occasion," Jentt admitted. "But the name Jentt came from Jentt the Brave, the first warrior to ever slay an edgewood worm, before they were driven to extinction. You know what they were? They had three heads, one that breathed fire, one that breathed acid, and one ice." He launched into the full story, while little Jen and Vivi stared at him with rapt attention.

Stran introduced the baby-almost-toddler as little Nugget. "We haven't decided on his final name yet. Luckily, we still have a couple months left until his official naming ceremony. Amurra's family tradition is to hold it at fifteen months, so he can walk to his name."

"Two months left, and he will walk to Evren," Amurra said. "After my grandfather."

"Or Olag," Stran said. "Respectable, strong name. Olag."

Zera chimed in. "I vote Evren. Olag sounds like the sludge at the bottom of a beer barrel. Which is only tasty if it's expensive beer."

Amurra nodded emphatically, but Stran looked hurt.

"It's wonderful to see you so happy, old friend," Jentt said. He slapped Stran on the shoulder, which required him to reach up. "We won't be in your hair long. Just need to get Marso up on his feet again."

"And able to read the bones," Zera put in.

Kreya wished she hadn't mentioned that yet. So far, Stran didn't know they were here for any other purpose than rest and recovery for Marso.

"You want him to read?" Stran said. "In this condition?"

From the couch, Marso whimpered. "He lives, he lives, he lives."

"Yes, that's right, buddy," Jentt said, sitting on the couch by his feet. "I'm alive."

But Kreya glanced at Zera, who met her look with widened eyes and pressed-together lips. Neither of them had to speak to know they shared the same fear:

What if he wasn't talking about Jentt?

Kreya knelt beside Jentt. "Get well, old friend. We need you. More than you know."

CHAPTER ELEVEN

Later that night, after a hearty dinner they'd all pitched in to cook, Kreya cuddled against Jentt's chest in bed. She didn't mind that the cot was too narrow for two of them—she had no intention of letting him be farther away than this. They were alone, Jentt was alive, and she didn't have to worry about the spell expiring in a day, two days, ten days, or ever again.

It would have been nicer, of course, if Jentt weren't angry with her.

"This is the first time we've been alone since you revived me," he said, whispering so they didn't wake anyone else in the overcrowded farmhouse.

Kreya deliberately misunderstood where he was going with that. "Sadly, we can't make love in Stran's daughter's bed. We have to be good guests."

"I'm not worried about that. I'm worried about you. We need to talk about how you risked yourself. And Zera."

She traced a heart on his bare chest. "Dead boys don't get votes."

He caught her hand. "You knew how I'd feel about it."

"Yes."

"But you did it anyway."

"Yes. And I'd do it again."

The bird construct whirred, and Kreya heard the rustle of fabric beneath the bed. She'd kept her creations hidden while they were visiting with Stran's family, but she'd let them out after all the lights were doused. She cooed at them. "Calm down, little ones. There's nothing to fear here."

Screaming cut off her attempt to soothe them.

Kreya shooed her constructs back under the bed with a curt order to hide, and she grabbed her coat as she and Jentt darted out the door. He had a knife in his hand that she'd never seen before—his belongings, the few there were, had burned with the tower. He must have helped himself to it while they were in Ocrae. She approved.

They burst into the living room to find Stran and his wife, Amurra, already there. Kneeling, Stran had his beefy hands on Marso's shoulders as Marso was screaming with his mouth open so wide that it made his face look distorted.

"Breathe," Stran was saying, his voice calm and soothing. "You're safe. You're with friends. Breathe, Marso. All is well."

Amurra had a mug near him and was wafting the steam toward Marso's nose.

Jentt tucked his knife back into whatever unseen sheath he was carrying. Kreya shrugged on her coat over her nightshirt so she wouldn't be carrying it, but it didn't look like there was an emergency, at least not the kind that talismans could solve.

A few seconds later, Zera burst into the living room. She had a talisman in each hand. Given how few she had left with her, Kreya wondered which talismans she'd chosen. "Anyone dying?" Zera demanded. "No? Great. Going back to sleep." She pivoted and disappeared into the hall.

Kreya noticed Stran's children, minus the littlest one, peering into the living room. She herded them back. "He'll be all right. Everything's fine." With Stran and Amurra and now Jentt hovering over him, she wasn't sure how much she could add to the mix. Marso didn't seem to be calming down much, though he did gasp for breath between screams. "He's having a nightmare, that's all."

Little Vivi nodded solemnly. "I have nightmares sometimes."

"Oh? What do you do to get rid of them?" Kreya asked.

"I bite them."

"Sorry?"

Vivi chomped on the empty air. "I imagine I'm biting all the things that scare me."

"That . . . is a completely sensible solution. I'll tell Marso to bite them."

"Good," Vivi said, and dragged her brother back toward the bedroom they were sharing while Jentt and Kreya used Vivi's room. From another room, the baby started wailing.

Amurra stood. "I don't want to leave while—"

"Go," her husband told her. "Thank you, but we'll take care of Marso."

Both Stran and Jentt continued to try to soothe Marso. It didn't seem to be helping. He was gasping for air now and shaking. His eyes were open and darted everywhere, not seeming to see anything.

Kreya gave them two minutes more. And then she stepped forward, grabbed Marso's face in her hands, and said, "Knock it off, Marso, and tell me what you see."

He quit screaming, and his eyes focused on Kreya.

Stran murmured, "I will never understand how you do that."

Without moving her eyes off of Marso, she asked, "Do what?"

"Make us listen to you. You are half my size, and if I sat on you, you'd squash like an ant, but when you give an order, I don't even think. Same with Marso. Even after twenty-five years."

"Naturally bossy, I'm told," Kreya said. Sitting beside Marso, she took his hands in hers. "You read something terrible in the bones, and you didn't want to believe it."

It was a guess, but it felt right.

Marso stared at her, and his eyes looked so much like they belonged to a lost child. "Every time I tried, I saw the same thing. It haunts me, even after the mist fades. My power is broken."

Jentt said, "Your power can't break."

"*I* am broken," Marso said. "I shattered like glass. Like pottery. Smashed. Crashed. Shards of me, scattered on the ground. That's what he said, when I tried to tell. My mind lies. So I tried to silence it." He was pleading with Kreya to understand.

Bones help me, I do understand, she thought. She'd felt shattered too. For so long. She hoped with Jentt back, she'd begin to heal.

Looming above her, Stran asked in his gentle voice, "Who said you were broken?"

"Guild Master Lorn. I thought it was a warning. He said it was false. He said I was broken. Said that by creating a false reading, I'd broken my mind. Or by breaking my mind, I'd allowed lies to cloud the mist. Can't tell which. Doesn't matter which. He was right. All I saw every time I read—no matter what question I asked, no matter what I tried . . . Useless. Broken. Damaged." His eyes flickered to Jentt and Stran as if he needed them to understand too.

Reaching over Kreya, Stran laid a hand on Marso's shoulder. "You aren't, my friend."

Kreya saw despair leaching into Marso's eyes—he knew he

was in pain, and Stran's denial of that hurt. She tilted his head so he was looking at her again. "Of course you are. You're damaged. We all are."

Stran objected. "Not all."

Kreya didn't buy it. Everyone had wounds. But even though she meant the words for Stran, too, she spoke directly to Marso. "Some of us are better at hiding it than others, but we are all broken. You can't live without breaking a few times. But that doesn't mean that's a bad thing. It just means you've lived in the world." She'd had her moments of despair, when Jentt first died, when she read Eklor's journals and realized what the spell entailed, when she tried it for the first time and failed. She'd shattered and glued herself back together more times than she could count. "What matters is you keep living in it, despite your broken bits—or even because of them."

Marso was listening.

"You saw what you didn't want to see. What no one wanted you to see. But I'm here with you—we're all here with you—and we'll look at the unseeable together. You won't be alone. But we need to do this."

He began to shake. "You want me to read the bones again. You think if I try this time, I won't see him. He won't be in my mind. This time I'll be healed and the mist will be clear, because my friends are with me."

Stran said, "Exactly!"

"I don't think that at all," Kreya said, ignoring Stran. "But I *do* think that whatever—*whoever*—you see, we'll believe you."

Now Stran's meaty hand was on Kreya's shoulder. "A minute, Kreya?"

She let him draw her out of the living room into the kitchen.

Moonlight spilled through the curtained window, creating lacy shadows on the floor. It still smelled like the herbed grouse they'd eaten for dinner, and the embers burned low in the hearth. A curl of smoke led up to the chimney. She felt a pang of guilt for interrupting Stran's peaceful home life, but where else could they have gone?

She knew Stran had questions, and she saw him marshaling his thoughts, preparing to ask. Saving him the trouble, she said, "Yes, it's necessary, and yes, it needs to happen now. Do you have any bones he can use?"

Whatever argument he'd been about to make died unspoken—as he'd pointed out, she commanded, he obeyed. Instead he fished the grouse bones out of the bin. Kreya was mildly surprised they were there—she'd expected Zera to have pilfered them after dinner to create more talismans by now, but perhaps they weren't high-enough-quality bones for her. The effectiveness of talismans depended on the type of bone, as well as the skill of the carver. But they'd do fine for Marso.

She washed them in the sink, carefully cleaning off any vestiges of the carcass, and polished them with a bit of sandpaper from one of her pockets. As she was working, Amurra appeared in the kitchen. "The kids are back to sleep, and your friend seems calmer now," she reported.

"He's had a difficult time," Stran said.

Amurra clucked in sympathy. "He didn't need to. He could have reached out for help. He's a Hero of Vos. You can't tell me that people wouldn't move mountains to help him."

It was, Kreya thought, kind of amazing how innocent Stran's wife was. He'd managed to find someone who seemed untouched by pain or loss. Unfamiliar with broken things that couldn't be mended. *She's lucky*, she thought. Amurra would have been a child during the Bone War, young enough that it all had to feel more like a story than reality.

Without turning around, Kreya said, "We found him mostly naked in a fountain. He's apparently been living like that for some time. People have short attention spans."

"Not me," Stran said stoutly. "If he'd come to me . . ."

"To us," Amurra said. "We'd have taken care of him."

"I know you would have," Kreya said. "But he doesn't need taking care of. He needs to face what's haunting him and know the truth." Cradling the bones in a dish towel, she carried them back into the living room.

Behind her, she heard Amurra ask, "She's going to have him read? But he needs to rest!"

"Trust Kreya. She knows what she's doing."

Kreya wasn't certain that was true, but she appreciated the confidence. She found Jentt sitting beside Marso, who looked more alert than she'd seen him these last few days. She hoped she wasn't pushing him too hard too fast. She knew she had a tendency to do that, and it didn't always work out well. But she didn't stop.

Dropping the towel with the bones into Marso's lap, she stepped back.

Jentt looked up at her. "Are you sure?"

No, she thought.

"Yes," she said.

If he read what she thought he'd read . . . *It will change the world.* But that wasn't precisely correct, because if he read what she thought he'd read, he'd be seeing that the world was already very, very different from what everyone believed. Reading about danger wouldn't create the danger; it would just make it so they couldn't ignore it.

"You can do it, Marso," she said.

He hesitated, then picked up one of the bones and spun it between his fingertips.

WHEN HE WAS SIX YEARS OLD, MARSO READ HIS first bone. A chicken bone. He'd been playing in the backyard with three of his friends. He couldn't remember now what their names had been, but he remembered one always had a smudge of dirt on his nose, as if he applied it every morning as an identifying mark. They'd been pretending to be bone workers. One friend had been the bone maker and had created a teetering structure of sticks he claimed was a water pump, despite the fact that it had zero of the features of an actual water pump. Another friend had played the bone wizard, claiming that he'd carved the chicken's skull into a talisman that would grant him super strength—it hadn't. And Marso was supposed to be the bone reader.

He'd seen a real bone reader in the market, offering readings for young men and women anxious about their future, or older men and women anxious about their past. His parents had forbidden him from lingering around the bone reader's tent, saying it did no good to know what ordinary people weren't meant to know, but he kept being drawn back, and his parents were distracted anyway, selling their dyed wool at their stall. He'd told them he wanted to watch the puppet show, and they'd given him a coin to spend on pies.

That day, he'd given up the pie—an unusual choice for a child his age in a market that tempting—and instead brought it clutched in his fist to the bone reader. "Will you read my future?" he asked, offering the now-sweaty coin.

The bone reader had taken the coin, tossed the bones, and said, "*Prynato*."

"What does that mean?" he'd asked breathlessly.

"Reveal," the bone reader answered. "Come to the bones with an open heart and ask them to reveal secrets, and—if you are open enough—they will." To the bones: "Show the boy's future."

A mist rose from the bones, swirling above them. He'd expected to see faces inside the mist or, well, he didn't know what. All he saw within the mist . . . was more mist.

"What do the bones reveal for me?" little Marso had asked. He liked the word "reveal." It felt magical in his mouth. "*Prynato*." He angled himself to see the bones beneath the mist, fascinated by the carvings on them, memorizing all the ones he could see.

The bone reader peered into the mist and then down at the bones. Scowled at them. Scowled at Marso. Flipped the coin back at him. "Read them yourself if you want to know so badly."

At home, he'd drawn on the chicken bone and tossed it out onto the yard, saying, "*Prynato!*" with as much pomp and gravitas as a six-year-old could manage. He then stared at the bone. And stared and stared.

And saw nothing. No mist. No answers.

His friends laughed and kept playing.

But later, after dinner, he came out to look again. This time, he hadn't come with any grand expectation. He'd come because he was curious. And in a wisp of cloud that swirled above the bone, he saw an image within the mist and simultaneously within his mind: a golden wheel. And with the image came the sense of *soon*. And *journey*. And *sickness*.

Two hours later, a cart with golden wheels pulled up to their door and handed his father a letter saying that Marso's grandfather was ill and the whole family had to come quickly. Marso was already packed and ready.

After that, he never doubted that he would become a bone reader. He won his apprenticeship with the guild easily, once he was old enough, and he advanced quickly to journeyman. He wasn't surprised either when Kreya chose him for her quest—he had foreseen that in the bones.

His was a rare gift. While most bone readers saw a sliver of the future or the past of whoever posed a question—and an imperfect sliver at that—Marso could cast his mind farther and wider. He didn't require the subject of his question to be present. The bones showed him hints of possible futures of whomever he wished, as well as the certain present. They answered questions, sometimes directly, often obliquely. But they always revealed truth, if not precise fact. He became adept at interpreting the images in the mist.

The truth spoke to him, he said.

It was he who identified the danger when other bone readers began to be murdered one by one. It was he who pinpointed the cause of the killings: constructs made by the bone maker Master Eklor. And it was he who predicted the location of the final battle.

He never doubted himself, and that was one of the things that made him the most powerful bone reader in generations—his unshakable belief that the bones would unfold the meaning of their images and patterns to him. Until they didn't. Until Jentt died and he hadn't seen it. Until that moment, he'd never imagined it was possible for him to fail his friends. But he had, and after the war, when they were all lauded as heroes, he knew he was secretly a fraud.

He quit trusting his readings.

Especially when every bone he cast gave the same terrible reading, no matter what question he asked, no matter how hard he tried to clear his mind and focus on something else, anything else.

And sometimes the bones would even speak to him when he hadn't thrown them, the mist forming only within his mind, which was why the only relief he'd found in recent years was in Ocrae, where the hideous noise of the city drowned out the relentless warnings in his head.

His mind felt too cloudy now to be open to a reading. He wanted to tell Kreya that, but she was looking at him again the same way she always did, as if she trusted him absolutely. How could she, when he'd failed her so badly, when his mistake had cost her Jentt?

Except Jentt was here, not lost. And Marso didn't understand that at all. He'd seen him fall. Seen him die. He knew it was no nightmare, even though he'd relived that moment night after night for months after.

Nothing made sense—nothing but the fact that Kreya was asking him to do something. And even though he didn't want to—wasn't even sure he *could*—he knew he had to try.

"Mint tea?" he requested.

If he could clear his head, he might be able to understand.

He felt a mug in his hands, though he hadn't thought enough time had passed for water to boil and tea to steep. Lately, he had been losing moments. He knew why, of course.

"Might not work," Marso said. In fact, it shouldn't. As confidently as Kreya looked at him, her faith in him couldn't fix a broken brain. "Broke myself."

"I told you," Kreya began. "You—"

"Read so much I broke myself. On purpose." *She needs to know that,* he thought. So she wouldn't be disappointed when he failed. He'd tried to drive the voices out of his head by allowing them all inside at once. The psychic equivalent of blowing out one's eardrums. It had mostly worked. And for the ones that still persisted, he'd drowned out the worst of them with the sound of the fountain.

He'd liked that fountain.

Nice *trickle, trickle.*

He felt a hand on his shoulder. "Marso, you still with us, my friend?" Stran asked.

"You're a father," Marso said. He'd seen that sometime, a long time ago. Stran liked to take care of people. That was one truth he was happy he'd seen. "Four children."

"Three, but yes, I am," Stran said. "You met my kids when you came in, though you weren't quite alert. You can meet them again in the morning."

Marso looked down at his hands and wondered why he was holding a bone. He didn't want to be holding one. He flung it across the room. And then his hands felt empty and sad. "I'm sorry," he said to his hands.

"Read it," Kreya said quietly.

He looked up, surprised.

"Just try," Jentt told him.

"You don't have to," Stran put in. "If it's too much—"

"*Read it,*" Kreya said.

"*Prynato,*" Marso said. And across the room, the bone vibrated and spun. Mist arose, like smoke from a just-lit fire. He closed his eyes and continued to see the spinning. He knew how it was done. Open yourself. And the bone would reveal an answer. But to what question? He couldn't focus his mind to ask. It was so difficult to hold on to where he was, what was happening, even who he was.

But Kreya asked for him, the one question he never wanted to ask yet was always asking:

"Is Eklor alive?"

The bone showed him, both within the mist that had risen above the bone and within the mist in his mind, and he was screaming again.

CHAPTER TWELVE

J oining the others for breakfast in the morning, Zera was wholly unsurprised to hear Kreya confirm that Eklor had appeared in the mist of Marso's reading. She was also unsurprised to hear Stran deny that it meant what they thought it meant. Readings were subject to interpretation, which was why you needed a fully functioning bone reader who could feel the intent of the bones as well as see the image. Without that, it wasn't proof of anything. They could have seen the past, Stran said. Not the present. Certainly not the future.

Waving Stran's objections aside, Zera told the others, "I need to take care of a few things at home if we're going to go off and save the world again."

Stran frowned at her, and she smiled sunnily back at him. He was spoon-feeding mashed peas to little Nugget, and the baby used his moment of inattention to grab the spoon and catapult the green mush onto the floor. They were all having breakfast in the kitchen, while Marso tried to sleep for more than five seconds at a time in the other room. Cleaning up the mush, Stran said, "We don't need to save the world again. It's already saved. Eklor is dead. Marso . . . He's caught in the past. That's why the reading showed what it did. He needs to let go and move on."

"There's no moving on while Eklor lives," Kreya said. She'd chewed her way through her breakfast as if it had personally wronged her. She was a bit on edge.

"*Might* live," Jentt said, correcting her.

Kreya shot him a hard look, and Zera resisted laughing. Didn't he know better than to contradict his wife when she'd obviously made her decision? *Really,* Zera thought, *was there ever any question about what we're going to do?* If she was being honest with herself, which she tried not to do as a general rule, she'd known since the moment she'd heard that laugh.

Jentt threw up his hands in surrender. "I'm only saying it's not solid proof. There's a possibility that Marso is not in the best state for interpreting a reading accurately."

"Exactly," Stran said. "Kreya, you know I would follow you through fire—"

"Then follow me to the forbidden zone!"

Stran began, "Grand Master Lorn—"

Stopping him, Zera said, "Work it out without me, people. I'll be back soon." She showed off two new talismans she'd made, from the bones of a rabbit, as proof she'd be quick, and then she breezed out the door before she had to listen to any more of their argument. She knew Kreya well enough to know that her old friend didn't have any intention of involving Grand Master Lorn. She wanted to take care of the problem herself. If Eklor lived, there was no way that Kreya would be content to leave him in that condition.

And that's fine with me, Zera thought. *But if we're going to have a chance of succeeding, we're going to need a lot more talismans.* She could help with that—but couldn't do it here. She needed access to her stockpile.

Outside, only a few yards from the farmhouse, Zera was intercepted by Kreya, of course, who could never just let someone do what she hadn't planned for them to do. Blocking the trail, she asked, "Are you coming back?"

"Of course, darling. I'd miss you too much to be gone long!" She beamed at Kreya, telling herself she wasn't *really* hurt that her old friend didn't trust her. It was understandable for Kreya to be paranoid. "Just need to pop on home for a few additional supplies, and then I'll pop back before you even have a chance to coax Marso into some more mint tea."

"You're lying to me," Kreya said. Annoyingly.

"I will come back." Zera meant it. Naturally, she was going to rejoin the team and see this through. She couldn't simply forget the fact that she knew Eklor was alive and her greatest achievement was, in fact, un-achieved. She was going to return and by then all the unpleasant arguing would be over. Kreya would have bullied the boys into accepting whatever plan she thought was reasonable, and Zera would swoop in to provide whatever support was needed, without having to deal with all the tedious angsting nonsense.

Kreya was studying her, and it was disconcerting. "You mean to, but will you?"

Ouch. This time it was impossible to pretend it didn't hurt. She'd gone into the forbidden zone with her. Didn't that mean anything? "You have so little faith in me."

Glaring at Kreya, Zera met her gaze with the same intensity. It was strange to see a mix of who her old friend was and who she'd become, combined in the creases around her eyes and mouth. She wondered if Kreya still considered them a team. "You used to believe in me," Zera said. "When no one else did, you were the one who had faith in me. What happened to that trust?"

"I still trust you," Kreya said. "I just think you're lying to yourself."

"Well, fuck you then." How dare she? After everything they'd been through together . . . after everything they'd just gone through . . . *How can she not trust me?*

"This is more than you ever bargained for," Kreya said. "More than you should have to face. You have your life now. I won't blame you if you want to live it."

Oh, really? She was couching this distrust as being understanding? Zera clenched her fists, unclenched them, and smiled sweetly. "It doesn't matter how little you think of me. I'll see you soon." She waved her new speed talisman at Kreya. She knew several shortcuts to Cerre, especially traveling alone and without heavy supplies and weaponry.

"I hope so," Kreya said.

"Then you *do* want me to come back! Go on, you can say it." As much as she tried to disguise it, even Zera heard the anger in her own voice.

To Zera's shock, Kreya didn't hesitate. "I want you to come back."

For a moment, they stared at one another, and then Zera flashed another fake smile at her, wiggled her fingers in a wave, and activated the speed talisman. She felt Kreya's eyes on her as she zipped away from the farmhouse and sped across the terraced farmlands. She even felt her eyes still on her after she was long out of view.

By the time she reached Cerre, though, Zera had half-convinced herself she felt pity for her old friend, not hurt. *I feel sorry for Kreya,* she thought. *I truly do. Unable to trust . . . that's an unpleasant way to live.* She passed quickly through the gates to the fifth tier and announced her presence before entering her mansion. Her people wouldn't have let it fall into disarray in her absence, she was certain, but she wanted to ensure a proper welcome.

She wasn't disappointed.

As she approached, lifted on a cloudlike mechanism, the doors of her palace flew open. Shirtless, with all his muscles on display, Guine filled the doorway. "Everyone, she's returned!"

Six or seven of her dearest friends—if she used a loose definition of the word "friend" . . . and "dearest"—poured out with him into her statue garden. They swarmed around her, weaving and cooing, and she guessed that they were all quite inebriated, even though it was barely noon. She wondered how much of her liquor remained, but luckily that wasn't the supply closet she needed.

She greeted each of them, granting them new nicknames when she forgot a few of the ones she'd already given them, before allowing herself to be swept inside and installed by the main fountain. One of the men fetched her fresh fruit and a lemon-flavored drink. Another dabbed her forehead and cheeks with a sponge. She supposed she had gotten warm and dusty from the journey. It felt nice, at any rate. For a few minutes. Zera swatted the girl's hands away. "Enough."

Guine positioned himself next to her with his harp and started to play. The others drifted to their couches and lounged on the pillows. One laughed, a sound like water falling over pebbles. It reminded Zera of the river. She tried to imagine any of these people in the valley. They'd faint dead away at the first roar of a river lizard.

It's nice being surrounded by people who don't put my life in danger, she told herself. She'd chosen this life and these people. Or at least people like them—who they were specifically seemed to revolve every few months.

"How's business been the past few days?" she asked Guine. "Any surprises?"

"Steady growth, as you predicted," he said, continuing to play a soothing melody. "The flight talismans are popular with those who want a novelty at their events. And the Messenger Guild would like to renew their contract for speed talismans."

"Very well. Is the paperwork on my desk?"

"Ready for you to sign."

"I will want to read it first." She hadn't become the wealthiest bone wizard in Cerre by skipping the details.

"Naturally."

She'd take care of a few business items first. See to it that she had a proper bath and a full night's sleep, and then she'd return to Stran's farmhouse. With luck, they'd be finished arguing by the time she arrived, and she'd have skipped all the tedious hand-wringing. She could already tell that Stran's wife was going to be a complication, no matter what Kreya decided. Amurra wouldn't want him to leave and it was clear she was in charge of the household, which was adorable, given that he was about three times her size and could crush a hornet's nest in one fist and a rock in the other.

Maybe Zera would give them an extra day to deal with all their issues. And an extra day to quit feeling so . . . she wouldn't say "hurt." That was giving Kreya too much power over her. An extra day to quit feeling so disappointed. But then she'd go back.

Of course she would.

Wouldn't she?

AFTER DEALING WITH A FEW BUSINESS DETAILS and soaking in a bath, Zera retired to her room. She collapsed into her bed with a sigh and then stretched like a cat. It felt wonderful after the last few uncomfortable nights. She was almost sorry when Guine let himself into the room—he'd take up a portion of the bed, and she wasn't inclined to share.

"You don't plan to stay in Cerre?" he asked.

She hadn't told him her plan to return to Stran's farmhouse. "What makes you say that?"

"You completed all the payment forms for the next three weeks. I know because I filed them."

Ahh, yes, he was not as dumb as he looked. Sometimes it was difficult to remember that. Zera smiled. "A vacation. It's been a while since I've taken one."

"You've *never* taken one. I'm pleased to hear it. I have thought for a while you work too hard." Dropping his robe, he climbed nude into bed beside her. She decided she didn't mind sharing the bed after all as he began to massage her shoulders. "But you were away already, and you don't seem rested. In fact, I see bruises." He gently kissed a bruise on her upper arm. She hadn't even noticed that one was there.

"It was a far more active visit than I'd expected," she admitted.

"And was your friend in danger?"

"She needed my assistance, and I helped her." *And him.* She thought of Jentt and how amazing it was to see him again. He was exactly how she remembered him. Prior to dying, of course.

"Does she need your help again?"

Guine was indeed smarter than he looked. Also, he excelled at getting the knots out of her muscles. She curled to give him better access to her back. "She might."

"Haven't you given her enough of your time? She was your friend decades ago. That hardly obligates you to jeopardize your health for her." He paused, adding as if afraid she'd be offended, "I only say this because I worry."

"I'm not as young as I used to be, am I?"

"You are twice as beautiful."

She smiled. "Good save."

He returned to massaging her. "What I mean to say is that you've built a life here. This is your future. She's your past. You don't owe her anything more, but you owe yourself, what you've built and created in the years since you knew her, as much as you can give."

Zera rolled over to face him, as a sudden thought occurred to her. "You missed me."

He took the opportunity to kiss her. She let the kiss continue for a while, nearly distracting her from the topic at hand, but then she pushed back and said, "Is that what this is really about? You missing me? I warned you not to fall in love with me. I bore easily and will break your heart."

"What about *your* heart?" He laid his hand on top of her heart. "I won't break that. Can you say the same about your friend, the same friend who abandoned you for twenty-five years? You were so angry with her. So hurt. I don't want you hurt again."

She considered that. What did she owe Kreya, Jentt, Marso, and Stran? Yes, they had been a team long ago. And together they'd done their best to protect Vos.

It was tempting to stay with Guine, be the successful bone wizard, and leave Eklor and the fate of Vos to the next set of heroes hungry to make a name for themselves. As far as she knew, that could be the very conclusion that her old friends were reaching in the farmhouse: perhaps it was time for another team now to step forward and sacrifice. If Eklor lived, then others should face him. He was no longer their responsibility.

Except that he was.

Defeating him was her greatest achievement. It was what she'd built her empire on. Once it was known he lived, all this adoration could disperse like a cloud in wind. *That's not true,* she thought. *My life's work is not so fragile.* There had to be another reason why she felt the pull to return. "You don't know Kreya. She wants me to come back, and I can't say no."

"You can say no to me," Guine said.

She wondered if she was truly breaking his heart by leaving again so soon, even though it wouldn't be permanently. She doubted it. "Yes, that's true, isn't it?"

"You're breaking my heart."

"But I'm not, am I? You don't love me, Guine, do you?"

"Of course I do!"

"The truth."

He hesitated. "I admire you. I enjoy you."

She should have been disappointed to hear it, but instead she felt relieved. He wouldn't suffer while she was gone. "Kreya needs me."

"I think it isn't about Kreya at all. I think she's an excuse. You want to go for you."

That was a troubling thought. It was much easier to simply blame Kreya. The idea that Zera would *want* to put herself in danger again . . . It was absurd.

I'm returning for the sake of my friends. And my reputation. And the future of Vos. She certainly wasn't returning to the farmhouse for any other reason.

"You want a second chance at being a hero," Guine said, far

too perceptive for a man who was so often shirtless. "But you don't need one. You're a hero in my eyes already."

"And you . . . talk too much." While her hands caressed his lovely muscles, Zera kissed him until he stopped talking and she stopped thinking.

AT DAWN, ZERA STOCKED HER COAT WITH ALL THE talismans she thought they'd need. She hadn't had time to make more, but she had a healthy supply to draw from. Plenty of strength talismans for Stran, plenty of speed talismans for Jentt, and an assortment of others that could come in handy if Kreya persuaded everyone to return to the plains.

Using a bit of a speed talisman herself, she departed Cerre without looking back and traveled across multiple mountains to Stran's farmhouse. She had plenty of time for second and third thoughts on her journey, and she also had plenty of time to decide that Guine was right:

She wasn't doing this for Kreya or Vos or even her reputation.

I'm doing it for me, she thought.

It was a somewhat extraordinary revelation. She had thought her hero days were long behind her. She'd become a businesswoman and had thought she was happy with her role in life. Who knew she still had an adventurer within her, yearning for a second chance to come back into the light and shine?

Waltzing into the farmhouse, Zera sang, "I've returned! Are we ready to save the world? You know, again?"

Everyone turned to look at her. And Marso burst into tears.

CHAPTER THIRTEEN

K nock it off, Marso," Kreya said.

He slumped into the kitchen chair, buried his face in his hands, and moaned more quietly, which was fine— Kreya could think with a little moaning in the background. Full-throated sobs were harder to ignore.

Zera dropped an embroidered bag on the table. It clattered with the familiar sound of bones. A beautiful sound. "Okay, well, *I'm* ready," Zera said. "I vote we give everyone ten more minutes to pull their shit together, and then we leave."

A smile tugged at Kreya's lips. She hadn't been one hundred percent certain that Zera would even return. It was good to have her here, especially since Stran and Marso continued to be resistant to the idea of trying to be heroes again. "I'm glad you're back," Kreya said. "About what I said before you left . . ."

"Forgiven and forgotten," Zera said breezily.

Kreya hesitated. She wasn't sure if Zera meant it or not. She'd seen the hurt in Zera's eyes when she'd left. Kreya hadn't meant to sound as if she doubted her. She'd only meant to say that it was her choice whether to return or not, but all her words had come out wrong. *I'm out of practice talking with people.* Truthfully, she wasn't certain she'd ever been good at it. Barking orders, yes. Handling emotions, not so much. "You're sure?"

"I'm sure we need to stop Eklor. Sooner rather than later."

That wasn't exactly an answer, but she'd take it.

By the hearth, Stran's children were playing with her rag doll constructs while their parents, set off again by Zera's return, argued in the other room, loud enough that everyone could hear every word:

"You already completed your destiny," Amurra was saying. "It's over. Eklor is dead!"

"Of course he's dead," Stran said. "Everyone knows this. Everyone except Marso and Kreya and Zera and Jentt. And that's why I have to go! For them!"

"But it's crazy!"

Kreya met Zera's eyes. She'd never been overly fond of that word. It had been used too often as a weapon against those she cared about. *And against me*, she thought. A better phrase might be: "experienced in the ways life can screw with a person."

"Amurra," Stran pleaded, "I had a chance to heal. You healed me! But they're still stuck in their old pain. If I go with them and prove that the past is the past, I can help them move on."

"Can't they move on in a way that doesn't mean breaking the law and endangering your life? There are guards posted on the wall! Why do you have to risk yourself?"

"If I didn't help my team when they need me, I wouldn't be the man you married."

"You don't have to prove anything to me!" Amurra cried. "You don't need to be a hero anymore. You're a father, a farmer, and a husband. Why can't that be enough?"

Stran's reply was lost beneath Vivi's squeal of delight when a rag doll construct danced with another—she had been trying to teach them to dance for the last few hours, while her brother Jen repaired some of their loose stitches. He was neat with a needle.

Quietly, Kreya admitted to Zera, "I don't know if Stran and Marso are up for this." She'd been talking with them, arguing with them, and listening to Stran and Amurra argue with each other ever since Zera had left.

Helping herself to tea, Zera sipped and added honey before saying, "We could leave them here. Just go ourselves. You, me, and Jentt. This time we're prepared—"

"We're a thousand times less prepared," Kreya said. "Zero training. Out of practice. Out of touch." Maybe she was a fool to think they could do this at all. They'd been heroes such a long time ago.

Zera chugged her tea, slammed down the mug, and upended her bag of bones. Glittering talismans spilled out onto the table. "We may be out of practice, but at least we have firepower."

Gawking at the array of hundreds of gorgeously carved bones, inlaid with gold and jewels, Kreya picked up one of the stealth talismans. She examined the markings, a variation on any she'd ever seen before, with rubies to enhance the grooves. Holding it up to the light, she admired it and barked in a voice loud enough to carry throughout the farmhouse, "All right, people. Enough dithering! Let's prep to move out! If you're coming, come. If you're not, fuck you." Belatedly, she glanced at the kids. "Pretend you didn't hear that."

Both Vivi and Jen covered their ears and grinned.

Kreya hauled out her pack and checked over her supplies. Knives, sharp. Canteen, fresh and full. She was certain Amurra would supply them with food, even if she didn't want to supply her husband.

While she weeded through her pack, Zera divvied up the

talismans: the strength ones for Stran if he came, speed for Jentt, and an assortment for Kreya and Marso. Each of them would take a few for emergencies, but as she'd done the last time they'd adventured together, Zera would hold on to the majority of them. They'd discovered it was much more efficient to have her distribute them than to ask the others to dig through their pockets in the heat of battle. She always doled out the appropriate talisman to the right fighter—she had an incredible instinct for it. She was like an archer's quarrel that always supplied the most perfect arrow. Finishing her own task, Kreya watched her. It looked as if Zera had chosen their supplies wisely.

Coming into the kitchen, Jentt added his emergency stash to the pouches that hung around his waist. "These look amazing, Zera."

"They *are* amazing," Zera said. "And worth a bloody fortune. So don't use them casually and don't waste the power. They're not infinite."

He winked at her, whispered a word to a speed talisman, and zipped around the kitchen as fast as a blur of light. When he stopped by the sink, he wore a rag doll construct on his head like a hat. The kids laughed and clapped. Bowing with a flourish, he deposited the construct on the floor. Wobbling, it toddled back to the hearth.

Opening her coat, Kreya whistled to her constructs. "Three of you. Volunteers only." She didn't know if they knew the word "volunteer," but they whispered to one another and three of them tumbled forward, climbed up the inside of her coat, and stuffed themselves into pockets. Raising her voice, she asked, "Amurra and Stran, may the rest of my constructs stay here?"

Vivi chirped, "Ooh, can they? Please, please, Mama! Please, Papa!"

Coming into the kitchen, Amurra halted when she saw her children playing with the remaining dolls, as well as the skeleton bird. Her eyes widened, but to her credit, she didn't scream. Kreya liked her even more for that. "Will you two be responsible and take care of them?" Amurra asked.

"We promise!" both Vivi and Jen chorused.

"Then yes, they may stay."

Vivi danced in a circle with one of the dolls, hugging it.

In a lower voice, Amurra asked, "They aren't dangerous, are they?"

Standing beside Amurra, Kreya watched the bird skeleton bump into a cabinet, switch direction, and bump into another cabinet. One of the rag dolls twisted its head halfway around to watch the bird. Even Kreya had to admit they were a bit unsettling. "I promise they won't harm your children. Or anyone. Unless I ask them to." She had a burst of inspiration. "On the contrary, I will instruct them to protect you."

Amurra looked surprised but then said, "Thank you."

As soon as Kreya finished instructing the constructs, Jentt crossed to Kreya's opposite side and murmured, "Kreya, I don't think Marso is up for the journey." She looked over to where the bone reader was no longer moaning, but he hadn't lifted his head off the table. He was tapping his fingers on the table in a random pattern that seemed to fascinate him.

"Did you ask him?" Kreya asked.

Jentt shook his head. "He's in no condition to—"

Kreya lifted her voice. "Marso? Want to come find Eklor with us?"

He didn't move. "If he lives, what do we do?" His voice sounded lost, but Kreya thought it was a sensible question. Maybe that was a good sign.

"Kill him more thoroughly," Jentt answered.

Amurra yelped. "Not in front of the kids!"

"Sorry. We'll . . . tickle him relentlessly." He winked at the kids, and Vivi and Jen giggled. "I didn't get a chance to help with . . . the tickling . . . last time. I have a few leftover feelings about Eklor's behavior that I'd love to work out . . . by tickling."

"He deserves it," Marso said, with more passion than before. It gave Kreya hope. *He'll come,* she thought.

She turned to Stran and picked up the talismans that Zera had set aside for him. "I know you don't believe he's alive, but in case you're wrong, I want you to be prepared."

He accepted the emergency talismans, securing them in pouches around his belt. With a shuddering breath, Stran said, "If he lives, we will ensure that Vivi, Jen, and Nugget will not grow up in a world where Eklor threatens the peace."

Amurra placed her hands on his chest and looked at him with wide eyes. "I love that you're brave. I love that you're noble. I love that you're strong and self-sacrificing and heroic. But if he lives, I want you to come home and inform Grand Master Lorn, not try to stop him yourself. Someone else can take a turn at saving the world. Your children need you here!"

Kreya had the strong sense that Amurra had never witnessed his facing true danger before. Stran's past must have seemed like a collection of adventure stories to her. Until Kreya showed up at their door. *I wonder if she regrets welcoming me in,* Kreya thought. She glanced at the pouches of food that Amurra had prepared for them and noticed hers lacked the blackberry muffins she'd packed in the others—that was an answer, of sorts.

"Kids, to your rooms, and take the constructs," Stran said. "Everyone else, outside, please. I owe my wife a thousand promises and apologies, and I'd prefer the privacy."

Scooping up packs, Kreya and Zera scooted outside. Jentt helped Marso out the door. They settled on a bench near a woodpile, while Kreya and Zera looked out across the terraced fields.

From here, Kreya knew the most obvious approach to the forbidden zone—the one they'd used twenty-five years ago. Unfortunately, since the war, it had become a popular historic trail. *So that's out,* she thought.

"You have a plan?" Zera asked.

"Do you have any leftover lizard bone?"

"Luckily for you, I do." Reaching into a pocket, Zera pulled out a six-inch shard and handed it to Kreya. Crossing to one of Strand's farm wagons, Kreya checked its bones. Outfitted with a few basic bones, it was designed for travel on well-worn paths, to the market and back. But she could fix that. Pulling out her tools, Kreya lowered herself to the ground and began tinkering. She hummed to herself as she worked.

"Speed?" Zera asked.

"Yep."

"And steadiness."

"Enough to keep us from flying off the mountain. Can't make wheels climb, though. We'll need to take the paths as far as they'll go, before descending into the mists."

Zera giggled.

Scooting out from beneath the wagon, Kreya glared at her. "What?"

"The boys are going to hate your plan."

THE BOYS *DID* HATE HER PLAN. BUT KREYA GAVE them all the option to stay at the farmhouse, which she thought was more than fair. Twenty-five years ago, she'd given them a choice too, whether they remembered that or not. They could have said no then. They could have said no now.

Amurra *did* say no, loudly and repeatedly.

But Stran kissed her and swore up and down he'd return unscathed, on top of whatever he'd promised her in the privacy of their kitchen, while the others politely pretended they weren't watching. Tearfully, Amurra turned to Kreya. "Promise me you'll bring my husband back to me, alive and unharmed," she pleaded.

Kreya replied, "Why in the world do you think I could make that kind of promise?"

That did not help.

Eventually, though, they were under way.

Marso, wrapped in blankets, was tucked into the wagon with Jentt. Stran took up his position at the back, facing behind them. He'd ensure they weren't chased, or if they were, that they were aware of the fact. Kreya sat with Zera beside her on the front bench. She'd steer while Zera assisted—or, more accurately, provided running commentary:

"You should slow on the corners.

"Gotta watch out for the branches.

"You ran through moose crap. Do you have any idea how hard that stuff is to wash off? We are going to be smelling it for days."

Finally, Kreya said: "How about you warn me *before* I'm about to hit anything instead of after it's too late, hmm?"

Zera sat up straighter. "You were listening to me? Okay. Great. Rock."

A half second later, Kreya hit a rock, and the wagon jostled up into the air a foot and then crashed back down, rattling as it careened onward.

"Thanks," Kreya said through gritted teeth.

She didn't touch the brakes, though, despite how many branches whacked the wagon and how many rocks bounced it. Speed was key as they zipped past farms, villages, and pastures. It was fine if people remembered an out-of-control wagon. It wouldn't be fine if they were stopped or even recognized. The fewer questions they had to answer later, the better.

If we're wrong about Eklor, Kreya thought, *it's best if no one guesses where we went.*

Going into the mist to certain doom would confuse most onlookers anyway.

Fortunately, keeping up their speed was easy—she just aimed the wagon straight down the mountain. She didn't even have to activate the speed bone. Gravity and momentum were all the magic they needed.

As they sailed over a larger rock, Zera flung her arms in the air and whooped. "This is amazing! We're doing this! And we're going to be awesome! We're not less than what we were; we're more! Eklor, we're coming for you!"

Kreya grinned. She kept her eyes on the path as it twisted between the trees. If she had read the map correctly, they had a few hundred yards before—

The path ended in a pleasant clearing, with clusters of wildflowers. Birds startled as they rattled into it. Kreya didn't slow. She'd seen the elevation markings and knew the contour of this part of the mountain. This should be the perfect place to descend.

"Wait, Kreya? Road? We lost the road," Stran called from the back of the wagon.

"No more road," Kreya said. She braced herself. "Hold on, everyone!"

She hit the opposite side of the clearing, where a flat boulder jutted out from the mountain slope, and she drove the wagon off it. Its wheels flew over empty air for a moment, and then they crashed down on a steeper slope.

Every bone in her body rattled, and she clung to the steering stick as they careened down the mountainside toward the mist below.

With luck, any onlookers would remember a tragedy: an out-of-control wagon that disappeared into the mist. They'd murmur about how it was such a shame, and then they'd dismiss it as an accident—certainly, they wouldn't expect anyone to intentionally drive *into* the mist.

"Stay alert, everyone," she called. With the kind of racket they were making, they were bound to draw attention. Without thinking about whether he could or not, she asked, "Marso, any predictions?"

"Death and doom," he replied. "I don't need bones for that."

"Helpful," she said through gritted teeth. "Stran, report." She glanced back at him.

"Movement to the east. Ten-foot predator. Make that multiple predators." He drew his knife but kept his seat. "Croco-raptors."

"They hunt in packs," Kreya said, focusing on driving again. "Expect the visible ones to be a distraction. Attack will come from either west or behind us."

"Or front," Zera added. "Could be front. For fun."

"Defend or outrun?" Stran asked.

Kreya scanned the clumps of bushes, aimed for the least dense, and drove the wagon through them. She ducked beneath branches. "Wait for it."

Ahead was the rush of the river. She heard it, calculated the distance, and angled the wagon so it burst out between the trees alongside the water. Vines stretched from bank to bank, knitted into weblike patterns, and Kreya saw the croco-raptors racing along the opposite side.

The attack would come from their side of the river.

"Two behind us!" Stran called.

Four on the opposite side of the rushing water.

"Now!" Kreya shouted.

Stran launched himself off the back of the wagon as one of the previously hidden croco-raptors attacked from the bushes on the side. He shouted, *"Ozri!"* to activate a strength talisman as he swung feetfirst to plow into one of the raptors.

"Ready for extraction!" Kreya called to Jentt.

"On it!" He leaped from the wagon, grabbed a vine, and swung to land on the riverbank. Zera tossed him a speed talisman, and Jentt activated it. He sped into a blur. In seconds, he was back, with Stran and the severed head of a croco-raptor.

"Stran, deliver it!" Kreya called.

Stran hefted the croco-raptor head up and threw it hard, fueled by a strength talisman. It soared over the water. Kreya heard shrieks from the croco-raptors as it impacted. Drawn by the fresh meal, the croco-raptors slowed to attack the head.

"Two still back there," Stran reported. "Keeping their distance."

"You got blood on your shirt," Zera informed him.

He ignored her. "By the bones, that was the most fun I've had in ages."

Kreya agreed. It felt like the old days.

"Strongly recommend not telling your wife that," Jentt said to Stran. He had his arm around Marso, cushioning him from the rattle of the wagon as they flew over rocks and fallen trees.

"I tell her everything," Stran said. "That's how our marriage works. No lies between us."

"Adorable," Zera said. "Absurd, but adorable. If she asked you whether you thought she was the most brilliant person you'd ever met, what would you tell her?"

"She wouldn't—"

"You'd lie and say she was as brilliant as the sun."

Kreya smiled at the thought of Zera's dispensing relationship advice. She hoped Stran was too sensible to listen. He was lucky to have Amurra, and vice versa. *And I'm lucky to have my team here with me,* she thought. *Together again.*

"And if she asked whether she had any habits that annoyed you, you'd tell her what?"

"She snores," Stran said. "She knows that. A marriage is a union—that means the two of you, united against whatever life throws at you. You share everything."

"You're not sharing this." Zera waved at the wagon, the wildness, the river, and the bloodstains on his shirt. She narrowly avoided whacking Kreya's arm.

"I'll share the story of this, when we return," Stran said, as if that were obvious. "And doing so will make us stronger."

Kreya thought of all the things she hadn't shared with Jentt, all the days that there hadn't been time to tell him about, all the hours she'd spent alone. She thought too of her greatest omission: the truth about the cost of the resurrection spell.

I'll share that with him someday, she promised herself. *After Eklor.*

Or . . . maybe she'd just wait until they were both on their deathbeds. He'd understand then and wouldn't blame her for choices she'd made when they were apart.

Right now, they had the future to share together. Who cared about the past?

And that future right now held an enormous venomous stone fish. "Hold on!" she called, and veered sharply away from the river toward the tangled mass of trees. "Jentt, to me! Zera, watch Marso."

Zera scrambled into the back of the wagon, replacing Jentt beside Marso. She cooed at him and put her arm around him. Jentt climbed up with Zera.

"Clear a path," Kreya said.

"Happily."

Standing, he drew two knives. Coming behind him, Stran braced him, holding his thighs steady while Jentt leaned forward. With blurring speed, Jentt slashed at the vines, branches, and greenery, clearing a path in front of them.

"When I met Amurra," Stran said conversationally, "I thought she'd never go for a man like me. You've seen her—capable, beautiful. She was running her parents' farm on her own since age fifteen and, when I met her, had already put in motion plans to purchase what is now our farm. Had no need of a partner."

"How did you win her over?" Zera asked.

They burst out onto a deer trail, and Jentt stilled his arms. He sat on the bench as Stran returned to lookout on the back of the wagon.

"I didn't," Stran answered Zera. "She wooed me."

"Attracted to the Hero of Vos mystique?" Zera guessed.

"She needed a tree removed but didn't have the equipment for it," he said. "I had a spare strength talisman, so . . ." He paused. Holding on to the back of the wagon, he swung himself out and kicked a croco-raptor in the face. It squealed as it hit a tree trunk.

"Got it," Zera said. "You impressed her with your muscles."

"Actually, no. It turned out there was a raccoon family living in that tree. I relocated them to a new home, and they scratched the crap out of my face as thanks. She said anyone who tried to cuddle a nest of baby raccoons deserved some cuddling without teeth and claws."

"Okay, that's the cutest story I've ever heard," Zera said. "I may throw up."

"River lizard ahead," Jentt said conversationally. "Should we kill it?"

Kreya heard the roar and caught a glimpse of its massive jaws through the canopy of trees. It was ahead of them, on the deer trail. "Still got any croco-raptors on our tail?" she called back to Strand.

"One left."

"Feed it to the lizard."

She glanced back in time to see Stran's enormous smile. Working together, Stran and Jentt caught the tail of the final croco-raptor. Activating her own strength talisman, Zera shouted out, "Now!" and joined them as they hurled the croco-raptor into the gaping maw of the river lizard as Kreya drove the wagon between its feet.

Stran whooped and punched the air.

Kreya smiled. *We're still a team, just like we used to be,* she thought. No other group she'd ever heard of could have navigated the deadly valley like this. But here they were, surviving, thriving. Together, they could conquer the impossible. *Eklor won't know what hit him.* Feeling more optimistic than she had since fleeing the plains, she kept driving through the valley, toward the forbidden zone and toward the future.

CHAPTER FOURTEEN

After a night switching off who slept and who was on guard—not counting Marso—and another day of traveling, Kreya and the others reached the wall. They stashed the wagon beneath a screen of matted vines and branches, and they used stealth talismans to sneak along the wall until they reached one of the grates.

It wasn't the same culvert that Kreya and Zera had used before, but the grate was just as rusty and barely guarded. That seemed to be a theme with the forbidden zone. No one cared about it anymore, which was why in twenty-five years no one had noticed Eklor's return.

Poor kids, Kreya thought, looking back at the guards who patrolled the top of the wall. *They have no idea how terrible they are at their job. Or how terrible their job is about to become.*

Using speed talismans, they left the poorly guarded wall behind. Kreya and Zera led the way across the plain, while Jentt and Stran marveled at how it had regrown. All the lush grass, the autumn wildflowers, and the just-beginning-to-turn trees made it look as if nothing terrible had ever happened here. But all of them remembered what had been, and Kreya felt a tightness in her chest as she thought of what was to come if she was right.

Stumbling along with them, Marso was muttering in a sing-song voice, "Going to the dead, going to the dead, going to the dead."

Zera whispered, "Can we gag him?"

"Absolutely not," Kreya said.

"You know I love him, but he's getting on my nerves."

"He's our early-warning system," Kreya said. "You don't gag an alarm. Besides, I think it makes him feel better." She glanced back and saw Jentt had his arm around Marso, comforting him. Her heart felt as if it thumped a little harder, seeing Jentt alive, here, and caring for their friends the way he always had. He'd always been the heart of their group, believing in them all even when they didn't believe in themselves.

After a few miles of walking, they spotted the tower. Broken and burned, it looked like the bones of a dead thing. It stood in sharp contrast to the abundant life all around it. Soon, in another few decades, the life would consume it. Already vines ran up through cracks in the stone, a tree jutted out at a crooked angle from the side, and moss coated its base.

"Looks abandoned," Stran said, stating the obvious.

"Looks like a trap," Jentt said.

"Regardless of what you believe, everyone is to treat this as if Eklor were functioning at full strength," Kreya said. "No stupid mistakes. No unnecessary risks. We assess the situation, and then we regroup and determine how to proceed. Got it?"

Nods all around, but no one looked at her—everyone was focused on the tower.

"Zera, your fastest talisman to Jentt," Kreya whispered. She crouched in the grasses. Beside her the others did the same. "Jentt, scout. Five-hundred-yard radius, then return."

Zera withdrew two silver bones from her pockets and pressed

them into his hands. He was gone with a rustle of grasses in his wake. Closer to the tower, the rustle disappeared, and Kreya couldn't even track him by his path. He'd combined a speed talisman with a stealth. She tried to ignore the way her heart squeezed at his absence and instead concentrated on counting her breaths. He should return in one, two, three—

He was back, only a minor rustle in the grasses as he slowed.

"Two patrols, six soldiers each, to the northeast and the south," he reported in a whisper. "Archer on the top of the tower, hidden between rocks."

"Take them out?" Stran asked.

Kreya shook her head. "Not yet. First, we see what they're guarding."

She heard a clink behind her. Silently, she spun, hand on the hilt of a knife. But it was only Marso, squatting between the grasses, making a pyramid with scavenger-picked bones he'd found nearby. "One dead, two dead, three dead . . . ," he cooed at the bones.

"Are you reading them or playing with them?" Kreya asked.

He stopped. "Can't promise I won't scream."

"Maybe don't try if you're going to scream, buddy, okay?" Jentt said.

Marso began to quiver.

Kreya had hoped that bringing him here, believing in him, would help restore some of his old self. She began to wonder, though, if she'd made a mistake. "Just stay hidden." She nodded at the tower. "Zera, with Stran. Guard Marso. If the patrols come near, take them out. Jentt, you're with me. We track the pattern of the patrols."

"Like the old days," Jentt said cheerfully.

"Hopefully not," Kreya said.

He sobered instantly.

Together, they activated stealth talismans, two of Zera's finest, and crept through the grasses. The patrols had left clear trails, tramping over the grasses and leaving skeletal footprints in the supple soil. Their more frequently used paths were obvious, and Kreya and Jentt followed them.

When she had a clear picture of their pattern, she signaled to Jentt to return to their friends. It was as she expected: all the patrols centered around the tower. There was no way to know whether this was a remembered pattern from the days when Eklor used it as his stronghold or if they followed new orders, but there was no doubt that they guarded the tower. The hidden archer was only extra proof.

The problem was that she'd been inside the tower, albeit quickly, and had seen no evidence of any recent occupation. Chewing on her lip, she considered it.

Her tower had burned too, and where had she gone? *Underground*, she answered herself.

The mountains were riddled with caves, so it was an obvious refuge for her. Here, though, on the plains . . . *He could have made himself tunnels*, she thought. Or used his skeletal labor to dig them. He'd had plenty of time.

And plenty of skeletons.

She would have bet heaps of gold that they'd find an entrance within the tower. She eyed it. She hated the thought of an underground lair. With Marso nonfunctional, there was no way to anticipate what they'd find, and with their only known exit through the tower, they could be easily cut off. It had been bad enough facing Eklor's forces on an open plain.

For the first time since they'd left the farmhouse, she felt a twinge of doubt.

She knew what they would face in the valley, because she and Zera had just survived it, but here, she felt as if she were flying blind. They lacked too much information, and it made her skin prickle with unease.

"Given the patrols, I can see why you'd believe he's here," Stran began. "But there's no structure other than the tower, and as you can tell from the ruins, no one—"

Kreya cut him off. "He's beneath it."

Jentt nodded. "You can dig yourself quite a large basement in twenty-five years."

"It would explain how he's kept himself and his soldiers out of sight," Kreya said. She deliberately did not look at Marso. It wasn't his fault she'd brought him here before he was ready. But they couldn't have waited, not if the worst was true. "Here's what I'm thinking: stealth and speed to enter the tower. Stran, you hide Marso inside the tower and keep watch—"

Marso's eyes widened. "I can't go in there. I'd scream for certain. Give you away."

She considered that for a moment. They couldn't leave him unguarded on the plain, but they also needed Stran to be lookout—it would be all too easy for the patrols to block their escape route without Stran to keep the way clear. "If you can't handle it . . ."

Zera rolled her eyes. "Obviously he can't handle it. I still say gagging him is the right move. Can't scream in mortal terror if there's a thing shoved in your mouth."

"That's inhumane," Stran said. "We don't gag friends."

Kreya weighed the options. She too didn't like the idea of gagging a teammate any more than Stran did. But Zera was in the right here, and she knew that. No matter how much like their old selves they'd all felt in the valley, she had to acknowledge that time had passed and they had all changed, most obviously Marso. Opening her coat, she extracted one of the rag dolls. "Marso, if you can't control yourself, my friend here can silence you. Would that be acceptable?" To the construct she said, "If he begins to scream, can you stuff yourself in his mouth without hurting him? Make sure he can still breathe."

Marso reached out a shaky finger and touched the cheek of the doll. He then nodded, and Kreya placed the construct on his shoulder. It wrapped its arm around the back of his neck to hold on.

"All right then," Kreya said. "Stran, you're on guard with Marso. Keep yourselves hidden. Any patrol comes, eliminate them."

"What about the archer?" Jentt asked. "It could sound an alarm and draw more patrols to the tower than Stran could handle at once."

"Take the archer out now," Zera suggested.

Kreya shook her head. "A patrol could notice its absence." She drew the other two rag dolls out of her coat. Addressing them, she said, "Once we're inside, sneak to the top of the tower. If the archer grows suspicious and tries to sound an alarm, bind his wrists so he cannot use his bow and fill his mouth so he cannot cry out. Do you understand? If there's danger, silence and still him."

Both constructs nodded eagerly.

"Jentt, Zera, and I will descend—"

"I do *not* like that idea," Zera objected.

Truthfully, she didn't like it either. The team functioned best with Zera supporting the fighters. Putting Zera on the front line risked the effectiveness of the whole team. But there weren't too many options, given the situation and all the unknowns.

"We don't know what we'll face down there," Kreya said. "You're the only one who knows exactly what firepower we have and how to use it. We need you."

Zera glared at her but nodded.

To Stran, Kreya said, "If we come out and say 'bury it' . . . be ready to pull down the tower. Destroy it down to the stones."

"But that's not Plan A," Jentt clarified. His eyes were fixed on Kreya's, as if trying to read her intent. "Plan A is still reconnaissance, then regroup and determine how to safely proceed."

She knew what he was asking: was she planning to risk herself? *All of this is a risk,* she thought. "If there's an opportunity, we take it. But we take no unnecessary chances."

"Agreed," Jentt said.

The others agreed as well, even the rag dolls.

KREYA DARTED ACROSS THE BARE, OPEN LAND BEtween the tall grasses and the tower. She knew that with Zera's combined speed and stealth talismans, she was barely a streak to the human eye. A whiff of cloud that could be confused for the haze of heat.

They slipped through the broken door into the shadowed interior. Last time she had been here with Zera, they'd run too quickly to explore. Now, as the two rag dolls scurried up the stairs to monitor the archer, Kreya examined the atrium.

This was the room where Eklor had issued his orders to his troops, where he'd planned his attacks. The walls had been covered in maps. There had been only one chair, a thronelike wooden seat. She crossed to where she remembered its being. Only a pile of charred sticks remained.

"See," Stran said in a whisper. "There's nothing here."

"Except memories," Kreya said.

"And this trapdoor into—and this is just a guess, but I'm going to assume it's accurate—a pit of horrors." Zera waved lazily at a strip of burlap that lay across the floor.

Stran scowled. "What door—"

She kicked the burlap aside, revealing a stone that lacked any of the burn marks that streaked the rest of the tower. "Shall we?"

Kreya grinned at her, though it was a tight grin. A small part of her had hoped she'd been wrong about an underground room, about Eklor, about everything.

"Any more specific plans than 'go in, see what's there'?" Jentt asked.

"Did you bring any cat-eye talismans?" Kreya asked Zera.

"Owl this time," Zera said. "They won't work in total darkness, but if we stick close to whatever light filters through the opening . . . Activation word is *nesca*." She handed one to Kreya and one to Jentt.

Kreya looked at each of them, her old friends whom she'd led back here, and gave them one last order: "Don't die."

Stran yanked up the stone.

All of them froze as the stone scraped against the nearest stone. He laid the cover as softly as possible next to the hole. No one moved. No one breathed. They waited, listening. But no alarm sounded, and nothing came out of the hole.

Silently, Kreya signaled: Jentt first, then Zera, then herself.

Jentt first, because he could flee fastest. Zera next, in case he needed a talisman they didn't anticipate. Her last, to relay any warning that they'd been discovered.

She hated sending Jentt first. Hated watching him lower his body, his newly alive body, into the darkness. He flashed her a smile that was meant to reassure her, but it was nearly enough to make her call him back and say this wasn't worth it, that they could still flee and pretend they'd never discovered what they'd discovered, that it wasn't their problem anymore, that they'd given enough . . .

She heard the soft *thump* of his feet hitting the floor.

They waited. No screams. No cries. Just one soft *coo* like a pigeon—Jentt's "all clear" call. Kreya nodded to Zera.

Zera glared at her once more, making it clear how unhappy she was about this plan, but then she lowered herself into the hole after Jentt. A second soft *coo*.

Climbing into the hole, Kreya dropped down and landed in a crouch in the darkness. She brought the owl talisman to her lips and whispered, "*Nesca.*"

The shadows sharpened. She saw Jentt and Zera beside her, crisp shapes of gray. Each movement was vivid as they examined where they were: a chamber that branched into five paths. She felt her stomach tighten—she'd expected to find a basement, not a network of tunnels.

Zera held two fingers together and then apart. *Split up?* she was asking.

Kreya shook her head. *No.*

You don't split up. Not when you don't know what you're up against. *And sometimes not even when you do,* Kreya thought. After Jentt died—

She cut off that train of thought. She wasn't going to think about that time. She had to stay rooted in the present, deal with whatever threat lurked in the darkness here.

The tunnels stank like rotten eggs, machine oil, and a long-dead rat carcass—all of which was worrying. What if all the soldiers weren't up on the plains? "Going to the dead," Zera whisper-sang, mimicking Marso. Kreya shot her a look, but Zera pretended she couldn't see it.

Wordlessly, they chose the tunnel with the strongest stench and crept along it. The stealth talisman masked their footsteps. Kreya kept reaching out to touch Jentt and Zera, as her brain shrieked that she'd lost them or was going to lose them. Soon, they *did* lose the light from the opening, and the darkness swamped them.

Another turn, and a sickly green light illuminated the tunnel. Creeping forward, they found the source: bioluminescent moss wrapped around a carved bone. "Clever," Zera murmured.

Indeed, Kreya thought. She'd never heard of such a thing.

Her heart thudded hard in her rib cage. She was torn between being grateful for the dim light and being afraid of what it meant. They crept slower, even more cautiously, alert for guards and traps. Her eyes swept the shadows in front of them, and her fingers trailed along the wall, feeling the chipped stone—these were man-made, not construct-made, tunnels. There shouldn't have been so much underground area to explore, and yet there was. She wondered how far they went, and what they'd find at the end.

And then she didn't have to wonder anymore, as the tunnel widened into a vast cavern. It glowed with the eerie greenish light, which bathed everything in an even glow that came from every direction, washing out but not erasing shadows. Filling the cavern were horrors.

Skeletal soldiers lined the walls, their skulls drooped on their necks as if they slept. Constructs cobbled from the bones of mountain lions, stone fish, river lizards, and bears dominated the center of the room. And then there were the machines. Killing machines, with knives for hands, metal jaws with tearing teeth, and saws locked into their torsos.

She'd expected a few. She'd never expected *this*.

"Shit," Jentt whispered.

She felt as if her blood had frozen in her veins. As commander, she always tried to think of every possible outcome, to believe in her team while still considering every worst-case scenario. But in all her imagining and all her planning, she'd never imagined anything of this scope. She wanted to run out of the tunnel screaming. Flee and never look back. But she didn't. They had a job to do.

"Count them," Kreya whispered back.

As Jentt counted and Zera invented new curse words, Kreya committed to memory the weaponry of Eklor's new army. If they had to muster a force against this, she wanted exact information on what they'd face.

In the Bone War, so many had died when confronted with an army like this . . . And that time, they'd been ready for it. They'd come with the finest soldiers that Vos could muster. *Focus on the task at hand,* she ordered herself. *Assess the threat, and get out.*

As soon as she felt they'd seen enough, she signaled for them to retreat. Creeping back through the tunnel, she signaled again for them to investigate a second tunnel. Ahead of her, Zera had halfway climbed back up the hole, using handholds carved into the rock. With a barely audible sigh, she descended again.

Kreya waited for her to rejoin them, and they crept along the second tunnel. It too opened onto a cavern filled with inert soldiers and machines. The third tunnel was the same.

He had created an army that would have overwhelmed his original force.

The horror of it made her feel as if her heart had stopped. Her blood felt sluggish with ice in her veins. This was beyond any nightmare she could have ever had. He'd made himself stronger than he'd ever been.

She shoved every bit of fear into a tiny knot that she stored at the base of her stomach. This was not the place for fear. It was the place for caution. Learn as much as they could. Retreat. And regroup. She could not allow herself to think about the scale of the horror that lurked underground.

He must have been assembling this since his defeat, she thought. So many years, and he'd been using them all to rebuild.

She abandoned any thought of confronting Eklor now. They didn't have the firepower to face such a foe. No one did. *The guild must be warned,* she thought. The cities would need to prepare.

If they could.

If it wasn't already too late.

All five tunnels were stocked with a battalion each. Every soldier and machine was inactive, but Kreya had zero doubt that they were fueled by powered bones. She wished there were a simple way to take one as proof, but touching one could activate all. It was too great a risk, even if she set aside the problem of safely transporting such a construct. She was acutely aware of how tremendously outnumbered they were. At peak strength, they never could have fought so many.

Better to leave them here and formulate a plan from a reasonable distance. With time, with space, maybe she could see a way forward. Besides, there was one question they hadn't answered yet: *Where is Eklor?*

Only when they'd searched all the tunnels did they return to climb back up into the tower. Kreya went first, not because it was sensible but because she had the sudden fear that she'd made a grave mistake and that both Stran and Marso were in danger and that none of them should have come here.

She felt a hand grab her arm. Only old training kept her from screaming. Stran helped her climb out. She turned to help Zera and then Jentt.

"What did you find?" Stran whispered.

Marso moaned softly. "Death."

The rag doll construct caressed his cheek.

Jentt pushed himself out of the hole—

And they heard a whirring noise, followed by clicking—the familiar sound of machines starting up. Screaming began from far belowground, high pitched, from throats that didn't exist and shouldn't have been able to cry.

"Oh, shit," Jentt said.

"Close it," Kreya ordered, unnecessarily—Stran was already throwing the stone over the hole. It wouldn't be enough. She thought: *Nothing we can do will be enough.* You could drop a mountain on an army this size, and it wouldn't stop them. "Bring the tower down."

Zera passed him a fresh strength talisman. He caught it and activated it as they all ran toward the door. Outside, he pivoted and slammed his fist into the stones at the base of the tower. It shook.

Above, the archer raised a horn to his skeletal jaw, and a rag doll knocked it from his hands. The other rag doll wrapped around his wrists.

"Return to me!" Kreya called to them.

Stealth was over.

Now was the time for action. And luck. *Please, let us survive this,* Kreya prayed silently. *Great silence, do not take my friends.* She'd only just found them again. She couldn't lose them.

Stran slammed his fists again and again into the base of the tower as the ground rumbled beneath them. One more hit, and it crumbled. The rag doll constructs tumble-ran down the side of the wall as it fell. They launched themselves into the air and spread their arms as if they were sails. Kreya caught them. She pivoted, ready to run.

And saw what they'd failed to discover in the tunnels.

"There was more than one exit," Jentt said.

Zera began swearing, colorfully and ceaselessly.

Across the plains, the skeletal soldiers and killing machines were clawing their way up through holes in the earth. They encircled the tower in every direction. Back-to-back, Kreya and her friends drew their weapons.

"Anyone see a weak point?" Kreya asked, her voice calm and steady. There had to be a way out of this. They'd faced terrible odds before and survived. They were the Heroes of Vos—this couldn't be their end.

I won't let us die in secret and in vain.

The horrors kept spilling out from at least five points across the plain. As they emerged, they spread, clicking and whirring and crying to fill in the space between them.

"There, where they're climbing out." Zera pointed. "Yes, it's less dense in between the exits, but those soldiers are prepared for us. The ones emerging are jumbled."

Kreya nodded. "Aim for the exits, then run straight for the wall." It wasn't much of a plan. In fact, it was a terrible plan. But they couldn't fight an army this size. Their only option was to try to flee before the enemy was at full strength. She hoped Zera had enough talismans. It had seemed like so many back at the farmhouse. Now she didn't know if it would be enough.

"Stealth and speed?" Jentt asked.

"No stealth. Unnecessary. The enemy knows we're here." And at this point, it didn't matter if the guards saw them. Especially if they also saw the army. They only had one goal this time: survive.

Stran flexed his muscles. "We do it like we did before. Jentt unbalances the enemy, and I take them out." He squeezed a talisman in one hand and adjusted his grip on a knife with the other.

"Not like before," Kreya snapped. "Only speed."

All that mattered this time was escape. She watched the nearest point—they had to hit it when it was at its densest and use the confusion. Even then . . . *We're not going to make it,* Kreya thought. *This is impossible. I led them to their deaths. All of us, this time.*

Zera passed out her strongest speed talismans. "These are carved for speed but not endurance," she warned. "You'll get a ten-minute burst out of each, and that's it. Use it well."

As Zera's fingers touched hers, Kreya could feel the power buzzing through it. Later, if there was a later, she'd ask what kind of bone Zera used. For now, though—

"*Run.*"

Marso took off first, a hair faster than the others, but Jentt knew how to use every bit of power inside a speed talisman. He soon stretched into the lead. The others were a blur around Kreya.

It took mere seconds, but Kreya felt as if her mind slowed to see it all: the blueness of the sky, the sway of the autumn wild-flowers, the deadliness of the force arrayed before them.

We can make it! We can—

And then she heard a voice behind them:

"My old friends, you must stay and visit."

His voice was soft and urbane, yet it carried, amplified, to all their ears, and beside Kreya, she saw Stran slow at the sound of Eklor's voice. Only a slight hitch to his stride, but it was enough.

Ahead of them, a construct with a metal frame, steel feathers, and the remnants of flesh clinging to once-human arms rose from the grasses—it had been hidden there, perhaps since before the earth opened up to disgorge the army of horrors.

In one hand, it gripped a three-foot blade, a narrow flash of silver.

Kreya saw it all in a millisecond. Less. But before she could scream a warning, the construct plunged the blade into Stran.

CHAPTER FIFTEEN

It was happening again.

She was going to lose someone she cared about. Someone she was responsible for. And it was her fault. She'd led them here, given the orders, and made the mistakes.

Kreya slowed to catch Stran as he stumbled, his hand over his chest. Red spread across the front of his shirt. Suddenly, the others were there too, supporting Stran.

The construct lunged with its sword a second time, and Stran lurched forward, out of their arms, swatting at the enemy with his own sword. The skull flew off the monstrosity's neck, as Stran landed hard on one knee.

"Where did it hit?" Zera asked, her voice shrill.

"Pressure on the wound," Kreya said. "Stop the bleeding."

It had sliced through his shoulder. She couldn't tell how close it had come to anything vital, but if they didn't get him out of here now, it wouldn't matter. They'd all be cut apart before he even had the chance to bleed out.

He's not going to make it, she thought. *None of us are going to make it.*

She twisted to spy Eklor—far enough away that she couldn't see his features but only his silhouette, standing atop the rubble that was his ruined tower, looking the same as he did in her memories: tall, with the arrogant posture of a wealthy man and the thinness of a starving one, his coat with its bone pockets billowing in the wind around him. And that snapped her out of her despair.

I'm not losing anyone, she thought.

"Zera, what happens if you use a flight talisman on the ground, combined with speed?"

"I . . . haven't tested for that." But she was digging talismans out of her pockets. "Flight word is '*renari*,'" she told Jentt as she dropped them in his hand.

"You'll know when to use it," Kreya said to him. "Zera, you and I will clear a path as far as we can. Jentt, come back for Marso when Stran is clear." As the team runner, Jentt was the fastest with the speed talismans. He knew how to eke out every bit of advantage from the boost of power, honing his body into an arrow through the air. His feet barely touched the ground. It was, he'd told Kreya many times before, akin to flying. Felt like it to him. Combined with the flight talisman . . . he should know exactly what to do.

"How can I help?" Marso asked.

"Scream," Kreya told him. "As loud as you can. Distract Eklor. Keep him from issuing new orders." Left to their own devices, the soldiers were stupid. Eklor, though, with his bird's-eye view . . . "But don't die. *No one die.*"

They sprang into action.

With the nimbleness of a goat, fueled by a steadiness talisman, Marso skipped over the top of a metal construct. He sang at the top of his voice, "Death to you, death to me, death above, death behind, death below!" He pointed at Eklor. "I see you!"

Kreya didn't wait to hear Eklor's response.

She strapped knives to her wrists and squeezed a talisman in each hand. Flanking Jentt, she and Zera ran, matching his pace. They both struck out with their knives, using strength talismans to power each blow, speed talismans to boost the strike speeds. They whirled through the enemy, slicing a path through the army.

Her muscles trembled as she felt the talismans give out. Short bursts, Zera had promised. She hadn't expected *that* short. She hoped it was enough. "Now!" she told Jentt.

Jentt, with the half-conscious Stran, shouted, *"Renari!"*

Carrying Stran, he propelled himself forward, leaping as he ran, and the flight talisman kicked into action. He flew between each footfall.

Knives ready and already blackened with filth from the undead soldiers' bodies, Kreya and Zera faced the army as it closed in on them.

"What now?" Zera asked.

Evading the soldiers' swords, Marso was still shouting, spinning out a prediction: "I have seen you, against the bloody sky! Your hand upraised! Severed! Until the white sun gleams and all is sand, sand, sand in your throat, as you swallow but do not drink. Your thirst unslaked. Your hunger unending, until the bones cast you down, down, down. Until death is not a door but a path you walk. Sunset after sunset, sweet but never tasted until your last day, unceremonious and unspoken."

Glancing toward the tower, Kreya saw that Eklor was focused on Marso, drinking in his words, trying to glean meaning from them. Kreya wasn't sure there was any. She was also sure that Eklor was exposed, secure in his belief that his army could defeat them. If she timed it right, she could attack, strike before he even noticed her—but then she'd be leaving Zera. Again.

She couldn't do that.

"What kind of talismans do you have left?"

"You want me to take inventory? Now?"

They had to do something the army wouldn't expect—the soldiers were prepared for them to run and prepared for them to fight. "Any steadiness?" Kreya asked.

"It's a flat plain—"

"All of them are wearing helmets. Think of them as stepping stones. Like Marso did. Flight plus steadiness—push off for lift. They won't see it coming."

"Love it."

Hate it, Kreya thought. There were too many risks. But the army had far too many swords, axes, and spears. Catch them by surprise, and they had a chance.

Out of the corner of her eye, she saw Jentt spurt toward Marso. Empty-handed. Either Stran was safely beyond the wall or . . . Or he was dead.

She thought of Amurra. And the children. How would she tell them—

As Jentt twisted to evade a soldier's spear, she saw his shoulder: an arrow was sticking out of it. Kreya faltered for an instant, and a skeletal soldier slammed against her. She shifted her focus back to fighting as Jentt scooped up Marso and sprinted away with him.

"Follow him," Kreya ordered.

Zera tossed her the talismans. Simultaneously, they activated them and ran up the nearest soldiers as if their bodies were ramps. She didn't let herself think how stupid this was or how bad the odds were. She called out to the flight talisman as she pushed off the helmet of one soldier.

Landing for only a second on the next one, she pushed off

again and felt the flight talisman propel her farther. Out of the corner of her eye, she saw Zera leaping as well.

They crashed down on the other side of the soldiers, beyond the edge of the army. Kreya felt every bone in her body jolt. She was going to pay for that later, she knew. *Please let there be a later!*

"Run!" Zera shouted.

Side by side, they both ran.

"Any more speed talismans?" Kreya called.

"Gave them to Jentt! We're out!"

Close behind, the army chased them. She heard them roar, like a howl of wind. Glancing back, she saw some of the soldiers were gaining on them.

She searched her brain for another clever plan. A new trick. Anything—

It's not going to work, she thought. *We're not going to make it.*

Ahead, in the distance, she saw the wall. It was at least two miles. She knew she couldn't outrun them for two miles. Maybe in her youth. Not now.

Her side ached. Her breath burned in her throat. *I'm sorry, Zera,* she thought. *Jentt. Stran. Marso. I'm so sorry.*

She hoped at least a few of them had made it, to spread the warning to the rest of Vos. It might be too late for her and Zera, but she had to hope it wasn't too late for the world.

"Kreya, they stopped!"

She shot a look backward and saw it was true: the soldiers had slowed, hanging back. She slowed as well, catching her breath. Every gasp hurt. "Why?" And then she guessed the reason: "Orders not to be seen."

Just like the patrol the last time. That was how Eklor had kept them secret. He'd kept them away from the wall. And they were obeying that order now, either because Eklor cared more about keeping them secret than he did about running down his prey, or because Marso had distracted him from remembering to issue a new order. Either way, she'd take it.

"Keep going," Kreya said, forcing her body to move again even though every step hurt. He could still change his order. "We're not out of this yet."

REACHING THE WALL, KREYA SAW THE GUARDS were alert. Probably for the first time in their tours here.

They were the ones who had shot Jentt, she realized.

And they would happily riddle Kreya and Zera with arrows as well. She spared an instant to worry about Jentt, Stran, and Marso—she didn't know what it meant that Jentt hadn't returned. His speed talisman could have failed. His arrow wound could have disabled him.

She refused to think he could be dead.

Or that Stran most likely was dead.

And Marso . . . She didn't know if he'd made it either.

But she had to focus on the immediate problem.

So far, the guards hadn't seen them yet. Unfortunately, the grate they'd used before wasn't an option anymore. She spotted at least two guards patrolling near the culvert.

Side by side, Kreya and Zera dropped into the grasses and surveyed the wall. Built at least fifteen feet high, it would be tricky to climb without being noticed, especially with the guards on alert. She didn't have access to any constructs that could blast through it or dig under it.

"I have an idea, but you're not going to like it," Zera said.

"I like any idea better than staying here." She couldn't guarantee that Eklor wouldn't risk the guards' seeing his soldiers.

In fact, several constructs could already be creeping up behind them, using the tall grasses for cover, the same way they were.

"I let myself get caught—"

"You're right. I hate this idea."

Zera held up her hand. "I can talk my way out of this. Bribe as many of them as I have to. You'd be surprised how much gold I've amassed over the years. Those poor guards should be better paid anyway."

"You're assuming they'll let you talk. And that they have no moral fiber."

"We're running low on talismans, and we still have to get through the valley. Let me sweet-talk the children on the wall."

Kreya studied the guards. Even from this distance, she could tell they were clutching their bows. "They shot Jentt. I don't think they're in a talking mood."

"Hard to be persuasive if you're riddled with arrows," Zera agreed. "Even if you're as charming as I am. Fine. How about a disguise? Knock out a guard and dress in his or her armor. The confusion might buy us a few precious seconds."

It wasn't a terrible idea. Well, yes, it *was* a terrible idea, but she didn't have a better one. And Jentt, Stran, and Marso needed them. *Or they could be beyond need.* She immediately shut that line of thought down. *Don't even think it. They're not dead. They can't be dead.* "Do it. Two guards at the grate. You get the one on the left; I'll get the one on the right."

"I want the one on the right."

"Why?"

"Absolutely no reason," Zera said. "You were just looking stressed so I thought I'd be arbitrarily ornery." Her voice was light and breezy. Wasn't she worried about the others at all? Or themselves?

Of course she is, Kreya thought. This was how Zera coped.

It was damn annoying.

Together, they crept through the grasses.

Kreya glanced behind them as they went, alert to danger both in front of and behind them. Using stealth, as minimal an amount as possible to preserve the talismans, they darted behind their targets, thumped them hard with rocks to their heads, and then pulled their unconscious bodies under the arched culvert, out of sight.

Quickly, they stripped off the most visible armor: chest plate and helmet. Zera swam under the grate first, and Kreya passed her the armor through the bars. Then she swam through.

"This won't fool them long," Kreya warned.

"Follow my lead," Zera said. She put on the chest plate and crammed the helmet on her head. Rushing out into the open, she shouted, "They went under the gate! They're on the plains! Shoot them!"

The archers on the wall pivoted to aim at the plains, and Zera, with Kreya close behind her, ran for the forest. They had only seconds before the archers realized they'd been tricked. Kreya and Zera plunged in between the trees as arrows thunked into the earth behind them.

The greenery and the mist closed around them.

They kept going. Kreya felt her arm throb. One of the soldiers' blades must have nicked her. She also felt a cramp in her side, but she couldn't let that slow her. "We need to find the others."

Zera produced a talisman from her pocket. "Bloodhound

bone. Not popular with buyers. Only have the one. Should be enough." She activated it and pointed. "This way."

In minutes, they found them—the boys hadn't made it deep into the valley before collapsing. Jentt was slumped against a tree, and his face looked ashen. Kreya dropped to his side. "My Jentt—"

"Tend to Stran," he told her.

She wanted to protest: He was hurt! Badly. But Stran was worse.

Marso was beside Stran, holding him up to elevate the wound. Kreya noticed a talisman was clutched in Stran's hand—stamina, she guessed, keeping him alive. But for how long?

The rag doll constructs pressed themselves over Stran's wounds, and their fabric bodies were saturated in blood. Zera unpacked the bandages and wound kit. Kreya joined her.

"Hold him still," Zera said. "I'll sew."

"We have to clean the wound first," Kreya said.

"I know that!" Zera snapped. "You command our missions, but the mission is over, in case you didn't notice."

Seeing Stran had shattered her cool façade. Now Kreya was seeing the tension that Zera hid beneath it. *She doesn't think he'll make it,* Kreya thought. A cold fear spread through her.

"Marso, can you fetch water from the river without freaking out?" Zera asked.

"Yes, ma'am," Marso said. Unsteadily, he got to his feet and wobbled between the trees. He stumbled over a downed log and crawled into the underbrush.

Kreya started a fire, a small one, clawing out a hole for it in between the roots of a tree. She used matted dried vines for kindling and struck a spark on a fire-starting rod. Blowing into the smoke, she grew the flame until it was a small fire.

Zera held a needle in the flame, sterilizing it.

Marso returned with water in his canteen, and they set it to boil. "Stone fish in the river," he reported. "Didn't die."

"Good, Marso," Kreya told him. "You did good."

He beamed at her, looking at once like a child who had seen little of the world and like a ghost who had seen too much.

Turning from him, Kreya examined Jentt's wounds as the water for Stran boiled. He had two arrow wounds, but thankfully, neither had pierced anywhere serious. Missed an artery in the thigh. Missed anything vital in his shoulder. He'd limp for a while, and he'd ache probably forever. *But he'll live.*

This time.

She wasn't as sure about Stran.

His breathing was thin and rough, and his skin bore a glossy sheen.

Once the water was boiled, they used it to clean his wound, dabbing the water on and then pouring it after it was just cool enough to not burn him. His flesh turned bright red anyway, and he screamed until one of the rag dolls stuffed its one unbloodstained arm into his mouth.

"How many stamina talismans do you have left?" Kreya asked. "Can they keep him alive long enough for us to get out of here? Long enough for us to get him help?"

"Yes. Maybe. I don't know. If we only use them for him, there might be enough." Zera sewed the wound quickly and precisely, as only someone who'd spent her life in careful and precise work could do. Stran bit down on the construct's arm, his eyes wide in pain, desperate to scream. Using a strength talisman, Kreya held him down so he wouldn't thrash.

When they'd finished, he'd passed out.

"Can't tell if he's bleeding internally," Zera said. "Even if we had all the stamina talismans in the world, I don't know if—" She cut herself off, unable to finish the sentence, and Kreya knew what she wasn't saying. Even after all they'd done, even after escaping the plains, he might not make it.

Kreya glanced up at the trees. A ruby-colored bird flew between the branches, and she heard a monkey cry. How long until the monsters of the valley noticed them?

Turning their attention to Jentt, they dressed his wounds. The arrows had stanched the flow, but once they were yanked out, his wounds needed to be sewn shut as well. He bit a hunk of wood to keep from screaming and alerting the valley predators.

Finishing, Kreya collapsed backward and realized that the forest had gone quiet. The only sound was the rush and tumble of the nearby river.

"They're coming," Marso whispered.

Kreya didn't know if he meant Eklor's monsters, the border guards, or river creatures, and she didn't care. Fleeing was their only option, regardless of who chased them. She knew it wasn't smart to move either Stran or Jentt, but she also knew they had no choice. "How far to the wagon?" she asked Jentt.

"Not far," he replied, and pointed, his arm shaking with the effort.

She had lost her sense of where they were, but she trusted him. "Strength, Zera?"

Zera tossed her a talisman. "It's just a minor boost—we used up all the good ones," she warned. "So move fast." She used one herself. Lifting Stran, she started in the direction in which Jentt had pointed. Kreya carried Jentt. Marso stumbled along with them.

Around them, Kreya saw the rustle of branches and the

familiar shadow of a croco-raptor. She swore under her breath. If she saw one, the others would be closer.

"Marso, take Jentt." She handed him her talisman. "It's my turn to distract."

Jentt objected. "We have to stick together—"

"You're not dying twice," she told him. To Zera, she said, "Battle conditions again. Obey me. If I can't rejoin you, get them to Stran's farmhouse. Then go to Grand Master Lorn and tell him everything."

Squeezing her shoulder, Zera didn't waste time arguing. She shepherded the boys through the greenery. The branches and bushes closed behind them.

Taking a breath, Kreya stood. Counted to three.

And then called, "Here I am! Come get me!"

Taking the invitation, the croco-raptors burst out of the trees, and Kreya sprang into motion. Calling on steadiness, she climbed a tree. She swung on a vine above the croco-raptors. Landed on the ground. Ran, with only her own speed to draw on.

Lead them away, she thought.

Give my friends time.

She ran toward the river, a plan forming in her mind. It was a terrible plan, and she knew her friends, Jentt especially, would have hated it, but she wasn't taking a vote. She never did.

She'd have to time it right, make sure that her pursuers believed they'd nearly caught her when, in fact, they hadn't. Slowing, she feigned a limp, as if she were wounded prey.

As two croco-raptors charged from the front, having circled her, she grabbed another vine and shot over them. One grazed her leg with its claws. She felt the jab of pain, but adrenaline pushed it back.

The river roared, invisible through the thick mat of trees

and vines. Slicing at the greenery with her sword, she plunged toward the crashing water.

As Marso had said, the stone fish was in the river, half-submerged and causing the flow to tumble around him. She led the croco-raptors to it.

Wild with certainty that they would catch their prey, the lizards failed to see the danger.

Two of them fell straight into its mouth, twitching once from the venom before the mouth closed around them. The other croco-raptors veered sharply away as Kreya raced over the back of the creature.

She moved as fast and carefully as she could. If only the soles of her shoes touched its toxic skin . . . she could ditch the shoes. Or use them as weapons.

On the other side, Kreya leaped for the riverbank.

She almost made it.

The stone fish sliced its tail through the water, and one scale brushed lightly against an exposed bit of Kreya's arm. It was the lightest touch, but she knew instantly that it was too late.

She kept running, though, telling herself not to think, not to look back, and for bones' sake not to slow. She heard her pursuers fall behind as they were forced to contend with the stone fish.

She was now contending with it in her own way. The poison permeated her muscles, and she felt them clench. Her vision swam, and the green around her swirled. Slowing, she dropped to her knees and swayed.

At least the others lived.

Or at least they had the chance to live.

Zera would get them to Stran's farmhouse. Amurra would nurse them back to health, probably cursing Kreya's name from her pretty mouth. Grand Master Lorn wouldn't ignore Zera's report—Kreya had faith that Zera wouldn't let him. It should have been enough to know she'd done all she could. But it wasn't. Oh, it wasn't.

"I'm not ready to die," she whispered.

She didn't even know for certain if she'd truly formed the words.

Everything plunged into blackness and silence.

CHAPTER SIXTEEN

Kreya woke to the smell of baking bread filling her nose. She opened her mouth and breathed it in before she opened her eyes. "Not dead?" she croaked.

"Not dead," Jentt said, relief clear in his voice.

She couldn't focus on him yet. He was a blob of blue in the middle of a sea of brown. Squinting, she tried to differentiate between his face and his body, but the effort made pain shoot into her head. She closed her eyes.

She must have fallen asleep again because the next time she opened her eyes, her face felt warm with sun, the smell of bread was (sadly) gone, and she was alone, almost. Her bird construct nudged against her hand, and she awkwardly patted his skull.

Her rag dolls were nestled around her. The three that had accompanied them into the forbidden zone had been scrubbed until their fabric faded to a pinkish off-white—the attempt to remove the blood not quite complete.

Gingerly, Kreya sat up. She'd expected to see her tower. *But no, that burned,* she remembered. Belatedly, her brain caught up to her eyes and named where she was: Stran's farmhouse.

She cleared her throat, testing her voice. "Hello?"

Bustling in, Amurra smiled at her. "You're awake!"

"Stran?"

Her smile dipped, and Kreya felt her heart squeeze. If Stran . . .

"He's alive," Amurra said quickly, seeing Kreya's expression. "Sorry. I should have said that right away. He's recovering. You were closer to death than he was."

"How close?" Her throat felt as if it had been stuffed with wool. She swallowed and changed her question. "How long was I out?"

"Eight days."

Eight! She'd never—

Amurra rushed to her side. "Steady. Just breathe."

Kreya got control of her breathing. She forced her muscles to relax until she sank back into the pillows. She was lying on a sofa in their living room, a crocheted blanket tucked around her.

Sitting on the edge of the sofa, Amurra waited while Kreya breathed. After a few moments of silence, she said, "I have a confession. When you first came back . . . I hated you. Stran was hurt, and I . . . thought you deserved what happened to you. And worse."

Eyeing her, Kreya reached for a pocket and felt only thin cotton. She wasn't wearing her coat or any of her usual clothes. She'd been dressed in a simple long shirt. All her weapons had been removed. Trying to appear calm, Kreya crossed her hands over her stomach. "Are you going to murder me now? Smothering with pillows is standard. It would cast the least suspicion on you." She wasn't certain she had the strength to resist, but if she could manage to scratch the other woman, there would be evidence.

Amurra sprang up. "Of course not! How could you think that?"

Kreya relaxed minutely. "You said you hated me."

"What kind of life have you had that you'd think that murder is the natural response to hate?" Settling down again, she sat, this time on a chair near the sofa. "I would never . . . You can't think that of me!"

"I don't know you well," Kreya reminded her.

"You know Stran," Amurra said. "Trust him, if you won't trust me."

"If you don't plan to murder me, could I have some water? And . . ." She thought about what she could stomach. She knew she had to eat. "Broth? If you have it? And Jentt . . . Is he here?"

Amurra sprang to her feet. "Of course! I'm sorry."

"Don't apologize. I assume the reason we're not all dead is because of you?"

"I did what I could," Amurra said.

Kreya fixed her with a look. "Don't do that."

"Do what?" Amurra looked genuinely confused. One foot was aimed toward the kitchen, but the other was planted unmoving.

"Make yourself smaller than you are," Kreya said. "Life will do that enough for you. Own your power. You created a safe haven here, and because of that, we're alive. Thank you."

A smile blossomed on her face. "You're welcome."

Then the smile faded, and she looked as if she wanted to say more, but she didn't. She fled into the kitchen. A few minutes later, Jentt emerged with a tray. He set it on a table near the sofa and smiled at her. "You're lucky—turns out you have some resistance to stone fish venom. You know how rare that is?"

Kreya drank in the sight of him: his shoulder bandaged, a slight limp, but otherwise he seemed well and whole. "You seem to have some resistance to being shot with arrows. That's good. You didn't used to."

Leaning over, he touched her cheek. She saw sadness in his eyes, wrinkles in the corners that hadn't been there before. She wanted to reassure him that she was okay. Both of them were okay. But she wasn't certain that the world was okay. "Has Grand Master Lorn responded to the threat? Has he assembled an army?"

"You nearly die," Jentt said, "and that's your first question?"

"Actually, my first question was to Amurra, who said you're all alive. So yes, this is my second question: is somebody out there doing what needs to be done to save the world?"

"Drink your broth," he told her.

"Jentt?"

He lifted the bowl to her lips and tilted it. With shaking hands, she took the bowl from him and did it herself. "You woke briefly enough to take in a little food and water," Jentt said. "You probably don't remember that."

She shook her head.

"You weren't coherent with the venom in you."

Kreya lowered the bowl. "Oh no, what did I say?"

"You seemed to be under the impression that I was a pear tree," Jentt said. "And you were very concerned about squirrels eating all my pears before they could ripen. Another time, you accused Amurra of stealing a shovel. Every time she walked into the room, you'd demand she return it before she broke it, because you didn't know how to fix a shovel."

Kreya began to laugh and then stopped when it hurt. She felt as if her torso had been trampled. "I don't know how to fix a shovel."

In a quieter voice, he said, "You also cried. As often as I told you I was here, you wouldn't believe me, and you cried."

"I'm sorry."

"I realized how rarely I've seen you cry."

She marshaled a smile. "It's not my favorite activity. No more tears. You're here. We're all alive, and someone is going to do something about Eklor, right? Grand Master Lorn must have approved action once Zera reported to him."

Jentt lifted the soup again. He didn't meet her eyes.

"Zera *did* report to him, didn't she? It couldn't have been you—too many questions. Marso would be considered too unreliable. And Stran was injured." Had Zera flaked on them? Surely she wouldn't have. She'd seen the danger. She wouldn't have retreated to her plush life and pretended none of this had happened. Would she have?

"She was the one who found you," Jentt said. "She saved you. But . . ."

He trailed off.

The silence of that unfinished sentence was worse than any words he could have said. Kreya struggled to push herself to sitting. "But what?"

"She didn't know what injured you . . ."

Before he finished, Kreya realized where he was leading. "She was exposed to the venom. How badly? Is she awake?"

He shook his head. "She hasn't woken at all. You, we were able to feed, even when you were delusional. But Zera . . . If she doesn't wake soon . . . I'm sorry, but there isn't much we can do. There's no cure for stone fish venom. The body either fights it off, or it doesn't. And usually, it doesn't."

"Amurra said Stran was recovering. She didn't say anyone else had been hurt!" Kreya would have asked if she'd thought Zera was in danger, but the last time she'd seen her, she'd been fine. She hadn't known to worry.

"Amurra didn't want to upset you."

"Help me to Zera," Kreya commanded.

"You need rest."

Kreya glared at him. "I'm giving you a look. Do you see me giving you a look? Carry me, if it makes you feel better."

"You're impossible," he told her, but he scooped her into his arms—she couldn't tell if his arrow wound hurt him or not—and carried her, blanket and all, down the hall. He nudged open a door and carried her inside.

It had been a laundry room, but the washing bucket was shoved to the side, the drying racks were empty, and a cot had been set up along one wall. Wrapped in blankets, Zera lay, breathing shallowly. Her face looked unlike itself, sunken and pale, without the bright spark of a sudden smile or eye roll.

She needs to wake, Kreya thought.

Gently, Jentt lowered Kreya onto the cot at Zera's feet. Kreya tucked her own blanket around Zera, and Zera gave a sigh that was more of a moan, as if she were caught inside a bad dream.

"This is your commander," Kreya said, "and I'm ordering you to get better. Do you hear me, Zera? You have no choice. You're going to wake up."

She heard a shuffling from the doorway and glanced over to see that Stran and Marso had joined them. They crowded into the tiny room.

"Zera, we're here," Kreya said, softer. "Your friends are here with you, and we need you to wake up. Can you hear me, Zera? We need you." Leaning over, she took her friend's hand. Jentt sat on the side of the cot and took her other hand. Stran put a hand on her shoulder, and Marso touched her forehead. "Can you feel us, Zera? This time, none of us left you. We're here, and we won't ever leave you again. Come back to us. Please!"

She didn't open her eyes.

But Kreya didn't stop pleading with her. Amurra brought broth. The others drifted in and out, but Kreya and Jentt stayed. They took turns talking to Zera, encouraging her to wake. At last, they both fell silent, with Kreya lying beside her on the cot and Jentt on the floor.

When she woke, Jentt was still asleep.

And Zera had worsened.

KREYA LISTENED TO ZERA BREATHE IN GASPS THAT stuttered, stopped, and then, eventually, painfully resumed. Each breath sounded shallow, and each time Zera's breath hitched, Kreya instinctively held her own breath, as if that would force her friend to keep living.

Gray predawn light filtered through the high window, and Kreya studied Zera's face. Her cheeks were sunken and gray, and her lips were tinged with blue.

She's not going to wake, Kreya thought.

Soon, her breath would stutter, and she wouldn't be able to draw another one.

Reaching out, Kreya touched Zera's cheek. Her skin felt clammy and much too hot. A fever was raging inside of her, and it wasn't getting better. "Please," Kreya whispered. She didn't know who she was begging anymore.

Whatever was inside Kreya that had enabled her to survive the stone fish venom, Zera, like ninety percent of people, didn't have that ability. She was going to die, and Kreya couldn't bring her back. With Eklor and his army on the plains, she didn't have access to enough human bones, even if she'd had the future years to spare. *I'd give it to you*, Kreya thought. *All I have left.*

If only Zera had been the one with immunity, instead of

Kreya . . . Zera didn't deserve this. She'd been loyal and strong and brave beyond anything she'd ever had to be. She had built herself her own life, all on her own, while Kreya had locked herself away, and then Zera had chosen to leave that life and all its comforts and successes for the sake of her friends.

"I'm sorry," Kreya whispered.

This shouldn't have been happening. It wasn't fair.

"It should have been me," she whispered. "I'd trade places with you in a heartbeat, if I could." Lightly, she touched Zera's forehead, cheek, and lips with her fingertips.

How could she ever say goodbye?

"It *should* be me." And then a thought—an impossible thought—blossomed inside her. "It *could* be me."

The spell to resurrect Jentt . . . There were variants. She'd read about Eklor's speculations in his journals, and she'd spent time speculating on her own. Years, in fact, of trying to understand the forbidden magic that would bring Jentt back to her. The theory of the magic behind the spell had two interpretations: In one, when she'd worked the magic on Jentt, she'd given a part of her life to him. But in another, she'd taken a part of his death into herself.

Huh.

If she adapted the spell just right . . . she could take Zera's illness into herself.

Kreya had already fought the poison once. She could do it again. Maybe. Her body still felt weak, and a second exposure could be fatal. But "could be" for her was much better than "would be" for Zera. *I might die, but Zera certainly will if I do nothing.*

"I'll take that risk," she whispered.

There was, however, one problem.

Well, there were many problems, but only one that mattered: to work any forbidden magic like this, it required human bone. She wouldn't need as much of it as she had for Jentt, since Zera still lived, for now. Just a shard of bone, a couple inches.

A finger bone, like she'd stolen from the dead girl in Eren.

Eyes glued to Zera's gray face, Kreya listened to her breath. And she listened to Jentt, lightly snoring on the floor. She hoped he'd forgive her for this. She hoped she'd survive for him to yell at her. She'd happily listen to days of his unhappiness, if this worked.

Carefully, she maneuvered herself on the bed so she could reach down to Jentt's waist. She withdrew his knife. He always kept it so beautifully sharp. The edge glinted in the predawn light.

She laid her left hand on the bedside table, spread her fingers, and raised the knife. She steadied her breath. Cleared her mind. "Sorry for the mess, Amurra," Kreya said.

And then she, in one hard swift stroke, sliced her own finger off.

Pain spread up her arm, as fast and terrible as lightning.

Hissing between her teeth, she wrapped her hand in a bedsheet, tying it tourniquet-tight. It continued to throb, so hard that her vision swam and then blackened.

Briefly, she lost consciousness. She didn't know for how long. Seconds, she hoped. The blood was still bright red and wet. And Jentt still slept beside her. She had managed not to cry out, which was good. Now, to complete the rest.

Pressing her severed pinkie finger against Zera's chest, she whispered, "Give me your pain, give me your poison, give me your rot, give me your sorrow. *Iri nascre, evert sai enrara. Iri prian, evert sai ken fa. Iri sangra sheeva lai. Ancre evert sai enrara. Sai enrara ray.*"

Some of the words were guesswork, albeit based on years of research and experience. None of it had been tested, though.

She held her breath, ignoring the pain in her hand and arm, and watched as her finger dissolved into Zera's body. Her blood stained Zera's nightshirt, the only trace left behind.

Then Kreya felt the venom flood her body, darkening her sight.

Before she plunged into pure darkness, she called out to Jentt, "She will wake!" She meant to add, *And so will I*, but she couldn't be certain her mouth had formed the words before she lost all grip on the world.

"I HATE YOU," KREYA HEARD ZERA SAY.

Eyes still closed, Kreya smiled.

"Hah, you're awake. Knew it." Raising her voice, Zera called, "Jentt, she's awake! Just faking it now to mess with us." Her voice sounded brittle.

Squinting, Kreya tried to open her eyes. Sunlight stabbed them, and she closed them again. She'd seen enough to know a figure loomed over her, probably Zera, which meant she wasn't dead. "It worked," Kreya croaked.

"If you mean you almost killed yourself, then yes, it worked."

"You're alive."

"I know I'm supposed to say thank you," Zera said, "but I'm too pissed at you. There was no guarantee you'd survive the venom a second time. You were unconscious for days. *Again.* Idiot. Selfish, stubborn idiot."

Her hand didn't hurt, she noticed. Someone must have

stitched up her wound and bound it properly. Her body felt like it had been flattened with an enormous rolling pin, but she could feel it, which had to be a good sign. "You're welcome."

She heard footsteps nearby and cracked her eyes open again. Zera was beside her, in a chair, and Jentt now filled the doorway. She managed a smile at him. "Are you going to yell at me too?" She was aware the question sounded pathetic.

"No," he said.

But he didn't come closer than the doorway.

"You're angry." It wasn't a guess. It was an obvious fact. "I'm sorry I risked myself, but Zera was on the brink of death, and I knew—"

"You didn't even wake me. Much less talk to me first."

That was true. But she'd been afraid of what he'd say, that he'd try to talk her out of it. Not talking it over first allowed her to be brave. "I thought you'd tell me not to do it."

"I could have helped you," he said. "Instead I woke to you bleeding and unconscious. And missing—" He sucked in air as if trying to compose himself. "You used my knife, and you didn't wake me. We're supposed to be a team, Kreya. All of us, remember?"

She closed her eyes, not wanting to see the pain in his face.

"I know you've been on your own for a long time, but I'm here now—"

"And that means I could lose you again." She opened her eyes, looked at Jentt, and then looked at Zera. "I could lose all of you. Nearly did. I can't bear that."

"And what if we lost you?"

"I—"

Amazingly, it wasn't something she'd ever thought about.

Zera patted her hand, the one that still had all five fingers. "I love you too, idiot." Leaning over, she kissed Kreya's forehead. "Get some more rest."

She left the room, and Jentt stepped back to allow her to pass. He lingered in the doorway for a while, looking as if he had more to say but pressing his lips together so he wouldn't say it.

Exhaustion pulled on all of her muscles like a heavy weight. "Do you forgive me?"

He was silent for a moment. "No."

Fine. She deserved that. "Will you forgive me?"

This time, he didn't hesitate. "Yes."

Good enough.

IT TOOK ANOTHER THREE DAYS BEFORE KREYA FELT up to her usual strength. By then, Zera was able to shuffle around without aid, and Stran seemed determined to prove he was as good as new, spending their recovery days chopping as much wood as possible.

The surprise was Marso.

In the wake of Kreya and Zera's recoveries, he skipped through the farmhouse as if each day were suffused with sunlight, and he rained smiles on everyone. He played with Stran's children, helped with nighttime feedings for the littlest one, took over cooking for the majority of the meals, and made the farmhouse sparkling clean.

Finally, when she felt sufficiently like herself again, Kreya planted herself in front of the kitchen sink and asked, "What is going on with you?"

He stopped. His smile was like Stran's daughter Vivi's when the rag dolls danced for her. "I was never broken. I was *right*. And as soon as all of us are well, we're going to destroy him, finally, permanently, and I'll be able to sleep the whole night without screaming."

"That sounds good," Zera said, coming into the kitchen. "Except I never want to sleep again. I did enough of that. Hey, Stran!" She called out the window, and the sound of chopping wood ceased. "Come in—we're ready to discuss our plan of attack!"

"About time," Stran said, coming into the kitchen and plopping himself into one of the chairs. It creaked beneath him. "First thing we need to do is plug up those bone-blasted exit holes. Keep the monstrosities bottled up in their tunnels."

Jentt joined them, coming in from the back rooms. "No, the first thing we need to do is ask those nice boys and girls on the wall to quit using us as pincushions and aim at the actual enemy instead."

"Coordinating with them might be key," Zera said. "After all, they must have seen *something* on the plain that shouldn't be there. We find out what they reported to their higher-ups, and what size army they can raise and how quickly they can be deployed."

Sinking into a chair, Kreya listened to them discuss how to approach the wall, how to contact the border guards without alerting Eklor's forces, and how thorough they intended to be in making sure he was dead and stayed dead this time. She said nothing, watching the faces of her friends as the arguments became more heated: approach openly or covertly, with assistance or without, target only Eklor or eliminate his forces first. She noticed Amurra hovering in the doorway, with Vivi and Jen clutching her legs. Little Nugget was in her arms, chewing on the ends of her golden hair. Kreya met Amurra's eyes.

When Stran took a breath to launch into another idea, Kreya said, "No."

They all stared at her.

"Excuse me?" Zera said.

"No to which part?" Jentt asked. "There are pros and cons to all the approaches—"

Kreya got to her feet. "No to all of it. Look at us. He kicked our asses when he was barely trying." With her bandaged hand, she gestured at Stran's shoulder and Jentt's limp.

"He caught us by surprise," Stran objected.

"He didn't," Kreya said. "I believed he was there. We all acted as if he was. Cautious. Thorough. We did everything right, and we nearly died. We have to face the truth: we aren't the heroes we used to be."

"Sure, we're out of practice, but the old instincts are there," Jentt said. He demonstrated by plucking a kitchen knife out of its block and throwing it across the room. It thunked into a knot in a beam of wood.

Vivi and Jen cheered.

"It's time for new heroes to step up," Kreya said. "We completed our destiny." Her eyes slid to Amurra. Those had been her words. She hadn't been wrong. *I just wasn't ready to listen*, Kreya thought.

Zera raised a finger. "A point? We actually *failed* to complete it. For evidence, I submit literally everything we just witnessed on the plains."

"I don't know how he returned," Kreya said, "or how he was able to build up his army again without anyone ever suspecting, but this isn't about unfinished threads that need to be neatened up. He presents a new danger to Vos, and he requires a new solution."

Marso piped up. "We won't make the same mistakes."

"You all act as if this is a chance at redemption," Kreya said. "But it's not about us at all. It's about Vos and what is best for the safety of those we love."

Amurra silently nodded.

"We have to do what's best for the innocent, for those we've sworn to protect," Kreya said. "And what's best is for us to step away, and let others—stronger, younger men and women—defeat him. Our role is to warn them, advise them, and prepare them."

Zera glared at her. "Aw, that's bullshit. I am not an 'advisor.' I am a damn warrior!"

Stran thumped his chest in agreement, and then winced—he'd hit not far from his still-bandaged wound. Kreya thought that proved her point. *Our time has passed. We need to admit that.*

"You're a businesswoman now," Kreya corrected her. "I'm a hermit. Stran's a farmer and a father. Marso . . ."

Marso spoke up. "Marso wants a second chance to be what he was supposed to be. I want a chance to not fail my friends."

"There are no second chances," Kreya said.

Quietly, Jentt said, "How can you look at me and say that?"

She opened her mouth and then shut it. Marshaling her thoughts, she glanced down at her bandaged four-fingered hand. "You're right. You have a second chance. *We* have it. Which is why I'm not going to allow us to throw it away. I can't lose you again. Any of you." She fixed her eyes on each of them.

Zera broke eye contact with her first. Studying her hands, she said, "You want me to go to Grand Master Lorn. Is that what you want me to do? Convince him to act? What if he won't? He may choose not to believe me. I have . . . a reputation for theatrics."

"We all go," Kreya said.

Amurra spoke up. "I'm coming as well. My parents can stay with the children here. But I'm not letting my husband out of my sight again."

Stran's shoulders slumped. "You truly believe we can't defeat him this time?"

"I do," Kreya said firmly. "Our time is over."

The others looked at her with a mixture of disbelief, disappointment, and . . . anger. And while she felt all those things too, she knew she was right, and in time, they'd come to understand that, too.

CHAPTER SEVENTEEN

If you had a complaint for the Bone Workers Guild, you went to the guild headquarters on the third tier of Cerre. All the clerks were stationed there, with the bulk of the teachers. The novices lived there as well, in quarters close by for training. But if you wanted to talk to the grand master about important matters, away from the riffraff, you went to the fifth tier, to the palace that served as the grand master's personal residence.

If you could get in.

Zera led the way.

She knew how to make a production of it. Sweeping into her own fifth-tier palace with all the force of a hurricane, she issued orders right and left, and her followers scrambled to obey.

When Kreya began to object, Zera cut her off. "You know how you get a powerful person to listen to you? You come to them as equally powerful. Out there, you command. Here, this is *my* battlefield."

Which was the truth. She knew how to maneuver in this stratified world. Choosing to stop in the center of her grand salon, rather than anywhere private, she held her arms out while Guine stripped her, washed her, and garbed her in her finest embroidered silks. She was patient while another painted gold swirls on her skin, decorating her chest and arms. Bangles were attached around her ankles, rubies affixed to her ears. Guine added gold strands to her multicolored hair.

She saw Marso watching her, eyeing the sparkle. "Same treatment for the bone reader."

Stran snorted. "Leave me out of it."

"Had no plans to dress you up. You must look like what you are: a warrior who has seen battle," Zera said. "Only pants. No shirt. No jewels. Can you remove the bandage?"

"Looks ugly," he warned.

"Perfect. Don't hide your wounds."

Quietly, Kreya said, "I won't wear Liyan silks. That's not who I am anymore." She had worried creases around her eyes, and Zera couldn't tell if they were new or not. She resisted the urge to fix Kreya's blemishes. It was best if Kreya stayed as she was.

"Obviously." Privately, Zera thought that was a trifle sad. And silly. You could be who you chose to be. It was immensely freeing once you realized that you could define yourself, provided you quit handing that power over to other people. "Cleaner would be better, though."

She oversaw all the preparations to her satisfaction:

Marso was decked out in over-the-top finery, with heavy eye makeup, black jewelry, and a silver robe—the picture of a man who saw the world as others did not.

Jentt was in shadow colors: a black and gray coat that concealed his body. No flash of jewelry for him. He was their runner, and he looked it.

Stran was a battle-scarred warrior, every wound he'd borne visible and stark against his muscles. His strength wasn't the same as a young man's. He did not look as though he'd pushed himself hard to become strong; he looked as though he had always been strong and his body knew no other way to be.

And Kreya . . .

She wore her battered, frayed, and faded coat. With her freshly washed hair gleaming like polished silver, she looked every inch their wise leader as she quietly surveyed the others. Zera did not try to hide the exhaustion or the age that Kreya wore on her skin with creams or makeups. Every crease was earned. She left the bandage wrapped around Kreya's left hand, showing clearly the recent loss of a finger.

Zera wondered if Kreya had any idea of how powerful she looked. She didn't look as if she'd become someone else. She looked like she'd become *more* of herself.

At last, they were all ready.

Lorn isn't going to know what's hit him, Zera thought smugly.

"Remember: we are the Heroes of Vos," Zera said. "The world owes us a debt it can never repay. But we are here to demand payment, nonetheless. We *will* be listened to. We *will* be heard. We *will* be believed. Also, we look amazing."

"Can we go now?" Kreya asked impatiently.

Zera rolled her eyes at her.

Stran kissed his wife and told her she'd be safe here, in Zera's home. Zera's servants would pamper her in any way she wanted—a fact that Zera confirmed. Amurra clearly wasn't pleased to be left behind, especially after leaving her children and accompanying her husband here, but none of them invited her to come. Not even Stran. Not for this. This was for the Five to do, and the Five to do alone.

Zera marched them out her front door, and they mounted the polished white stones that carried them skimming over the streets of the fifth tier. She knew the way to the guild master's palace, though she'd had little occasion to visit him. Even Guild Master Lorn came to *her* when he wanted to purchase one of her talismans.

For him, she'd brought a gift: a new flight bone, carved from a shard of river lizard. She'd wrapped it in red velvet, and Guine carried it in a gilded box. She took the box from him when they reached the guild master's door. Her followers would not be joining them inside.

"Announce us," she told the guard at the door.

"Your names?" the guard said.

Zera fixed her with a look. "You know us."

A second guard whispered to her, and the first guard's eyes bulged. She yanked the door open, and Zera and her friends swept inside as the guard shouted their names.

Inside, the palace of the grand master was opulent in the extreme. Every massive marble pillar upholding the vaulted ceiling had been carved to resemble a skeleton, the floor was inlaid with diamonds encased in gold, and the walls were a mosaic of rubies as red as blood.

"Makes your house look tasteful," Kreya murmured.

"He got the idea for the skeleton pillars from me," Zera whispered back. "Shall I take the lead?"

"Yes, until we reach Lorn. Then he's mine."

A servant was bustling up to them. The look on the man's face was a cross between terror and awe, which Zera found gratifying. Always nice to see their reputation still carried weight, even after all these years.

"You'll take us to speak with Grand Master Lorn now," Zera said in her most imperious I-will-not-be-denied tone.

The servant bowed so low that Zera thought his head was

going to bop on the floor. "Forgive me a thousand times, but Grand Master Lorn is currently busy—"

"There is nothing he could be doing that is possibly more important than the news we bear," Zera said. "Unless he's dying. He's not dying, is he?"

The man swallowed hard. "Ahh, no, Your Greatness."

"Delightful," Zera said. "Then tell him to put his pants back on and greet us."

As the servant scurried away, Stran shifted uncomfortably. In a low voice, he said, "I thought you were going to be diplomatic."

"Whatever gave you that idea?" Zera asked.

Jentt defended her. "She *did* allow him a warning to put on pants."

She swept forward, following the servant. The others fell in behind her, except for Kreya, who matched her pace. She knew Kreya did it instinctively, but it was exactly right.

"Anything I should know before we go in?" Kreya murmured. "Has Grand Master Lorn changed at all?"

"Everyone changes," Zera said, "but I believe in essentials you'll find him much the same."

"Pity," Kreya said.

And then they were standing before two massive brass doors, carved with scenes of battle, specifically their battle, when they first confronted Eklor and his army. Zera reflected that she should have perhaps warned the others about this choice of décor. Marso in particular looked a bit green. She hoped he held it together. *On the other hand, if he breaks down shrieking, it could underscore our point.* She had no doubt that a bone reader freak-out could be spun appropriately, with a little effort.

The servant expected them to wait at the door, she knew. But Zera was not the type to wait. Those days were long over.

She pushed through and heard the clack of the mechanism at the top of the door—a construct was employed to make the doors swing as lightly as if they'd been made of hollow wood instead of solid metal.

The servant was conferring with Grand Master Lorn at the far end of the room. Zera's eyes swept over everything, noting the heavy red brocade drapes were pulled shut, the usually brilliant chandeliers were extinguished, and the only light came from a trio of candles in a candelabra that stood on the grand master's desk. Even the fire in the marble fireplace was out.

Perhaps he'd been taking a nap? she wondered.

Grand Master Lorn smiled at them as they approached, though she knew they'd given him little time to compose himself. A deliberate choice to keep them in control of the conversation. She wondered, though, if he was as caught off guard as she'd hoped. He dismissed the servant and came around his desk to greet them. "This is both a surprise and an honor!" His voice was rich, with a pleasant burr to it. He could have been a singer, if his life had taken him on a different path. His manners and appearance were equally cultured. He wore a purple velvet robe with silk trim and a large silver pendant with the symbol of his office. His manicured beard was a silvery gray, matching his braided hair.

Kreya stepped forward, and Zera wondered what she'd do. After all, Zera had gone through a lot of effort to ensure they appeared before him as equals in power, if not in rank, and Kreya could easily ruin that with a polite bow or other servile pleasantry. *Tread carefully, Kreya. Show him no deference.*

"You got old," Kreya said.

Perfect. It took all Zera's willpower not to smirk.

Behind her, she heard Stran groan softly.

Kreya continued. "Given your ego, I'd have thought you'd try to hide the natural passage of time. Refreshing to see you've embraced your mortality so openly."

Grand Master Lorn did not let his smile dip, which impressed Zera. It took concentration to remain pleasant while Kreya was being her most unpleasant. In a light voice, he said, "I am delighted to see all of you again." His eyes swept over them and then his expression did, at last, change as he saw Jentt. His mouth dropped into an O.

Kreya said, "It is mortality that we've come to talk to you about."

Awe in his voice, he said, "Jentt lives again."

"He does, and he has come as proof that what we're about to tell you is possible." Kreya took a breath, and Zera noticed that Jentt shifted his weight so that he was there to support her without looking as if he was supporting her. Zera approved of that. "Eklor lives. And he has amassed a mighty army to march against Vos."

Grand Master Lorn tore his gaze from Jentt to study Kreya. "Indeed?" He sounded curious but not alarmed.

"We have seen it." She gestured to the others.

One by one, they stepped forward to verify the truth. Succinctly, Kreya described what they'd seen and experienced, leaving off the true reason for their first trip to the forbidden zone and also excluding the fact that she'd been responsible for Jentt's return. She kept her report focused on Eklor's forces, the size and strength and readiness.

"And what do you wish me to do about it?" His voice was neutral, and Zera could not read whether he believed them or not. In his shoes, would she? Leaning a hair forward, she glimpsed his shoes—heavily beaded sandals. *Not my style.*

"Send heroes," Kreya said. "Raise an army. Eradicate the threat in a way we never did. Our expertise and guidance will be at your chosen heroes' disposal."

"And if there is no threat?"

"Eklor lives," Kreya repeated. "There's a threat."

Grand Master Lorn considered them gravely for several minutes. He clasped his hands behind his back and crossed to one of the draped windows. An unseen construct rolled the curtains back with a soft whirr, and sunlight flooded in. For an instant, Zera could only see the light, but when her eyes adjusted, she saw the mountain range that lay beyond the glass. "It has been many years."

"Enough time to rebuild his army."

"Enough time for a man to change profoundly," Grand Master Lorn said. "I have seen many things in my tenure as the head of the Bone Workers Guild. Many changes. Many bright-eyed young students who believe their workings will fix the world. Many bleary-eyed old masters who have lost the ability to affect that same world."

Kreya opened her mouth to respond, and Zera elbowed her.

Grand Master Lorn was leading somewhere, and there was a chance he would end up where they wanted him to. They needed to give him space to pontificate. It was his way of feeling in control of the situation, and it cost them nothing to grant him that.

Kreya gave her a subtle nod, to say she'd be patient.

"I believe in second chances," he said. "And I hope, in time, you will too." Raising his voice before any of them could ask what he meant, Grand Master Lorn called, "Enter."

Soundlessly, the brass doors swung open.

And Eklor walked in.

CHAPTER EIGHTEEN

It's the poison left in my body, Kreya thought.

That was why she was seeing things. Things like Eklor's strolling into Grand Master Lorn's office and smiling at them as if they were old friends. She must still have had stone fish venom in her blood. Except that the others saw him too.

Beside her, she felt her friends tense. Stran swore loudly and colorfully. Marso whispered, "I saw it, I see it, I saw it, I see it . . . ," and then devolved into humming under his breath in a minor key. As much as she sympathized, Kreya wished she could ask a rag doll to silence him. She had to *think*!

A bone was pressed into her palm, and Kreya glanced to see that Zera was subtly handing talismans to all of them. Closing her fingers around it, Kreya felt the grooves of the strength carving. She didn't stop staring at Eklor the whole time.

He looked the way she remembered, for the most part. A few more creases in his face but still handsome, with sharp cheekbones, gray-tinged skin, and hair so black that it gleamed blue in the candlelight. He wore a bone worker's traditional ankle-length coat, with embroidered pockets. He did not look, and never had looked, like a man who dealt out death the way a card player dealt out cards.

"Grand Master Lorn," Kreya said evenly, "it appears that there is a genocidal war criminal in your office. Are you aware?"

The grand master circled his desk and sat. He folded his hands and rested his chin on them. "I admit I had a similar reaction to you when Master Eklor requested an audience a week ago." To Eklor, he said, "Perhaps it's best if you explain?"

She didn't want to listen to an explanation. His blood should have already been spilled on the marble floor, and it was only the shock of seeing him here, in what should have been the safest place in all of Vos, that stayed her hand.

Jentt broke his paralysis first and was moving faster than Kreya could think. He darted toward Eklor, a flash of silver in his hand, and his knife impacted on a marble sculpture. Stone chips clinked on the ground. Spinning around, Kreya saw that Eklor now stood beside the grand master's desk. Lorn held a talisman in his hand and was panting slightly, though he quickly got control of his breathing and sat at his desk again. Clearly, he'd moved Eklor out of Jentt's path.

But . . . why?

Kreya felt as if she were screaming from within her skin—her mind, her soul, her very blood felt as if it were screaming. She couldn't make sense of this. Eklor, here! And the grand master, protecting him?

"Excellent speed there, Grand Master," Zera said drolly. "One of *my* talismans, I presume? Delighted you're a customer."

Of course the grand master had been ready for an attack. He hadn't risen to his position by being naïve or stupid. He'd predicted their response.

Eklor held up his hands, palms out, as if that made him look innocent. "What I have done is unforgivable. Yet I am here, to ask for forgiveness."

"For killing Jentt?" Kreya demanded. "For slaughtering hundreds? Or for rebuilding your army to do it all again?"

"There's no army," Grand Master Lorn said with the supreme confidence of a man who, to the best of his knowledge, had never been wrong. In the face of such a declarative statement, Kreya cycled through a half dozen responses, none of which were respectful of his office.

Before she could say anything unfortunate, Stran stepped forward into the sunlight that poured through the window. He displayed his chest, and the ugly red of his wound gleamed in the light of day. "With all due respect, great sir, there is."

"You can't say he was scratched by a kitty-cat," Zera said lazily. She made cat claws with one hand. Kreya noted that her other hand rested casually in a pocket, undoubtedly a pocket with a powerful talisman. She felt a surge of gratitude for Zera. Her friends were willing to go up against the grand master of their guild, if Kreya gave the word.

"The guards at the wall reported thieves breached the wall," Grand Master Lorn said. "They fired upon and injured the intruders—*that* is where you received your wounds. Illegal activities."

"We saw his constructs with our own eyes," Jentt said.

"Remnants from the war," Lorn said dismissively. "I've known they still roam the forbidden zone. That is, in part, why it is still forbidden."

"Hundreds of them?" Kreya said.

"Only the few that remained after the battle," Eklor said. "A handful of guards, for my own protection. They would not have harmed you if you hadn't trespassed. I can assure you my remnants will harm no one else."

"Oh?" Kreya asked. "And we're supposed to believe you? You made those soldiers to kill—you're saying they're harmless now?"

"They're harmless because I destroyed them," he said promptly. "I directed them to gather in one of the tunnels and then I collapsed earth and rock on top of them, and for good measure, I set fire to the plains. They're buried and burned, as they should be."

"You believe this nonsense?" Zera asked Lorn.

Kreya wished she could ask Marso to read the truth, but she wasn't about to ask anything of him while they stood here with the grand master and their worst enemy. She saw that Marso hadn't moved so much as a twitch. As still as a mouse seen by an owl, he was staring motionless at Eklor. She regretted bringing him here, but how could she have known?

It seemed the last few weeks had been a series of "How could I have known?" moments.

But the thing was, she was their commander. She *should* have known.

"I did not, at first," Lorn said. To Eklor, he said, "Show them."

Kneeling smoothly, as if he'd expected this, Eklor withdrew a handful of bones from his pocket. He scattered them on the rug before him and said, "*Prynato.*"

Reveal. A bone reader's command. But Eklor was a bone maker, like Kreya, not a bone reader. She knew of no one who had both skills. They each required too much training and specialized skill, not to mention innate talent and affinity for the kind of bone work—

Mist arose from the bones.

She took a step backward.

Within the mist: Flames. An undead soldier. A charred tree. The soldier screamed, silent, but still Kreya flinched as the fire licked over him. It wavered in the mist, and she saw the ruined tower. Then the image melted into swirling gray.

All of them stared at the mist as it dispersed.

"Well, that was conveniently clear," Zera said. Her tone was flippant, but Kreya could hear the tremor in her voice. It was difficult to dispute what the bones had just shown. The vision had been sharp and unambiguous.

No wonder Grand Master Lorn believes him, Kreya thought.

"You know a bone reading shows only the truth," Eklor said. "The truth of the past, the truth of the present, the truth of the future."

"Unless it doesn't," Marso whispered. "Unless it's warped."

"Ahh," Eklor said with a smile, "but such a warping would warp the mind of the reader, and look at me. I am sane, whole, and here."

Kreya doubted "sane," but she couldn't deny "here" as much as she wanted to. Still, he was right—deliberately twisting a bone reading was known to endanger the mind of the bone worker. Given what she knew of Eklor's narcissism, it was unlikely he'd take such a risk . . .

But it *had* to be a lie!

Or a partial truth. "It doesn't mean he destroyed the whole army."

Grand Master Lorn spoke. "The guards at the wall reported smoke blackening the sky. In the aftermath, I had my best soldiers scour the entirety of the forbidden zone. Master Eklor's bone reading shows the truth. The tunnels have been collapsed, and all remnants of his ancient army have been destroyed. The past is burned and buried."

Jentt caught her eye. By his thigh, he held his hand with two fingers out. She knew what he meant—if two of them rushed at Eklor with a speed talisman, Lorn wouldn't be able to stop them. Zera nodded once to show she'd seen and understood. *They're waiting for me*, Kreya thought. A nod from her, and they'd attack.

But this was the grand master of the Bone Workers Guild. As much as she disliked him personally, as much as she disagreed with some of his decisions, she'd never truly questioned him. She'd been a loyal soldier, honored when he'd chosen her to select and lead her group of heroes to confront Eklor when the extent of his depravity was first discovered.

I trusted him.

So she held off for the time being. "Why?" Kreya asked Lorn. She packed everything into that word: why was Eklor here, why was the grand master defending him, why were they being asked to accept the ludicrous idea that he sought redemption.

"Is he threatening you?" Zera asked. "Blackmail?" She made a show of studying her nails. "Eklor, you should know that Grand Master Lorn has many, many friends who would hate to see him used in an unscrupulous way."

"I hope to someday count myself as one of those friends," Eklor said. He was all politeness and charm, and Kreya didn't believe it for a single second. It was all she could do to keep from screaming in frustration.

The army *had* to still be there. It had to all be a trick! Even if she couldn't figure out how he'd done it—crafting a false reading, hiding all trace of his forces from the guards on the wall, faking a fire, and persuading Grand Master Lorn, who was no fool, to trust him after everything he'd done.

Why was he not in chains?

"Grand Master Lorn," Stran said stiffly, "tell us in plain terms: is that man under your protection?"

Kreya translated. "We want to kill him, but we don't want to piss you off. Give the word, and he stops breathing." She felt as if her muscles were vibrating, every inch of her wanting to attack the monster in human skin who stood before them.

"He is indeed under my protection," Grand Master Lorn said.

Eklor smiled.

"Why?" This time it was Marso who asked, his voice quivering.

"Because I believe in second chances," Lorn said loftily. "Our guild did him a grievous wrong that led to a tragedy that cost us all so dearly."

She knew Eklor's tragic backstory. Everyone did. It was part of the legend, entwined in theirs. His wife and child had died in a terrible accident—a cable car wire had snapped, and they hadn't survived the fall—and he'd turned his rage and helplessness on the guild who'd created the technology that failed. "Lots of people experience loss," Kreya said. "They don't use it as an excuse to turn into a mass murderer."

"But they do find it pushes them to extremes they'd never have previously considered." Eklor gestured at Jentt. "I thought you, of all people, would understand."

Kreya opened her mouth and shut it. The idea that she could be anything like this . . . this inhuman monster, this seething mass of hate disguised as a person. She shook, wanting to protest—but she *had* used Eklor's research to create her spell. And worse, Eklor knew it.

"*She* never hurt anyone," Zera piped up. "You, on the other hand, *murdered* hundreds—thousands!"

That was true. There was a vast difference between violating the law to help a loved one, with zero harm done to others, and violating the law to slaughter innocents in an act of mindless revenge. Surely, Grand Master Lorn saw the difference.

I'm not like him!

"But she still broke the law, all of you did, as witnessed by my guards on the wall, and all of you are in need of forgiveness," Grand Master Lorn said. He held up his hand when Jentt stepped forward to protest. "Which will be granted, *if* you will all agree to allow Master Eklor the chance to earn his own forgiveness."

He'd done the unforgivable.

Before she could say so, Zera clutched her hand. "Consider it."

Kreya gawked at her. How could . . .

"By your own admission, you crossed the border into the forbidden zone, violating the law," Grand Master Lorn said. "Your transgression will be forgiven, each of you, if you agree to leave Master Eklor unharmed."

The five of them *might* be able to overpower the grand master and take down Eklor. She couldn't guarantee it, though. She didn't know what surprises Grand Master Lorn had up his sleeves, literally. Or Eklor. And if they tried and failed . . .

"I repeat: he is under my protection," Grand Master Lorn said. "An attack on him is an attack on me. You know the guild council would not forgive that." He smiled benevolently.

He's right, she thought. If it were only Eklor they'd be fighting, that would be one thing. The Bone Makers Guild would understand an attack on their mortal enemy. But it would not forgive an attack on their grand master, no matter the excuse or provocation—the laws were clear and unyielding on that point.

Regardless of whether or not the other bone workers believed they were justified, the five of them would be hunted until the end of their days. At best, Stran would lose his farm and endanger his family, and Zera would lose her wealth and all she'd built. At worst, each of them would lose their life.

It's not worth it, she thought.

Killing Eklor to protect Vos was one thing.

Killing him for revenge . . . It wasn't worth their lives.

She knew Eklor must have seen his victory in their faces, and she refused to look at him. She only looked at Grand Master Lorn. "He's deceived you, and he will destroy you. When you are ready to face that truth, we will do what needs to be done. Until then . . ." She turned to each of her friends, reading in their faces that they saw what she saw: they had no choice. "You have your second chance."

THEY DIDN'T SPEAK UNTIL THEY REACHED ZERA'S palace.

Inside, Kreya crossed to the fountain and stared at the water while Zera dismissed her followers, shooing them away as if they were gnats. When it was only the five of them left, Stran slammed his fist into one of the skeleton-shaped marble pillars. Unfueled by a talisman, he only chipped it.

His wife rushed in at the sound. "What happened? Is he sending heroes? An army?"

Kreya didn't respond.

"Did he not believe you?"

She didn't listen while Stran explained in low, tight tones. She heard Amurra cry out in shock and disbelief. Kreya felt numb. But that was good—she could think instead of feel.

"Insanity," Zera said. "That's what it is. Batshit crazy. It has to be blackmail. Or a threat of some kind. Eklor has something on Grand Master Lorn."

Kreya heard Zera pace back and forth behind her, her silk robes swishing over the floor. The others threw out wilder and wilder explanations: Eklor was threatening the city, Eklor was threatening Grand Master Lorn, Eklor was bribing him, Eklor was poisoning him, Eklor was controlling him, Lorn had been replaced by a mechanized construct made by Eklor who only looked like a human, which of course wasn't possible, but Eklor was a genius so who knew what he could achieve . . .

Only when they finished did Kreya turn to face her friends.

All of them were looking at her expectantly. Certain she'd have a plan. Certain she'd at least have an explanation. But she had neither. Just a conviction that they needed one, quickly. "I assume we're all in agreement? Eklor still plots to destroy the guild, taking all of Vos with it if it suits him. He doesn't care about 'forgiveness' or a second chance."

Amurra ventured, "Perhaps he does? You said he showed a bone reading as proof. And that the guards on the wall saw the smoke from his fire."

"He watched while his creations sliced your husband open," Kreya said bluntly. "He could have stopped them with a single word. He didn't. He merely watched."

Blanching, Amurra touched Stran's chest, near his mostly healed wound. It would scar, adding to his collection of many scars. "Perhaps he was afraid? You'd killed him once before. He could have felt he needed to defend himself."

They all stared at her.

"What?" Amurra took a step backward. "I don't *forgive* him. I'm only trying to understand why Grand Master Lorn, who is

supposedly wise and clever, sees a change in him, despite this"—
she waved at Stran's torso—"evidence."

"Told you," Zera said. "It's blackmail or—"

Kreya cut her off. "You're right. He must have something
on Lorn." Yes, the bone reading was convincing, as was the fire
on the plains, but even with all that, Grand Master Lorn had
to have suspicions. This was Eklor, architect of the Bone War.
You didn't take his claims at face value, no matter what proof he
produced.

The others agreed. Jentt sat beside the fountain and rubbed
his shoulder, the one that had been shot by an arrow. Kreya
wondered how badly it was bothering him. He never complained
about it. "It's likely most people will follow the grand master's
lead," Jentt said. "Unless his reputation has gone down since the
last time I was here alive?"

"He's beloved," Zera said. "And you're right—the people will
want to believe him. No one wants to believe their life is in danger and that one of their grandfatherly leaders has been misled.
Or, worse, has betrayed them."

"It's been twenty-five years," Amurra ventured. "To most of
us . . . to many, Eklor is a legend. You are all legends. There aren't
many who will believe the dangers of the past have anything to
do with them and their lives. As you said, they want to believe
it's over."

"So how do we save a world that doesn't want to be saved?"
Jentt asked.

She hadn't planned to save the world again. She'd intended to come to Cerre and hand the responsibility to the
next generation. No one would blame them if they did exactly
that. After all, they'd only be following their guild master's

orders. They were the Five Heroes of Vos—they were supposed to obey the leaders of the city and behave in only virtuous, righteous ways—and they were supposed to be retired from the hero business anyway. But Kreya read determination on every one of their faces. This wasn't over yet, for any of them. She'd never been more proud of her team. And she'd never been so grateful that they weren't throwing everything she'd said back in her face. After all, she'd been the one who'd wanted to give up and dump the entire problem onto younger heroes' laps. *Looks like I was wrong*, she thought. "We can start with me saying I'm sorry. I owe all of you an apology. You were right. We aren't done with being heroes yet. It was a fool's dream. Feel free to say 'I told you so.'"

"We'd never say that," Zera said. "We'd think it. Loudly. Often. But we wouldn't *say* it." Jentt grinned at her, and the others nodded in agreement.

Stran punched one fist into the palm of his other hand. "What's the plan, Commander?"

She smiled at her team, grateful for everything they weren't saying. She'd made so many mistakes, and they still trusted her. *To work then*, she thought. "Before we can make any kind of reasonable plan, we need two pieces of information: One, what does Eklor have on Lorn? And two, where is Eklor's army?"

"You . . . want me to read for it?" Marso asked, his voice quivering. "You want me to counter Eklor's reading in front of the guild master?"

Kreya shook her head. "Thank you, but no." She saw relief in his eyes. "Grand Master Lorn has already discredited you. Claimed your false readings drove you mad. That rules you out as an effective witness."

Zera patted him on the shoulder. "Yeah, it would be your

reading versus Eklor's, and while he has a history of genocide, you have a history of sleeping naked in city fountains."

"We need tangible proof," Kreya said. "Only then will we have a chance of convincing Grand Master Lorn to withdraw his protection."

Stran volunteered. "Send me to find his army."

Amurra yelped. "Stran!"

He wrapped his arm around her. "I won't engage. Only scout."

Kreya glanced at Jentt, who nodded. "Fine. Jentt will accompany you. Take the direct route to the plains, not through the valley. There's no need for secrecy. Both Lorn and Eklor will expect us to check for the truth. More than that, they'll *want* us to. Send word to Lorn that you require official permission to cross into the forbidden zone, and go as soon as he grants it. Make your search thorough. And be alert—we don't know where on the plains Eklor stashed his army or what he intends them to do."

Jentt promised Amurra, "I will speed us out if there's a whiff of danger."

"If—or should I say *when*—you find evidence, make sure you have as many witnesses as possible," Kreya said. "I don't buy for a moment that Eklor could have, or would have, destroyed his army. He'll have his soldiers hidden somewhere underground, ready to erupt out when he needs them. As soon as you find proof that his monstrosities still exist, expose the truth to the border guards and then bring whatever evidence you can back to Cerre." She turned to the others. "Amurra—"

Stran jumped in. "My wife is not part of this."

"She's part of Vos," Kreya said. "She's as much a part of this as anyone, and she has a strength that none of us do: she's unknown here. She can go where she wants, talk to who she wants, and learn information that none of the rest of us can. Amurra, I need you to find out what the people know and what they believe. If it comes to it, we need to know if the people will side with us or with Lorn. And we'll pray it doesn't come to that."

Stiffening her shoulders, Amurra said, "I can do that."

"Zera, you need to unearth what Eklor has over Lorn. Poke all your contacts. Call in favors, if you're owed them. Bribe people, if you aren't. We need to know, and we need to know *fast*, before Eklor makes his next move. Right now, he has the advantage."

Zera smiled, but there was no humor in her eyes. "I'll shake the trees so hard, people will be telling me their grandmother's secrets."

"And you?" Jentt asked Kreya. "What are you going to do?"

"I'm going to distract Eklor from all of you." She did not meet Jentt's eyes as she said it. She knew he wasn't going to approve of this part of her plan. "He wants forgiveness? He can begin by facing me."

She was right: Jentt didn't like that idea. None of them did. All of them began talking at once, arguing with her. "You can't attack him," Stran said, louder than the rest. The others echoed him.

"I'll only talk."

None of them believed her.

Kreya held up her hands, silencing them. "He'll want to talk to me." She hesitated for a moment. She wasn't sure how they'd react to the reason for that, but she plunged on. They deserved to know. "He'll want to know how I brought Jentt back. Eklor has always believed he's the smartest in the world, but his research into resurrection was flawed and incomplete. It must be eating him up to know I achieved mastery of what he considered his life's work. And it will hurt him even more when he learns I used his own notes to do it." According to his notes, Eklor had never brought back the dead, at least prior to bringing himself back to life. He'd merely theorized it. She'd both completed his studies and applied them. He had to be curious about how.

There was a silence.

Marso, who had been silent, spoke up. "That's how you did it? Using his knowledge? Did we know that?"

"We strongly suspected," Zera told him. "We weren't asking questions because we didn't want to know. It was enough that we had Jentt back. And me." Her eyes rested on Kreya's hand, the one with one less finger.

All of them fell silent, looking at her hand.

"Either condemn me for it, or let's get to work." Kreya held her breath but tried to keep her face placid and confident. She resisted the urge to also look down at her hand. If they turned on her for what she'd done to save Jentt and Zera, then so be it. *I don't regret it. Even now. Even with Eklor here, in the heart of Cerre.*

Jentt addressed Marso. "Are you well enough to go with Kreya?"

"I . . . don't know if I can read the bones like I used to," Marso stammered.

Kreya had deliberately not given him any tasks. She'd wanted him to focus on recovering. She'd ripped him out of his stupor and forced him to face things she knew he hadn't wanted to face. Asking more of him now felt cruel, but Jentt didn't hesitate.

"You don't have to read any bones," Jentt told him. "You

just need to accompany her when she faces Eklor again. She'll want to make sure you aren't killed, so that means if you're there, she'll be careful."

Kreya smiled. Clever man. He knew her well. "Everyone happy with the plan?"

"I'm not happy about *any* of this," Zera said.

Kreya one hundred percent agreed with that, as did they all. But they set about doing it anyway.

Because that's what heroes did.

CHAPTER NINETEEN

Marso retreated to the room that Zera had designated for him, while the others packed and prepared and plotted. He sank cross-legged in the center, on top of a plush bear-skin rug. He sank his fingers into the fur and concentrated on breathing evenly and smoothly.

He should have seen this.

If he'd been himself, at his old strength, he would have read the bones and known to expect Eklor in that palace. They'd have been able to be prepared. Instead, he'd failed them.

It had been kind of them not to point it out. He'd forgotten that people could be so kind. After the war, it seemed the entire world had expectations for what he could do, what he must feel, what he'd think and want. Keeping up with them had been exhausting—and impossible.

Concentrating on breathing, Marso tried to pull his mind out of the swirl of memories. There had been one lover he'd had who wanted him to use his powers as a parlor trick. All low stakes, so Marso hadn't seen the harm: what will such-and-such restaurant offer for dinner, what will a friend wear to the night's party, which runner will win the sprint. It was only when Marso realized that the young man was using the predictions to gamble that Marso broke it off. His next lover had been fascinated by his gift, but she hadn't pushed him to use it. He ended it because he read her death in the bones and couldn't bear to tell her. He'd tried once, but she'd stopped him. She hadn't wanted to know what the cryptic images in the mist had meant, and he couldn't live with both her and the knowledge. He'd tried once more, with a beautiful man who wasn't afraid of what Marso might see. It was with him, though, that Marso had first widened his gaze to read the plains and seen a glimpse of Eklor alive.

That time, the man broke it off with Marso.

I have failed so many, Marso thought.

He didn't know whether it was the endless failure or the never-ending fear that had driven him to the fountain. His memories of that time were fogged, and he didn't care to stare too closely at them.

He was not there anymore. He was here. And his mind was clearer than it had been in a long, long time. And though Kreya had not given him anything to do—and he had said he couldn't do it—he felt the need to cast.

Perhaps it was seeing Eklor read the bones. It was disturbing to think that someone like that, a vector for destruction, should be gifted with the ability to summon the mist, while Marso, who had dedicated his life to the truth the bones could reveal, failed.

Reaching into a pocket, Marso drew out a handful of old chicken bones. They'd been polished smooth years ago and felt light and familiar in his hands. Even at his worst, he hadn't been able to part with them. He spun them around, manipulating them with his fingers, twisting them over and under his knuckles until he was juggling them one-handed.

Marso had lost the knack of clearing his mind. It was a jumble of thoughts, fears, worries, and memories, but if he could quiet it for just a moment . . . He focused on building up a picture of the plains in his mind, not as they used to be but as they were in the present, with tall grasses, wildflowers, and the rubble of the tower. If he could predict what waited for Jentt and Stran, that would be a help.

Bringing the bones to his lips, he whispered, "*Prynato.*"

He spilled them onto the floor.

Leaning over them, he let his eyes absorb the pattern as mist rose above them. Images began to appear both in the mist and in his mind. Earth, erupting upward. Machines, clawing their way out of the ground. Jentt, young, being hit by arrows—no, Jentt now, being hit in the shoulder by an arrow, which he had been, but he'd lived. *He's alive,* Marso told his mind.

A dead soldier lurched to its feet.

Another old memory. He tried to cling to that fact, to separate past, present, and future, but the images assailed him. He heard screaming, and he clapped his hands over his ears. But it didn't fade. The screaming was within him, echoing through his veins. He saw soldiers—innocent men and women who only wanted to defend their homes and their families—torn apart by Eklor's army. He saw the grass trampled, steeped in blood. Then he heard the silence, the wind, the wails, all at once, and the plains were both empty and full.

Stop!

He tried to pull his mind back, and he was in Cerre, hovering above it like a hawk. Below, the city burned. Blackened bodies lay in the streets.

Future? Past? Imagination?

He didn't know.

When the images fled and the mist melted away, he wept.

⟲

"QUESTION IS: AT WHAT POINT DO I QUIT BEING civil?" Pacing back and forth across one of Zera's lesser and more private salons, Kreya seemed to be talking more to herself than to Zera, so Zera didn't answer.

I don't know what the answer should be anyway, Zera thought. "No luck getting an audience with him?" she asked out loud. She knew Kreya had sent her initial request hours ago, with a follow-up each hour after. Zera too had sent out feelers to her contacts, paving the way to pry for information about the grand master. Both of them were waiting, though Zera privately thought she was being much more patient about it.

"Normally I'd insist, but that could be seen as an act of aggression," Kreya said, before punching a pillow on a divan. "So I am politely and patiently waiting for my request to be honored. But there has to be a limit."

With a clenched jaw, Kreya looked as if she wanted to bite someone, and Zera spent an enjoyable minute imagining her friend biting the crap out of Eklor. Obviously harsher punishments would follow, but that would make a delightful appetizer. Zera opened her mouth to suggest she consider it, and she heard a tentative clearing of a female throat.

"Not hungry, not thirsty, go away!" Kreya called. "Honestly, your servants think if I don't try a 'nibble' every thirty minutes, I'll starve to death. How many meals a day do you eat?"

"None and all," Zera said airily.

A soft voice carried through the curtained archway. "It's Amurra. I thought—"

Zera swung her legs off the couch. "Oh, goodness, girl, come in!" She crossed to the curtain and shooed her inside. "You're always welcome, love."

Amurra scooted inside. She was dressed in some of Zera's clothes, since her farmwear wasn't appropriate in the city, and she tugged at the blouse, trying to force it to cover the skin it bared. Zera thought she'd feel more confident if she added a few tattoos, but she wasn't going to mention it. She herself had a lovely golden lizard skeleton inked on her left ankle. She'd gotten it at a time when she hadn't felt as comfortable in her own skin. Getting it had felt like hanging a painting in a new house, claiming it as hers. She spent a pleasant few seconds imagining what kind of tattoo would look best on Amurra, as if Amurra were a blank canvas and she a painter. Perhaps an apple tree, in blossom.

"I've been to the lower tiers," Amurra began. She twisted her hands as if she were a nervous student in front of two harsh teachers.

When did I go from being a friendly bone wizard to someone intimidating? Zera wondered. She hadn't noticed the transformation happening, even though of course she'd worked for it. She tried to put on a more encouraging face and waited for Amurra to continue.

"No one I spoke to knows Eklor is here, so at least it's not common knowledge among the average citizens. I thought about slipping the information, you know, to see how people would react, but I wasn't sure if that would be wise."

Kreya nodded. "You acted correctly. We don't know what Eklor's game is. Until we do, it's better to be cautious."

"The great Kreya, advising caution," Zera said.

Kreya glared at her. "I'm always careful."

Zera laughed and then stopped. "Oh, you're serious?"

Gingerly, Amurra sat on the plainest chair, only occupying the edge, as if she were afraid of soiling the cushions. "People remember the war. Many lost loved ones. I can't imagine they'd be happy to know Grand Master Lorn is sheltering Vos's greatest enemy."

Lounging back on her sofa, Zera considered the matter. "We could reveal him and throw him off guard. Remind people of the war as loudly as possible. Demand to know his purpose here. Put him on the defensive."

"Not until we know where his army is," Kreya said. "We wait for Jentt and Stran before we make any kind of move."

Fair enough. Twirling one of her bracelets, Zera thought more. "What if we're subtle?"

"Subtle is not our strong suit," Kreya said.

"Thank you for saying 'our.'"

Kreya grinned at her, and Zera grinned back.

"I am serious, though," Zera said. "What if we—*subtly*—remind the people how terrible Eklor's war was? I could make donations to theater troupes, on the condition that they stage the tragedies and war dramas. Singers, always in need of more funds, could be encouraged to sing ballads in the streets."

Amurra perked up. "You could commission artists! A mural, memorializing those who were lost. Ooh, a mural on every tier."

"Statues, too," Kreya suggested. "Place them in plazas and on street corners. Or at least encourage street performers, if statues would take too long to create. Buskers in every square, singing, dancing, playacting about the Bone War."

Zera loved all these ideas beyond measure. She rubbed her hands together. "This is going to annoy the shit out of Eklor." And prime the public to reject him when he finally revealed himself from whatever corner of Lorn's shadow he was lurking in.

In the end, that could be as powerful a weapon as any sword

or arrow. Zera called for Guine, as well as several of her servants. After a moment's thought, she also called for Marso.

"Why Marso?" Kreya asked. "He needs to rest."

Zera disagreed. "He needs a new hobby. Something to distract him from screaming his head off." It would be good for him. All of them had heard his screaming, so no one objected.

Once all her lovelies were assembled, she set their plan in motion.

Now everyone had something useful to do while they waited for Zera's contacts and Lorn to respond. And more important, Jentt and Stran to return.

THE WORST THING ABOUT HAVING BEEN DEAD, Jentt thought, *is the lost time*. He'd died countless times, knowing each could be the last, but he had no memories of the days, weeks, months, even years before Kreya was able to wake him again. She had been accruing experiences, but he . . . had simply not.

I have a lot to make up, he thought.

Standing outside the city of Cerre, he filled his lungs to capacity. Pine trees. The dusty sweetness of fallen aspen leaves. A whiff of garbage, as the wind blew over the first tier behind him.

After all this was over, he wanted to travel. See the world with Kreya. Sail the seas beyond the borders of Vos. Maybe learn to sail first. Taste food neither of them could name. Explore bits of the maps that were so obscure no one had bothered to label them.

Leading two mountain horses, Stran joined Jentt to overlook the road, the pine forests, the mist-coated valley, and the expanse of peaks that lay before them. "Ready for an adventure?"

"Oh yes," Jentt said fervently.

Stran grinned back at him.

They mounted and set off. So close to the city, there was a steady stream of travelers on the road. Jentt bought a bag of apples from a farmer who gawked at both of them in obvious curiosity—you could practically see him trying to figure out who they were, where they were going, and what they planned to do. Neither Jentt nor Stran enlightened him. Later, the farmer might realize he'd met legends. *Or maybe not,* Jentt thought. Maybe he had better things to do than muse over the identities of two strange travelers, such as sell his fruits in the market, meet with old friends in the city, and return home to a family who loved him.

A quarter mile from the city, they activated the speed talismans that Kreya had built into the bridles, and they galloped like wind through the pine forests, beneath waterfalls, and past orchards and farms.

They stayed in an inn under false names, and Stran swore they weren't recognized, though the musicians played several of the old ballads about the Five Heroes of Vos, which Jentt didn't think was a coincidence. At dawn, they continued on.

"Did you ever think you'd be the father of three?" Jentt asked midmorning.

"Never thought I'd want anything but the battlefield," Stran said. "At least until I was on one, and then I knew I never wanted to see another. You ever see yourself as a father?"

"Once. But I missed that chance. Apparently I can cheat death but not time." He and Kreya had never talked about whether or not they wanted kids. Before the war, it had felt like they had eternity to decide. After . . . well, he was dead. "Probably would have made a terrible dad."

"Nah, you'd have been great. It's not hard. All you gotta do is love them every second of the day and make sure they don't burn themselves on the kitchen fire, fall off a cliff, fall out of a tree, have a tree fall on them, get trampled by farm equipment, or eat anything poisonous. Actually, parenthood is extraordinarily stressful. Babies come out so tiny and helpless. Horses plop out and are able to walk instantly, but not babies."

"Regrets?" Jentt asked.

Guiding his horse around an outcrop of boulders, Stran said, "None. Except for not asking Amurra to marry me the second I met her. I wasted a year thinking she couldn't possibly love me before finally she cornered me and told me the wedding would be in two weeks, unless I said no. I didn't say no."

Jentt laughed. "Wish I could've been there."

Stran grinned. "Her parents insisted I wear silk. And bells. Tiny bells sewn into the fabric. Couldn't even sneeze without setting them all off."

"Now I *really* wish I could have been there."

Even fueled by bones, it took them another day to reach the plains. They rode straight for the outpost at the wall, stabled their horses, and presented themselves to the head guard, who was barely more than a boy with an uneven mustache.

Stran introduced himself first, and the guard's eyes bulged.

"I . . . I would need authorization from the grand master . . ."

Jentt stepped forward and presented the official paperwork that they'd obtained before they'd left—Kreya had been correct that Lorn would grant them permission without a fuss, even if he refused to meet with her directly. He wanted them to cooperate with whatever his agenda was, and that required them to believe Eklor's claims.

Gawking at Jentt, the young guard lost his ability to speak.

"We need shovels," Stran said, helping him out. "Can we borrow two?"

Sweat poured off the poor boy's forehead. "Sh-sh-shovels?"

Stran patted his shoulder. "No worries. We'll find them ourselves. Assign someone to feed and water our horses, will you?"

As he passed him, Jentt also patted his shoulder. "And sit down before you faint, hit your head, and split it open. Dying isn't as fun as it sounds."

They located a less overwhelmed guard, one who was too young to recognize who they were or comprehend what their presence meant, and obtained the shovels. Crossing the plain, they aimed for the tower, or what was left of it. They left the horses chowing down on oats—they deserved a rest after the journey here—and they took several of the guards with them.

Witnesses or backup, depending on which it would turn out they needed.

A mile from the wall, on the way to the tower, Jentt saw a scorched tree. Around it, the grasses were shriveled and blackened. "Definitely a fire here," Stran noted.

"But what did it burn?"

Eklor could have set the fire to make his claims more plausible. It didn't mean he'd actually burned anything.

One of the guards piped up. "Bones, sir! There are human remains here."

The other guards bowed their heads and murmured a prayer that their souls had reached the great silence. Crossing to the guard, Jentt knelt beside a charred rib cage. The burned bones lay beside a rusty sword with a Vosian hilt. "One of ours," Jentt said.

Stran huffed. "Proves nothing. Not until we find *his* soldiers burned to a crisp."

Very true. Standing, Jentt said, "Stay alert, everyone."

The guards saluted. Clutching their weapons, they fanned out, tromping across burnt grass that crackled under their footsteps.

Closer to the tower, the meadows had been torn up. Ugly scars of dirt and rocks ran in five lines radiating into the rubble. *Collapsed tunnels*, Jentt thought.

Another point in Eklor's favor.

Again, though, it could all be a show staged by Eklor to hide the truth.

"You really think his army is buried under there?" Stran asked.

"You really have to ask that?" Jentt said.

"Fair enough. Let's prove those tunnels are as empty as his promises."

At random, they picked one of the lines of dirt. Assuming that the machines and soldiers had returned to the chamber at the end of the tunnel, then the best spot to dig should be at the end of the line, farthest from the tower. "Here?" Jentt suggested.

"Sure." Stran swung his shovel off his shoulder and planted it in the churned-up dirt. "You use speed, and I use strength? Winner buys lunch?"

Jentt grinned. "You're on."

They activated their talismans and began.

Dirt flew. Rocks were tossed. Jentt felt sweat pour off his body. He felt his muscles strain. He inhaled the dirt-saturated air, and he had never felt more alive. Beside him, Stran was shifting massive amounts of earth but at half his speed. Jentt pushed himself harder, faster. He flew, his shovel a blur.

At last, they reached bedrock.

"Halt!" Jentt called.

He slowed himself. His body still felt like it was vibrating.

"Tired?" Stran said.

Jentt grinned back. "Never." He turned in a circle to look at the hole they'd dug. They'd cleared enough that they were well below the level of the meadow. Deep enough that they'd reached what had been the floor of the chamber. The air was cooler within the shadows of the hole, and it smelled like rich earth. "See any monstrosities?"

"Not a one," Stran said.

Heaving himself out of the hole, he got to his feet. Several dozen guards from the wall were there, spread in a semicircle, gawking with mouths dropped wide open.

"No trace of Eklor's army so far," Jentt reported to them. "You're witness to this."

Starting with one, then spreading to the rest, the guards applauded. Jentt and Stran exchanged glances and started toward where they knew the next tunnel used to be. Trailing behind, the guards followed, jovial, joking back and forth, happy not to find any horrors. *They don't get it*, Jentt realized. The fact that nothing had clawed its way out of the earth to attack them wasn't a good thing.

If the army wasn't here—either broken or intact—that meant it was somewhere else.

The question was where.

He didn't know what Eklor had planned for his army, but it didn't take a genius to know it would be bad for Vos. And for their dreams of a peaceful future.

Determinedly, Jentt and Stran began digging out the next tunnel and chamber. They'd promised Kreya they would search as thoroughly as possible, and that was exactly what they were going to do: remove every excuse, rationale, or argument that

Eklor could make. Force Grand Master Lorn to withdraw his protection.

As the hours passed, their audience grew in size as more guards gathered to watch, cheer, and make bets on who was the more effective shoveler. And as the hours passed, they still found no trace of any inhuman soldiers.

It was late into the night of the third day when they began on the fifth and final tunnel. Stars speckled the blue-black sky, and many of the guards carried lanterns so that both they and the two diggers could see.

And that was when they found the remains of Eklor's army.

Jentt hit the first crushed soldier with his shovel.

"Stran!" he called.

His friend jogged closer. "Everyone, clear this dirt!"

Together, Jentt, Stran, and the guards from the wall cleared away the dirt to expose a tangle of burnt bones and scorched metal—a fused-together mass made of the unnatural bodies of his constructs.

"He didn't lie," Stran said, shock in his voice.

But . . . he couldn't have told the truth. Could he? He had to have a nefarious plan. Jentt refused to believe his murderer could be reformed. There had to be another explanation.

"He could have sacrificed these soldiers to hide the fact that the rest of his army lives," Jentt said, but the words rang hollow. As mangled as they were, it was impossible to count the number of undead soldiers in this sunken tunnel, but given the size of the tangled mass . . . It would have been hundreds.

To destroy so many . . .

It was possible that Eklor had herded all his soldiers into one tunnel to crush and burn them—certainly that's what this was supposed to look like, and he'd specifically said he'd gathered them before crushing them. But it was also possible that he'd only destroyed a portion of his forces. After all, the other tunnels had been empty.

"This could be a decoy," Jentt said. "To throw us off the scent."

"Then let's find the scent," Stran said.

They spent several hours with lanterns combing the area, looking for evidence of which way any potential remaining army could have marched—without luck. If Eklor had found another way out with any additional soldiers, he'd destroyed all trace of it.

Returning to the guards, Jentt and Stran found them piling the burnt bones of Vosian soldiers into the newly dug pits. They'd left the mangled mass of undead soldiers where it had been found and marked off the area with flags.

Under his breath, Stran said, "We proved the opposite of what we came here to prove."

"Looks like we did," Jentt said. Certainly the guards would testify that Eklor's army had been destroyed, exactly as Eklor had claimed. Grand Master Lorn would feel even more justified in his trust of Eklor. Still . . .

He wished it were possible to tell exactly how many had been destroyed here. Was it truly hundreds in that mangled mass? Or was it a much smaller number?

"There has to be something we're missing," Jentt said. "I can't believe he's reformed."

"The ache in my shoulder says he hasn't," Stran agreed.

This was a setback, though, undeniably. "Maybe Zera will have uncovered some useful information." She was supposed to be looking into possible ways Eklor could be blackmailing the grand master.

"Kreya will have a plan," Stran said, certainty in his voice.

"She will," Jentt agreed. "And this time, we all survive. Together." He clasped his hand on Stran's shoulder. "Consider that a promise."

ZERA PLOPPED ONTO THE COUCH IN THE ROOM she'd given to Kreya. Her many silk scarves fluffed out around her, and her jewelry clinked like wind chimes. She'd been to seven parties in six hours, and if she ever saw another rare, exotic shrimp wrapped in rare, exotic antelope steak, she might vomit all over someone's rare, exotic rugs. "It's his son," she said.

Frowning in concentration at a bone she was affixing to a new cat-size mechanized construct, Kreya didn't glance up. "Who?"

"He's ten years old, and his name is Yarri. Cute as a fat rabbit. He likes to play ring ball, or whatever that ridiculous sport is called, you know, the one with the targets on sticks . . . Anyway, everyone agrees that he's a bright, charming, and delectable child, and isn't it so sad that he is oh-so-very sick."

Kreya put down the construct. She twisted in her chair. "Grand Master Lorn has a child."

"A very sick child. A few people I talked to believed he might already be dead, but they hadn't been invited to view the pyre, so that was roundly dismissed as gossip."

"Shit."

"Yep." Zera liked that she didn't have to spell it out to Kreya.

Stretching her arms up, Zera felt the ache in her back ease. She twisted her torso and then her neck, rolling it around in a circle. Grand Master Lorn had a son who was likely to die. If Eklor had convinced Lorn that he'd conquered death—and the very fact that he was alive was convincing proof of that—it would explain why Lorn was committed to protecting him. But it didn't explain what Eklor wanted in exchange for a promise to save Lorn's son. Or what Eklor's plan was in lieu of saving the boy.

She didn't for a second believe he planned to help anyone, least of all the son of his enemy.

We need proof that his army exists, Zera thought. *If we can't prove Eklor has nefarious plans, then Lorn will never believe us over hope for his son.*

Without proof . . . all they had was their paranoid suspicions about Eklor. And a reason to distrust Grand Master Lorn. "Any word from Jentt and Stran?"

"Not yet."

KREYA EYED THE CROWD OUTSIDE OF ZERA'S palace.

Word had spread: the Five had returned.

Of course, the only people allowed on the fifth tier were the very rich and famous and their servants, but just because they were wealthy, it didn't mean they weren't voyeurs. In fact, the two things went nicely hand in hand, as they had plenty of time to loiter. Kreya and her friends had used their real names to access the fifth tier, and they'd paraded through the streets to Lorn's palace looking every inch the parts they'd played. "I should have expected this," Kreya said.

All the work they'd been doing with artists and theater groups had resulted in renewed interest in the Heroes of Vos, as well as hatred of Eklor. She hadn't thought about this side effect.

Sitting on one of the sofas, Amurra said, "I think it's nice. You still have the support of the people. You could go out and meet them."

"I'd rather swallow glass."

Amurra laughed. "Stran feels the same way about a fuss being made over him. He always said I rescued him. It's part of why he loves the farm so much. The sheep are unimpressed with his fame."

A cheer went up outside, loud enough to penetrate the walls of the palace. Marso strolled in to join them in the grand salon. "Jentt and Stran are back," he said conversationally.

"At last!" Zera jumped to her feet.

Startled, Kreya twisted to look at Marso. She'd thought he wasn't going to read the future anymore. "You saw it in the bones?"

"I saw it out the window. Didn't you hear the cheering?"

Squeezing through the crowd were Jentt and Stran. They shook hands and were pulled into hugs. Quite a few touched Jentt as if he were a kind of lucky charm. Amurra laughed. "He's a miracle. They probably think it'll rub off on them."

They watched for a few minutes more. The crowd pressed closer to the two heroes, cutting them off from the palace. Kreya waited for them to use talismans to push through, but they didn't. Possibly they were trying to be polite.

Ugh, they were both entirely too nice. She wanted them here *now*. While they'd been gone, Eklor had had another week to push forward with whatever his agenda was. Another week of access to Grand Master Lorn. Another week to worm himself into the heart of Cerre, to plan his traps and tricks, to spin his web. Plus, of course, the week he'd been here before they were even aware. He could have caused so much damage already, and every minute of glad-handing was a minute not plotting how to stop him.

"Someone might want to rescue them before people start

carving off chunks of our boys as souvenirs to take home," Zera suggested.

"I'll do it," Kreya said with a sigh.

She stalked to the door and threw it open. With a gasp, the crowd turned to look at her. A few began shouting her name. Others rushed forward.

"Stop!" she commanded, hand out.

Not everyone could hear her over the roaring crowd, but those in front saw her motion and saw the look in her eyes. They skidded to a halt, and the crowd was forced to stop behind them. They quieted, watching her expectantly.

"Let them through!"

A little shuffling, and then the crowd parted. Jentt and Stran walked through. Kreya held the door open for them as the crowd watched her, rapt.

If she knew what to say, it would have been the perfect moment for a speech. She had the attention of the upper crust of the city. She could sway them however she wished. Tell them of Eklor's presence, of Grand Master Lorn's betrayal in allowing such a viper into the heart of Vos. With all the plays, songs, and revivals, the citizens were primed to listen to her.

I don't know enough yet to act, she thought.

And so she said nothing, and when Jentt and Stran entered the palace, she shut the great doors behind them. If the crowd reacted, she didn't hear it. "Give me good news," she said. "You found his army? Please tell me we have proof."

She knew the answer before he said it.

"We found burnt constructs within a collapsed tunnel," Jentt said. "No way to tell if it's all of them or not, but also no way to tell that it isn't."

"Searched the area thoroughly, too," Stran added. "No evidence that any soldiers escaped the plains. The wall guards will undoubtedly report our findings to the guild, bolstering Eklor's claims."

Closing her eyes, Kreya tasted disappointment, bitter on her tongue. She'd been counting on this. With hard evidence, maybe they could have convinced the grand master to set aside his concerns for his son and see reason. But without evidence . . .

"I'm sorry, Kreya," Jentt said, "but all we found is proof that Eklor is telling the truth. We failed."

CHAPTER TWENTY

Five days later, they still had no proof that an army was marching on Cerre or even that Eklor's army had ever existed. And Kreya was getting very, very tired of failure. So far, Grand Master Lorn had rebuffed her every attempt to speak to Eklor, and Amurra and Zera hadn't unearthed any new useful information about the connection between Eklor, Lorn, and Lorn's son, Yarri. The only one who'd had any luck was Marso, who'd sparked a revival of artistic interest in the Bone War.

Of course they weren't giving up, but Kreya couldn't help feeling they were running out of time. And when the invitation from Grand Master Lorn arrived, she knew the clock had run out.

The invitation was delivered by a vaguely birdlike construct with gauzy wings and written in gold ink on elegant stationery that felt soft and thick. Kreya read it and handed it to Zera, who read it, snorted, and said, "It's a trap."

"Obviously, but is it a trap for us or for the people of Vos?" Taking the paper back, Kreya scowled at it. The invitation had come for all five of them to join the masters of the Bone Workers Guild and other luminaries in front of Grand Master Lorn's palace on the fifth tier for a "presentation of great import" that would be of "benefit to all of Vos."

Concerned, Amurra joined them and read the invite. "I'll get Stran and Jentt—they were planning to search east of the city today, but I don't think they've left yet." She scurried out of the room, past the fountain.

"At least there's no more waiting," Zera said.

Shooting her a glare, Kreya sat at the workbench with her half-finished constructs. She hadn't expected to run out of time so quickly. Jentt and Stran had been spending hours searching the mountains around Cerre for Eklor's missing army, while Kreya and Zera had been feverishly creating new constructs and talismans. Marso and Amurra had paired with Guine to spread word of Zera's donations to the various theater and dance troops around the city. Everything was in motion, but it clearly wasn't enough.

Jentt and Stran burst into the grand salon, with Amurra and Marso behind them. "What's happened?" Stran demanded.

"We're out of time," Kreya said.

Zera showed them the invite, while Kreya performed triage on her creations: those too far from completion were pushed aside while she focused on the few that were close to done. She'd have to cut corners, make them slightly less agile and slightly less aware, but so be it.

There had been no sign of Eklor's army hidden in the forests around Cerre. So Kreya was designing these constructs to search through the vast network of caves beneath and near the city. If Eklor was setting his plan into motion, they needed to find his army as quickly as possible—they'd sent a report of their concerns to Grand Master Lorn, highlighting the fact that there was no way to be certain that Eklor had burned and buried *all* of his constructs, and he had replied that perhaps the "army" had been exaggerated in their minds, due to the stress of the situation. He asked them to consider the possibility that Eklor was truly repentant and that their own past experience was coloring their view of the present.

Murderers who try to destroy the world should not get the benefit of the doubt, Kreya thought.

She worked as quickly as she could, adjusting legs and inserting bones. She'd modeled these after the spiderlike crawler, but they were much smaller. They had to be fast, agile, and capable of escaping detection if they did find any trace of the inhuman soldiers.

And then get back to her with that information.

Behind her, the others were tossing ideas back and forth—what Eklor wanted, what they could do about it, and who was in the most danger. Zera loaded up on talismans, filling all her pockets.

"I want you to stay here," Stran said to Amurra.

"You know I'm coming with you," she told him. "I didn't leave our children for me to hide behind fancy walls, and I didn't like being left behind when you talked to Grand Master Lorn before. We face this together."

"Amurra, we don't know what we face. I can't let—"

"Let? There's no 'let' in marriage. You ask. We discuss. I convince."

"If I were to lose you—"

"You can't wrap me up in blankets and preserve me like a glass vase. That's not how love works. I know there are risks. I want to take those risks with you."

Kreya activated her constructs, and they chittered as their legs began to vibrate then move. Jentt opened the nearest window, and together they watched the fist-size spiders climb out and flow down the side of the palace. "There are a lot of caves," Jentt said. "This could take a while."

"We have to try," Kreya said. She turned to face the others and noted that Stran and Amurra were still arguing. "Amurra, you're the only one not mentioned on the invite. You do not have to come."

A smile blossomed on Stran's face. "Listen to Kreya."

Amurra frowned. "With all due respect to Kreya, she's not my commander—"

Kreya wasn't finished. "But I am Stran's. And, Stran, I am ordering you to let your wife, a grown woman, make her own choices about what she's willing to risk or not."

"Then I'm coming," Amurra said firmly.

Kreya nodded approvingly. *All of us could choose to stay behind,* she thought. *We could all decide to go somewhere "safe" and pretend none of this is our responsibility.* After all, they'd warned Grand Master Lorn, so that should absolve them of their duty. But that didn't remove the danger to Vos, and if their country was in danger, there was no way to truly flee this. "Nothing we do is safe. You make the choices you think you can live with and hope you do get to live with them. This is my choice. Each of you gets to make your own." She stalked to the door. "Come on, everyone who's coming. We have a disaster to witness."

She walked outside.

Glancing back, she saw all of them had followed her.

The crowd cheered as soon as they saw the heroes, but they parted when Kreya and the others stalked forward. Kreya didn't know what kind of expression was on her face, but she didn't question it. Nor did she stop the crowd from trailing after them.

"Is an audience wise?" Marso asked nervously.

"The more people who see us go, the more who will know if we don't return," Jentt said, low enough that the crowd couldn't hear.

Amurra was close enough to hear. "Is that truly a fear?"

"You can still stay behind," Stran said. "It's not too late."

Kreya didn't hear Amurra's response, but she noticed that Amurra was still with them when they stepped onto the white stones and rode up toward the guild master's palace, and was proud of the diminutive woman, who may have been even braver than her massive husband. She then focused back on what was ahead of her. Kreya hated not knowing what to expect. At least when they'd gone to battle, they'd known who the enemy was and what he wanted. Here, they still knew who the enemy was. But after that . . . it was up in the air.

When they reached the guild master's residence, a crowd had already assembled: bone masters in embroidered coats that marked them as members of the guild's ruling council, additional non-council bone workers in masters' coats who must have gotten special permission to access the fifth tier, several members of the city's parliament, and the grand masters of a few other prominent guilds—she recognized the mantle of the grand master of trade, the grand master of agriculture, and the grand master of artisans.

She shivered as she surveyed the assembly. This was a gathering of a lot of important people. If Eklor somehow managed to get his army within Cerre, the devastation it would cause just from the perspective of leadership would be incalculable—a power vacuum that could only mean chaos. She wished she'd been able to finish her little scouts faster. They could have been searching all this time and been able to give them advance warning.

"Be ready to supply us," she whispered to Zera.

"I'm always ready," Zera whispered back.

"You think this is it?" Stran asked.

"It could be. The conditions seem right if I were setting up an ambush."

To Amurra, he said, "You should have stayed where you'd be safe."

"Kreya already said there's no place truly safe," she said. "And I'd rather be with you."

"There's safer."

Kreya shot them a glare. "Stop arguing, and be alert."

The luminaries whispered to one another as the five heroes arrived. Even among such exalted company, the five were impressive. The men and women parted for them, and Kreya led her group toward the vast brass doors.

"I hate this," Jentt muttered.

Kreya reached out and took his hand, as much to assure him as to bolster herself.

Zera stepped up beside them. "So, do we knock?"

Before Kreya could decide on an answer, the doors swung open. She tensed, ready for soldiers to spill out, but instead Grand Master Lorn emerged from the shadows with a hooded man beside him. Kreya knew instantly it was Eklor, though his face was hidden, but what she hadn't expected was that Lorn carried a small body, wrapped in linens.

Wordlessly, his face stiff, Lorn carried the body past the five heroes. The crowd shifted, also silent, and Kreya saw that up a small set of stairs was a pyre built on a marble pedestal.

She felt Zera's hand grip her wrist. Jentt already squeezed her other hand.

All of them had guessed who the small body was: Lorn's son.

Lorn laid the body gently on the pyre, as if laying him down to sleep in his own bed. Tenderly, he unwrapped the linens. Amurra gave a soft gasp-sob. Others behind them whispered. From the bits she gleaned, a few had guessed they'd been summoned to a funeral.

The tension leached out of the crowd, replaced by sympathy. Everyone respected Grand Master Lorn. Even if they didn't agree with all his policies, even if they didn't know him personally, they all respected the office, and all Vosians mourned the loss of a child.

But Kreya did not relax. Nor, from the grips of Zera and Jentt, did her friends. She watched Eklor. His head was bowed, hidden within the shadows of his hood, and his hands were clasped piously in front of him. The crowd hadn't yet guessed who he was. He stood a respectful distance behind Lorn as the grand master bent over his son's body and kissed his forehead. *Any second now*, she thought, *he could signal his army*. This funeral could turn into a massacre without any warning at all. It was a brilliant plan: promising to save Lorn's son would get him a front-row seat to a funeral guaranteed to be witnessed by dozens of Eklor's prime targets. Given the solemnity of the event, none of the attendees would be prepared to defend themselves. He could slaughter the leadership of the city, as well as decimate the ranks of the Bone Workers Guild, before anyone properly understood what was happening.

"Who will confirm my son's death?" Grand Master Lorn's voice was soft, but still it carried, sweeping across the crowd that had gathered.

The grand master of the trade guild, one of the most influential guilds in Vos, climbed the steps to the pyre. "I will confirm." She bent over the body; touched his forehead, neck, and wrist; and then stepped back.

Second, the grand master of agriculture presented himself. "I will confirm." He completed the ritual and then returned to the crowd.

One by one, ten of the highest masters of the Bone Workers Guild—all council members—also confirmed they'd serve as witnesses.

Kreya noticed a line of novice bone workers stretched from the doorway to the pyre. From within the shadows of the palace, a flame emerged. A novice carried it, passed to the next, and then he passed it to the next, and she to the next—hand to hand, until it reached Grand Master Lorn.

"Long have we believed this was the only way," Grand Master Lorn said.

In Kreya's ear, Zera whispered, "Do we stop him now?"

"Archers," Jentt whispered from her other side.

Kreya glanced up to see that city guards in black leather armor were mounted at the top of Grand Master Lorn's palace. All of them held bows, their arrows trained not on the crowd or searching out an unidentified threat. The arrows were aimed at the Five.

With speed talismans, they *might* be able to evade them. But she didn't doubt Lorn had anticipated that. He knew the only ones who might stop him were Kreya and her friends.

Lorn was prepared for them. As if they were the enemy. Not Eklor.

She looked back at the pyre and was certain that Eklor was looking directly at her, even though she couldn't see his face beyond his hood. She began to calculate the odds of reaching him before Lorn's security measures took her down.

He hadn't made a move, though. *What if the army isn't coming?* Kreya thought. *What if we're wrong? What if he was telling the truth?* But . . . Eklor couldn't have changed so drastically. You couldn't be a mass murderer one day and then the next day say "Sorry, my mistake." Except that it had been twenty-five years. She'd changed in that time.

"We have believed and we have burned and we have mourned, but I have learned that there is another way." Grand Master Lorn pivoted and threw the flaming torch behind him, over the expanse of nothingness between the mountains. It sailed into the sky, higher than it should have been able to for an ordinary torch thrown by an ordinary man.

Why all this theater? Kreya thought. *What does Eklor get out of this?*

Because he still hadn't revealed any hidden army. He hadn't even revealed himself.

He couldn't be planning to work the spell that Kreya had used on Jentt. It would require his giving up years of his own life, and he'd never do that. He was far too much of a narcissist.

Unless there was something he wanted badly enough in exchange. But *what?* The only thing that had ever driven Eklor was his conviction that the world owed him for every wrong, every slight, every accidental twist of fate, and every tragedy that befell him.

Kreya wished again that she'd succeeded in getting an audience with Eklor. Maybe she could have shaken out of him some clue as to his goal. If he wanted revenge against the Bone Workers Guild, this was the perfect opportunity: deny Lorn his child and then eliminate the masters, as well as the leadership of other guilds. Yet she wasn't sure that was what was happening here, and that made her even warier.

As the crowd around her gasped and whispered, Grand

Master Lorn stepped aside for Eklor to approach the pyre. He still did not remove his hood. He bent over the boy's body.

Kreya couldn't hear what he said, but she knew the words. She didn't see a knife, but she saw him pour a vial over bones and then press each bone one by one into the body. The bones he was using were too shattered and small to identify as human, though she knew they had to be. She wondered where he'd gotten his. *The plains, most likely.* Jentt had reported burnt bones, but like with the constructs, there was no way to be certain Eklor had destroyed all of them.

The whispers around her grew into shouts. The vast majority of the crowd didn't know what was going on, but they knew this was a violation of one of their most sacred rites. Yet no one moved to stop them—a bone maker was clearly manipulating the body, but he was not stealing from it. He was *giving* to it. No one knew what it meant.

Except Kreya.

She knew exactly what he was doing. She just couldn't believe it.

Again, Zera asked, "Do we stop him?"

Kreya shook her head. She felt as if frozen water had poured into her veins, displacing the blood. What she was seeing . . . It didn't make sense. She'd expected a trap—a battle at best, a massacre at worst. She hadn't expected *this.* A sacrifice by Eklor of his own future.

Eklor stepped back, and Lorn's son's mouth opened. He sucked in air. His chest filled and rose. The crowd fell silent. And the dead boy sat up.

Not a sound beyond the breathing of the crowd and the breathing of the boy.

"Who will confirm my son lives?" Grand Master Lorn asked, his voice booming across the fifth tier.

Hesitantly, the same men and women who had confirmed his death each stepped forward, one by one, and verified that the boy, impossibly, was alive.

"Papa?" the boy said, his voice small. Lorn enveloped him in his coat, embracing him, and then helped him climb down from the pyre. The boy clung to his father.

"You have witnessed a miracle," Grand Master Lorn said, addressing the crowd. Tears streamed down his cheeks. "And I present to you a second miracle: the bone worker who has achieved this. He was on the verge of discovering the secret of resurrection when the guild interrupted his efforts. In the clash, we destroyed the bodies of his wife and child. This act plunged him into rage and despair, and he sought revenge."

There were murmurs around Kreya—they didn't know who Lorn was talking about, but she did. She also knew that wasn't the story she'd been told about Eklor's past. He'd lost his family in a cable car accident. An accident, due to mechanical failure. He, in his grief and narcissism, had blamed the guild for what was merely the hand of fate.

Softly, Jentt said, "We were lied to."

"That doesn't excuse what he's done," Zera replied just as softly. "Nothing does. And besides, how do you know we aren't being lied to now?"

A valid point, Kreya thought.

Raising his voice to be heard above the rumbling crowd, Grand Master Lorn continued. "He knows now, though, that revenge was not the path he should have taken. And so, contrite and seeking redemption, he has returned to offer us a gift:

life beyond death, for ourselves and our loved ones. A second chance to all who deserve it."

He did it, she thought. *He really did it.* Eklor had given a portion of his own life to Lorn's son. She'd never imagined he was capable of such an act. The Eklor she'd known wasn't capable of that kind of self-sacrifice or empathy. She'd always believed he'd abandoned his research into resurrection magic because of the cost. Yet here he was, paying it.

Could it have been some kind of trick? Maybe the child hadn't been dead. Except the other masters had confirmed it . . . What if Eklor had somehow fooled them too? Or maybe there was some other explanation she hadn't thought of yet. A conspiracy? Some kind of mind manipulation? Smoke and mirrors?

So many possibilities, and yet the proof was here, now.

At Lorn's command, Eklor stepped up to the pyre again and pushed back his hood. Immortalized as the greatest evil ever embodied by a man, Eklor was instantly recognizable. His face had been carved into statues, vilified on murals, and transformed into theater masks.

"I seek forgiveness," Eklor said. "And I bring, to all of Vos, the gift of second life."

CHAPTER TWENTY-ONE

In the stunned silence, Grand Master Lorn shepherded his son and Eklor back into his palace, with the promise that more information would follow. As soon as the brass doors shut, the crowd outside exploded into chatter—awe, confusion, shock. It all swirled around her as Jentt tugged Kreya's hand.

He murmured in her ear, "We should leave."

Nodding, she let herself be led away from the pyre. But they only made it a few feet before the crowd closed around them. One older woman in a master's coat patted Jentt's arm. "You were dead, weren't you? But now you're alive again, too!"

"Just seriously injured," Jentt said. He flashed her a smile, and Kreya had to resist the urge to step in front of him, knives drawn. She felt prickles over her skin as the crowd pressed closer.

"How are you alive?" a man shouted.

"Coma," he supplied. "Totally unresponsive for years until one day, a miracle, I woke. It was amazing luck and great nursing care. Nothing to do with anything that happened here today."

Another bone worker pushed closer. "Who revived you? Was it Eklor?"

"You *were* dead," another said. "My uncle fought in that battle. He saw you fall."

"All of Vos mourned you!" another, a man in heavy finery, cried. "Did Eklor bring you back to life? Can he bring my wife back?"

Kreya and her friends clumped around Jentt and pushed through the crowd. Marso was shaking hard, and Kreya thought it had been a mistake to bring him. It had been a mistake for any of them to come at all.

"He was dead." The words spread through the crowd. "How is he alive? Did you bring him back? Do you know what Eklor knows? Is that why you returned now? Are you working with him?" And over and over: "Did Eklor bring him back?" until Kreya wanted to shout at them all to quit asking and leave them alone.

Before she could break, though, Zera did:

"Yes!" Zera shouted. "It was Eklor! Ask him!" She pointed to Lorn's palace, and the crowd, as if pushed by a giant hand, rotated and shoved toward the doors.

Kreya grabbed Zera. In a low voice, she demanded, "Why did you say that?"

"Because soon they'll learn *how* he did it," Zera said, also in a whisper. "They'll learn about the key ingredient. I'd far rather *he* were burned alive than you."

She couldn't argue with that. Still, she felt a tug of unease, giving credit to their enemy. They still didn't know what he truly wanted. Fame? He had that. Forgiveness? Eklor deserved to be arrested, tried, and convicted. You didn't kill hundreds, then turn around and say, "Oops!" But then again, with an ego the size of Eklor's, he could see forgiveness as possible.

Maybe this was his plan for changing his fate. Maybe he wanted to be granted a chance to return to civilization. Live a normal life. *Or maybe he wants to quit all bone work and become a traveling acrobat*, she thought. She had no way of knowing what his thinking was. The last time she'd encountered him was twenty-five years ago, and she hadn't understood him then. If only she could talk to him, maybe she could get some insight into what they were dealing with.

"Any ideas for getting in there?" Kreya asked, with a nod at the brass doors.

"Later. Right now, we need to get Jentt away from the crowd," Stran said. "Also Marso."

She weighed her odds of forcing her way into the palace and glanced again at the archers. They'd lowered their bows and were no longer focused on the Five. *We didn't do whatever they were afraid we'd do*, she thought. Did that mean they'd failed once more?

"Kreya, we need to go," Zera insisted. "Regroup. Replan. The show's over—"

The brass doors swung open. Caught by surprise, the crowd fell backward. A servant appeared. "Grand Master Lorn requests to speak with the leader of the Five Heroes of Vos, Master Bone Maker Kreya Odi Altriana."

Her friends flanked her. "Not alone!" Jentt said.

The servant frowned. "Only Master Kreya Odi Altriana."

"He harbors our enemy," Stran said. "We all come, or none."

The servant didn't move. "He is your guild master. He requests the presence of the bone maker Kreya Odi Altriana. You are sworn to obey your guild master. Failure to comply could result in fines, or the withdrawal of your bone worker license."

Kreya put her hand on Jentt's shoulder. "I'll be fine," she said softly. "Look at all the witnesses. If I go in and don't come out, Grand Master Lorn will answer for it."

"That's a 'what to do after you're dead' plan," Zera said. "Not an 'avoid dying' plan."

"He wants to talk," Kreya said. "I want to hear him explain. We've been wanting this—more information, some clue as to what Eklor plans." She looked at each of them. "In the meantime, keep searching for his army. I'll be back soon."

Zera flew forward and hugged her, and Kreya felt her slip two new talismans into her pant pockets as she whispered, "Speed and flight. Break a window and fly out of there, if you need to."

Kreya nodded.

The crowd parted for her to walk up to the brass doors. She glanced back to make sure her friends were safely away. They were still standing there, watching her, when the servant closed the brass doors with a soft clang.

"Follow me, please." The servant bowed and led the way down the hall. "Grand Master Lorn requests you leave your coat. He doesn't wish for there to be any misunderstandings. He knows emotions are fraught." He gestured toward a rack.

She briefly considered protesting, but she didn't. If this was her chance to gain information, she wasn't going to waste it. She also wasn't going to show fear. Reassuring herself that Zera's two talismans were safely hidden in her pants pockets, Kreya hung her coat on the rack.

Lorn might have been the grand master. He might have been housing her greatest enemy. But his agenda surely didn't include being accused of her murder and being separated from his newly resurrected son. She could count on his self-interest to protect her. *He wants to talk*, she told herself. She had no reason to think he meant her harm.

His guest, though—that was another matter.

She followed the servant past Lorn's office door to a polished silver door. He opened it and bowed. Kreya took a step inside and tried to ignore how hard and fast her heart was beating. *This isn't a battlefield*, she told herself. Her thumping pulse did not believe her.

She scanned the room first, checking for exits. One other door. One wide window, drapes open, with a view of mountains beyond. In the center of the room was a table with a teapot, steam curling out of it, and two teacups. Two upholstered chairs sat on either side of the table. One was occupied, though the person's back was to her.

"Grand Master Lorn?" She stepped into the tea room, and the servant closed the door behind him, leaving her alone with the grand master. "Congratulations on the return of your son. I know that must be a great relief and joy to you."

The man in the chair stood, and it wasn't the grand master. Eklor faced her.

She didn't let a hint of surprise show on her face. In fact, she wasn't certain she *was* surprised. She noted he wore his bone worker coat, while she'd been required to disrobe, and he was playing with a talisman in his right hand, spinning it between his fingers. Crossing the room, she positioned herself near the window. Every muscle was tense, every breath sharp.

"Join me for tea?" Eklor requested.

"Is it poisoned?"

"If I kill you, it will undermine everything I've achieved here." Eklor resumed his seat and poured tea in his cup and hers. He placed his talisman down to do so. "Everyone saw you enter. Everyone heard you summoned."

"Grand Master Lorn summoned me. Perhaps you seek to frame him for my murder?" She eyed the talisman, trying to decipher the carvings—not strength, not speed, not any one she was familiar with. If she knew what he intended, she could counter it.

"After I went through all the trouble of granting his dearest wish? Kreya, I know you believe me evil. At least do me the courtesy of also believing me logical." He added sugar to his tea and stirred, then picked his talisman back up.

Kreya sat carefully on the chair. She picked up the teacup, added sugar, and stirred. She didn't sip it, though. She wasn't stupid. Instead she set it back down on the saucer and studied Eklor. He looked well, especially for a man who should have been dead. "You expect me to believe you've reformed? I saw your army."

He sat back, spinning his talisman again. "There was no army."

She snorted.

"Only remnants left over from an old, nearly forgotten war. As your pet warriors saw, I destroyed them, as my first act of good faith."

"Is it good faith to threaten me with whatever that is?" She waved her hand at the talisman.

He quit fiddling with it. "Ahh, a nervous habit." Neither his voice nor his face betrayed any hint of nervousness. "My deepest apologies for making you uncomfortable."

"You still existing makes me uncomfortable," Kreya said. "You with a talisman makes me feel like slitting your throat and being done with it." Especially a talisman she didn't recognize. She wished Zera had come with her—she could have identified it.

With a smile, Eklor tucked it into one of his pockets. "Better?"

"Not entirely. You're here. How are you even alive?"

He wiggled his fingers. "Magic."

"Fuck you. How did you do it?"

"What did your lover tell the crowd? It was a miraculous recovery."

Kreya stood. "I'm not playing your games. If you won't answer my questions, we're done here."

He held up a hand. "No more games. Ask me another question. A different one. Those moments when I lay near death . . . they're painful for me to remember."

Fine. She had plenty of other questions. They could come back to that rather important one. Sitting again, she asked, "Is it true about your wife and child? Were you trying to bring them back?" She had long wondered why he had ventured down this line of forbidden research. And why he'd abandoned it. "We had been told you sought revenge because of a cable car accident."

He flinched, but his voice was still smooth and steady. "There was indeed an accident, but I reclaimed the bodies and was seeking to restore my loved ones. I was on the verge of success when my experimentation was discovered by the guild. I had been . . . less careful about concealing the source of my supplies than I thought I had been."

"Your murders were discovered." It was a guess, but knowing what she knew about him, she felt confident it was correct. He hadn't obtained bones the way she had, from the naturally dead. He'd sped the process along himself. "You're responsible for many deaths, Eklor. Grand Master Lorn might be grateful to you for his son's life, but that won't erase the crimes you've committed."

"I don't seek to avoid punishment," Eklor said. "But I do seek to redeem my soul before I face the great silence. I have done grievous harm, and if I can pay back even a fraction of what I owe to the people of Vos, then I have to try."

"How noble." She lifted the teacup to her lips, pretended to sip, and lowered it. If he was going to pretend they were having an earnest, honest conversation, she'd play along. "And what brought about this change of heart?"

"Time," he said simply. "My wife and daughter died in an accident, and I did the unthinkable in a bid to bring them back. When their bodies were destroyed by the guild before I could revive them, all I had left was hate and anger."

"Are you expecting me to feel sorry for you?"

"No. But I am expecting you to understand me."

The trouble was she *did*. He had done the unthinkable. *But so did I*, Kreya thought. After Jentt had been killed, she'd abandoned her friends in order to avenge him. And then later, she may not have murdered anyone to save Jentt, but she had broken the law again and again.

"You killed innocent people," Kreya said.

"Yes. But you crossed a line as well," Eklor said. "And you've been flouting the proof of that, bringing Jentt here to the city with you, allowing him to be seen in public. You don't believe you did anything wrong, and you don't regret what you did."

"You crossed a much more serious line. Mine was a taboo; yours was a *war crime*."

"Yes, I know." A hint of irritation colored his voice. He took a deep breath. Calmer, he said, "Let me spell this out for you. I committed horrible acts. I will die for them. But before I die, I want to do as much good as I can. It won't erase what I've done. I know that. But I feel I owe it to the world to try."

He sounded so earnest. Kreya looked into his eyes, the eyes

of the man who had killed her husband, and didn't know what to believe or what to feel. "You feel *guilt?*"

"Guilt and remorse."

"When?"

He blinked, confused. "What?"

"When did you start to feel guilt and remorse? Was it after the twentieth death? Or the hundredth? Was it after you were killed? After you'd finally faced the consequences of your actions? Or was it even later than that? You rebuilt your army, whether you deny that fact or not—so it must have been later. What did it?"

He didn't answer at first. Instead, he placed his teacup in his saucer, rose, and crossed to the window. *My exit,* she thought. She glanced at the silver door. With the speed talisman, she thought she could make it to the door while he was at the window, if she needed to.

Or with the speed talisman, she could run *toward* him instead. Break the window with his back and shoulders, and then release him midflight. She doubted he had one of Zera's special talismans, and it was a long way down to the mist-cloaked valley.

"It was a sunrise," Eklor said softly. "Like any other. After the war, I used to sleep beneath the tower, in the tunnels, but this one morning, I woke early and climbed out . . . The sun was just rising, and I thought, as I always did whenever I saw the sunrise, that here was another sunrise that my wife and daughter would never see. And the sun"—he raised his hand as if tracing a beam of light—"hit the bones in the meadow, and I realized they would never see the sunrise again either."

"Yeah, that's what happens when you kill people."

She saw his shoulders tense and then he took another breath. But he continued in the same urbane, slightly wounded voice. "Before then, I was so consumed with grief and rage that I couldn't see them as real people. I saw them only as the ones who had stolen my happiness. I was a wounded creature striking out with every weapon and bit of knowledge I possessed. I wanted to hurt those who hurt me. Make them suffer."

"You succeeded," she said. "Congratulations."

Eklor faced her again. "You are infuriating. I am baring my heart to you—"

"You're giving a speech. It's lovely. I like the bit about the sunrise on the bones. Nice touch." Rising, she again calculated the distance between the chair, him, and the window. But she knew she wouldn't do it. She'd promised Jentt she'd return to him alive, and attacking Eklor here and now . . . She couldn't guarantee she'd survive that. Plus there was so much she didn't understand. "What do you really want, Eklor? Why are we even having this conversation?"

"Because you are the only other person in Vos who knows how to perform a resurrection," Eklor said. "You know what it costs, and you know what ingredients it uses."

She didn't tell him that her team knew the "ingredients" as well. "Yes?"

"I plan to resurrect as many of the recently dead as are worthy," Eklor said. "There's little I can do about those whose bodies were burned, but those who lose their loved ones to illness, age, or accident from now on . . . I want to save as many of them as I can. But if the public knew how the magic is done, I would be stopped."

"You want me to keep quiet about the fact you use human bones," Kreya said. "And that they only gain as many years as you have to give?"

"I am hoping Grand Master Lorn will see fit to change the

law on the use of certain bones, but until then . . . yes. I invited you here to ask for your silence on this matter."

She was tempted to say no, run out the door, and scream the truth to all the masters and wealthy who no doubt still lingered outside the grand master's palace. But the fact was it could implicate her too. Zera had been right to worry about that. "Where are you going to get the human bones? I won't condone more murder, and I doubt you're going to have much luck sneaking around to steal them from city dwellers. They're far too careful with their pyres." She'd only succeeded because she stole from remote villages where there was plenty of room for escape.

And because she went to the forbidden zone. Which was when she understood.

"I brought the dead with me," Eklor said, as if seeing her dawning realization. He added quickly, "Not the army. As I told you, I destroyed all the bones that I used for my constructs—that was no lie. But the untouched bones of the noble dead, as many as I could bring . . . It felt fitting that they should go to grant new lives."

"Show me," Kreya commanded.

He hesitated, studying her as if reading her thoughts.

She kept her face implacable.

"Very well," he said at last.

He led her out of the room and to a passageway painted in subdued blues, with glints of diamonds. She'd never been to this part of the grand master's palace. It felt odd that the greatest traitor to the guild, the man known in legends and songs as the Betrayer of Vos, should be more familiar with Lorn's home than she was, but it wasn't the strangest thing of today. *The fact that I'm not stabbing him between the shoulder blades right now is the strangest.*

She remembered the rage and grief she'd felt after Jentt's death—and now that she'd learned it was the same kind of rage and grief that Eklor had felt, she didn't know what to think or how to feel.

She shuddered. *By the bones, I'm not the same as him.*

Reaching a nondescript wooden door, Kreya tensed as his hand dipped into a pocket, but he only drew out a key. He unlocked the door and swung it open. Inside was a storeroom. Scanning it, she saw there were no other exits or windows. She stayed in the doorway.

He went inside and unwrapped a bundle of velvet. Inside were human bones. He'd cleaned them, removing all the flesh so they'd be odorless and ready to use. There was no question that they were older bones—she could tell from the sun-bleached color and the fine cracks. She stared at them, nodded, and he rewrapped them and placed them carefully, respectfully, back on a shelf. The shelves were full of them. Returning to the hallway with her, Eklor relocked the door. She noticed he was again twirling the same unfamiliar talisman. So long as he didn't activate it, she could choose to ignore it. Perhaps it was a nervous habit.

"You killed my husband," Kreya said softly.

"I know."

"There is no apology you can make, no act of redemption, that will ever be enough for the pain you have caused me and the people of Vos. You know that, don't you? You can drain your life force giving it to others, but it won't erase what you did or undo the harm you caused."

"You are still angry, even though you have your husband back," Eklor said. In the dim passageway, his face was shadowed. She thought he looked sad, though. A strange look on his face.

She only ever pictured him contorted by rage. She hadn't ever known it was fueled by grief. "You don't want me to feel any relief from my guilt."

"I don't. But . . ." She thought of the bones that lay in that storeroom, wrapped in velvet as if they were precious treasures. "If you want to give what remains of your life to others so that they never feel what you—what you and I—felt, I won't stop you."

He exhaled, and she thought she saw the flicker of a smile touch his lips. It was gone before she could be certain. She never wanted to do or say anything that would cause him to smile or feel even the briefest hint of joy. But she meant what she'd said. If he wanted to use these bones and drain his life force to save others, that was a far better way for him to die than in a violent act of revenge.

"But if you're lying to me," Kreya said, "know that my team and I will tear you apart and burn every trace of you so that there is no chance of you ever coming back again."

"I understand." He held out his hand.

She didn't shake it. "How are you alive?" she asked again.

"I was never dead," he said. "Merely seriously injured. Eventually, with the aid of my constructs and with the use of medicines I'd stored in my tower, I recovered."

"Huh." She stared at him, trying to read his face for any lie. She didn't believe him, but she also didn't know what the truth could be—there was no way he could have resurrected himself. *We should have burned him then*, Kreya thought. "And your army?"

"I told you—there was no new army, only the remains of the old, and I destroyed them all thoroughly," he said. "After one of my constructs harmed Stran, I wanted no chance of their resurrection. I wished I'd destroyed them sooner, before any of my creations could hurt anyone."

"You expect me to believe you."

"I don't," he said, and she could read nothing but honesty in his eyes. He was spinning the talisman again. Still hadn't activated it. "I expect you and your team to keep searching. But I know you will find nothing, because there's nothing to find. And eventually, I hope you will come to believe me. I *am* a changed man."

"We'll see," Kreya said.

With a bow, he walked away from her. She watched him until he disappeared around a corner, and then she returned to the main hall with the massive carved pillars, retrieved her coat, and walked out into the sunlight. She answered no questions and spoke to no one until she reached Zera's palace.

Her team rushed forward as soon as she walked inside. "You're alive! Did you see Eklor? Did he hurt you?" "What did Lorn want? Did he have an explanation?" "Did you kill Eklor? Half-hoping you didn't and half-hoping you did." "What did you learn?" "You should never have gone in alone. Was it worth the risk?" "What's his plan? What does he want?"

Kreya looked at her friends. Really looked at them. Marso, his face anxious, his body skeletally thin, his hair escaping the braids that Zera had forced it into. He still seemed so fragile, as if wind would shatter him, but he was coherent now, improving every day. Stran had his arm around Amurra. The years hadn't shrunk his great heart, only expanded it. Zera, her face painted and her body bejeweled, looked the same as she had when Kreya had intruded on the life she'd built, but Kreya knew she wasn't the same. *She forgave me*, Kreya thought. Zera may not have said it in so many words, but she'd shown it again and again by staying with them and by being here now. They were like sisters again, something she had thought wouldn't happen.

And then there was Jentt.

Eklor was right. She had gotten her husband back. Eklor had never gotten that chance. It didn't excuse what he'd done, but . . . For the first time ever, she thought perhaps she understood better what had happened and why.

If she understood the past, could she begin to let it go?

All of her friends were here, now, changed but here. *Maybe it's time for me to live in the present too. And the future.* "I spoke with Eklor," Kreya said. She described everything he had told her and shown her. Finishing, she said, "He wants a chance at redemption. I think we should give it to him."

CHAPTER TWENTY-TWO

That's a fucking terrible idea."

Zera could not believe what had just come out of Kreya's mouth. She must have fallen and hit her head. Or eaten a hallucinogenic mushroom and was experiencing delusions. Or maybe she'd finally lost it.

Kreya defended herself. "I am not saying forgive him. Or trust him."

"Good. Because that's not happening." Zera put her hands on her hips. "No more going off to chat with genocidal maniacs without supervision. You come back with your brain messed up." She was relieved when her friends nodded their agreement. They may have all reverted to following Kreya's lead, but at least there were limits.

Concerned, Jentt took Kreya's hands in his. "What did he say to you? What could he have possibly said to cause this change of heart?"

"He pointed out that he crossed a line. Many, many lines. But I've crossed them too." She drew his hands to her lips, kissed them, and then released them. "If he can be redeemed even a little, if someone so broken and twisted can find some measure of forgiveness and peace, maybe I can as well."

Jentt cradled her face lovingly, and Zera contemplated vomiting on their shoes. Instead, she shouldered between them. "Okay, false equivalence. What you did"—she waved her hand expressively at Jentt—"is in no way the same as what the Betrayer of Vos did."

"She's right," Amurra said.

Zera glanced at her, surprised she'd volunteer an opinion. It was obvious the woman was intimidated by Kreya, though she had relaxed a bit recently. It was nice to hear her speaking up, especially to speak sensibly.

"You acted out of love," Amurra continued. "He was fueled by hate."

"Yep," Zera agreed, nodding vigorously and pointing. "That."

"He'd lost his wife and daughter," Kreya said. "When I lost Jentt, I lost my mind. I abandoned all of you on the field, wrecked our plan, and chased after Eklor by myself."

Rolling her eyes, Zera groaned dramatically. "Not. The. Same. This is absurd. He's playing you. Can't believe you fell for it."

Softly, Marso said, "People can change. Heroes can stop being heroes. Villains can stop being villains." It was obvious he was talking about himself as well as Eklor.

Zera rolled her eyes at him too. "You know, the last time we saved the world, you people didn't have so many issues." She'd imagined reuniting the old team dozens of times, but she'd never once imagined it would be so annoying. Seriously, defending Eklor? *Eklor?* It was like . . . like . . . she couldn't think of a comparison; that was how absurd it was.

With a sad smile, Kreya said, "That's just it, Zera. Maybe the world doesn't need saving this time. Maybe we do. We deserve a future beyond Eklor." She turned to Marso. "Think of it: You don't have to be a bone reader anymore. You can declare that part of your life done and pursue whatever you want."

He fidgeted. "But if I'm not a bone reader, who am I?"

"You could discover that," Kreya said. "You could travel."

Marso shuddered.

"Okay—how about a career in the arts? You've liked coordinating with artists and theater troops in Cerre. That could be a future to explore." She turned to Stran and Amurra. "And you have a future to return to, one that you already built." To Zera: "You as well. You've built a life here. Let Grand Master Lorn handle Eklor. He's as much as said it isn't our concern anymore. Maybe we're seeing problems that don't exist."

Zera stared at her old friend for a long moment. At last, she said, "That's bullshit. You need to get yourself together and quit letting genocidal maniacs mess with your mind. You already tried dumping this problem on someone else's lap. Remember how you had this lovely epiphany that that was wrong? Nothing has changed since then. *Nothing*." To emphasize her utter disgust at Kreya's idiocy, she walked out the door.

She instantly felt silly for stalking out of her own house. But she was also convinced she was right. Yes, people could change. Yes, people could seek forgiveness and redemption. Blah blah blah. But not everyone. Some got worse. She was willing to stake a lot on the conviction that Eklor was firmly in the "got worse" category.

After all, she'd heard him laugh on the plains as his soldiers chased them. How could Kreya have forgotten that? *She wants to forget*, Zera thought. *She wants there to be no threat, for this all to be over, for her to have her happily-ever-after where she can ride off guilt-free and responsibility-free with Jentt into the sunset.*

"Arrrgh!" she shrieked out loud.

A small crowd of voyeurs beyond her yard gawked at her.

"Shoo," she told them. "Hero stuff going on here."

"Master Zera?" one called. "Did you see the miracle on the pyre? Is it true that Grand Master Lorn's son died and now lives again?"

"Go ask him," Zera told him.

Because certainly no one here knew what was going on.

SHE'LL COME AROUND, KREYA THOUGHT, ONCE *nothing disastrous happens. Or she'll revel in saying "I told you so" if it does.* Either way, Kreya didn't intend to relax her guard completely. She wasn't going to recall her constructs or ask Jentt and Stran to stop searching for signs of Eklor's army. If Eklor betrayed her, she wasn't going to be caught by surprise.

But she *was* going to allow herself a moment of peace.

She turned to Jentt. "Have dinner with me?"

He kissed the back of her hand. "Of course."

She toyed with the idea of visiting one of their favorite restaurants, if any were still in business after all these years, but in the end decided it wouldn't be private enough. Not with the public so interested in the "miracle of the pyre" or whatever they were calling it. Bringing Jentt out into the open wouldn't be wise.

So she talked with several of Zera's servants. As she suspected, they had zero problem with preparing an elaborate dinner—apparently, what Kreya described as a gourmet meal was just an ordinary snack for Zera. After confirming the menu, Kreya retreated to her room to dress. Again, she asked a servant for assistance. A few moments later, the man brought her a silk dress, the kind she'd sworn off, then bowed and retreated.

Holding the dress up to the light, she twisted it. It shimmered, forest green and sky blue. Minuscule diamonds had been sewn into the hem, delicately, so as not to tug on the silk.

She shed her bone worker coat, hanging it by the door, close just in case, but still separate from her. She felt fifty pounds lighter without it. Changing into the silk dress, she let it flow around her, along with the memories of who she had been long ago, the last time she'd worn silk. This time, she found she could bear the memories.

Just one moment of peace, Kreya thought. She might have been deluding herself into thinking she'd have more, but she wanted this one.

Crossing to her hanging coat, Kreya fished in one of the pockets and took out one of her rag doll constructs. It had rolled itself into a tight ball and was, if such a term could be applied to a nonliving creation like this, asleep. "Are you okay?" she asked it.

Unrolling, it looked up at her, and Kreya would have sworn it looked happy, though she hadn't designed the rag doll to show emotion.

"It's good to see you too," she told it. "Jentt and I are going to be spending the evening together. Will you stand guard for us? Let us know if we're about to be murdered."

It chirped as if it understood.

She retrieved the other two rag dolls. After she instructed them all, they chittered to one another in their singsong made-up language. "We'll be on the balcony," she told them.

They followed her, tumbling out of her room and down the hallway, to Zera's infamous balcony. One doll scurried out, climbing a trellis onto the roof, while another ducked within a potted plant. The third draped itself over the edge, disappearing from view. She was certain it was clinging beneath. She hoped

Jentt wouldn't mind their chaperones. She felt better knowing they were there. *I'm not naïve*, she thought. *I'm hopeful. And tired of living with fear and sorrow.* After everything, she deserved this, didn't she?

Walking out on the balcony, Kreya admired the view. Night had fallen while she'd prepared, and the mountains were cloaked in stars. Three peaks were overlapping shadows that merged into pure darkness below. She walked to the edge. The lack of edge didn't bother Kreya. Lifting her arms to her sides, as if she were a bird about to take flight, she felt the night breeze caress her. The silk whispered around her.

"You remember the first time I kissed you?" Jentt's voice, behind her.

Kreya closed her eyes and tilted her head back, breathing in the night air. "*I* kissed *you.*"

"Sure, for our first kiss. But by the fifth, I'd figured out that you might be interested in me." She heard his footsteps behind her and then felt his arms wrap around her. His breath was warm on her neck, and she leaned against his torso. She lowered her arms to rest them on top of his. "Our fifth kiss, the first time *I* kissed *you,* we were on top of a mountain."

Kreya smiled. "That doesn't narrow it down."

"The very top. You'd wanted a view."

She remembered. "For strategic purposes. As I recall, you complained the entire climb because you hadn't worn thick enough socks."

"'Come for a walk with me,' you said. You left out the fact the walk would be near vertical up an ice floe. I used up a third of a steadiness talisman."

She twisted her neck to see his face. "You did? You said you didn't need any talismans."

"I was lying to impress you. Were you impressed?"

Kreya laughed. "Very," she lied.

"Do we need to talk only about the past?" Jentt asked. "Or do we dare talk about the future? Our future?"

The future. *Our future*. She had imagined it a thousand times, but they'd never spoken those dreams out loud, when they'd lived in stolen bits of time. The future felt too fragile, as if making plans would shatter any chance at happiness. Now, though, did she dare?

Before she could answer, a servant cleared his throat from the doorway. He held a covered tray. A second servant carried a crystal pitcher filled with tangerine-colored liquid. Neither ventured onto the balcony.

Kreya and Jentt crossed to them and thanked them, before carrying their dinner and drinks to the table in the middle of the balcony. Bowing, the servants retreated, obviously relieved not to be required to set foot on the open balcony. Kreya and Jentt sat. He uncovered the dishes, while she poured their drinks into spiral flute glasses.

Both of them stared quizzically at their plates. On each was a tiny . . . Well, it looked like a squishy white square. Jentt poked it with a fork. It was framed by curls of carrot. "Vegetable, animal, or mineral?" he asked.

"It sounded like a kind of fish? I asked for an appetizer appropriate to the night air. Probably should have been more specific."

Jentt began, "Do you remember—"

Kreya cut him off. "We can talk about our future."

He smiled. "If Eklor gave you hope for that, then I'm grateful to him."

"We aren't talking about him." She sliced the squishy square, and it collapsed under her knife, spronging back to its original height as soon as she was done.

"Fair enough. What do you think about traveling?"

"Where to?" She stabbed half the square with her fork, lifted it, and examined it. It didn't smell like fish. It smelled like herbs and vaguely of soap. She wondered if they'd mistakenly served them homemade soap.

"Everywhere."

She liked the sound of that. "Are you waiting for me to try it first?"

"Together?" he suggested.

Together, they popped a slice of soaplike fish into their mouths. Together, they spat it out into their napkins and washed out the taste with their tangerine-flavored drinks. They laughed, and they ate the other courses while they talked about all the places they'd love to see someday and all the things they'd love to do, if they were given the chance.

Silently, the rag doll constructs kept watch through the night.

CHAPTER TWENTY-THREE

Zera flopped onto a couch in her workroom, adjacent to her bedchamber. Beside her, Guine strummed on his harp. "You seem unhappy," he said.

"No shit."

"Tell me." He played an arpeggio that should have calmed her nerves but instead made her feel like chewing on a pillow with all her excess frustration. "Perhaps talking it out will help."

"Definitely not. How about you strip off your clothes and then mine and make me think about anything but how much I'd like to knock sense into Kreya's thick head?"

He smiled but didn't move. "You don't want a distraction."

"Oh? You're the expert on what I want?"

"Yes," he said calmly.

Okay, I'll bite. She rolled onto her side to study him. She didn't think he loved her, not truly, but maybe he *knew* her. *And maybe that's better.* "What do I want?"

"Answers," he said.

Huh. She hadn't expected him to be quite so on-the-nose, instantly right. But that was exactly what she needed. "You're right. Thank you, Guine." She'd never been the type to mope, and now wasn't the time to start. "Gather everyone. Not my

old team—they're too busy being idiots. Summon our friends."
Getting to her feet, she proceeded to pace impatiently while
Guine stuffed all of her current followers into the suddenly-not-
as-spacious room.

It only took a few minutes until the room was full to bursting. She stood up on one of her stools to be heard, holding on to
Guine's hand to stay steady. It wouldn't do to fall off the stool.

All of her followers looked up at her adoringly. She was
pleased she recognized the majority of them. She gave them her
most charming smile.

"You all delight in gossip, don't you?"

A few tittered. A few looked concerned.

"Of course you do," Zera said. "We all do. It's human nature to be curious. Well, we have the opportunity to delve into
the juiciest bit of gossip going on right now. I assume you've all
heard the rumors of the 'miracle of the pyre'? Eklor has offered
to extend that miracle to others. I want to know who he's offering it to and if he's delivering. Lurk around the grand master's palace. Let me know who comes and goes. Pull whatever
strings you can to learn who is benefiting and who isn't from
Eklor's presence." She thought of one specific request. "And
get me a list of the recently dead. We can start there, with
the hospital, with the mortuary. Especially keep an eye out for
any recent dead with politically powerful relatives, but let's be
thorough. I want to know who that asshole plans to revive next
and what he might gain from it."

She dismissed them, all but Guine.

He stroked her multicolored hair. "You still seem tense."

She gave him a flat look.

He quit petting her. "Understandably tense."

"I don't trust Eklor. And now I'm not sure I trust Kreya, at least when it comes to this. He's up to more than 'redemption,' and I don't know what it is or how he plans to do whatever it is. But whatever he plans, I don't want it happening in my city to people I care about."

Guine smiled. "Like me, I hope?"

She didn't want to smile, but he looked so charmingly sweet that she couldn't help it. "Yes, like you. Now scoot. Get me that list of the dead."

He headed for the door. "Most lovers request chocolate or flowers . . ."

"Scoot!"

MARSO COULDN'T CONSIDER ANY FUTURE WHILE Eklor was sinking his teeth into the throat of the city. He tried—he desperately tried—to imagine a life without fear of him, but his brain stuttered to a halt.

When everyone dispersed, he wandered the lush halls of Zera's palace. He'd always seen himself as a bone reader. Before he'd even heard Eklor's name, he'd known this was his destiny: to read the shifting shadows of possibilities and reveal the truth.

Surely, that wasn't over.

He wasn't done.

But he felt shredded, as if he were wisps of himself. *Maybe Kreya is right*, Marso thought. *Maybe I need to find a new way to be.*

But not until Eklor was gone.

After an hour of fruitless pacing, his feet took him to Stran's door. He didn't know what his old friend could do, but he knew he didn't want to be alone with his thoughts. It was too tempting to try to drown them. Safer to be with another. He knocked.

Stran's wife, Amurra, opened the door. "Marso? Is everything okay?"

Yes. No. It hadn't been okay in a very long time, and it wasn't okay now, but he was trying. *Look at me, trying.* "Is Stran here?"

"He went out again to search for any traces of Eklor's army." She widened the door. "Do you want to come in?" He saw she'd been having tea. A half-eaten sandwich lay on a plate.

"I don't want to bother you."

She smiled, her cheeks dimpling. "No bother. I'd like the company."

He came in and stood awkwardly in and her Stran's room. It was a converted music room, with instruments on the walls and several chairs for an audience—the chairs had been stacked in one corner to make room for Stran and Amurra to sleep and live while they were in Cerre.

Sitting at a tiny table, Amurra poured tea into a second cup. "You look like you need to talk. Come. Sit. I feel like I haven't gotten a chance to get to know you yet."

"I feel the same way about myself right now."

She nodded sympathetically. As she did, he eyed the chair and the tea and knew, with more certainty than he'd known anything in weeks, that he did *not* want to talk. "I want to read the bones again. But . . . I don't want to, too."

She nodded again, as if this were a perfectly normal thing to say. "I have to confess that I've never been clear on what it means to 'read the bones.' You toss them down and mist appears? Poof? And images within it? How does that work?"

"It . . . uh, has to do with your connection to the bones. You, well, activate them. Like how you activate a talisman. But you do it with a question, not a command."

Amurra clasped her hands together. "Can you teach me?"

"I . . ." He'd never taught anyone. "It requires innate power, to summon the mist. Unlike bone wizardry or bone making, which are more skills. And art. They're art too."

"Pretend I have it, the innate magic. Walk me through what I'd do to read bones." Leaving her tea, she moved to sit cross-legged on the floor beside a marble and gold hearth. "You don't have to read them yourself. Just demonstrate for me what you would do if you were to read them."

Marso hesitated.

"Don't read. Just teach."

He . . . he could do that.

Marso dropped to the floor across from her. The carpet was plush and soft. He wasn't sure why Amurra would want to learn if she didn't have power, but it was nice to have something to think about that wasn't dire and serious. He drew a handful of chicken bones from one of his pockets. "First, you need to introduce yourself to the bones."

He held them out, but she folded her hands. "Show me?"

Feeling a bit silly, he lifted the bones to his lips so they'd feel his breath. "I am Marso of Vos. I am . . . broken inside. And . . ." He tried to think of what else to tell the bones, to imagine he'd never held them before. "I like chocolate. And the sound of wind in the pine trees. I once danced naked in a waterfall."

"Only once?" Amurra teased.

It was commonly thought to be lucky to dance naked in a waterfall. "Did you do it more?"

"I have three children," she said. "I danced for luck before every birth. What else do you need to tell the bones?"

"The more they know, the better they'll respond to you. But these bones already know me." He tried to hold them out to her again.

Gently, she curled her hands around his and pushed the bones back toward him. "Tell them something new about you. Something from today. Or this week."

He hesitated, but she was smiling brightly and innocently at him. So he told the bones what Zera's palace looked like, what the city of Cerre smelled like. He told them how he'd felt in the crowd outside the grand master's palace and how he'd felt seeing Eklor again. He told them about what Kreya had said, only an hour ago, and how he didn't need to be a bone reader anymore but that was scary because he didn't know any other way to be. He forgot that Amurra was there and just talked.

When he quieted, she said, "Now what?"

Startled, he flinched.

"If you were a new bone reader, what would be the next thing you'd do?"

"An experienced bone reader opens himself up to the bones. And a corrupt one tries to manipulate them. That is the line one must never cross. That's the line I thought I'd crossed, the line Grand Master Lorn said I'd crossed. But I didn't. Because Eklor lives. I should have trusted . . ." He trailed off, caught up in the tangle of what could have been.

"Pretend none of that ever happened," she said. "Pretend you've never done this before. You're a new bone reader, and it's your first time reading the bones."

His hands shook. He knew what the first step was: throw the bones. But he couldn't predict what would follow, what he'd see.

"Would you like me to do it with you?" Amurra asked.

He nodded.

She closed her hands around his again and together they dropped the chicken bones between them, on the plush carpet.

They scattered, tumbling together. Marso saw them and then squeezed his eyes shut before the visions could come.

"A novice would ask a single question," Marso said. "Instead of keeping himself or herself open to the visions." He felt as if he were humming. Every bit of him was urging him to open his eyes, open himself, look at the bones, see what they wanted to tell him.

"Ask as if you were a novice," Amurra coaxed. "One question."

"Is Kreya right?" he asked. He tried again, making the question even more specific. "Can we trust Eklor to not intend harm?"

Opening his eyes, he saw the mist rise over the bones. Images blazed in his mind, mirrored in the mist: a body rose, and another fell. A body rose, and another fell. A body rose, and . . . He swam in the vision, in its simplicity.

One died, and another lived.

He wondered what else he could see, who the bodies were—and the images piled onto him faster than he could see, and he was back on the plain and then in the fountain and here in the palace and back . . . until he felt as if he were ripping into pieces, and a scream burst out of his lips.

He felt hands over his eyes. Not his mouth. Just his eyes.

And the images went away.

He quit screaming.

She removed her hands, and he squeezed his eyes shut.

"Once I was picking apples out in our orchard," Amurra said conversationally, as if she hadn't just been confronted by a screaming man and a cascade of chaotic images, "and I thought some of the best apples, the ripest and juiciest, were on the highest branches. I'd been picking apples all my life. I've climbed hundreds of trees. I thought nothing of it as I pushed myself up into the branches. I plucked an apple—and I don't know what happened, but I slipped. I fell through the branches, and I hit the ground hard. My hip broke. My ankle twisted. My wrist snapped. I'd never been in so much pain in my life. More than that, I was alone. Out in the orchard, and no one was around. It was the worst feeling I'd ever experienced.

"Soon, though, Stran found me. He carried me back, so gentle for such a big man, and nursed me back to health. It took months before everything healed, and I still feel a twinge in my hip sometimes if I twist the wrong way. But the hardest part was learning how to climb trees again. I had to do it step by step, as if I'd never done it before. I'd never had a fear of climbing trees before, so first I had to learn to conquer that."

"You . . . were helping me. On purpose." He opened his eyes. On the carpet, the bones had been swept away, out of sight. Amurra had them cupped in her hands where he couldn't read them. She was looking at him with the kind of concern he remembered seeing on his mother's face, every time he did something that scared her.

"You said you wanted to read the bones," she said. "Did I help?"

"Yes." He thought of the vision he'd seen—the clear one, before all the shadows of his fears had destroyed everything. He could still do this. "I want to try again."

ZERA'S PEOPLE BROUGHT HER WORD:

He'd saved six more lives.

Six more miracles.

There's a line at the guild for his services.

Yay. Hooray. Cue the parades.

While the people of Cerre celebrated, Zera pored over gossip papers, news reports, and every scrap of information she could find that might connect the "miracles" to Eklor. It was all very unpleasant and not at all how she wanted to spend her days, but if Kreya was going to be unreasonable, then Zera had no choice. Yet, so far, she couldn't find anything the six had in common with either each other or the corrupt bone maker. Her followers had collected dozens of rumors and anecdotes. All of them led nowhere.

She was glaring at yet another report when Marso knocked tentatively on her open door. Waving him in, she put down the latest bit of vapid gossip, detailing what fashion miracle number three wore, as if that mattered to a genocidal monster like Eklor.

"You look better," she observed.

Color in his cheeks. Clothes that didn't hang off his skeletal frame. It had undoubtedly helped that he'd been eating and sleeping with more regularity. *Nice to see our reunion has made at least one of us happier,* Zera thought.

"You look worse," Marso said.

She grimaced, though she couldn't argue with that. "Lack of sex."

"I can't help you there, but . . ." He hesitated. Behind him, Amurra popped her head up over his shoulder and whispered, "Go on, tell her what you saw."

That is one tiny woman, if she can hide behind Marso.

Zera waved them inside and shooed them onto couches. She signaled to one of her followers to fetch refreshments and wondered when she'd last eaten. She remembered Guine coaxing her into slurping down some whipped duck liver, but that could have been hours ago.

Marso studied his hands as if he'd written the words he wanted to say on his palms. She peeked but they were clean. Glancing at the report again, she waited until Marso spoke.

He didn't, though. Instead Amurra did. "He's been reading the bones."

"A little," Marso said. "Not like I used to."

"But regularly," Amurra said.

"Good for you?" Zera tried to sound encouraging, though she didn't know why Marso wasn't just spitting it out. She flipped to a new report. "Any chance you found our stray enemy army?"

He hung his head. "Not that. But: one dies and another lives."

She put down her papers. "What do you mean?"

"I don't know what it means. But I see the same vision over and over, with every question about Eklor and his miracles: one dies and another lives."

Zera digested this.

"I know I'm new to bone magic," Amurra said hesitantly, "but I watched him do his readings, saw the images in the smoke, and it seems to me there's a clear interpretation. If we could pair it with evidence . . ."

"Yes," Zera agreed. She dug into the piles on her desk. In seconds, she'd located a list of the dead. "Do we know exactly the time of each resurrection?" When Amurra and Marso were silent, she raised her voice. "Guine!"

He entered as if he'd been lurking just outside, which he might have been.

"Exact times of Eklor's 'miracles,' please?"

He joined her at the desk. Sorting through her notes, they compiled a list of the six new resurrections, plus Lorn's son. Zera and Guine then pored through the lists from the hospital and mortuaries.

"I think—" Amurra began.

"Shhh," both Zera and Guine said.

Zera handed him a page. "Look at this." He handed her one. "You look at this." They traded pages back and forth until they had found matches for every single time.

For each resurrection, there was a death recorded at the same exact time.

All were from the same location: the hospital on the third tier, all from the recovery wing, a mix of men and women in their early twenties. "Look at the causes of death." Zera waved the papers in front of Guine's nose. "'Inconclusive.' 'Heart attack.' 'Unknown.' Another 'heart attack.'"

He intercepted the papers. "All the dead were young."

"Young and not hospitalized for anything that should have been fatal. No prior histories of heart problems. None were under any kind of special near-death watch. You can't convince me this is a coincidence: at the exact time Eklor works his spell, a hospital patient, one who shouldn't have been in danger of dying, dies."

Marso exhaled a loud breath. "One dies and another lives."

"It's not proof enough for Lorn," Zera said. "But it's proof enough for me. Eklor hasn't repented.

"He's killing again."

AT DAWN, KREYA WOKE TANGLED IN JENTT'S ARMS. With her head on his chest, she listened to him breathe. It was the most beautiful sound in the world. So alive.

She matched her breathing to his. He smelled like a mix of soap and sweat, sweet and sour and woodsy and distinctively *him.* She wasn't sure why she'd woken so early when they'd fallen asleep so late, but she was grateful for the extra moments.

Every moment still felt stolen. She knew it shouldn't—that had been the entire point of the last resurrection spell and everything she had gone through all these years to reach that point—but every time she looked at him, it seemed like a new miracle. She couldn't shake the memory of him gray and lifeless, wrapped in linen strips. She'd gotten her second chance, and she was determined not to waste it by feeling as if she didn't deserve it.

She heard a *click-click* from near the window. The last of her constructs—the only one that hadn't reported in yet—had returned. That must have been what woke her.

She felt her breath seize in her throat.

Please, no army. She wasn't ready for this to end yet. She wanted to go on pretending that she could have peace—that her happiness wasn't an illusion.

Careful not to wake Jentt, Kreya slipped out of his embrace. She crossed the room and knelt beside the construct. It was clogged with reddish-brown dust, picked up from the caves within the mountains. Grabbing a towel, she wiped down its gears. This particular construct looked like a mechanical tree squirrel. "Did you find something, little one?" she whispered.

Say no, she thought at it.

It shook its head.

Relief flooded through her. *Maybe there is no army.*

Maybe we get a future after all.

"Have you finished searching the caves?" she asked. She'd assigned each of them a portion of the tunnels that burrowed through the mountain, and this construct had the final unexplored region.

It nodded.

She smiled at it. "Excellent work. You've done well."

Straightening slightly, it seemed proud of itself.

"You can rest now. You deserve it."

It shook its head. It didn't want to rest.

"Everything has been searched," Kreya said. "Jentt and Stran have explored the forest around the city, you and your brethren have looked below the city, and there's nowhere to hide an entire army within the city." It seemed as if Eklor had told the truth: there was no army. He'd destroyed it, as he'd said. She'd let paranoia fuel her convictions.

The construct drooped as if disappointed. She'd built it to search. She wasn't allowing it to be itself if she forced it to stop. "You want to search more?" she asked.

It perked up, waving its metal tail at her enthusiastically. Carrying it to the window, she looked out at the city, the mountains, the valley below . . .

She hadn't considered the valley. A tight knot seized her stomach. Far below, she could see a hint of mists. The mists were thick enough to hide an army, and Eklor could have taken his monstrosities from the plain through the valleys to below Cerre.

Just because no one ever traveled through the mists didn't mean it was impossible. After all, they'd done it themselves to reach Eklor. He could have had the same idea. "How about you search the valley, within the mists?" she said, with fake cheer in her voice. "Nothing there would be interested in eating you. You're much too crunchy." She patted its metal body. "Would that make you happy, to search more?"

It nodded, clicked at her, and then waddled out the window. She followed it, watching it climb down the side of Zera's palace.

Please let me be wrong. She hated that her imagination was so good at supplying new horrible possibilities. It was highly unlikely an army could have survived passage through the deadly valley. Made of partial flesh, Eklor's soldiers would have drawn too many predators. Unless Eklor took steps to keep them concealed. Which he couldn't have, right?

But he shouldn't have been alive, either. Yet here he was.

"It won't find anything," she said out loud, as both a promise and a prayer.

Behind her, from the bed, Jentt said, "It's good to be thorough."

"Yes, but I'm not convinced it's healthy to be paranoid. The war is over, and Eklor isn't our problem anymore. He's Grand Master Lorn's. And Grand Master Lorn made it clear he doesn't want our help. Or our paranoia."

"You want to leave the city now, then? Say we're done, and begin our traveling?"

She couldn't tell from his voice whether he was hopeful or critical. His tone was bland, as if he had only a passing interest in her answer. Returning to bed, she climbed in with him. "Maybe we could. Maybe it's time." Except it didn't seem right to leave yet, while Eklor still lived. He had to expire soon, given the rate at which he was doling out his future years, and then she'd finally feel free. "Soon," she said. "Let's let the construct search the mists first, just to be sure."

He kissed her forehead. "Whatever you think is best."

Yet he sounded relieved. She pushed back, her hands on his bare chest. "Do you think I'm being selfish, spending time with you instead of pounding on the grand master's door, demanding a report on Eklor's every move?"

Jentt hesitated for the barest of seconds—*He's going to say*

yes, she thought—but instead he said: "If you're selfish, so am I."
Lifting one of her hands, he kissed her knuckles. "I've loved this
time with you. Vast improvement over being dead." He hooked
his other arm around her and pulled her closer so she could feel
the hardness between his legs. "Let me demonstrate again how
much of an improvement it is."

She laughed and returned his kisses.

Still, a worm of doubt twisted inside her: the army could be
in the valley, Eklor could still be planning to destroy the guild,
and the Five could be the only ones with both the awareness
and the experience to stop him. Or it could be all in her head.
And memories.

A brisk knock sounded on the door, and they broke apart.

"Clothe yourselves," Zera demanded as she opened the door.
"It's all of us, and we need to talk." She barged in, followed by
Stran, Amurra, and Marso.

For a brief instant, Kreya was annoyed, but that faded fast.
For all of them to be here so early, something had to be wrong.
She swung herself out of bed as Jentt wrapped a sheet around his
waist and sat up. She noticed the others were all dressed, though
they could have been wearing the same clothes as last night. She
kept her voice calm and even, despite the way her heart rate had
increased. "You have my attention. Talk."

"There are a lot of unknowns," Zera began, "but here is what
we *do* know. Eklor has resurrected eight people, the latest revival
occurring this morning—"

Kreya cut her off. "Eight?"

That was impossible. Even if his body had another fifty
years left of life in it, how could he have resurrected so many?
Unless he was only giving a few years to each. Or less. *That's
possible*, she thought. He'd said he was giving them new life,

but he could have been lying about the *length* of that new life. "Sorry. Continue," she said.

"We believe that for every person he saves, he's murdering another." Zera waved papers in the air. "The dates and times of the resurrections and deaths line up exactly."

Amurra gently pushed Marso forward. "Tell them what you saw."

"I can confirm the connection," Marso said. He was trembling as he spoke, his eyes flitting back and forth as if he wanted to flee to the comfort of a fountain. "I read it in the bones. For every life Eklor gives, he's taking another."

A few decades ago, Kreya would have believed him without question, but she'd seen what happened when he tried to read the bones now. "You read this?"

"I . . . It's not the same as it was. I can't . . . But I can answer a single question. Amurra helped me. I'm not . . . healed . . . but I'm better. And Eklor is killing to heal."

"All the murders—yeah, I'm calling them that, even though they're recorded as natural," Zera said, "happened in the hospital on the third tier."

"What we don't know is *why* he's killing them," Amurra said.

"Bones?" Stran suggested. "Could he be using their bones for the resurrections and counting on no one making the connection?"

"Except he'd need the bones *before* the spell, which should mean the deaths are occurring *before*," Zera said. "Plus he should have plenty of bones from the plains. Kreya saw them in Lorn's palace."

Kreya had a thought. A terrible thought. It shouldn't have been possible, of course, but this was Eklor . . . "Did you check with the hospital? Were the bodies missing?"

"No, but—"

That was not the answer she was hoping for. "Were the bodies missing bones?"

"Not that the hospital reported, but—"

"You said that the deaths occurred at the precise moment of resurrection."

Zera waved her papers again. "Yes. All the times line up exactly, and we confirmed with the hospital that the victims weren't sick or injured enough to die. Their deaths are all unexplained. Their bodies untouched."

"Shit," Kreya said. She closed her eyes. "He's not taking bones. He's taking blood." Probably sent a construct to infiltrate the hospital. It wouldn't have been difficult to design one to perform that task—she could've done it in a few hours. You could even make it look like a typical cleaning construct, like the kind that she'd had cleaning the tower stairs. It could have passed unnoticed, retrieved the blood, and delivered it to Eklor for use at a later date.

In a satisfied voice, Amurra said, "I told you we should tell her. She knows more about the resurrection spell than anyone."

Except she clearly didn't. He must have stumbled onto, or more likely intentionally developed, a new variant of the resurrection spell, one where his own life force wasn't affected.

Actually, now that she thought of it, she could see how such a spell would be crafted. A few tweaks to the words. Substitute in your "donor's" blood. *I just didn't think of it, because I'm not pure evil.* Someone like Eklor . . . He could have created a spell to do exactly this.

No—he *did* create such a spell. That was apparent now.

"What is it?" Jentt asked. "What's wrong?" He added, "Aside from everything."

Kreya opened her eyes and looked at Jentt. She didn't want to tell him. Not now. Not like this. Not when she wasn't alone with him, to explain, to beg him to understand. She'd thought she'd have years to explain what she'd done and why she'd done it.

Jentt laid his hand over hers. "Kreya?"

"Try to understand," she said to him. She stared into his eyes and tried to will him to forgive her for what she'd done. "I've lived life without you, and I couldn't bear it. Not when I had the strength to save you."

He withdrew his hand. "What are you saying?"

"The resurrection spell requires three things: the right words, human bones, and the life essence of the caster. Not all of it. But as much as you choose to give."

Jentt's voice was hushed. "Tell me you didn't."

But she couldn't tell him that, as badly as she wanted to. "In order to bring someone back to life, you have to give them some of yours. That's why I believed Eklor—I thought he was sacrificing his future to give a future to an innocent child. But eight . . ."

"How much?" Jentt asked.

"If the people in the hospital are dying, he must be draining—"

He interrupted. "How much of your future did you give me?"

She looked at him. "Half. I'll die when you die."

Jentt stood up abruptly and walked to the window, his back to her.

"That still could be many, many years away," Kreya called after him.

Zera waved her hand. "You two have plenty to discuss, I

know. But do it later. Right now, we have to focus on Eklor. You think he's stealing other people's lives?"

Kreya steeled herself. She didn't want to have to think about Eklor in this moment, with Jentt in pain, but she had no choice. As Zera said, she had to focus on their enemy and only on him, if they were to find a way to defeat him. She forced herself to drag her gaze away from Jentt's angry eyes and look instead at the others. "Yes, that's exactly what I think." And she explained what had come to mind as soon as she'd heard the news. As she spoke, another piece of the puzzle clicked into place. "If he used such a spell on himself while he was close to death and stole the life of another . . ."

"There were plenty of wounded on the battlefield," Stran said.

"Or he could have prepared in advance," Zera said. "He was always a fellow who liked to plan. He could have had all the necessary ingredients already with him."

"Ingredients," Amurra said. "You're talking about a person."

"But Eklor wouldn't have thought of them like that. And right now, we need to think like him."

Amurra shuddered.

Stran punched one fist into his other hand. "We should have made certain he was dead."

"We did," Zera said. "He was. We're not idiots. Kreya examined the body. Stuck him with a few knives, as I recall, and before we left the plains, Marso read the bones and saw him dead."

Kreya nodded.

"He could have drafted a flunky to work the spell after we were gone," Zera said. "But how about we ask Eklor about the nitty-gritty details *after* we take him down? Plenty of opportunity for reminiscing about the past once he's behind bars."

All of them looked at Kreya, expecting her to command them as she always did. Yet at the moment, her heart ached to go to Jentt, talk to him, try to fix what she knew she'd broken. Her head knew her duty, however. There was no question what the right thing to do was: Report Eklor immediately. Expose his crimes, and keep him from fleeing as the bone guild and the city authorities came down on him. "It's time for another visit to Grand Master Lorn."

"He won't listen," Zera objected. "Eklor saved his son. He'll dismiss this is as circumstantial evidence, not proof."

"He'll listen to the truth if we make him listen—the coincidences with the deaths in the hospital should be at least enough to cast suspicion," Kreya said. "The guild will *make* Lorn investigate, if we present this publicly enough. The council will insist on it. I assume he still visits the masters and novices on the third tier once a week?"

Zera smiled. "I happen to be on close terms with the clerk who sets the agendas for his meetings. He likes to use my strength talismans. Or, more accurately, his wife likes it when he uses my strength talismans."

"I did not need to know that detail," Kreya said. "Can you arrange for all of us to speak with Grand Master Lorn in front of the council of masters and as many other guild members as possible? Without anyone figuring out we're planning to do so?"

"Absolutely," Zera said. She swept to the door and then paused, looking back at Kreya. "Better brush off your public speaking skills. And maybe find some less transparent clothes."

CHAPTER TWENTY-FOUR

Kreya and the others descended to the third tier, where all the guild headquarters were housed. They hid their bone worker coats in a pack that Stran carried, and they used false names as they passed through the gates. *Paranoid, maybe*, Kreya thought, *but it pays to be cautious when your enemy has such a causal relationship with death.*

Only Amurra remained behind at Zera's palace, with Guine and Zera's followers. This time, she hadn't argued or asked to come. They were about to piss off the grand master of their guild. It would be best if outsiders weren't present.

Squatting on the east side of the third tier, the Bone Workers Guild headquarters were made of stone carved to resemble the rib cage of a beast, larger than any that had ever lived. The walls had been polished until they gleamed the white of sunbaked bone. The five heroes entered through a stone skull, beneath empty eye sockets.

Already, the headquarters were humming with activity. Sliding into a side corridor, Kreya signaled to her team to keep quiet. They didn't want to draw attention to themselves. At least not until they entered the great hall.

Zera whispered, "How impressive an entrance do you want us to make?"

"Options?" Kreya asked.

"Anywhere from joining the queue of supplicants to arriving like a firework."

Kreya considered it. "We want all eyes on us. But no advance notice. Grand Master Lorn would prefer to see us privately, but we can't count on him being reasonable one-on-one. We need the other masters to pressure him into listening."

Zera grinned. "Firework then. My specialty. Follow me."

As Zera led the way, Kreya fell in beside her, with the others behind them. She was acutely aware that Jentt had chosen to take up the rear, as far from Kreya as possible, but she shoved thoughts of him into a knot to be untangled later. *He'll forgive me*, she thought, *once he's had the chance to accept that done is done.* She couldn't let herself believe anything else. Especially now. She had to stay focused on the task at hand.

After they saved the world, she could turn to saving her marriage.

The corridor was mostly empty, except for a few novices scurrying here and there. None of them gave Kreya and her team more than a glance. All five heroes knew the trick of walking with purpose, looking as if you belonged.

We do belong here, Kreya thought. *Or we did.*

The white-as-bone walls were coated in memories. She'd been a novice here, racing through the halls to be on time for class, sneaking spare bones out of the labs to practice when no one was watching, obsessively studying for exams until her entire body ached. She'd met Zera in one class—the teacher had been taunting a student with a stutter, telling him he'd never amount to anything if he couldn't speak his spells right, and

Kreya had informed him that she was reporting his attitude to his superiors. The teacher had tried to suspend Kreya for talking out of turn, and Zera had "accidentally" blown up a shelf of chemicals. In the chaos, Kreya and Zera had bolted for the head of the department, and within twenty-four hours, the teacher was on sabbatical, and the students had a much better teacher.

To be fair, they'd both been given detention, but it had been worth it.

She'd met Jentt here too, when they were older. Maybe it had been in the library? She knew vaguely when but didn't remember the exact moment. She wondered if he did.

She'd recruited both Stran and Marso after, but this was the place that had set them all on the path to their future. She felt as if the memories were welcoming them back, and she began to feel confident: the council of bone worker masters would listen to them, and Eklor would be exposed and defeated.

This is it, Kreya thought. *We defeated him once with strength of arms.*

Now we'll defeat him with strength of words.

Zera pivoted, leading them through a classroom with several bird skeletons suspended from the ceiling. All the rooms still smelled the same as Kreya remembered—a mixture of mildew, dust, and body odor, all undercut with the ever-present and unmistakable scent of blood. It was a comfortingly familiar smell, and she felt the muscles in her shoulders relax minutely.

Through the classroom, Zera chose a narrow stairwell. Windowless, it wound up two levels to emerge in a hall that led to the balconies overlooking the great hall. She held up a hand, stopping them before they approached the balconies.

They shed their plain coats and donned their bone worker coats. Stran stashed the pack behind a pillar. Creeping closer, they heard voices drifting up to the balcony. A crowd was gathered in the great hall, with Grand Master Lorn seated on a dais. He was lit by the muted light that poured through twenty stained glass windows, above the balcony. Each window was decorated with past glories of bone workers in colored glass thick enough to block all noise from the city outside but thin enough to allow sun to seep through.

Fourteen masters were seated beside Grand Master Lorn, in chairs carved to resemble an array of tusks—they comprised the Council of Bones, an advisory board that served the grand master. Each throne was in its own pool of muted light.

If we can convince them . . .

With a jolt, Kreya spotted Eklor between the masters, as if he'd earned the right to sit with such great men and women. It hadn't occurred to her he'd be here. She'd pictured him skulking around Lorn's palace. *No matter,* she thought. *Same plan.* She felt a hand squeeze her shoulder and glanced back to see Marso, stricken. She nodded to him and wished she had the words to reassure him.

Zera passed out talismans to each of them. "Say 'renari' and try not to crash."

Kreya crept forward, listening. Addressing a man in a bone worker's coat, one of the masters was expounding on his theory of why the current crop of novices needed more structure in their curriculum. She had a vague memory of the master who was speaking—his beard had been burgundy when she'd known him. It was straggly and white now, and his shoulders curved toward his chest as if he carried a heavy pack.

Grand Master Lorn let him complete his monologue, and then when he inhaled to launch into another point, the grand master raised his hand. "Thank you for your input, Master

Subene. We will discuss and consider your points as they pertain to the complaint at hand. But it's time to move on to the next order of business, even if it means waking Master Epsana from her nap."

A few laughed, and one lightly tapped Master Epsana, an elderly woman who had been slumped in her chair, on the shoulder. She straightened herself and blinked owlishly, as if she believed that fooled anyone into thinking she'd been paying attention all along.

Grand Master Lorn beckoned the next in line.

"Now," Kreya whispered.

All five of them stepped up onto the railing, whispered "*renari*," and soared off the balcony. Below them they heard surprised gasps and shouts. Following Zera's lead, they circled once before landing in a line in front of the masters.

Straightening stiffly in his thronelike chair, Grand Master Lorn opened his mouth to speak, but Kreya did not give him the chance to either welcome them or berate them for their interruption.

"Eklor has lied to you," Kreya said with no preamble. "He is granting life for a chosen few by taking life from unconsenting innocents."

"He is a murderer," Zera put in. "Not in the distant past. But now. In this city."

Everyone broke out in shocked chatter, both from the supplicants in line behind them and from the council. Kreya focused solely on Grand Master Lorn and the other masters. Their response was what mattered, and their expressions ranged from shock to disbelief.

"Impossible!" Grand Master Lorn said. "He has been nowhere but my palace and the guild headquarters since the moment of his return to Cerre." He signaled to the guards, and they herded the supplicants out of the hall.

She glanced back at them and the heavy doors. He'd reacted quickly, almost as if he'd been ready for them. But they could do this without an audience. The only ears they truly needed were the council's.

"With all due respect, Grand Master, we believe he has found a way to circumvent you," Jentt said with a bow. "He has deceived you."

"We believe he is stealing blood from victims convalescing in the second-tier hospital and using it as a conduit to transfer their life force to the dead for his 'miracle' resurrections." Kreya switched her gaze to their nemesis.

On his chair of tusks, Eklor looked unfazed. He hadn't moved, not even to flinch when they flew in from the balcony. *He couldn't have been expecting us*, Kreya thought.

Or maybe he had. After all, he knew what crimes he was committing. It couldn't have been a surprise to him that someone eventually noticed.

"These are serious accusations," Grand Master Lorn began.

"For serious crimes," Kreya cut in. "And we count on you and the council to investigate them. Master Eklor has caused great pain to the people of Vos. We must learn from our past mistakes and not allow history to repeat."

A small smile was playing on Eklor's lips. She wished she could charge up to him and wipe it off his face. What did he have to smile about? They were exposing him, and yet he seemed like he was about to get a commendation!

"Ah, but we must also not be blinded by our past," Grand Master Lorn said. "Master Eklor has come to us with open arms, confessed, and repented. In exchange for forgiveness, he offers us a blessing: a second chance at life for our loved ones."

"By murdering innocents," Zera said. "You caught that part, right?"

A few chairs down from Lorn, Master Subene scowled at them. Kreya recalled that the master had never liked her. Called her arrogant and pigheaded, which may have been accurate but the master shouldn't have said it publicly. "Such a serious accusation requires serious proof. Do you have proof?"

Presenting her death list, Zera indicated the eight hospital patients who had died. She shared it with all the council members, walking to each one of them. "Note the times of death. Each corresponds to the exact time of one of Eklor's resurrections. Also note the causes of death: inconclusive. In all cases, according to their records, the patients were not in the hospital for life-threatening causes. Furthermore, all were located in the same floor and same wing of the same hospital."

"Coincidence," another master scoffed. Kreya had forgotten her name. She didn't think she'd made an enemy of her. Zera, though, who had obviously expected a greater reaction to her presentation, looked rattled.

Master Subene agreed with his colleague. "I only hear speculation. Do you have any proof beyond this coincidence?"

Kreya had expected outrage. Confusion. Questions. She hadn't expected anyone on the council to sound so immediately dismissive of their charges. She eyed Master Subene, wondering why he would want to defend Eklor. Fear of his own death, or fear of a loved one's? That fear was a powerful thing. She began to wonder if she'd misjudged the council members.

She wondered if she'd misjudged humanity.

I was willing to sacrifice myself, and desecrate the dead, to reach my goal. Who's to say others wouldn't willingly kill for their loved ones—or themselves—to live?

Still . . . was that true for all of them? Surely, at least one council member had to harbor doubts. She glanced again at Eklor and saw he was twirling the same unfamiliar talisman. She wondered again what it was. A backup plan of some sort? A way to escape, if all turned sour for him?

"Furthermore, I, for one, do not appreciate the theatrics of it," Master Subene continued. "There is a process here." He waved his wrinkled hand at doors, now closed to the line of supplicants. If they were still out there, it was impossible to hear them through the thick wood.

"Kind of thought the seriousness of the issue warranted a deviation from the usual process," Zera said. "Again, murderer. Mass murderer. Of innocents."

"If you had actual proof, you wouldn't have resorted to theatrics," Subene sniffed.

What was wrong with them? This was *Eklor*. Mass murderer. Cause of the Bone War. Enemy of the people. Why were they being so obstinate?

"Investigate however you choose," Kreya said to the council, directing her words to the members who were *not* Master Subene. "Speak to the doctors who treated the victims. Review the causes of the deaths. Interview the hospital staff and determine who had access to these patients prior to their deaths. There is proof to be found, now that you know where to look. All we ask is that you find the truth and proceed accordingly. If we're wrong, we apologize. But if we're right, isn't that worth confirming?"

She met the eyes of the other masters, looking for agreement. To her shock, she saw only doubt, suspicion, and resistance.

He's corrupted the council, she thought. She didn't know how, but somehow he had won them over. It made no sense. These were masters of their craft, respected, educated, and smart. *Well, except Master Subene.* But the others shouldn't have been so easily swayed. Most of them were old enough to have fought in the Bone War against Eklor, to have lost friends and family.

"We sympathize with all you have suffered," Grand Master Lorn said with what he must have meant as a pitying smile—it came off as a caricature of one—"but Master Subene and Master Anitra are correct. This is the thinnest of evidence you present for the gravest of accusations. With respect to all you have given to and suffered for Vos, your desire for revenge is overwhelming your grasp on reality. Correct me if I am wrong, but as I see it, you have no concrete evidence that Master Eklor's gift is anything but that: a gift."

Jentt stepped forward. "I know how grateful you must feel for the return of your son. But no gift is free." He did not look at Kreya as he said this, but Kreya felt the words burrow into her. She had been willing to pay the cost, though, with full knowledge of it. Those people in the hospital had not even been given a choice.

Stran spoke up next. "It's not your fault someone died so your son could live. You didn't know. Not knowing—well, I would've done the same as you. But now that you do know, you cannot stand by and do nothing—"

Grand Master Lorn interrupted, his temper beginning to fray. "We do not do nothing! And believe me, Master Eklor is being carefully monitored. He is not a free man, forgiven of all past wrongdoings. But thus far, we have seen no *true* evidence, beyond wild speculation, that Master Eklor is still the man he was. All of us have seen the bone reading showing clearly and indisputably the destruction of the last of his soldiers, and the guards on the wall have reported to the council of your own team's findings in the forbidden zone. Master Eklor has shown every sign of change, and I believe it is right for our souls, right for the healing of this land, to open ourselves to the gift of forgiveness. And to allow Master Eklor to gift us with the benefits of his skills."

Master Subene sighed in obvious relief, and Kreya narrowed her eyes. She studied each of the masters, all of whom were nodding in agreement.

Yes, everyone feared death. But was *everyone* willing to pay such a cost? She wouldn't have believed it. Could it be denial? Perhaps they could pay anything if they could deny the cost existed. Pretend there wasn't a problem. Pretend they didn't see. How willingly would people delude themselves if it meant saving the life of one they loved? How many lines would they cross? And if all they had to do was refuse to look at the lines they were crossing . . .

She had to shake them into facing the truth!

"He uses human bones," Kreya blurted out.

Beside her, Zera hissed in her breath.

Kreya plowed on. "That's what the spell requires: words, a life force to give, and human bones to create the link. Even if he used his own life force and the hospital deaths were only a coincidence, he would still be breaking the law."

"Lies!" Grand Master Lorn shot to his feet. "I witnessed my son's rebirth, and no human bones were used!" She read shock and disbelief on the faces of the other masters. If she could just make them listen, make them believe . . .

"I have seen the closet where he keeps them, in your palace," Kreya continued relentlessly. "He has been using the bones taken from the fallen soldiers—*our* fallen soldiers—in the forbidden zone. Search your palace, and you'll find them. In the third hallway."

The masters chattered to one another, and she could feel the outrage rising. *Good,* she thought. *Now we have their attention.* Eklor had committed multiple atrocities. The masters couldn't ignore them all. Surely, they'd investigate now.

At last Eklor spoke. "There are no bones from the war. I burned the bodies on the plains, along with the remnants of my soldiers, and mourned them. Whether you wish to see it or not, I have repented and come to Cerre a changed man."

"Your hatred of Master Eklor has blinded you to the truth," Grand Master Lorn said.

"And your love for your son has blinded you," Kreya countered. Lorn had been standing at the pyre when Eklor performed the spell. He *had* to have seen the bones Eklor used, and he was far too educated a bone worker to mistake them for anything but what they were.

Zera asked the question. "Why protect Eklor now? Your son already lives. Discovering you were tricked by a vicious worm disguised as a human being won't undo that."

Grumbling spread up and down the council, but it wasn't in agreement with Zera. *We have no allies here,* Kreya thought. She hadn't anticipated that. She'd thought they'd at least be met with neutrality, if not open minds.

Drifting closer to Kreya, Jentt whispered in her ear, "We're missing something. There has to be a reason they're not listening. They aren't being rational. He got to them somehow."

Kreya nodded. Just the suspicion of wrongdoing should have been enough to launch an investigation. It wasn't as if they'd demanded Eklor's immediate arrest. All they wanted was for the masters to act sensibly and cautiously—and then, obviously, toss him in jail and swallow the key.

Jentt's right. Eklor has something on them, Kreya thought. *Blackmail. Threats. Or a bribe? A promise to resurrect them and their loved ones? There's something we're missing . . .* Seemingly unconcerned, he was twirling that valley-damned talisman again.

"What is that?" Marso whispered to Zera.

"Not one of mine," she whispered back. "Unfamiliar pattern."

If Zera didn't recognize it . . . But there were more pressing matters than solving the mystery of one measly talisman. Whatever it was, he hadn't used it to attack them or to escape. She focused back on the council.

"You must at least consider the possibility—" Jentt was saying.

"Enough," Grand Master Lorn said. "Your baseless accusations, combined with your theatrics, are making a mockery of all of us. All of Vos is grateful for your past efforts against a true threat to our world and lives, but you must accept that time as past, lest you who were once Vos's heroes become our villains."

Master Eklor rose, his face somber, his hands clasped piously in front of him, cradling the talisman. "I assure you all that I come in peace with only a hope of achieving, if not forgiveness, then at least some measure of atonement before I breathe my last breath. My methods hurt no one, either living or dead." Turning to the Five, he said, "Master Kreya, Master Jentt, Master Stran, Master Zera, and Master Marso, Heroes of Vos . . . I deeply regret the pain I have caused each of you, and I know that your forgiveness is impossible. But I hope that you, in your zeal, will not be the cause of needless suffering. You have heard of my miracles with resurrection. But here is what you do not know, the reason the council has voted to support me."

Yes, she wanted to hear this. What reason could possibly be sufficient for them to turn their back on the past, on the future, and on the innocent?

"I have in my power the ability to extend the life of every bone worker in this guild, as well as the lives of their loved ones. This is what I have come to offer every bone worker. A chance for they and their loved ones to defeat death *before* it comes for them!"

A hush fell over the hall.

Kreya felt as if all the oxygen had been sucked from the room. She stared at Eklor. *This* was how he had won them all over. At least she understood. He wasn't offering a nebulous promise of future resurrection. He was offering them and their families longevity. He was offering them *life* now.

Still . . . Still, didn't *any* of them have reservations? A suspicion that it was too good to be true? Concern about the consequences?

"The cost—" Kreya began.

"The cost is mine to bear," Eklor said.

"If you were truly paying it, you'd be dead by now," Kreya shot back. She wished immediately she could recall the words. She did not want the council asking how she knew the details of the spell so well. It was important to tread carefully. But to her surprise, no one on the council questioned her.

Eklor shook his head sadly. "You speak out of a lack of knowledge. I have refined the resurrection spell well beyond my clumsy attempts years ago. I am able to perform it without draining the life of myself or anyone else."

"Tell them how you know," Zera whispered.

But Kreya shook her head. With the council set against them, she was not about to reveal that she had violated the law. Far too risky. "Prove it," she said to Eklor. "Show me the spell."

"You will understand if I don't trust you," Eklor said.

"Then show another master. Teach it to Grand Master Lorn. Show Master Subene. Or Master Rabkin. Demonstrate the spell to the entirety of the Bone Workers Guild. If it's as innocent a spell as you claim, then share it. Let all bone workers grant extra life to the people of Vos."

He smiled, and she knew she'd made a mistake, though she didn't know what the mistake was. "I have already shared the spell with Grand Master Lorn. He has approved its use and already shared his conclusion with the council. Would you contradict the verdict of the grand master?"

"I have indeed reviewed and approved the spell to my and the council's satisfaction," Grand Master Lorn pronounced.

Kreya gaped at him.

"If you want proof of my goodwill," Eklor said, seeming to enjoy Kreya's disbelief, "come in two days' time. On that day, I will be giving the miracle of extended life to all bone workers and their families. Grand Master Lorn has summoned bone workers from across Vos. They are traveling here as we speak."

Prickles ran up and down Kreya's neck. There were hundreds of bone workers of varying skill levels across the vast mountains of Vos. The number of deaths it would take to extend all those lives . . . Kreya gawked at Eklor, then at all of them. "So you're just going to *believe* him? Believe the man who waged war against all of us? The man who caused the deaths of your brothers, sisters, parents, children? You're going to accept that this miracle of a second life comes with zero cost, with no review or oversight?"

"No," Grand Master Lorn boomed, "what we will not do is let old hatreds destroy this golden opportunity! Without proof, actual solid proof, of ill intent, we would be fools to refuse such a rare and precious gift."

Beatifically, Eklor spread his arms wide. "This is my act of redemption. Allow me to take this risk, give this gift, and bless the bone workers whom I have caused such pain."

Kreya could only gawk at him.

"It's a trap," Zera said to the council. "Obviously. I bet he has no intention of working this miracle spell. He just wants to gather all his enemies in one hall and unleash his army."

"Clever plan," Jentt agreed. "Appealing bait."

"He'll kill you all," Stran said. "Succeeding where he failed before. Please, masters, listen to Kreya, listen to Zera, listen to us! You're in danger!"

"We have listened to you," Grand Master Lorn said. "This 'army' doesn't exist. We have listened to you out of gratitude for your past deeds and sympathy for what you have suffered, but you have presented us only conjecture and fear. Produce evidence of this 'army,' show us proof of Eklor's misdeeds beyond mere coincidence, and we will act. But unless you have concrete facts to back up your wild claims, I suggest you remove yourself from this hall and cease spreading baseless fear."

Kreya opened her mouth to yell louder that they were being idiots . . .

And heard Zera suck in a gasp. She whispered to Jentt, and Jentt laid a hand on Kreya's shoulder, silencing her. Kreya shot a look over at Zera. What was it? What did she know? Or guess?

In a voice wavering with age, Master Epsana, the woman who had been asleep earlier, said, "We are not fools, Master

Kreya. We will not walk into darkness with our eyes closed. If Master Eklor brings evil, we will not accept it. But if he brings hope and life . . . then do not deny us the right to choose it."

Master Subene chimed in. "Find proof and return."

"We told you where to find proof!" Kreya said. "Grand Master Lorn's palace! The bones are there, right now, if you send someone—"

Leaning over, Eklor whispered a word to Grand Master Lorn.

"Enough!" Grand Master Lorn said to Kreya. "I know what lies in my palace, and there are no human bones within. I have had enough of you questioning my integrity and my intelligence. Heroes you may be, but you have worn out your welcome here."

She was about to launch into arguing more, to go through it all again, but Kreya's team urged her backward, with Jentt pulling her hand and Zera guiding her other elbow. Bowing, Jentt said to all the masters, "We thank you for your time, and hope you will consider what we have said and proceed with caution."

Kreya turned to glare at him and noticed that several guild soldiers were flanking them. They looked nervous but resolute. If she didn't want this audience to turn into a brawl, then leaving gracefully now was their only option.

Part of her *wanted* to turn it into a fight. Knock sense into their heads, before any more innocents died. But that wouldn't make them see reason. *Fools. Damn fools.* Grinding her teeth, she stalked out of the great hall and didn't stop until they were out of the guild headquarters full of uncaring masters, only to find herself standing beneath the uncaring sun.

OUTSIDE, KREYA STALKED THROUGH THE THIRD tier, away from the guild headquarters and its obstinate, delusional, selfish, shortsighted, moronic—

"It was a persuasion talisman," Zera said.

"A what?" Marso asked.

"Remember the mindcloud jaguar in the valley," Zera asked Kreya, "the one that hypnotizes its prey and nearly killed me? I bet anything Eklor's talisman is carved from a mindcloud jaguar bone."

"Mind manipulation talismans are forbidden," Stran said.

"So is corrupting a bone reading and claiming it's truth," Marso said. "And using human bone in a bone-making spell. And raising an army of constructs to try to kill everyone. We know Eklor will cross any line. Why not this one?"

"But he's not a bone wizard," Kreya said. He was a bone maker, like she was; that was how he'd made the constructs for his army. Of course, he had been alone for twenty-five years, plenty of time to hone new skills. And he was undeniably a genius. She'd read his journals.

She wondered if he'd used the talisman on her, that time in Lorn's palace when she'd agreed to give him the benefit of the doubt. She remembered he'd put it away when she'd noticed it, but had he already messed with her mind? Or were all her mistakes her own?

"He's not a reader, either. But he showed at least some proficiency there."

"And he might not be at my level as a wizard, but he could be good enough to craft an effective talisman—he had plenty of time to work on it, especially if he focused on perfecting just that one type," Zera said. "Think about it. Persuasion talisman to soften up Lorn and the council. Bone reading to show them what he wants them to see. And resurrection spell to prove he can do the impossible. Combine all of that with an irresistible offer of eternal life, and there you go."

"We need to destroy that talisman," Stran said. "Free the council from his influence."

"How?" Jentt asked. "We'd never get close enough. He's under Grand Master Lorn's protection, and it looks as though the protection of the entire Council of Bones too."

"Plus we just got kicked out of there, if you noticed," Zera said.

"If he works his longevity spell," Marso said anxiously, "innocent people will die."

"And if he *doesn't* work the spell and instead orders his army to attack the guild," Stran said, "innocent people will die. Either way, whatever he plans, it is a tragedy waiting to happen."

Both of them are correct, Kreya thought. It almost didn't matter what his end goal was, since either result was unacceptable.

"What do we do?" Zera asked.

And all of them looked at Kreya.

Kreya took a deep breath. She quit raging. And she started planning. "Master Subene said we can return if we come with proof. So we need to obtain proof. Use that to either shake Eklor's hold on the minds of the council, or to at least get close enough to him to destroy the talisman." She turned to Jentt and Zera. "I need you two to get to the hospital. Zera, you charm your way inside. Convince the hospital to increase their security. Donate enough for a private security force if you have to, to protect the patients. Instruct them to watch for unauthorized constructs. Cut off Eklor's access to his favorite victims." She turned to Jentt. "Jentt, you need to identify which doctors treated the patients who have already died. Speed them out of there. We'll need to protect them from Eklor. He'll go after them, if he can. He won't want to risk their testifying against him—there's a chance they may have witnessed a construct stealing the blood from his victims. At the very least, they can testify that the deaths were unexpected. Anyone know a safe house they can hide in until we're ready to bring them before the council?"

"I know a few places," Zera said. "I can direct Jentt, after I talk to security."

"You think the doctors will be able to provide enough proof?" Stran asked. "Exactly how powerful are persuasion talismans? Will the testimony of witnesses be enough to counter its effects?"

Zera shrugged. "Never experimented with illegal talismans. But based on my work with non-horrifying ones, my guess is that we can break his hold if we present enough tangible evidence to create cognitive dissonance. He's influencing their minds, not controlling them. They need to want to believe him, at least on some level. Shake that up, and we may have a chance."

"And if we can't . . . well, then our goal becomes destroying the talisman," Kreya said. "But to do that, we have to be close to Eklor. And to get close, we have to have proof, as I said. So let's go get it. Marso, Stran, you're with me." She kept walking toward the gateway between the tiers. She didn't even glance at Zera and Jentt as they split away.

With luck, Eklor would be stranded at the headquarters for a while longer, placating everyone and acting the innocent, possibly twirling that blasted persuasion talisman some more. Grand Master Lorn would stay as well to reassure people that the accusations were baseless, either because he was in thrall to the talisman himself or because he'd been persuaded by his son's fate. Or both. Regardless, Kreya and her team would have a slim window in which to act.

Stran caught up to her. "What are you going to do?"

"Get the bones, obviously," Kreya said. "Keep up, Stran."

Eklor needed two things to complete the resurrection spell: bones and blood. Best case, they'd be able to use the bones from the plains to discredit him and stop him. Worse case, Eklor would have to find replacement bones, which would slow him down.

If they could at least make Eklor have to delay his miracle-for-every-bone-worker plan, then they'd buy time to prove the price for his "gift" was too high. And they'd buy themselves time to find that damned, thrice-rotted army, which would be the most compelling proof of all.

In the meantime, every delay helped. He'd be asked to continue his daily "miracles," and the more people he had to kill to work those miracles—and the greater the risks he had to take to do so—the greater the odds he'd be caught. Kreya didn't delude herself into thinking they could prevent more deaths. Even if they protected every single doctor and patient in the hospital, Eklor would find other victims. He could have his constructs prowl the streets to prey on the homeless, he could seek out victims in the prisons, or he could range wider and find his victims in remote farmhouses and sparse villages. But she'd save as many as she could until she could force the guild to see the threat for what it was—to see him for who he was.

She put together a plan as they moved up the tiers.

It was a sloppy plan, built on surprise and strength, but she had zero doubt that Eklor would move quickly to secure his bone supply. She had to get there first.

A crowd flocked behind them as they strode through the fourth tier to the fifth. She didn't bother to hide their identities. There wasn't time for any of that. They gave their real names to the guards at the gateway, and they rode the white stones directly to Lorn's palace. She marched up the stairs.

Marso stopped her. "I can't read in battle conditions. Not yet."

"You don't need to," Kreya said.

"What do you need me to do?"

"Lie," Kreya said. "On my cue and loudly."

Stran was on her other side. "And me?"

"Get us in."

He eyed the two armored guards who stood on either side of the brass door. "You want me to sweet-talk our way in?"

Kreya leveled a look at him. "I want you to knock down the damn door."

He smiled. "Got it." Charging up the steps, he roared as he activated a strength talisman.

Running behind him, Kreya shouted, "Out of our way! Emergency!" She hauled Marso with her. "He's seen danger within!" Lower: "Now, Marso."

With all the intensity of a consummate theater performer, Marso began to howl, "Danger! Doom! Horrors!"

Startled, the guards sprang back as Stran plowed through the brass doors. They popped off their hinges and crashed with an echoing clang. Kreya called to the guards, "Don't let anyone in, even Grand Master Lorn—it's too dangerous! Everyone must be kept outside, where they'll be safe!"

"But what—" one began.

"We'll take care of it!" Kreya shouted with authority. "You protect the innocents! Do your duty!"

He saluted. "We will! Good luck!"

Marso shuddered visibly. "We need it." And then they barged inside, joining Stran.

Charging down the hall, Kreya led the way unerringly. Stran bellowed, "Emergency! Run for your lives!" Marso continued to rant loudly about danger, and the servants and other bone workers cleared out of the way.

"Follow me!" she called to Marso and Stran, and together they ran down the corridor.

She yanked on the door—locked. Pushing her aside, Stran punched through the door. It shattered. She stepped inside. "Shit."

The shelves were empty.

Of course they are, she thought. Eklor must have moved them shortly after he showed her. He was a smart man, and he had to know showing her his stash was a risk. Kreya pivoted. "They have to be close. He wouldn't have hidden them outside the palace where he couldn't easily access them."

"We'll never be able to search it in time," Stran said. "If we had Jentt to speed-search it . . ." As a former thief, he would have known exactly where to look for valuables.

But she'd sent him to the hospital to, hopefully, save lives and secure witnesses. Unless Eklor was one step ahead of them there as well. "We'll have to persuade the guards to help—"

In a small voice, Marso said, "I think I can do it."

Both Kreya and Stran looked at him.

"It's a single question: where are the stolen bones? I can ask that. I can't read in battle conditions anymore, but if I have quiet and one straightforward question to focus on . . ."

Kreya hesitated for only half a heartbeat. She trusted Marso to know what he was ready for. Gesturing to the closet, she welcomed him in. "We'll guard you."

"Don't watch," he requested. "I have to concentrate."

Both Stran and Kreya stood in front of the broken door, backs to the interior, their arms crossed. The palace was eerily quiet. Everyone had taken their advice and either fled or hidden. Kreya tried to keep her thoughts from chasing in circles.

If Eklor had anticipated they'd come for the bones, he had to have anticipated they'd find out about the hospital. What if Jentt and Zera were walking into a trap? What if the doctors were already dead? What if Eklor had a backup source for his blood already lined up?

And: what if she'd guessed wrong? All their evidence was thin at best—Grand Master Lorn wasn't wrong about that. She'd hoped, though, that they'd investigate Eklor and, with the might and intelligence of the entire guild, uncover what he planned in time to stop him.

Now it's up to us, Kreya thought.

Behind her, Marso gasped.

Leaving his post by the door, Stran knelt beside him. He put his hand on Marso's back. "Deep breaths. Breathe. That's it. Even breaths."

"What did you see?" Kreya asked.

"All their lives, all their deaths," Marso gasped. He doubled over, his forehead touching the floor. His chicken bones scattered as he caught himself on his hands. Stran helped him sit. He rubbed his back until Marso was breathing evenly instead of in short gulps of air.

"Did you see the bones?" Kreya asked.

He looked up at her. "Yes."

He led the way. Stran supported him every time he wobbled, but he headed unerringly down the hallway to a stairway. Again, they faced palace guards. This time, though, Marso looked so haunted that they didn't hesitate to withdraw when he told them there was danger within.

In a burst of inspiration, Kreya told the guards, "Come with us. Be ready for anything."

One guard unlocked a door and threw it open.

Inside, a young boy jumped to his feet. He dropped the book he'd been reading. Kreya stared at him, and he stared back.

"You're the dead boy?" Kreya guessed. "Grand Master Lorn's son?" She remembered Zera had told her his name. "Yarri?"

"Don't hurt me!" he squeaked.

"Don't be afraid," Kreya said. "All we want are the bones."

His eyes widened. "I don't know what you're talking about."

"Marso, where are they?" She didn't take her eyes off the boy. Damn Eklor for involving a kid in all this. And damn Grand Master Lorn, for putting his own heart above the good of the world. *He knows*, she thought. The persuasion talisman could only excuse so much. On some level, Lorn had to understand what he was doing. *He knows the cost of it all. But he doesn't care because his son lives.*

She asked herself what she'd do if it were Jentt, and then she ruthlessly banished that thought. She'd crossed lines, yes, but there were limits. There had to be.

With a shaking arm, Marso pointed at the bed.

Kreya drew her knife and stalked toward it. Falling back, the boy screamed, but she ignored him. She stabbed the mattress and dragged the blade back, slitting it open. Beside her, Stran yanked at the quilted top until it was open.

Inside lay the bones.

CHAPTER TWENTY-FIVE

Amurra paced in front of the ridiculous artificial water-fall. Zera's servants had given up offering her refreshments after she refused them again and again, and she'd been left in peace with her own thoughts and worries.

She wasn't certain that was a good thing.

Without the children and the farm to distract her from Stran's absence, she couldn't stop imagining everything that could go wrong, from the guards at Lorn's palace arresting Stran to an army of the undead cornering him and killing him. She hated being stuck without anything to do except worry. The whole point of coming to Cerre with her husband was so that she could be useful. In marriage, you were supposed to face life's challenges as a team. *It's supposed to be the two of us, together,* Amurra thought. *Not me here, useless and worried sick.*

She had made the choice to stay, however, so this time there was no one to blame but herself. She wasn't a bone maker, and besides, someone needed to be here in case Kreya's constructs returned with news of Eklor's army, as unlikely as that was. But still, she wished . . . *I don't wish I were one of them. I don't wish I were fighting alongside him. I wish we were both home, in the life we built, in the life we chose, with the family we made.* He'd left all of this behind—happily, she'd thought. She missed her children so badly that it felt like a physical ache. *Why are we here?* Why was Eklor his problem again? Couldn't someone else do this? He'd risked enough!

Often at night, Stran still woke, covered in sweat and shaking, and when she asked, he said, "Nightmares." But she knew they weren't. They were memories. When they'd married, she'd sworn she'd help him make new memories, better memories. And they had! Was all that about to be erased by fresh trauma that neither of them had asked for?

She told herself that she was being selfish. She should be proud that Stran was noble and selfless. *But I don't want him to be noble and selfless,* she thought. *I want him to be home! I want all of us home, a family together.* Whatever Eklor did in Cerre wasn't going to affect them way out on their farm.

She scolded herself for such thoughts. Lives were at stake. Other people's husbands, wives, and children. She merely had to be patient. After this was over, they'd go home and be with their children again.

Across the room, Amurra heard a clicking noise. She crossed to the window and opened it. One of Kreya's constructs, a mechanical creature made of gears and bones that loosely resembled a tree squirrel, climbed inside. As it chittered and whirred at her, she felt a cold horror close over her heart. The search had been going on for days with no results, and she'd expected that to continue. However, the Five had gone to poke the hornet's nest.

She knelt beside the construct. "Master Kreya isn't here right now."

A confused chirp.

"But you can tell me what you found."

Another chirp, this one with a down note, as if it were agreeing with her.

"Did you find Eklor's army?"

It chirped, whirred, and nodded its mechanical head so hard that it toppled over. She righted it, while her heart hammered hard in her throat. She pivoted toward the door and shouted, "Guine!" *Please don't let it be too late yet*, she thought. There had to still be time to warn Stran and the others. "Guine!"

Behind her, the window shattered. She screamed and ducked as shards embedded in her skin. And a monstrous construct leaped through the broken window. It was massive, with spiderlike legs like a crawler but also tentacles made of twisted wires extruding from its back. Its head spun and its mirror eyes fixed on her. Amurra ran for the door, still screaming for help.

A tentacle shot out and wrapped around her waist.

She grabbed the nearest pillar, but the pull of the tentacle was implacable. She felt her hands slip as it dragged her toward its maw. "Help! Someone help!"

Another wire wrapped around her waist and then another. She felt them squeeze. It was hard to suck in air. *Crunch*—the massive construct crushed Kreya's scout, the one who'd tried to bring a warning. A warning she'd failed to deliver.

Stran . . .

She heard footsteps pounding in the corridor outside.

Then she heard shouting.

Then Guine's voice: "Get it off! Grab her!"

They hammered at the construct with whatever they could find—someone shattered a pitcher on its side, another hit it with a chair. A few ran. But those who stayed pounded at the horror.

Amurra struggled, but it was becoming harder and harder

to breathe. Black spots danced in front of her eyes. *Stran*, she thought, *I'm sorry*. She didn't know why she was sorry—that she wasn't able to help, that she wouldn't be able to say goodbye, that they didn't have more time, that she was leaving him alone to face the world, to be a father alone, to be a man who had lost his wife, to have pain when he should have had joy. And her, she'd wanted more time, more time with him, more time with her children, to see them grow, to help them and hold them and love them. More time in the world. More springs, to see the buds on the trees, the fresh shoots bursting out of the ground. More summers, lying side by side looking up at the stars with the warm breeze all around them. More autumns . . . Her thoughts scattered as the tentacles squeezed harder.

She tried to form words. "Tell. Stran." But then there wasn't air. She couldn't force the words out of her throat. Air, water, blood gurgled in her throat.

She heard Guine begging, "Don't kill us. Please, don't kill us."

"You will not all die," a man's voice said—the construct? She hadn't known they could speak. She wondered at that, clinging to the question as if it were a rock in a raging river. "You must deliver a message. The five so-called heroes will recant their false accusations immediately, and in exchange, Master Eklor will restore this woman's life."

"Don't—" Guine began.

And then Amurra felt a sharp pain in her neck as a wire pierced her throat. Darkness consumed her vision, and death swallowed all else.

IN YARRI'S ROOM, KREYA WRAPPED A BUNDLE OF bones, including an obvious human skull, in a sheet and tucked it under her arm. "Proof of what we've witnessed here," she told the boy and the guards. "We'll present these to the guild. Let Eklor try to squirm out of this now."

The boy was whimpering. "Bones. In my bed. My father—"

"Don't blame your father," Kreya told him. "Master Eklor is the one who brought horrors into your home. And our city." *Blame your father for inviting him inside,* she thought, but she wasn't going to say that to Yarri, who seemed traumatized enough. Imagine sleeping on a cache of human bones and not knowing it. Nightmare fuel for years. "We'll burn the rest."

"Of course, Master Kreya," one of the guards said. He looked nearly as wild-eyed as the boy. "We'll bring them to the pyre."

She stopped him. "It's not that I don't trust you. But I don't trust Master Eklor. He'll be here any minute to check on his supply. We need to destroy it before he gets here." Every second mattered. She wasn't taking any chances with Eklor. *Never underestimating him again,* she promised herself.

The guards didn't argue. At all. One rushed out into the hallway and returned with a lit torch. The others helped her, Stran, and Marso shift the furniture away from the bed.

Taking the torch from the guard, Kreya lowered it to the bedding and the bones. Dry as kindling, it lit easily, and the fire spread, skipping from bone to fabric and racing across it all. She watched it burn. Only when she was satisfied that the bones were charred enough to be useless did she feel the tightness around her chest loosen. This would have to slow down Eklor. "Keep the fire going until they're ash," she instructed the guards. "And see that the fire doesn't spread beyond this room."

The boy began to cough.

"Don't breathe in smoke," she told him. "Outside. Now."

Shooing the kid out of the room, she strode into the hallway. Stran and Marso fell in behind her. Now they had proof.

They just had to get it to the guild headquarters and present it, ideally jointly with the testimony of the doctors from the hospital. Combined, it had to cast doubt on Eklor's claims, perhaps even enough to overcome the effects of the persuasion talisman. "We'll regroup with the others. Present everything at once for maximum impact. If we can keep him off balance enough, we might be able to create an opening to destroy the talisman. At the very least, we should be able to delay him."

Outside, by the broken door, Kreya informed the guards about the fire. They saluted and rushed in to help. Belatedly, she noticed that Lorn's son was still following her. A young boy shouldn't be wrapped up in all of this. "You need to stay here," Kreya told him.

He blinked back tears. "But what if Master Eklor comes back? What if he's angry? What if he blames me? What if he blames my father, and uses me . . ."

He's right, she thought. Master Eklor wouldn't hesitate to use Grand Master Lorn's son as a hostage against him. In fact, he'd already done so. "Fine. Come with us." The boy could stay at Zera's palace until this was all over. He'd be safe enough there.

"I want my papa."

Stran put his arm around the boy. "We'll get you back to your father as soon as we can, okay?" he promised. "Until then, we'll keep you as safe as if you were one of my own kids." He helped Yarri onto one of the floating stones, and they rode away from Lorn's palace toward Zera's.

Shepherding Yarri inside, Kreya didn't see the chaos at first. Stran halted, and Kreya had to peer around him. Instantly, adrenaline flooded through her. She rammed her hands into her pockets, pulling out talismans, and half-crouched in a defensive position with the boy behind her. Every muscle tensed. "Stay behind me, kid."

Stran was already in motion, crossing the vast room.

On one side, Guine was tending to the servants. Bodies lay under curtains. A window had been shattered. One pillar was damaged. Juice and blood mingled on the marble floor. Kreya cataloged it all fast.

Whatever had happened here was over.

She slid her talismans back into her pockets and straightened. Her heart was thumping painfully hard in her chest. Whatever had happened here . . . It shouldn't have happened.

It's my fault, she thought. *I miscalculated. Again.* She should have predicted this. Set guards. Made plans. Had contingency plans in case those plans failed. Everyone knew their team was staying in Zera's palace. She should have realized that would make this place a target. And anyone in it.

Stran strode between the bodies, yanking back the sheets and bellowing, "Amurra!"

Behind her, Yarri's voice quivered. "Who did this?"

"Three guesses, and they're all named Eklor." Kreya stepped forward, and Yarri caught her arm. His grip was so tight that if she raised her arm, he'd dangle off it.

"Don't leave me!" he squeaked. "You said you'd keep me safe!"

"I won't abandon you," she reassured him. Yet another person she was responsible for. "But you need to stay by the door. If anything dangerous happens, run outside. Okay? Can you do that? Run instead of freeze?"

He nodded. Tears flowed freely down his cheeks.

She wasn't certain she believed him, but she also thought it wouldn't be an issue—this was the aftermath of a disaster, not the start of one. Still . . . She stalked through the room, checking out the window, around corners. "Any threats remain?"

Guine shook his head. He swallowed hard and looked at Stran. Kreya followed his gaze. The big man looked terrifying as he exposed the dead bodies, looking for his wife.

Kreya shifted so that she blocked Guine's view of Stran. "Tell me what happened." She kept her voice calm and even, as soothing as she could manage. They could fall apart later, but now she needed to assess the scope of the disaster.

"I heard her calling to me," Guine said, focusing on her. "And then she was screaming. We tried to fight it, but we're not warriors."

"Take a deep breath, and define your pronouns."

His eyes were wide, as if he were reliving the memory. She read the terror etched in his face. "A construct," he said. "Huge. Lots of metal legs. Wire tentacles protruding from its back."

She remembered facing such constructs on the battlefield. Eklor's specialty. Absolutely terrifying in close quarters. And supposedly burned on the plains. *I was right*, she thought.

The thought didn't comfort her at all.

"Amurra?" Kreya said.

"It had her." He dropped his voice to a whisper, as if afraid Stran would hear. "We tried. You have to believe me. You have to tell him. We tried!"

Kreya wanted to shake him. If Amurra had been captured, they had a very thin window in which to rescue her before the trail grew cold. Even if she'd been injured, hope wasn't lost. They could use flight and speed to chase after the construct. Catch it before it returned to whatever hole it had crawled out of. "Guine. If you don't tell me what it said and did, I will feed your harp to you piece by piece, string by string. *What happened?*"

Guine began to weep. "It killed her. Right in front of me. She's dead."

Kreya heard a roaring in her ears. She kept her voice very, very even. "Dead?"

Across the room, by the waterfall that still burbled as if nothing ever happened in this room except mindless frivolity, Stran stopped moving. Kreya saw him out of the corner of her eye, but she kept her focus on Guine. "And then?"

"It took her body out the window." He pointed.

She was moving before Guine finished speaking, running toward the window. Stran met her there. Climbing onto the windowsill, Kreya commanded, "Keep me from falling." She felt her back twinge, and she winced, but she didn't stop. Stran wrapped his arms around her legs, and she leaned forward.

Gouged into the stone were claw marks. After that, the trail vanished over the side of the fifth tier. Of course. Eklor would have imbued his creation with a stability bone. She signaled for Stran to pull her back in.

"Anything?" he asked.

She shook her head. "Gone."

Inwardly she swore as colorfully as Zera—at the construct, at Eklor, and at herself. She hadn't fortified the palace against attack. She hadn't predicted any kind of retaliation, when retaliation was Eklor's trademark move.

She'd been so certain. So arrogant . . . *All of this is my fault.*

She'd poked the hornet's nest, and it had stung them where they were most vulnerable.

Kneeling, she picked up the remains of one of her own constructs. She recognized it, even though the metal gears were warped—it was the scout she'd sent into the valley, the squirrel-like one that had been so eager to search more.

Had it returned with news? Had Eklor's atrocity followed it here?

My fault, she thought again.

"We know who did this," Stran said. "We go to guild headquarters. Force our way to Eklor, if we need to. If the masters side with him, then they're complicit in this, and we force them to face their guilt."

"No!" Guine jumped to his feet. Both of them spun to glare at him. He gulped. "It talked. I didn't know such atrocities *could* talk, but it did. It said if you withdraw the false accusations, then Master Eklor will bring her back to life. If you go on fighting, you could lose her forever."

Sagging against a pillar, Stran seemed to deflate.

Kreya understood.

Revenge was one thing. She remembered how it felt when she charged into the tower on the plains long ago, intent on tearing apart Eklor, wanting to make him feel the kind of pain she'd felt when Jentt died. But this . . .

Amurra, whether dead or alive, was a hostage. Entirely different situation.

Crossing to the fountain, cradling the crushed scout in her arms, Kreya let the burble of the water drown out all else: Stran's sobs, the servants' moaning and crying, Marso's comforting them, the boy Yarri's worried chatter, Guine's continuing to explain he'd done all he could . . .

She cleared a space in her mind to think.

I failed my team. I have to fix this. I owe it to Amurra. To Stran. To all of them.

But how? I've been trying my best, and my best hasn't been enough. Eklor had outsmarted her every step of the way. He'd been more ruthless, more prepared. How could she hope to beat him? *I'm outmatched. And I failed to see it.*

And Amurra paid the price.

Dimly, she heard the door open and registered that Jentt and Zera had returned. She heard Marso fill them in, and all of them began to yell and argue about what to do next.

"We can't do it," Zera was saying. "It's what he wants. If we withdraw our accusations, if we don't have the doctors testify, if we don't get that talisman out of his hands . . . Stran, you can't want him to go unpunished!"

"I want Amurra back," Stran said. "Whatever the cost. If that means capitulating to that monster, I'll do it in a heartbeat. She's my wife, the mother of my children. She's my life!"

"He's trying to neutralize us before his big show," Jentt said. "He sees us as a threat."

Zera smacked her fists together. "Then we *be* that threat and we stop him!"

Stran raged, "I will not risk my wife! If there's any chance of saving her—"

"You'd sacrifice all of Cerre for the chance that Eklor will honor his word?" Zera shot back. "I am sorry, deeply sorry, but there is no real chance of that. You've met Eklor, right? Never honors his word. And even if he did, remember the cost? An innocent would die. You want that on your conscience? You want it on Amurra's? Eklor isn't making an offer we can take. He offers false hope. You know that. We can't negotiate with him—we have to take him down!"

In a shaky voice, the boy Yarri whispered, "She's right. Listen to her. Master Eklor hid human bones in my bed. You saw them. You can't trust him."

Zera spun. "Thanks for the vote, but who the hell let a kid in here?"

Yarri shrank back, and Stran crossed to wrap an arm protectively around him. "He's innocent. We're keeping him safe." To all of them, he said, "I know we can't trust Eklor. But what choice do I have? Amurra is my *wife*."

Kreya turned away from the waterfall and faced her friends. "It's my fault."

"It's Eklor's," Zera said flatly. "And he'll pay."

"I always think I know best," Kreya said. "I always think I know exactly what to do, how to keep everyone safe, how to win . . . I was so consumed with needing to beat Eklor." Holding the scout tightly, she closed her eyes and let the full force of her guilt wash over her.

"Love that you're having a personal epiphany," Zera said, "but right now, we need you to lead. Stran here wants to capitulate to a war criminal, while I think Eklor needs to be punished."

"He's won," Stran said. "He has my Amurra. He holds her life in his hands."

"He's not offering a way to save her," Zera snapped. "He's offering a trap. You walk in there and capitulate to what he wants, and we lose. But if we stick together . . ."

That was it.

That was what they had that Eklor didn't: a team. A team that could work together and trust each other and lean on each other's strengths. If they could unite in a single purpose.

But that depended, right now, on Stran.

Kreya focused on Stran and only on him. "What if we could get her body back? What would you do to save her? How far would you go?"

He understood what she was asking. "You broke law after

law to bring back Jentt. Believe me when I say I would do the same. I'd do anything for her. Give up anything for her."

Kreya studied him. "You're certain?" Next to Amurra, whom she couldn't ask, he was the one who'd been hurt the most. Not Kreya. Not this time. She'd made too many decisions for her team without listening to what they wanted and needed. She'd spent too long thinking she knew what was best for all of them, for Jentt, for Zera, for the world. This time, the choice was theirs. And she wanted it unanimous, beginning with Stran.

"In a second," Stran said.

Jentt jumped in. "No."

Stran glared at him. "You can't choose this for me—"

"She won't thank you," Jentt said, and Kreya felt as if he'd stabbed her in the heart and twisted. She should have told him from the beginning what the cost was. She shouldn't have let this lie grow between them. She should have given him a choice. "If you sacrifice your life for her, even a portion of it, to bring her back—"

"She'd do the same for me," Stran said. "As you would for Kreya."

Zera let out a mirthless laugh. "Jentt gave up his entire life for me, and I'm only a friend. Of course he'd give up his life for Kreya. Without a second's hesitation."

"Exactly," Stran said. "Look me in the face and tell me you wouldn't. You'd die for your wife. I know you would. So how dare you tell me I can't do the same?"

Jentt opened his mouth and shut it.

Good, Kreya thought. *Maybe he's beginning to understand my choice.* Maybe in time, he'd forgive her. She hoped they had that time. To all of them, she said, "I have a plan, if you'll trust me." Eklor wanted all five of them to withdraw their accusations. He'd expect them to either charge in recklessly and demand Amurra or capitulate to his demands. He wouldn't expect Stran especially to show restraint and trust his team.

"Always," Stran said.

"The army exists. The construct that attacked"—she wouldn't say the word "killed"—"Amurra proves it. It's coming." Even though, yet again, they had no proof. She looked down at the little crushed scout in her arms. This also wasn't proof, though it was enough for her. The army was coming from the valley. She'd have bet her life on it.

"So we fight?" Jentt asked.

"Not yet," Kreya said. "We're not ready yet. Zera?" Her friend grinned and rubbed her hands together in gleeful anticipation. "Choose your strongest talismans for Stran and Jentt, and leave me your spare, unused bones for my constructs. We will need to all work together to be ready, after I get back."

Jentt frowned. "Back from where?"

Back from atoning for my mistakes, she thought.

Out loud, she said, "I'm going to get Amurra."

"How?" Stran demanded.

"I'll give him what he thinks he wants. Lie as much as I have to." Her eyes landed on Grand Master Lorn's beloved son. She'd try the truth too, if she could, but whatever she had to say, she'd say.

"You do know diplomacy isn't your strongest skill?" Zera said.

"An old dog can learn new tricks," Kreya said. "I can change. For Amurra. For us. But only if we're all agreed that saving her comes first, before anything else. If I go down this path, then we're committed."

"Committed to what?" Marso asked.

"War," she said bluntly. "If I do this, there will be no more words that will save us or Vos. Only the spilling of blood."

Her team was silent for a moment, chewing over their memories and their fears.

At last, Zera said, "I think . . . that was always our fate, from the moment we heard his laugh on the plains."

"Then we're agreed?" Kreya said. "First I lie, then we fight."

Around her, her friends nodded, one after another, with Jentt last, reluctant but agreed. Unanimous.

CHAPTER TWENTY-SIX

Holding the boy's hand, Kreya walked through the stone skull into the guild headquarters. She gave their names to the guards at the front but spoke to no one else. It was crowded—Grand Master Lorn had summoned bone workers from across Vos to experience Eklor's "miracle," and they'd obviously begun to arrive, clogging the hallways and filling the great hall.

"Are you scared?" Yarri asked in a small voice.

"Of course," Kreya said. "Only fools aren't scared."

"Oh." His voice was even smaller.

"But that doesn't mean we don't do what needs to be done anyway. Fear just means you're alive. And that you care about staying that way. It's a good thing. You just can't let it make your decisions."

"Will Master Eklor be here?"

"I certainly hope so." She tried to keep the viciousness out of her voice and knew she'd completely failed. She gripped the boy's hand harder and increased her pace. She wore her best don't-fuck-with-me expression, and the clumps of bone workers reacted accordingly—they parted to let her through.

As she passed by, a few bone workers called to her by name.

She glanced over, and their names clicked into her head as she recognized them: Uvi, Penrek, Briel. But she didn't stop to greet them. One of them, Briel, jogged up to her. Once, they'd been students together here. Now, the years had carved craters into Briel's cheeks. "Master Kreya!" Briel sounded delighted to see her. "It's been years! How have you been? Is it true what I heard, that Jentt lives?"

"You should leave," Kreya told her. "Quickly and quietly, with as many as will go with you. No matter what you've heard or may hear. If you value your life and your soul, leave."

Briel recoiled and let out a nervous laugh. "Surely you jest. Grand Master Lorn has assured us in no uncertain terms there's no danger, no matter what gossip we may hear from the uneducated masses beyond our walls—"

Kreya kept walking. She'd delivered her warning. If others chose to disregard the lessons of the past, that was not her problem. Or it wasn't her problem right now. *It will be my problem later,* she thought. But right now, she had a single goal: Amurra.

Stran had made his choice to save her, and Kreya was going to honor that choice. She had the team's approval to do what needed to be done.

Besides, I do not leave teammates behind. Never again.

She'd lost one once. She wasn't about to lose another. And Amurra had become one of them, even if she wasn't in any of the ballads about the Five Heroes. She'd joined their group by her own choice and become a part of it by both words and actions.

Kreya walked straight to Grand Master Lorn's office. He'd be there, she guessed, preparing for the miracle. Giving her name to the guard, she waited while he knocked. The guard stepped inside and then emerged. "He will see you." Eyeing her, the guard hesitated for a second before adding, "Master Eklor is with him."

"Good." Still holding Yarri's hand, she entered the office.

Both Lorn and Eklor were there. Lorn was seated at his desk, papers arrayed in front of him, while Eklor stood behind him, also looking down at the papers.

"Papa!"

Grand Master Lorn rose to his feet. "Yarri, what—"

Kreya did not release the boy's hand. Instead, she tightened her grip. "Stay by me," she said softly. Seeing Eklor, Yarri stopped willingly. He clung to Kreya's side, and she wrapped her arm around him as if that would protect him from all of life's disappointments and betrayals. She knew it wouldn't.

"Ahh, Master Kreya, you've come to withdraw your false accusations?" Eklor guessed.

Kreya didn't try to keep her hatred off her face. "I have."

"You will admit to Grand Master Lorn that you have no proof?"

"I have no proof," she agreed.

Eklor broke into a smile. "And you will testify to this in front of all the bone workers?"

"I will. You stand falsely accused. My past blinded me to the truth."

He looked as if he wanted to rub his hands together and start chortling, but he restrained himself. "And your team? Will they testify as well?"

"Unfortunately, my team is in mourning," she said. "The wife of Stran, my friend and Hero of Vos, was murdered earlier today."

Grand Master Lorn's eyes flicked from his son up to Kreya's face. "Stran's wife?"

"What terrible news," Eklor said. "Of course, I had nothing to do with her death. As Grand Master Lorn can attest I have been in the guild headquarters since your embarrassing display of paranoia this morning." He said this as if it proved anything, when it was known he could create and command constructs.

"I didn't claim you killed her."

"Good. Because it seems to me that would be adding an accusation instead of recanting one." Eklor was studying her, as if trying to figure out her intent. She wished she could trust Grand Master Lorn to side with her if she did accuse Eklor, but given what they suspected about the persuasion talisman, she didn't dare take that risk. Her number one priority right now was Amurra. Everything else had to wait.

"It has come to my attention that you have her body," Kreya said. "I want it back."

Grand Master Lorn flipped his focus from his son to Eklor. "What has happened? Why would you have Stran's wife's body?"

Eklor spoke quickly. "Her body was delivered to me, along with a request for resurrection. I plan to revive her as part of tomorrow's grand miracle." He leveled a look at Kreya, as if daring her to contradict him.

"You will not revive her," Kreya said. "You will return her."

"You do not wish to accept my offer of life beyond?" Eklor said. "A pity. She could be back with her husband in a mere day. Be mother to her children again."

Kreya didn't reply.

"You still believe in the 'cost' of my resurrections?" Eklor sounded amazed. *He should have been on the stage,* she thought. He'd mastered his wounded-innocent act. "You'd truly rather she stay dead than admit you were wrong? I am surprised. But perhaps I should not be, given our history." He sighed theatrically.

"Very well. If you want her to experience true death, we will burn her body on the pyre, as is tradition. That can be arranged, can it not, Grand Master Lorn?"

"Of course," Grand Master Lorn agreed.

"Thank you for the honor," Kreya said, willing her voice to stay steady and low—she should have guessed he'd make that play—"but I will take the body."

Eklor's smile was back on his face, and Kreya resisted the urge to punch him in the mouth. He thought he held all the cards. "You cannot refuse such—"

She didn't let him finish. *Now* was the time to play her cards. "Grand Master Lorn, your son has had quite a scare."

Lorn rounded the desk. "Yarri—"

"Ahh, I see. How sad," Eklor said. "The hero has become the villain. You are holding him hostage, in case I refuse you. You want to trade this innocent boy for the body of your friend."

"I am not the villain here." As proof, Kreya stepped aside and released Yarri's hand. The boy ran into his father's arms. "*I* wouldn't use someone's loved one as a hostage to get what I want." Now it was her turn to smile pleasantly. He was mistaken: she hadn't brought Yarri to use against Eklor; she'd brought him to use *on* Lorn. Encouragingly, she said to Yarri, "Go on, tell your father what you saw."

"There were bones in my bed, Papa," Yarri said. "Human bones. Lots of them." The boy began to cry. "And then . . . and then . . . I saw dead people. They'd been attacked by a construct in a fifth-tier palace, where it should be safe. I . . . I . . ."

Lorn gripped his son's shoulders. "Are you hurt? Did anyone hurt you?"

Crying full out now, Yarri couldn't speak. He shook his

head. His father checked him all over, reassuring himself that he was unharmed.

"No one hurt him," Kreya said. "And no one will hurt him. Right, Eklor?"

"Indeed," Eklor said. His smile was more strained, but it was still fixed on his face.

"Here's the deal, Eklor: I will withdraw my accusations. Publicly, as you wish, on behalf of all five Heroes of Vos. And you will give me the body of Amurra, to be mourned and handled by her loved ones. If anyone asks, we will say her husband was not present at the time of her death, and he wishes to say goodbye. If you are as innocent as you claim to be, what's the harm in being gracious and kind?"

Grand Master Lorn rose. His face was a thundercloud. "You hid human bones in my son's bed? You made my son a target, after you swore—"

"Your son is unharmed," Eklor said. "And there is no proof the bones were mine, or even that they were human bones. Kreya has come to withdraw her accusations, not make new ones. Note that she carries no evidence of such a find with her. Only the word of a boy, untrained in the bone arts."

"My son does not lie!"

"But he can be mistaken."

She saw Eklor's hand slip into a pocket. Withdrawing it, he twirled a talisman between his fingers. Glancing at Lorn, she saw the second his eyes glazed. Eklor's other hand rested casually on the hilt of a dagger at his waist, as if daring Kreya to challenge him.

She weighed the odds and schooled herself to be patient. Amurra first.

"All I want is Amurra's body," Kreya said placidly. "If you are reformed, as you say, you will respect her family's wishes."

"Burning on a pyre in the guild headquarters is an honor—" Eklor began.

Yarri tugged on his father's arm. "Papa, he put bones in my bed! Why aren't you arresting him?"

For a moment, Lorn's eyes cleared as his son's truth broke through Eklor's lies. *A moment is all I need to save Amurra*, she thought.

"Grand Master Lorn, you know my request is not unreasonable," Kreya said. "Tradition is on my side. Her body should be handled by those closest to her."

Grand Master Lorn asked, "What happened to the bones in my son's bed?"

"Your guards burned them, as was appropriate," Kreya said.

Eklor flinched. But he recovered quickly. "How convenient. But your accusations are beside the point—Grand Master Lorn has witnessed the spell up close and knows it breaks no taboos."

He must have been using the talisman during the boy's resurrection, Kreya thought. She wondered how often he'd used it and when it would run out of power. He could have created dozens of them, for all she knew.

"You saw with your own eyes," Eklor said to Lorn.

He swayed slightly. "I . . . did."

"Grand Master Lorn, I am not here to cause trouble," Kreya said. "Your son is safe, and the illegal bones have been destroyed. All I ask is for what tradition owes me: my friend's body so we may mourn her properly."

Despite the effects of the talisman, Grand Master Lorn was not an idiot. She was counting on that. With Yarri here to deliver the news, he couldn't have missed hearing the unsaid truth: Eklor had murdered Stran's wife, and Kreya was withdrawing her accusation under duress. Whether Lorn believed that also meant that Eklor intended to harm the Bone Workers Guild or not, she couldn't say, and she wouldn't count on it. As Eklor had pointed out, she came with no proof. As preposterous as it might have seemed, under the influence of the talisman, Lorn could probably be persuaded human bones just *happened* to show up in Yarri's bed. She just had to hope it was enough—hope that hearing it out of the mouth of his own son was enough—to break through Eklor's hold on his mind and tip the scales in her favor just this once, for Amurra's sake.

"It's a reasonable request," Grand Master Lorn said.

Eklor frowned. "Grand Master!"

"You saved my son's life, Eklor," Lorn said. "Don't undo the good you have done through petty stubbornness. You will let Master Kreya take the body."

He looked as if he wanted to object more, but instead he inclined his head. "Very well, Grand Master Lorn. If Master Kreya will address the assembly of bone workers, then I will prepare the woman's body."

"Body first," Kreya said.

Grand Master Lorn held up his hands to stave off further argument. "I will have her brought to you. Let us have no more distrust, and let us use today to demonstrate to the entire guild that we have put the past behind us."

IN HER YOUTH, KREYA NEVER COULD HAVE DONE IT: stand in front of the entirety of the Bone Workers Guild and claim that her sworn enemy, the man who was responsible for her husband's death, was noble and good. Her pride, her stubbornness, her innate sense of justice never would have allowed her to let the words fall from her lips. She would have punched her fist into the sky and declared she'd never defile the truth.

Now, knowing what it was like to lose Jentt and knowing what it felt like to have him back again . . . If lying would give Stran back his wife, she'd lie until her tongue turned blue. She owed it to him, to all of them.

Standing between Lorn and Eklor, Kreya plastered a false smile on her face. She met the eyes of her colleagues, the masters, the novices, and the students. They were bathed in the thin light from the thick stained glass windows that muffled the sounds of the outside world. *Not unlike the way their minds are muffled.*

"I was blinded by my own pain," she said. "Stuck in the past. Unwilling to let go of my old anger and hatred. It poisoned me, and it nearly enabled me to poison you against Master Eklor, who stands before you a reformed man."

Without moving his mouth, Eklor murmured, "Don't overdo it."

"I still hate him. I will always hate him."

"Better," he murmured.

She continued as if he hadn't spoken. "To tell the complete truth, I want him dead. I will not be free until his heart stills, his breath stops, and his eyes stare sightless at eternity."

"You are terrible at this," he murmured.

"But it was wrong of me to let that hatred and anger cloud my judgment," Kreya said. "He owes an insurmountable debt to the Bone Workers Guild and to Vos itself, and I have no right to prevent him from whatever small amount he can do to repay that debt."

That didn't elicit a comment from Eklor. She guessed she'd met with his approval, at last. Kreya continued: "I have no proof that an army exists. He claims he destroyed it on the plain. I have no proof that he uses human bones. There are no bones in his possession. I do not know that his spell of resurrection causes harm to anyone. That was mere conjecture. And so I officially, formally, all other ways, withdraw my baseless accusations, on behalf of the Five Heroes of Vos."

She heard Eklor exhale beside her. *He didn't think I'd really do it,* she realized.

She wondered what would have happened if she hadn't, if she'd plunged forward convinced her own righteousness would carry the day. But she knew the answer to that. She'd have failed. He'd wormed his way too deeply into the guild.

"You must now use your own judgment as to whether to trust this man," Kreya said. "Do not trust to mine. And please forgive me, an old warrior, for still aching with the wounds of battle and allowing the past to color my perception of the present." She bowed to the assembly and then retreated while Lorn addressed the council.

Behind the dais, she discovered she was shaking. She clasped her hands together so no one would notice and turned to face Eklor, who had followed her. "Now it's your turn to keep our bargain," she told him.

"Very well." He gestured for her to precede him.

Side by side, they walked through a quiet corridor. "One question, Eklor."

"Ask," he said, with a significant look at the guards who trailed behind them. His message was clear: if he didn't like her question, she wouldn't be walking out of here, despite her performance.

"Why not use it on me?" She didn't say the words "persuasion talisman."

He knew what she meant anyway. "I tried, multiple times that day in Lorn's palace. But you . . . You don't want to believe me." He swept his arm out to encompass the guild. "Others do."

"It won't last forever," she told him. She meant the talisman, his hold over the guild master, and Eklor's own life.

"It will last long enough."

"So you're aware this isn't over."

"Oh, it will be over sooner than you think."

Under Eklor's watchful eyes, she claimed Amurra's body by the mouth of the headquarters. Unwrapping the linen over her face, she checked to be sure it was her.

It was. Silent, dead. It hurt to look at her. She remembered Amurra's smiling when she opened the farmhouse door to welcome Kreya in, shouting at Stran to not be a hero anymore, insisting on coming with them to the city. She didn't deserve to be treated like this, as a bargaining chip.

"I hope you will consider joining us tomorrow," Eklor said, "to receive my gift."

Kreya very, very briefly contemplated gutting him here and now. She'd be arrested instantly, though, and lose any chance of saving Amurra. "I hope you will consider going out back and fucking yourself," she said pleasantly.

Activating a bit of a strength talisman, Kreya lifted Amurra's body over her shoulder. Without another word to anyone, she carried her new friend out of the headquarters, adding a bit of speed to her movement. They all had a lot to do before tomorrow.

CHAPTER TWENTY-SEVEN

Zera ordered her followers to stand guard by every window and posted several by the doors. Plenty of onlookers, eager for a glimpse of the Five, still lurked beyond the statue garden outside—they'd serve as an early-warning system as well. "Let me know if you hear any screaming," Zera told her followers. "Unless it's by Marso." She flashed him a smile. "You be you, old friend."

His chicken bones were clutched against his chest. He gave her a tight nod.

While she waited for Kreya's return, she weeded through her collection of bones, separating them by source and strength. Stran paced back and forth in front of the waterfall, as if motion would speed time along. Jentt sat still. *As still as death,* Zera thought. He refused to watch for Kreya's return, yet Zera could tell that every nerve in his body was attuned to the door, ready for it to open.

"Knock it off," Zera told him.

He startled. "What?"

"Blaming her."

"She shouldn't have sacrificed her future for me."

Zera rolled her eyes. "You know how they call us the Five

Heroes of Vos? Literally our job to do that kind of shit. Get over it."

"I want her to live a long and happy life."

"Yeah, well, she chose happy. So get over yourself and stop making her miserable. It was her choice to make, and she made it."

"It was my choice as well—"

"You were dead."

"Not always," he pointed out. "She could have told me the cost any of the times she woke me. She knew how I'd feel about it, she knew it was wrong, and that's why she hid it from me. We're supposed to be a team, facing the world united—that's the point of marriage! And here she is, unilaterally making decisions that affect both of us and deciding for me what facts I can and cannot handle. How do I know she's not lying about anything else?"

"She probably is, given your attitude. I know I would."

"But—"

Zera held up one hand. "No. You took an arrow for me. You died for me. Did you consult Kreya first?"

"There wasn't time—"

"So? Same decision. You gave me a gift. You gave me a life, a future, hopes and dreams, and all that." Waving her arms, she indicated her palace, the waterfall, the skeleton pillars, all of it. "I didn't think I'd ever get a chance to say thank you. So I'm saying it now: *thank you*. And now I'm giving you a gift: don't be a dick."

Jentt looked startled again, and then he laughed.

Zera took that to be a good sign. It had been one of the foundations of her life that while he'd lived, Kreya and Jentt

were together, always united, ludicrously healthy in their relationship. It would be a shame to lose that in Jentt's second life.

Guine called from the door. "Master Kreya approaches!"

"Let her in, obviously," Zera ordered.

Crossing the foyer in three large strides, Stran flung open
the door and charged outside, shoving Guine out of the way.
Shooing her followers back, Zera cleared a path. Everyone was
bubbling: "Be careful!" "Let them through!" "By the bones, she's
dead!" "Give them space." "What did you do? How did you get
her?" "I can't bear to look at her." And from Stran: "Can you
make her live again?"

Kreya's lips were pressed tight together. She carried Amurra's
linen-wrapped body in her arms, and she didn't look at Stran.
She did, though, meet Zera's eyes.

Zera nodded. "This way. Everyone else, clear out." She asked
Kreya, "Anyone following you?" She had no idea who Kreya had
made an enemy of this time: Eklor, Lorn, the entire guild, an
undead army, all of Cerre. Really, with Kreya, the possibilities
were endless.

"Not that I know of. Might as well assume the worst,
though."

"Guard the doors and windows," Zera ordered.

She shepherded her friends into the closest bedroom, a
confection draped in silks and strands of crystals that Marso
had been using as his room. Kreya laid Amurra on Marso's
bed. Stran hovered over her shoulder as Kreya unwrapped
her body.

Amurra's face was gray tinged and still. Her eyelids were,
thankfully, closed, but she had that terrible empty, motionless
look of someone who had turned from a person to a thing. Zera

knew without needing to touch her that her skin would feel *wrong*—cold, stiff, and yet still with a hint of softness.

Stran dropped to his knees and made a noise that didn't sound like it could have come from his throat, a broken moan that hit Zera hard in her sternum. She laid a hand on his shoulder but knew he didn't feel it. Marso was close on his other side. Jentt lingered back by the door, and Zera tried to imagine what he was thinking.

For the first time, he was seeing a loved one the way Kreya had seen him for so long. He was witnessing how it affected Stran. *Good,* Zera thought fiercely. *He needs to see this so he can stop being an idiot.*

"Take my life," Stran said, his voice thick with a sob. "She must live. The children . . . They need her. The world needs her. Take all of my life."

"She won't thank you for that," Jentt said quietly.

Kreya raised her head, and Zera saw the pain in her eyes— pain that Jentt had put there, or maybe memories. *Let's blame Eklor,* Zera thought. He was easiest to blame for all of this, since it was, unarguably, his fault. "What would you have me do?"

"Half his life, if he wants to give it," Jentt said.

The pain in Kreya's eyes cleared. A little.

Zera spoke without even considering it. "Or some of mine."

"And mine," Marso said. "Take some from me as well." He attempted a smile. It looked awkward on his face, as if his cheeks were stiff from lack of practice. "I'm not doing anything better with it."

Stran looked up and clapped his hands over Marso's and Zera's hands on his shoulders. His eyes were red, and tears were pouring openly down his cheeks. He nodded his thanks, unable to speak.

"If I'd known the cost with Jentt . . . ," Zera began.

Kreya interrupted. "You're all very noble, but I don't know how to pull life from more than one source. There might be a way, but it's a significant enough change to the spell to pull from someone other than myself. If I had enough time to experiment and research, I might be able to figure it out, but if I delay and Eklor attacks . . . Stran, this has to be your choice."

"Do it now, and take half of whatever years remain of my life," Stran said without hesitation. "I don't want her dead a minute longer."

Zera wanted to counsel them to take the time, do the research, and find a way to share the burden. But she was also acutely aware of how precarious everything was. Kreya was right: this could be their only chance to bring Amurra back.

"The spell takes from your natural life span, from now until the moment of your natural death," Kreya told Stran. "It does not account for either of you being stabbed, falling off a cliff, or dying from anything other than your body simply failing. So don't think this will make either of you invincible. It won't guarantee you a happily ever after. You could sacrifice half your future, and she could still die from a random accident or another violent attack next week."

"I'd rather have the chance of living with her than the certainty of living without," Stran said. He held out his arm. "Take my blood."

"It may require a lot," Kreya said.

"I'm a big man. I have a lot. Take as much as you need."

"I mean you should lie down, because you'll probably faint. As you said, you're a big man—it would be a pain to try to move you." She shooed him onto the bed, next to Amurra. "I'll need the bones we took from Eklor's stash. All of them."

Without a word, Jentt darted out. He returned in a moment, carrying a bundle. He laid it on a table inlaid with onyx and gold, and he unwrapped it.

"Will it be enough?" Marso asked anxiously.

Kreya drew out a knife and tested its sharpness. "Water and bandages."

"I'll fetch them," Zera offered. She knew best where her supplies were. Letting herself out of the room, she strode down the hallway. She tried to keep from worrying about what Eklor was doing now. He wouldn't be waiting idly for them to finish their task and come back to deal with him; he'd be using this time, enacting whatever his plan was, putting pieces into place to counter whatever they'd do once they were ready. Even knowing that, for now, their only priority had to be Amurra.

She reached the linen closet and pulled out a pile of gauze and bandages, as well as a kit with medical thread and a sterile needle in case whatever wound Kreya inflicted needed to be sewn up. Closing the closet door, Zera jumped—Guine was standing a few inches away.

"You're supposed to be watching for danger," Zera scolded.

"Is the danger already within?" Guine asked.

"What do you mean?"

"Your friends are working unholy magic, aren't they?" His eyes were pleading, as if he needed her to comfort him and reassure him that everything was perfect, she'd never do anything remotely morally ambiguous, and he didn't need to worry about anything.

"They're saving the life of one who didn't deserve to die," Zera said carefully. She didn't want to lie to him, but she also didn't want to burden him with a truth that could endanger him. "I wouldn't call that unholy."

"Word is that you found human bones in Grand Master Lorn's palace."

"Word travels quickly," Zera said. "And yes, Eklor had bones he'd taken from the plains." Carrying the bandages, she strode back toward Marso's bedroom. She had to hope that her trust in Guine wasn't misplaced, and that his trust in her was intact. She felt vulnerable, which was not a sensation she liked. "Eklor's still the bad guy. We're still the good guys. You need to watch to make sure the bad guys don't come to kill the good guys while we're busy, okay?"

Guine laid a hand on her arm as she went to open the door. "Tell me: are you working illegal magic in that room?" His voice shook, as if it unnerved him to question her.

She raised both her eyebrows. "Are you going to try to stop me?" It would be inconvenient if she had to use a talisman to fight him—fight Guine? The very idea sounded ridiculous when she thought it. He was devoted to her, even if he wasn't in love with her. But she'd do it if she had to, though she'd rather not drop all the sterile bandages on the clean-but-not-sterile marble floor.

He hesitated, as if he hadn't considered the matter all the way through.

"You don't need to approve," Zera said, "but you do need to get out of my way."

"People aren't meant to live after they die." He looked terrified as he said it. "Such magic shouldn't exist. It violates all the laws of nature and decency."

"The laws of nature and decency say friends don't give up on friends," Zera said. "No matter what tragedies happen. No matter how many years pass. People are meant to keep loving each other, even after death." She might not have been sure about the ethics of what Kreya could do, but she believed in the goodness of her friend's heart. Jentt was a part of her, and in saving him, she'd saved herself. Now she wanted to do the same for Stran.

"If I died, would you try to save me?" Guine asked.

Zera didn't hesitate. "Yes."

"Even though you don't love me?"

"You're my friend. Like Kreya. Like Jentt. Even when you're behaving like this, the answer is still yes." Maybe it was a choice no human should be able to make, but if it was available to her, she'd do it. *Hey, Kreya, I understand now.*

And she also understood why Kreya said the knowledge would die with her.

Guine wasn't wrong. It was a terrible and wonderful power that no one should possess. She could think of six dozen ways to abuse the spell before dinner, and unlike Eklor, she wasn't even trying to be evil.

He let her go.

She raised her eyebrows at him. "You don't care if I'm using illegal magic so long as I'm willing to use it on you too? Impressive ethical gymnastics there."

"I assumed I was replaceable to you."

"Well, you aren't." She wasn't certain how or why this should affect Guine's attitude toward their breaking the law, but he was looking at her as if what she'd said changed everything. "You are important to me, a fact I would've thought was obvious. But maybe it wasn't. A fact I can make obvious *after* the current crisis, if you're willing to give me a second chance to be less of an asshole."

"I . . . misjudged you. Please—"

"Apologize to me *after*," Zera told him. "For now, go make

sure no one comes to murder us while we engage in our 'unholy' behavior."

He still looked dazed.

"Guine, I am trusting you with all our lives. Don't make me think *I've* misjudged *you*."

"Yes, ma'am." He fled down the hall.

She pushed her way back into the room and shut the door behind her. Dumping the bandages on a chair, she locked the door. For extra measure, she withdrew a strength talisman, activated it, and shoved a wardrobe in front of the door. Jentt helped her. He didn't ask any questions. Neither of them spoke.

Kreya had already begun.

She'd cut a slit in Stran's arm. Coating the old soldiers' bones with blood, she was pushing them into Amurra's sternum. As Kreya chanted the words of the spell, the bones sank into Amurra's flesh, like sugar dissolving into water.

Bone after bone.

A femur, a rib, a vertebra.

Clavicle.

Humerus.

More ribs. Another vertebra.

Last, Kreya pushed a skull into Amurra's body, and it melted into her, jaw first, nasal cavity, empty eye sockets, crown, until every last trace of it was gone. Zera realized Kreya hadn't answered Marso's question—would it be enough?

I guess we'll see, she thought. Every bone had been used. It had to be enough.

A sheen of sweat glistened on Kreya's face. Zera wished she could help. She stood ready with the bandages. But Stran still needed to bleed.

Silent, Marso had sunk to the floor to sit cross-legged beside the bed. He was stroking his chicken bones without looking at them, as if afraid to see what they'd say. She was oddly glad that he couldn't read them as well as he used to. Somehow not knowing if they'd succeed or fail made this mean more.

There's beauty in trying, Zera thought.

That was the difference between them and Eklor. When they lost a loved one, they . . .

Well, he *did* try to save his own loved ones first, and only after he was stopped did he seek revenge. Like Kreya on the plains. Maybe they weren't so different. They'd all crossed lines. *We have yet to resort to attempting a massacre, though,* Zera thought. *So we're winning.*

Staggering backward, Kreya gasped for air. "Done."

Jentt caught her and steadied her.

Moving quickly, Zera pressed gauze against Stran's wound. It was deep, and the blood still surged sluggishly from it. It would need to be sewn, and he'd need to rest. She readied the needle and surgical thread.

Beside Stran, Amurra's chest rose and fell. Color had spread to her cheeks. Her eyes fluttered open as if she were waking from a peaceful night's sleep. She turned her head. "Stran?"

His voice was choked. "Amurra."

"You're going to kill that bastard, aren't you?" she rasped. Her voice sounded as if all moisture in her throat had evaporated. She swallowed painfully.

"Absolutely," he swore.

"I didn't like dying."

"I won't let it happen again," Stran said.

Kreya murmured, "Don't make promises you can't keep."

Amurra sat up. "What did you do, Stran? What did all of you do?"

Jentt answered. "He shared his remaining life with you. Half of all his future years."

When Stran struggled to sit up with her, Zera poked him in the shoulder until he lay still. "I'm sewing you up. Don't move unless you want me to miss." Focusing on the wound, she knit together the flesh. Blood stained her fingers, but she ignored it. He lay still as she made neat, even stitches.

But his wife did not lie still. She pressed herself against his side, turned his head so he faced her, and kissed him thoroughly. He smiled, she smiled, and it was a lovely moment that would have made Zera roll her eyes if she hadn't been so focused on making sure he didn't bleed out. Finishing the stitches, she cleaned the blood as best she could and then wrapped the wound in clean gauze, covered in bandages.

When the two of them finally quit staring into one another's eyes as if they'd each invented the sun, Amurra asked, "How many years?"

"No way for me to know," Kreya said. She sounded extremely tired, and Zera was happy to see that Jentt had his arm around her, supporting her. Maybe they were past their issues, at least for now. Certainly there couldn't have been a better object lesson for Jentt for how he should have behaved. *At least something good has come out of this*, Zera thought. She thought also of Guine and how she'd never told him he mattered to her. Of course, in that case, he was an idiot for not realizing it.

"Can you ask the bones?" Amurra asked Marso.

He hugged the chicken bones tighter. "Are you sure you want to know?"

"Yes," she said without hesitation. Stran agreed with her.

"We have children," Stran explained. "If we can't take care of them, then we need to know to make other arrangements."

"Again," Kreya said tiredly, "you could still die randomly."

"Marso, please?" Amurra asked.

He sighed, and his shoulders sagged, but to Zera's ears, it didn't sound like a defeated or dejected sigh. More like relief, which was odd. She eyed Amurra and decided the woman was smarter than they'd given her credit for. She somehow knew she wasn't asking too much of Marso.

He tossed the bones on the carpet, and his eyes shifted, taking on that looking-elsewhere expression he wore when he was seeing more than what anyone else could see. He rocked side to side, and his lips moved without sound.

All of them watched and waited.

Mist rose above the bones, and images flashed within, too fast for Zera to see and too jumbled for her to make any sense of. But Marso was enrapt. The silence felt like the moment before a vase fell and shattered on the ground. It was the breath before the scream.

At last, he looked at them. Smiled. "Eighteen years."

Stran let out a gusty sigh. "It's enough."

"We'll see our kids grow up," Amurra said. "We'll be there for them, through their childhoods. It is enough. Thank you, Marso. Kreya . . . There are no words."

Kreya straightened. She had more color back in her cheeks, now that she'd rested for a few moments. "First we need to survive Eklor's—"

Jentt interrupted. "Read us. How many years do we have?"

"Does it matter?" Kreya asked him. "Would you live any differently if you knew it was eighteen years or eight months?"

A muscle twitched in his cheek. "I don't know."

"I do," Kreya said. "I plan to use every day to its fullest, no matter how many we have left, because I lived too many days waiting for things to be right again. I spent years with my heart in the past and the future. From here on, I just want the present."

"I need to know," Jentt said.

They stared at each other for a long moment.

"Fine," Kreya said, clipped. "If you need to know."

Marso gathered the bones, whispered to them, and then tossed them again. He swayed, his lips moving as the mist rose, and Zera thought about stopping him. She knew that haunted expression in Kreya's eyes, and so she wasn't surprised when Marso opened his eyes and answered:

"Three years."

KREYA HAD KNOWN IT WOULD BE SHORT. FRANKLY, she'd feared it would be less.

She felt Jentt rock backward as the words hit him, as if he'd been struck. But she merely let the knowledge sink into her. She'd used up bits of her life for years, resurrecting him piecemeal. It didn't surprise her that she hadn't had much left to spare. Actually, it felt right. Of course she should pay a price for defying the laws of the universe.

"Only three," Jentt whispered.

"What do we do?" Zera asked.

Kreya thought the answer was obvious. "We live. We live and we love, and we do our best not to stop doing either before our time is up."

Wrapping his arms around her, Jentt pulled her close. "I'm sorry."

"Just try not to get hit with an arrow this time." Kreya rested her cheek against his shoulder and breathed in the wonderful scent of him. He wasn't angry anymore, which was a small miracle. "And don't mourn our deaths before they happen. We have time."

Amurra let out a gasp. "Time! How much time since I died? The army—did it come? Eklor's army! The construct, the little scout, found it! Did it tell you? Do you know?"

"The construct that murdered you kind of made that clear," Zera said.

"I tried to tell someone before I died. My, that feels so strange to say."

Stran kissed her golden hair. "Don't think about it. You're alive now."

"I'll always think about it," Amurra said. "I was *dead*. No more days with you. Never returning home. Never seeing Vivi, Jen, Nugget . . . We're naming him Evren."

"Whatever you want," Stran said.

"I want to not die again," Amurra said. "I want no one to die. What is Eklor planning, and how do we stop him?"

Key questions, Kreya thought. She liked Amurra even better after death. She had a practical streak that was even more noticeable. "All the bone workers from across Vos will be gathering tomorrow morning to receive his 'miracles.'"

"But we destroyed his stash of bones," Stran said. "That should slow him."

"Only if he intends to work the spell," Kreya said. "We don't know that he does. In fact, I doubt it. The resurrections were bait for his trap. I think it's more likely he's lured them to the guild headquarters with the promise of a miracle, and then he'll use his army to massacre them."

Jentt nodded. "Makes sense."

Amurra shuddered. "It's horrific. How do we stop it?"

Kreya turned to Zera. "Did you find spare bones for me?"

"Plenty," Zera said.

Next question: "Do you mind if I destroy your palace?"

Zera blinked. "Sure."

She didn't ask any questions, which was like the Zera of old, trusting Kreya. She felt the weight of that trust, and she silently swore not to squander it this time. Years ago, she'd taken Zera's friendship for granted, and then in the aftermath of the Bone War, she'd assumed she'd lost it. This time around, she was going to treasure it as it deserved to be treasured. "Your pillars," she explained, because Zera deserved answers even if she didn't ask, "the ones carved to look like skeletons, I'm going to turn them into our army."

"I love you," Jentt said.

She smiled. "I know."

CHAPTER TWENTY-EIGHT

For her first warrior, Kreya chose a stone pillar carved like the skeleton of a rampant lioness. She studied it for a moment. Felt its strength. Behind her, Zera and the others were evacuating the palace. Once she took the pillars, it was likely the ceiling would collapse.

"Can it be done?" Jentt murmured behind her.

No one had ever used bones to animate a stone statue. Most constructs were machines, compilations of gears and useful attachments. Or else they were powered devices like cable cars or lifts. She was the only bone maker she knew who had ever used bones with dolls. *The techniques should be the same,* Kreya thought. "Yes."

"Kreya . . ."

"You don't need to say it."

"I do, though. I have left too much unsaid."

She waited, and she felt the weight of the silent seconds while Jentt searched for the words he wanted. It was a strange sensation to know exactly how much time she had left. Every moment felt like it had to matter. There were so many moments she'd wasted in the past. So many moments she'd simply forgotten or that had blended into other memories.

She didn't like how much pressure it put on each moment. And so she forced herself to still, to breathe, to wait until he was ready to speak. It was only a handful of seconds, but choosing to take them felt somehow rebellious.

It made her want to kiss him.

And so she did, brushing her lips against his cheek and then his mouth. He kissed her back hungrily, as if he were afraid he wouldn't ever kiss her again. He felt the moments slipping away too.

When their lips parted, she asked gently, "Do you still need to say whatever you need to say?"

"Yes," he said, and drew a breath. "I'm sorry. Deeply, truly sorry."

"Me too. I should have told you about the cost."

He studied her. "You don't mean that."

She smiled. "True. I would have lied to you until we died. Sometimes honesty is cruelty, and love is lies."

"That's shitty relationship advice." But he was smiling too.

"Good thing I'm not a role model. I'm just a hero past her prime who, very literally, loves you as much as she loves life itself. And I'm trying to learn from my mistakes. So how about we save the day before we walk off into the sunset?"

He passed her the first bone, the femur of a black bear. Taking it, she drew her knife and then activated a speed talisman. She'd been carving bones for so long that she didn't need to think—her hands and muscles knew what to do. And so they moved faster than she could think, carving symbols into the soft bone. Three bones for the first pillar. She installed them with wire, tying true bone to the spines made of stone. The second pillar was a twelve-foot upright lizard. She used four bones on it. Methodically, she worked through every pillar in the great room before she moved to the jeweled skeletal statues in the yard. Sweat dripped from her, and her muscles shook. She'd never worked so fast or so hard, but she didn't allow herself to slow, reactivating the talisman as needed. Jentt stayed beside her, passing her bones, forcing her to drink water at intervals.

Mountain lion bones.

Croco-raptors.

Owl.

Elk.

Wolverine.

One statue, she laced with a hundred mice bones. Another she infused with the strength of a dozen badgers. Another carried eagle bones.

At last, when her muscles ached and her head throbbed and she'd lost all sense of time, she finished, with bones installed on every statue in Zera's garden and every pillar within the palace, over fifty statues total.

Quietly—who knew how long she'd been standing there—Amurra asked, "Will it be enough? If Eklor's army comes . . . will it be enough to defeat them?"

She'd seen his army on the plains. Fifty statues wouldn't be enough to defeat it. Five hundred wouldn't be enough. "No."

"Then why—"

"We don't need to defeat his army. We just need to hold them back long enough to get all the bone workers Eklor is trying to surprise on our side. Then *they* can defeat them." If they could buy the other masters enough time to recognize the danger, gather their strength, and defend themselves, that could be enough. She hoped.

It's always about time, isn't it? she thought.

"Okay—will these statues be enough to hold his army back?"

"Not yet." Luckily, though, Zera was not the only fifth-tier citizen with a statue garden. She didn't even own the only house with skeletal pillars. Calling across the salon, Kreya asked, "Zera, do you think your neighbors would be willing to give up their statues?"

"Not likely," Zera said. "Unless we bought them all, of course. And before you ask, even I don't have access to that much gold. My neighbors have expensive tastes."

Kreya considered options. One, she could make do with what she had. She nixed that immediately, having just told Amurra that it wasn't enough. Two, she could ask Jentt to steal them. She rejected that idea as well. She wanted the largest statues for her stone army, so theft wasn't practical. Three, she could threaten Zera's neighbors and force them to cooperate . . . "What do you think we should do?"

Zera gawked at her.

"What?"

"You're asking our opinion," Zera said. "It's refreshing."

Marso spoke up. "Everyone in Cerre has been hearing the music, seeing the plays, and retelling the stories of the Bone War for days. They remember us, and they remember him. I think Zera's neighbors will listen to reason."

"We can't rely on people." She thought of the villagers from Eren who had burned her tower and would have burned her and Jentt if they could have. She thought of Marso, who'd been pushed away by the guild, disbelieved and denied to the point where he tried to shred his own mind. She thought of Eklor . . . Okay, he was a lousy example of how to treat people.

Glancing across the room, she saw Zera's followers, clumped together, cowering, eyeing Kreya and her friends as if expecting them to breathe fire.

No, she thought. *It's up to us. Again.*

She'd thought they were done, but she'd been wrong. There was no "done." Not until the day you died. And sometimes not even then.

"Forgive me," Guine said, extracting himself from the clump of scantily clad followers and servants. "But you should have more faith in the men and women of Cerre. We can reach out to all our neighbors. Maybe we aren't warriors or bone workers, but we can convince people to help."

Zera blew them a kiss.

Kreya opened her mouth to say she couldn't expect ordinary people to grasp the severity of the situation and rise to the challenge. But then she shut it. Maybe it wasn't her call to make. Maybe they should have a chance to have a say in their own fate. She gave a tight nod to Guine.

It was Marso, to Kreya's surprise, who spoke again with his old confidence in his voice, this time to Zera's friends. "Go to every palace on the fifth tier. Tell them we need their statues. And when you're finished, go to the theaters and the music halls on the other tiers. Tell them to help spread the word: the bone guild is in danger."

GUINE AND MARSO'S IDEA WORKED.

In the wake of Guine and his friends, Kreya approached Zera's neighbors, especially those who sported the largest sculpture gardens, and with the owners' blessing, she carved bones and installed them in their statues. Jentt accompanied her, carrying the bag of fresh animal bones.

Statue after statue.

Garden after garden.

She installed her bones in them all: sculptures of giant men and women, soldiers, wild animals, mythical monstrosities. Any statue that looked as if it could fight, she inserted her magic. "You have a new purpose now, my beauty," she whispered to a marble carving of a wild boar.

At last, they reached Grand Master Lorn's palace. She still had unused bones—Zera's collection had been extensive—and she knew exactly how she wanted to use them. Every muscle felt as if it were quivering, but she couldn't stop now.

The guards recognized them instantly. "Master Kreya! Master Jentt!"

"We need Lorn's pillars," Kreya said bluntly.

"Your friends approached us with your request, and we'll tell you the same as we told them: Grand Master Lorn has not returned from the bone guild headquarters. Without his approval, we cannot grant you access to his palace, but we will notify him of your request when he returns."

That was very polite, but she wasn't going to take no for an answer. The army on the plains, hidden beneath the earth, had been vast. Eklor had had many years to build it up. She needed every statue she could get.

She peered at the closest guard. "I remember you. You helped me burn the bones."

"Yes, Master Kreya."

"You saw them for yourself," Kreya said. "Do you believe Eklor means no harm?"

"I . . ."

The other guard asked, "Do you mean harm to Grand Master Lorn or his property?"

"Yes," Kreya said.

The guard was not expecting that answer. Her stoic face twitched in surprise, and Kreya felt a stab of sympathy. The guards' job was to keep uninvited visitors out. They hadn't signed up to be asked to decide who to trust to save the world.

Jentt jumped in. "What she means is: she intends to harm Eklor, the monster who deceives our grand master and threatens the lives of our colleagues."

"So she don't mean to harm Grand Master Lorn or his palace?"

"I will most likely destroy his palace," Kreya said.

Jentt shot her a look. "You're terrible at this."

"I need the pillars, and I had enough of diplomacy at guild headquarters." She turned back to the guards. "Let me do what needs to be done. Meanwhile, you evacuate the building. It will most likely collapse without the pillars, since they're holding up the ceiling, and I don't want to be responsible for unnecessary deaths."

This did not reassure the guards. "We cannot allow—"

Jentt cut him off. "You have a choice: Take a risk and trust yourself. Help us. Or close your eyes to the obvious truth—Eklor is offering a fool's dream. A second chance at life comes at a terrible cost, and Eklor is making the innocent pay. Worse, he's using that dream as a trap."

"You know we could force our way in," Kreya said. "This is a courtesy only." Of course, if they had to force their way in, they'd use resources they couldn't spare fighting against people who weren't their enemy. She'd rather the guards cooperated.

The two guards stepped back to confer.

"Do you *ever* try tact?" Jentt whispered.

She gave him a tense half smile. "Not if I can help it."

"Fair enough."

For a second, her vision clouded. Kreya rubbed her eyes. *Overtired?* she wondered. It had already been a long night, but tomorrow would be longer still. She had to keep pushing herself. The more statues she could prepare, the fewer innocents would die. She hoped.

When the guards stepped forward again, they looked resolute. The female guard spoke: "We are deeply sorry, Master Kreya and Master Jentt, but our responsibility is to Grand Master Lorn and without his approval, we cannot grant your request." They looked scared at the possibility this might end in violence, yet they also stood firm.

Kreya opened her mouth to argue more, but Jentt drew her back. "Not the right battle to fight," he whispered. Replying to the guards, he said, "We respect your dedication to your duty." He kept pulling her down the stairs.

She wanted to race back up and force their way in. He stepped onto one of the cloud lifts. "Jentt, the pillars in there are twice the size of the ones in Zera's palace. You know how useful they would be—"

His lips close to her ear, he whispered, "That's why I stole their keys."

Ahh, he'd been the blur that had clouded her vision—it hadn't been exhaustion. She should have realized it. Leaning forward, she wrapped her arms around his neck and kissed him.

After they broke apart, he said, "East of the palace. Servants' entrance."

Using the cloud lift, they skirted around the grand master's palace. Jentt spotted the servants' entrance, tucked behind several topiaries. He swung the bag of spare bones over his shoulder as if he were carrying supplies for the kitchen, and he strode with purpose down the path. Kreya followed.

In seconds, they were inside, and Jentt had slipped the keys back into one of his many pockets. With Grand Master Lorn on the third tier, the palace was nearly empty. Kreya heard the clink of pots and dishes from the kitchen, as well as a low hum of chatter, but once they reached the grander halls, it felt abandoned.

They used speed and stealth talismans to dart through anyway, and Kreya added carved bones to the massive skeletal pillars, using up the last of the supply. She gave these colossi her strongest, deepest carvings, throwing every bit of power she could into them.

In total, there were twenty-four.

When she finished, she surveyed them. In the shadowy hall, they looked both menacing and beautiful. Coming up beside her, Jentt kissed her neck. "Ready to wake them?" he asked.

"We have to evacuate everyone from the palace first," she said.

"On it," he told her.

He zipped away.

She walked between the pillars. If this worked . . .

For one beautiful moment, she let herself bask in hope and silence. It was the first time she'd been alone in weeks, the first time she'd held still when she wasn't asleep, the first time she'd allowed herself to breathe without a hundred thoughts tumbling through her head, and it felt almost peaceful.

And then Jentt was back. "Everyone suddenly found themselves in the topiary garden." He rubbed his hands together. "Let's do this. Are you ready?"

Was she? Such an interesting question. Years ago, she'd felt ready for whatever the world would throw at her. With Jentt by her side, she'd felt as if she could face anything and of course good would triumph and happiness would be her reward. But then she'd lost him, and everything she'd thought she knew about the world—all that certainty—had drained out of her. Now, could she ever say she was "ready" again, knowing how badly it could all go and how much was beyond predicting or controlling?

Hell yes, I can.

She took his hand in hers. "Ready."

"You know, if we pull this off, there will be ballads about us today."

"There are already ballads about us," Kreya said. "Best we can hope for this time is that they'll rhyme." She faced the pillars. "*Vasi rae. Lindar rae. Abrutri inari rae!*" She released Jentt and raised both her hands over her head as she called to them, "Follow me, my friends! Fight for me! Fight for the bone workers of Cerre!"

For a moment, nothing happened. And then, slowly, the pillars lurched forward. Chunks of ceiling rained down as they yanked themselves off their perches. Kreya and Jentt backed toward the massive doors.

More pillars ripped themselves from the floor and ceiling. Their skull faces were sightless, but still Kreya felt as if they were focused on her. She guided them out of the grand master's palace. Their massive stone feet shattered the marble as they walked, and the first through the doorway smashed into the door frame. Stone and gold plummeted onto the steps below. Jentt waved an apology to the guards, but Kreya ignored them, marching to the cloud lifts.

They rode ahead, with the behemoths marching behind them. As they passed the other palaces, Kreya awakened the statues in their gardens. Soon, they filled the gold-flecked streets of the fifth tier. Reaching Zera's palace, Kreya ordered her statues to halt.

She woke those inside and led them out to join the others. "It's a simple plan: the statues defend the guild, and while they hold back the army, we slip inside and alert the bone workers. Then the bone workers fight the army while the five"—she glanced at Amurra—"six of us find Eklor. Any questions?"

Amurra raised her hand. "What about the persuasion talisman? How can we be sure the bone workers will listen?"

Good question. They still didn't know how powerful the talisman was. But she'd seen Eklor's grip on Lorn slip when his son told him about the bones. "Enough proof should break through whatever hold he has on them."

"If they need proof, we're about to have a lot of it," Zera said. "Just have to make sure they're paying attention."

Stran asked, "Marso, can you predict where Eklor's army will emerge?"

"I . . . I don't . . ."

Kindly, Kreya stopped him. "Not necessary. They'll emerge as close to the headquarters as possible. He'll want to keep as much of the element of surprise as he can before he attacks. He won't want the bone workers to be ready to defend themselves." More quietly, she said, "It's what I would do."

It was disturbing how easy she found it to predict his actions. She liked it better when she couldn't imagine his thoughts and feelings so easily. *I am not like him*, she thought. *There are lines I have never and would never cross.*

"Okay, great, we need to make sure the bone workers see the army, ideally before they're crushed by it," Zera said. "You're right that that should weaken the effects of the talisman—no talisman, even one made by a genius, is all-powerful. We weaken the effects, free the bone workers, grab Eklor, end the war. Piece of cake."

Taking a breath, Kreya looked at all her friends. This felt similar to the moment in the abandoned farmhouse, before they began their assault on the plain. They'd prepared as best they could, felt full of self-righteous optimism, certain they couldn't fail. Not knowing what they were truly walking into.

"I'm sure absolutely nothing will go wrong," Zera said with a straight face.

Shooting her a sharp look, Jentt reached toward Kreya and took her hand. "It will be different this time."

"Yeah," Zera said more seriously, "we're older, wiser, and cuter."

Kreya wanted to believe that was true. Not the cuter part, although it did momentarily make her smile. No, she wanted to believe they weren't just making all the same mistakes, underestimating their enemy and overestimating themselves. Closing her eyes, she saw Jentt fall, pierced by an arrow, as fresh a memory as if it were yesterday. She couldn't bear losing him again. Not when she knew how little time she had left to gift him, if he fell. And if she fell? Leaving him alone? Or if Zera fell, after Kreya had just found her again? Or Stran and Amurra, leaving their children alone?

"This time, we aren't going in order to be heroes," Stran was saying. "This time, we're going for the people we love. *That's* why it will be different. *That's* why we'll win."

It was a beautiful thing to say, and Kreya let it warm her. She reached out her other hand, and Zera took it. Stran took Zera's and Amurra's, Amurra took his and Marso's, and Marso took hers and Jentt's, completing the circle. Kreya felt as if strength were flowing between them. She let it fuel her.

"Let's save the world," Kreya said. "And this time, let's finish the job."

CHAPTER TWENTY-NINE

Their mistake was simple: they believed Eklor hadn't changed.

Kreya and the others assumed he still only wanted to target the bone workers. If he had, then Kreya's prediction would have been correct. He would have ordered his army to attack the guild headquarters on the third tier as soon as all the bone workers were gathered within. Kreya's statue army then could have descended from the fifth tier and surrounded them, fighting from the outside while, warned by Kreya's team, the bone workers fought from the inside, squeezing the enemy between them.

But he *had* changed.

Now he hated them all.

Not a single citizen of Cerre had sided with him against the Bone Workers Guild. Not one man, woman, or child had shown a drop of understanding of what he'd suffered and what he'd achieved, or at least not that he perceived. The people of this city—every man, woman, and child—had cheered and celebrated Eklor's defeat. They had turned the execution of his apprentice into a festival, and they had glorified the five so-called heroes who had destroyed his dreams of justice. And so, he determined, they should all pay the price for their lack of compassion for his pain.

His army had crept close to the city through the mists and then clawed their way through dirt and stone, climbing high within the mountain itself, both using the existing tunnels and creating new ones. As dawn touched the peaks and ridges and bathed the rocky slopes in lemon-gold, hundreds of metal, bone, and decaying flesh soldiers burst into the city of Cerre, *not* on the third tier, where the guild headquarters were and where Kreya's team expected them, but instead on the first and second tiers, through the homes of ordinary people.

The part-machine, part–flesh-of-the-dead soldiers ripped through the walls of kitchens and bedrooms. They destroyed shops and schools and markets. Several climbed to tear down the arches that held the aqueducts. Hundreds of gallons of water flooded the streets.

And as they destroyed the city, they killed its people.

Ensconced safely within the guild headquarters, the bone workers had no idea of the massacre in progress on the lower tiers. They were enrapt, seduced by the persuasion talisman and by their own fears and desires, listening to Master Eklor spin promises of a deathless future: the lure of immortality for themselves and their families.

But on the fifth tier, high above, Kreya and her team heard the screams of the dying.

And it didn't matter if they felt hopeful or hopeless, youthful or every bit of their age, trained or not, strong or not, ready or not. The war was no longer in the past. It was here, now.

"SHIT." KREYA SELECTED A FEW MORE CHOICE words as well.

As horrible as it was, though, there was the tiny whisper of satisfaction at the fact that her first instinct had been right. Eklor *had* assembled an army, he *had* brought his soldiers to Cerre, and he *wasn't* seeking redemption any more than a croco-raptor was seeking to apologize to his dinner. If she were lucky, if they were all very lucky, she'd be able to say "I told you so" to Grand Master Lorn.

She wished, however, she'd been right about Eklor's target. "Okay, change in plans. We split up. Half of us protect the in-nocent. Other half rouse the bone workers." She paused for a second. "Everyone agree?"

Zera flapped her arms at her. "Yes! For all that's holy, yes!" The others chimed in. Yes, they had to protect the people. Yes, do it now. There was no need, or time, for debate.

They still trust me, she thought. *And I trust them. We can do this.*

Or at least we can die trying.

Spinning away from them, Kreya shouted orders to her statue army: Fight. Protect. Defend. Destroy. And then to Stran: "Lead them to the lower tiers."

To Jentt: "Evacuate everyone you can."

To Zera: "Supply them with the talismans you think they'll need."

To Amurra, Guine, and Zera's followers: "Warn as many as you can on the upper tiers. Keep civilians away from the lower city."

"And you?" Zera asked.

Grimly, Kreya eyed the third tier. Unharmed so far. "I'll tell the bone workers I was wrong—they don't need to save them-selves.

"They need to save everyone else."

Zera distributed talismans to each of them, Stran first. "Carved from a bull femur, this one will give you fifteen minutes of four times your strength. You should be able to get three uses out of it before it fails. Watch for cracks. This one, half an hour but twice your strength." She waved another in the air before passing it to him. "And this beauty, ten times your strength but you only get a single thirty-second burst. Don't waste it." She gave him several more, then loaded Jentt with strength and speed talismans as well, describing each of them. "This one doesn't look like much, but it's carved from a peregrine falcon. Fastest bird there is. Crap durability, but you'll love the rush." She also handed talismans to Amurra, Marso, Guine, and her other followers, for emergency use.

As soon as Stran finished pocketing his talismans, he saluted. "Don't worry, Kreya. We'll get your army where it needs to be." He embraced his wife. "Stay safe."

"I won't die again," she promised. "You don't die on me either."

Stran, Kreya noticed, didn't promise what he couldn't guarantee. "I love you. Stick with Kreya. Unless she does something dangerous, then you hide. Understand? You stay alive."

He jogged to the front of the statues.

Jentt took Kreya's hands in hers. She felt the calluses and the softness. His hands were as familiar as her own. "We'll save everyone we can," he promised. Pressing her hands to his heart, he looked as if he wanted to say more, but she already knew everything he could say. That was the lovely thing about loving someone for who they were, not who you wanted them to be.

"Go," she told him.

But he didn't go. Instead, he kissed her, and she kissed him back, memorizing every second of how it felt. She'd kissed him thousands of times, so often worrying that it would be the last.

She told herself that if this was the last, she'd be grateful for all the extra stolen moments that they'd had—but she knew that was a lie. She wanted more. There would never be enough moments, and they'd already had too many goodbyes.

"Come back alive," she ordered him.

"You too."

He jogged after Stran, joining him at the front of the army of skeletal statues. Together, they strode through the gate, and the statues marched with them, crashing through the arch. The carved marble tumbled from the gateway as the massive pillars from Lorn's palace shoved their way through. The smaller statues skittered up and over the wall, spilling down into the fourth tier, and then scurried quickly to the third. Below, the sounds of Eklor's army, the crash of falling stone, and the screams of the people rose to meet them.

"My turn," Zera said. "What are my orders? You had me give them their talismans. So I take it that means you aren't sending me to fight the army?"

Kreya reached out and took her hand. "Last time I was stupid. This time, how about we defeat Eklor together? Stopping Eklor won't stop his army, but it will free the bone workers to join the fight. Come with me to the third tier and help me knock sense into the guild?"

Grinning, Zera squeezed her hand back. "I'm in. Flight?"

"Let's do it."

Amurra stepped in front of her. "I'm coming with you. Stran said to stick with you unless you went into danger."

"I am literally going into danger," Kreya said.

"The army isn't on the third tier yet. I"—she switched pronouns when Marso stepped forward—"we can spread word to people there, while Guine and the others warn the upper tiers. Take us with you. Please."

Kreya only hesitated for a moment. She'd sworn to herself that she'd trust her friends from now on, honor their right to make their own choices. Here, then, was a test of that. She nodded sharply at Amurra and Marso.

"Hope you aren't afraid of heights," Zera said as she gave them talismans. "Come on!"

Running with a spurt of speed, the four of them circled Zera's house. The grand salon, which had been supported by pillars, had collapsed, but the balcony that overlooked the valley was perfectly intact. Hand in hand, the four of them ran onto it without slowing—and off.

"*Renari!*"

Simultaneously, they activated their flight talismans. They soared over the city. From above, Eklor's army looked like hideous rats swarming over the buildings, destroying and devouring all in their path, chewing their way through the city's lower levels. She saw the leading edge of her statue army charging through the gates to the second tier—a marble lioness in the lead. With a silent roar, the statue leaped onto her prey, and a half dozen inhuman soldiers slammed onto the street beneath her massive stone paws. The other statues poured into the lower city behind her, joining the city guards.

Kreya thought she glimpsed Stran and tried to see Jentt, but the spires and aqueducts blocked her view of the city below. He was somewhere in the chaos.

Swooping low, they landed on the steps of the bone guild headquarters on the third tier. As they did, they were spotted. Citizens poured through the street to fill the steps.

Kreya shouted to them. "You need to evacuate! The fighting is on the lower levels. Get higher!" As she scanned the crowd, she noticed something strange. *They're holding weapons,* she realized. Swords for some. Kitchen knives. Metal bats. Shovels. Bars. "Wait, what are they thinking?" she asked her companions. "They can't fight. They're not soldiers!"

"They are today," Marso said.

"This is amazing!" Amurra cried, her face glowing. "They heard the old stories! They listened!"

Kreya opened her mouth and then shut it. She hadn't thought hearing the old stories again would inspire this. After a moment, she said, "They could die."

"They know heroes sometimes die," Amurra said. "They know there's always a cost."

Hearing them, a woman holding two kitchen knives said, "You paid it for us before. This time, we pay it together!" Around her, men and women cheered, hoisting their weapons and makeshift weapons into the air.

Zera interrupted, raising her voice. "Or, better idea: make the enemy pay instead!"

An even louder cheer at that.

"Fine," Kreya said. This wasn't the same as before. Maybe the outcome wouldn't be either. "Help us tear down this door! We get the bone workers, show them the truth of what's happening around them, and then together we all stop Eklor's army!"

Without further prompting, the third-tier citizens surged forward, throwing themselves against the great double doors to the guild headquarters, beneath the carved skull. It creaked on its hinges.

"Harder!" Kreya called.

She heard it the moment the hinges gave way. The great

doors fell inward, and the citizen army surged inside. They flooded into the halls of the bone workers.

At the front of the wave, Kreya ran through the hallways until she reached the great hall. Bursting through the inner doors, she saw it in a moment: full of bone workers, from novices to masters, from all over Vos, with the council in their throne-like chairs.

Insulated from the city, they had heard none of the battle.

One of the masters sprang to his feet. "What is the meaning of this?"

"The city is under attack!" Kreya cried. "Eklor's army has come!"

But she saw they didn't believe her. The great hall was too far from the entrance for them to hear the sounds of battle as anything more than an indistinct cacophony. And they were still in the grip of Eklor's talisman. It had fed on the fact that they didn't want to believe the old danger had come again and, worse, this time had come to them. She tried to find the right words to open their eyes and ears and minds, but none of those words came.

It was Marso who stepped forward. He climbed on top of a table carved of granite and shouted to the council, louder than the shouting citizens, "You have been shown lies! I will show you the truth!"

Other masters began to shout at him.

Kreya thought he'd try to read the bones. She stepped forward, unsure how to stop him—he couldn't do it, not in this kind of chaos. He wasn't ready for this yet. And if he tried and failed, they'd never convince the masters to listen.

But Marso didn't reach for his bones. Instead, he raced up to the balcony, to the thick stained glass windows. Lifting a heavy, iron candelabra, he bashed at the closest window. The ancient ruby and sapphire-colored glass cracked. He hit it again. Harder.

Bone workers called to him to stop.

Some ran up toward the balcony.

But Marso didn't stop. He hurled the candelabra at the window, and at last the glass shattered. Colored shards scattered everywhere, like rain made of jewels.

And the sounds of battle poured through.

He went to the next window and the next. Sunlight streamed through the cracks, along with the cries of the dying and the thunder of the unholy army. Kreya saw the change in the faces of the bone workers as the screams and cries broke through whatever hold Eklor had on them.

"We're under attack!" Amurra called. "From Eklor's army!"

The citizens echoed her.

Now, at last, the bone workers believed them. Maybe they would never have believed Kreya and Zera, but they believed the proof Marso had provided, they believed the people of Cerre, and they believed their own ears as the sounds of battle reached through the broken windows. The bone workers surged out of the hall.

As they flooded out into the city, Zera shouted words of encouragement, "Go! Fight the enemy! Save the people! Don't be idiots! Go, go, go!"

Marso and Amurra joined the surge, shouting directions, guiding them toward the battle. Kreya lost sight of them almost immediately. She sent a silent prayer after them, hoping they'd stay safe. She had to trust they'd be smart.

Now that the bone workers were unleashed, she'd have to leave it to others to handle the army. She had another goal. She scanned the hall—where was Eklor? And Lorn?

Plunging forward, Kreya tried to force her way through the surge. She was knocked backward. "Where's Eklor?" she shouted. "Where is he?" She recognized a bone worker who was rushing past, and she grabbed the woman's arm: "Briel!"

Briel tried to yank out of her grip.

"Stop, Briel. Tell me: where's Eklor?"

"Is it true? Is it his army? Why did we trust him?"

"It wasn't your fault," Kreya told her. She could tell the other woman didn't believe her. There wasn't time to explain. "But you can help now. Tell me where to find him."

"He's with Grand Master Lorn," Briel said. "They're preparing the blood."

Kreya gave her a little shake. "Whose blood?" She'd thought there wasn't going to be a spell. She'd been so certain it was a diversion. He had no bones, anyway. And the army was here, which proved her right. So why was Eklor preparing blood with Lorn? "What innocents are going to die?"

They'd guarded the hospital. Had he sent his constructs elsewhere? Certainly his army was spilling blood now, but if Eklor already had blood, then who—

"Our blood," Briel said. "He said it was needed for the immortality spell. Why did I give him blood? Kreya, I don't understand. Why is Eklor here? Why did I listen to him? He seemed so reasonable . . . And Grand Master Lorn seemed so certain . . ."

Kreya released her arm as the horror of it sank in. *I was wrong*, she thought. *Not about the fact that Eklor meant harm. But about how much harm he intended.*

He'd taken the bone workers' blood. And they'd been so enthralled they'd let him.

By the bones. "Briel, you have to—"

Around her, bone workers began to fall. In front of Kreya, Briel crumpled to the ground. As bone makers, bone wizards, and bone readers collapsed, one after another, Kreya called to Zera. Together, they ran through the guild, to its heart.

Please, don't let us be too late.

Body after body fell.

She heard her own voice mocking her: *There's never enough time.*

"One more chance," she whispered. "That's all I ask."

CHAPTER THIRTY

Y ou first this time," Kreya said.

"My pleasure. Ooh, I'm using strength." Activating a talisman, Zera slammed her fist into the grand master's office door. The wood shattered around the hinges. "Ow. Nice." She then kicked it open. "Grand Master Lorn, we're back with proof! Eklor's army is attacking the city, and bone workers are dropping dead where they stand!"

Kreya saw the room in a flash: books and papers shoved to the floor to clear the desk for row after row of silver cups, each half-full with ruby-black blood. Eklor behind the glasses. Lorn in front, crouched in a protective stance with a knife in his right hand.

But as Zera's words penetrated, Lorn lowered his weapon. He blinked as if waking up from a dream. "Eklor, is this true—"

"Literally no time to deal with lengthy explanations," Zera said. "Army. Outside. Lots of dying. And they need the grand master of the Bone Workers Guild to do his job and defend this city." She darted in and yanked him out by his robes. As he resisted, she added, "Your son is somewhere out there, in danger."

That got through to him.

Pulling Lorn out of the room, she said to Kreya, "Kick his ass."

Sparking a nod to Zera, Kreya pushed inside the office, kicking aside the shattered remains of the door. "Eklor, stop!"

But Eklor was leaning over the silver cups, chanting faster and faster. He plunged his fingers into the blood of one and pulled out a knuckle bone. He slammed it against his already blood-soaked chest and continued to chant a mix of familiar and unfamiliar words, a warping of the spell that Kreya had studied and used for so long.

"Silence him," Kreya ordered.

Her three rag dolls crawled out of her coat pockets. Fast, they scurried across the room and climbed his coat. One swarmed up his bloody chest and crammed itself into his mouth, cutting off the spell. He reached up and yanked the doll out, and another rag doll wrapped itself around his wrists. The third wormed itself through his fingers, forcing him to drop the knuckle bone, as the one that had been in his mouth tied itself around his ankles.

He struggled against them but then stilled. "Master Kreya," he greeted her, urbane as always. "Glad you could join me. A pity you were too late to participate in the spell."

"You're taking their years for yourself," Kreya said. There was no question in her mind about what was happening here: each cup held the blood of a bone worker. Stepping forward, she plucked the persuasion talisman out of one of his pockets.

Such a little thing that had done so much harm. Opening one of the sconces, she dropped the bone into the flame. It began to burn. Whatever power remained within it would be leached away. And then she checked his other pockets, relieving him of six more persuasion talismans and destroying them as well.

"So thorough. I see you have at last learned not to under-estimate me." He sounded like a proud teacher, and she'd never wanted to punch someone in the throat so badly. "Grand Master Lorn never did figure it out, you know. But then he was such easy prey for my talisman that I barely had to waste any of its power on him. He wanted so badly to believe that I'd conquered death that he refused to believe that time is finite—for anyone to have more, another must have less."

"And this is how you survived your own death. You stole from others?"

"I only took from those who didn't deserve the time they were given," Eklor said. "From those whose existence put more evil into the world than good."

And she thought her years alone in a tower had messed with her mind. Being alone had not been good for him. "You think *you* are the best judge of who adds evil to the world. *You.* How can you be so stunningly deluded as to believe you aren't the villain in all this? You killed innocents. In a hospital. In their sleep! You unleashed an army on civilians who never hurt you, who only know your name through ballads and plays. You have no right to say who lives and who dies."

"Neither do you. And neither did Grand Master Lorn, when he issued the order to have my wife and daughter's bodies burned. Neither did all the bone workers when they condemned my apprentice to die. Neither did the 'good' citizens of Cerre when they celebrated that boy's death. He was a child!"

A thought occurred to her. "Was he the one who resur-rected you? He was nowhere near the tower when you died. He was caught miles from the battlefield—"

"He was caught miles away *after* he saved me. In case of di-saster, he had the blood and bones ready and stayed hidden until you'd confirmed your handiwork. When you left, he saved me, as he'd been taught. He was then supposed to escape and live a long and happy life. But the 'innocent' people of Cerre saw fit to make an example of him. Because they couldn't punish me, they settled for him, a child who had done no wrong, a child who grew up without a mother and a sister."

And was about to live without a father, she realized. *The boy . . . he was Eklor's son . . .*

She'd known he wouldn't trust just anyone, but she hadn't guessed he'd had a son. And Lorn had ordered his son's execution. No wonder . . .

Stop. Do not feel pity for him. There was no purpose in understanding why he had done what he'd done. Only in stopping him from ever doing evil again. "Are we really playing who-is-more-evil? Your army is slaughtering children right now! If you're the hero, stop your war. Order your army to withdraw."

He smiled. "Let me complete the spell, and I will stop my army and tell the good people of Cerre who saved them: the *new* grand master of the Bone Workers Guild, who foiled a plot by the Five Heroes of Vos to—"

Kreya held up her hands. "I am going to cut you off right there because that's absurd. Correct me if I'm wrong, but your plan is to make yourself essentially immortal by stealing the lives of all the bone workers, slaughter as many people as you can, and then announce that you're actually the hero? And you expect people—meaning the ones you haven't killed—to believe you?"

"They will when I use that stolen immortality to bring their loved ones back to life."

"Except the bone workers, because they'll all be dead. And whoever else you need to kill to give the select few life. You'll be the one who says who gets to live and who gets to die. Basically, your plan is to become a god." It was an awe-inspiring plan, both in its arrogance and in how close Eklor was to pulling it off.

She spared a thought for Jentt and Stran and the people in the thick of the battle.

"The good will live, and the evil will die," Eklor said placidly, as if his whole explanation weren't enough to make her feel ill. "I am so pleased you understand me. And I am equally pleased that I understand you." His eyes flickered to the shadows on either side of the office, and she heard the whirr of gears as his mechanical constructs lurched forward.

One was as Amurra had described: with wire tentacles emanating from its back. The other was a grotesque human-shaped soldier, with a skull that was half metal and half bone. It held a rusty sword in each hand. She took a step backward and lifted her own knife in front of her chest, blade out.

"Oh, Kreya, always so angry, always so unbending," Eklor said, his voice dripping with false pity. "Once again, you have come alone to defeat me. And once again, you will fail."

She took another step backward into the arch of the doorway.

The wire construct sliced through her rag dolls, and they fell from his wrists and ankles. "No!" she yelled as they dropped to the floor. They hadn't deserved that fate—they'd been loyal and brave. But there wasn't time to mourn them now.

Leaving the now-free Eklor, the construct scuttled beetle-like around the desk. Both monstrosities advanced on her. She took another step back, one foot still in the room and one foot in the hallway.

Eklor lifted a silver cup of blood as if to toast her. "We are not so different, you and I. Violating the rules for the sake of love. Making our own future, though no one understands our choices. Needing to be the one who alone rights the wrongs—"

Beyond him, through the glass panes of the window, Kreya saw a hint of movement. "I'm going to cut you off again," she said. "Because I am *not* the same as you. And this time"—the glass shattered as Zera burst through, feetfirst—"I'm not alone."

Eklor dropped the silver cup.

Blood spattered onto the floor.

He opened his mouth to say a word, one that would activate a talisman—perhaps to fight, perhaps to run, perhaps to fly. He didn't get a chance to say it. Zera plunged a blade directly into his heart, shoving against it until the metal was buried up to the hilt.

"See, I did change," Kreya said. "This time, I didn't need to be the one who killed you."

Zera shoved Eklor's body backward, and it crashed into the desk. Cups scattered everywhere, and the blood of a hundred bone workers splashed over the floor.

Kreya then turned her attention to the two constructs as they attacked, and Zera joined her. Together, they fought, the old muscle memory returning with each strike, as the spilled blood of the bone workers stained the stone.

CHAPTER THIRTY-ONE

J entt ran and then slid, his knife out. He sliced the ham-strings of one inhuman soldier, stabbed another in the groin and a third in the ankles. He rose and winced—he was going to pay for this later in aches and bruises, if there was a later.

He spun to face the next one as one of Kreya's statues—a granite slab carved like a bear's skeleton—plucked a soldier off the street and ground it between its stone paws. Another three soldiers hurled themselves at the statue's legs. Knocked off balance, it crashed onto the street, and the constructs swarmed over it, hacking at the stone with axes and swords until one of them hit the bone that powered it.

Another one down, Jentt thought.

Her statues were strong but not fast. And they were vastly outnumbered.

Like us.

Beside him, Stran was using up talisman after talisman. Powered by two at once, he was an unstoppable bull. Every construct he encountered fell to his fists and blades. Yanking a chunk of a stone out of the wall, he hurled it at a spider-shaped automaton. It crashed into the creature with such force that the spider tumbled off the edge of the tier to smash into the ground below. Glancing over the edge to make sure no innocents had been harmed, Jentt saw citizens from the first tier swarming over the spider, bashing at it until it quit twitching.

He wanted to feel good about that.

He hadn't died (again) yet, which was excellent. Neither had Stran. He wanted to feel good about that too. But for every one he and Stran brought down, another three escaped them. The mountain kept disgorging more and more of them, a seemingly endless stream from the caves beneath the city. It was clear that the tangled mass of metal and bone they'd found on the plain had been a trick—he bet if they'd chiseled into its heart, they could have found mere dirt and stone and bones gathered from the forbidden zone. Eklor had saved the vast bulk of his army and brought it here, via the valley and then through the caves beneath the city.

Jentt caught a glimpse of a line of city guards, marching against a construct with a torso of twisted metal and arms like claws. It swung a mace of thick iron, catching the first guard in the chest and hurling him back against the second. Two houses down, a giant horse statue was being pulled to the ground by a swarm of vicious beetle-like constructs with saws instead of pinchers.

We can't fight them all, he thought.

Seeing a blur out of the corner of his eye, he dodged right. A massive blow slammed into the ground where he'd been standing, the fist of a massive construct. It fractured the paving stones. He sped around the giant. "Hey, Stran, got another one for you."

"Excellent," Stran replied. "I was getting bored over here." He shoved back three machine-men with a horselike kick. Across the way, another of Kreya's statues—a former pillar carved like the vertebrae of a snake—bashed into a line of Eklor's soldiers, before the mechanized soldiers leaped on it. The stone snake reared once, knocking them aside, but more attacked. It would be overwhelmed soon.

"We need an endgame!" Jentt said. He tossed aside a drained speed talisman and withdrew another. He was running dangerously low on talismans and knew Stran's supplies had to be even lower. Using it, he zipped across the plaza and extracted a city guard a second before a spear would have skewered him. "Watch your swing. You leave your left flank open."

The guard stammered thanks.

Across the street, Jentt saw another bone worker wielding a tree trunk as if it were a mace. But he didn't see the smaller construct made of gears and wheels roll behind her until it was too late. The bone worker stiffened as needle-thin blades sprouted from her chest.

Jentt swore as he darted to her. He smashed the construct and caught the bone worker as she fell. He laid her gently on the street and then whirled around to duck beneath the blade of a bearlike horror with a face of twisted metal.

A horrible thought hit him, with certainty: *We're losing.*

It didn't matter how fast he moved, how hard he fought. There were simply too many of them, and they kept coming and coming. Sooner or later, he'd make a mistake. He'd run out of energy or out of talismans.

Time would defeat them.

We need a new plan, he thought. But what? He had no answer, and he couldn't stop moving or stop fighting to think of one. It was all he could do to keep up with the endless stream of enemies. If they could trap the army somewhere . . . Or lead them out of the city . . . Or force them back into the caves and collapse the caves . . . He wished Kreya were here to see the possibilities and make the call. In the middle of fighting, he couldn't clear the space in his mind to plan anything larger than the next strike or parry. He tried not to worry about Kreya, facing Eklor. She had Zera by her side. The two of them could handle themselves.

He wished he'd taken the time to tell Kreya that he finally understood. After seeing Stran nearly lose his wife, he knew why Kreya had made the choices she had. He even understood why she hadn't told him. In her place, he'd have done the same—it had taken him a while to admit that, but he'd gotten there at last.

He wanted to say he was sorry for being angry, sorry for dying and leaving her alone, sorry he hadn't swept her away from all of this before Eklor came back into their lives.

He swore that if they survived this, he would devote every day he had left to making it up to her.

Across the street, Stran was cornered by three multiarmed constructs. His blades were blurred, moving quickly to parry and strike. Sweat poured off his face. Jentt darted toward him, jumped onto a cart, and launched himself in the air.

He landed on the back of one of the constructs and drew his blade across its neck, severing the wires that connected its head to its spine. He then yanked out the bone lodged in its chest. The construct collapsed beneath him.

Springing out of the way, he went back-to-back with Stran.

"I'm out," Stran said.

"What?" Jentt heard him, but he didn't want to believe it.

"Last talisman failed."

"Then we stick together," Jentt said. "Protect each other."

He scanned the street. "Need to find a defensible position. Can't fight them all at once."

Stran grunted as he beat back the closest construct. "Need to find Amurra. And the others. If we're going to die, I'd rather"—he ducked beneath one of a construct's many arms—"die together."

It wasn't a plan for victory. But it was better than what they were doing here. At least if they found their friends, they could protect one another.

But first they had to make it out of the second tier.

"Cart," Jentt grunted as he swung his blade at a half man lurching toward him. He sprinted for the cart that he'd vaulted over. Stran jumped into the front. Whirling his blades, he carved a path through as Jentt used the last of his talismans to push them toward the gate to the third tier.

"You!" Jentt called to one of Kreya's statues, a marble elk that was twice the size of a live elk. "Clear the way!"

The elk obeyed, bashing through the gate, and Jentt and Stran followed in its wake. As they passed through the gate, he felt as if he were abandoning the citizens, statues, and bone workers that still fought on the second tier. But then the feeling vanished as he saw the state of the third tier: the battle was here too.

And the people were losing.

Littering the street were the wounded and the dead. Constructs lay between them as well, broken or twitching, but the fighting raged in the streets around them. He spotted another one of Kreya's statues—only for an instant, as a pack of constructs lifted it off the ground and tossed it into an aqueduct. Both the statue and the aqueduct shattered in a spray of stone that rained down onto fighters below. One boulder crashed through a roof.

"Shit," Stran said.

All the work they'd done, all the fighting, to contain the enemy in the first and second tiers . . . It had been pointless. The constructs they hadn't defeated had poured into the third tier, and Jentt didn't doubt they'd reached the fourth tier as well, and would soon reach the fifth.

"The city is lost," Jentt said.

"But we aren't yet," Stran said, and charged forward through the street, with only his own strength in his body.

With a roar, Jentt chased after him.

The hopelessness of it began to sink into his bones, and he fought harder with tears blurring his eyes. This was a fight they couldn't win.

KREYA WAITED FOR A MOMENT TO FEEL SOMETHING: Eklor was dead. Finally. And this time, she was going to make sure he stayed that way. Whispering to a strength talisman, she hoisted Eklor's body over her shoulder and carried him over the two mechanized constructs that she and Zera had sliced through, with the help of the talismans.

"Bonfire time?" Zera guessed.

"Oh yes." Like the fire that had burned her tower.

Together, they carried Eklor's corpse through the corridor. They encountered no one—everyone was outside fighting the army, she guessed—but she remembered the way. There had been funerals while she was a student, each of them burned into her memory.

They climbed to the roof, where the pyre was ever ready.

From here they could see the city. Dawn had risen, and light had spread across the tiers. The fighting had spread from the first and second to the third, fourth, and fifth to engulf all of Cerre in screams and smoke.

Together, they laid Eklor's body on the pyre. The wood was stored in a dry cabinet on the rooftop. Zera unloaded it and carried bundles that she placed beneath the pallet the body lay on. The pallet was a latticework of iron, able to be used and reused.

Kreya tried to focus on the task at hand—making sure Eklor couldn't return—but her eyes kept being drawn to the battle that raged on every tier. She spotted several of her stone giants, and as she watched, one was yanked down to the street. Constructs swarmed over it as if devouring it. It didn't rise. Her heart squeezed as she thought of Jentt and Stran in the middle of the chaos. She prayed they were all right.

I should be with them, fighting alongside Jentt and Stran and Marso. Zera should be feeding us all talismans. We should be back-to-back, watching one another.

This didn't feel right.

We should all be together. Never mind that she was the one who had ordered them to separate, and never mind that it had been the right decision, even the *only* decision. They couldn't have both stopped Eklor and fought the army if they'd stayed together.

Instead of a talisman, Zera offered her a fire rod. It was stamped with the symbol of the Bone Workers Guild. "You want to do the honors, my dearest friend?"

Kreya felt the weight of the fire rod in her hand. It had been used to light many pyres. She wondered if it had been used for anyone she knew. Staring at it, she didn't move. She heard the sounds of the battle—the screams, the scrape of metal on stone, the crash of walls collapsing. She tasted smoke in the back of her throat, of fires that burned in fallen homes, and she inhaled the coppery metal tang of Eklor's army.

Destroying Eklor wouldn't end the battle. He'd built his constructs to last.

"First Eklor, then the army," Zera coached her.

Still holding the fire rod, Kreya crossed from the pyre to the lip of the roof, looking out across the city. Not far from the guild, she saw the body of a child, twisted unnaturally. A woman lay not far from him, her throat torn. A man in a bone worker's coat was clutching his leg, and even from far above him, she could see he was spattered in blood. Another of her statues tumbled, falling from the third tier to the second. A guard fought, outnumbered, by the gate. She saw a construct's spear pierce his throat.

We're losing, she thought. *Eklor may be dead, but he's still won.*

There were too many of them, and the city was ill prepared. It was going to fall, Kreya realized. Maybe not in the next hour. Maybe not this day. But she could see it already beginning to turn. So many bodies already lay strewn in the streets.

"The aqueducts will run with blood, and the city will fall," Kreya said. "There's no way for any of us to stop it." Only the army's creator could stop it. "No one alive can stop it."

She hated what she was thinking.

But she could see the battle and the future stretched before her in blood and smoke.

"*He* has to stop this."

"Oh no. Kreya, no, absolutely not. You have had terrible ideas before. Trust me when I say this is your worst yet."

Kreya turned to face her, the battle at her back. "I can't think of any other way. His creations . . . they won't stop, they won't slow. At least not soon enough to save the city. You know that. He built them to last for years."

"He'll never agree to help. He wants this, his revenge!" Zera waved at the destruction. "He already has everything he wants!"

She was right. What could they offer him to get him to agree to help? "He doesn't just want that," Kreya said. "He wants to be seen as a hero. You heard him. He wants to be a benevolent god, who was wronged by the evil people he destroyed."

Yes, it was a terrible idea. But she didn't have any other. And if they didn't stop the army, she'd lose them all. Jentt. Stran. Marso. Amurra. All the people who had risen to help defend their city. The bone workers, the guards, the innocents.

Lowering the fire rod to the ground, she approached the pyre. She'd have to cut out the bone he'd pushed into himself while casting his warped spell so that he couldn't reactivate it, and then she'd have to give him some of her life.

Jentt, forgive me.

She took a breath, and Zera caught her arm. "If this is the only way, then use me," Zera said. "It's my turn. Let me be the one to sacrifice."

"I've hurt you enough." She'd abandoned her. Doubted her. Taken her for granted. At least she could spare her any more pain.

Zera snorted. "I've forgiven that, or haven't you noticed? Kreya, you aren't doing this alone, remember? Besides, we don't need to revive him for long, right? We're taking moments, not years, long enough to stop the army. A few minutes is not such a great sacrifice to save the lives of the people we love. And, you know, everyone else. Please, Kreya. I want to bear this burden."

Kreya shook her head.

"It's my choice," Zera said. "Not yours. This is it, Kreya—the moment you prove whether you've changed. Respect my right to make this choice about my own life."

Kreya couldn't refuse her, but she hated herself for having this plan. She switched her knife from one hand to another. "Hold him down," she ordered.

"He won't twitch," Zera said. "He's dead."

She knew that. Of course. But . . . *Stop delaying*, she told herself. This had to be done. Her thoughts flew again to Jentt, Stran, Marso, and Amurra. To the people of Cerre. Of Vos.

Bearing down on Eklor's torso, she sliced along his sternum. It was a precise incision, and her hand didn't shake. She knew where the extra bone had entered his body. He hadn't completed enough of the spell to absorb it, she hoped.

Separating the skin, she plunged her hand in. Her fingers wrapped around the loose bone, and she drew it out. Blood coated her hand.

Efficiently, Zera began to sew him up. "Not sure he'd survive this kind of wound if he weren't already dead."

"It doesn't need to be perfect," Kreya said as she cleaned the extracted bone in the buckets of rainwater left to extinguish any pyres. "I'm not giving him more than a few minutes of your life." She hoped. She ran over the words in her head, determined to get every syllable right. This was not a time for mistakes.

Finishing, Zera rolled up the sleeve of her coat.

Again, Kreya hesitated. "You're certain?"

Her friend didn't even bother to reply. Just held her arm out, wrist up, veins exposed. Kreya drew the blade over her skin deep enough that the blood welled in its wake. She wiped her blood over the used bone and hoped she'd cleaned it well enough. She couldn't do anything about the blood from others that had already dispersed into his system—the bone workers he'd already killed. But he shouldn't be able to kill any more. She just had to hope that Zera's fresh blood, combined with her spell, would enable her to control and limit the life transfer.

Pressing the bone against the freshly sewn wound, Kreya whisper-chanted in Eklor's ear: "Take her breath, take her blood. Sixty breaths, she gives you. Sixty breaths, you'll take. *Iri nascre, murro bey enlay. Iri prian, esa esi roe. Iri sangra. Iri, iri, nascre enlay.*" She finished the incantation and then stepped back.

Eklor sucked in a breath.

Her hand shook. She wanted to pull that breath out of him.

Struggling to sit, Eklor was bound too tightly to move. "*Iri nascre—*" Shit, if he worked the spell with Zera's blood—

Zera laid a knife, blade flat, hard against his throat.

He stopped.

Kreya leaned over him, opposite Zera. "You have three minutes to live. You will die at the end of those minutes. That's inevitable. But we have granted you three minutes so that you can stop your army. Command them now."

Eklor croaked a laugh, beneath the press of the blade. "Why would I?"

"Because if you do, I will grant you what you want."

Zera eased the pressure on the blade minutely so he could speak. "I want my family back. You can't grant me that." Bloody spit pooled in the corner of his mouth as he rasped out the words. His body shuddered with each stolen breath. They didn't have much time.

"I can tell the world you were the hero, though," Kreya said. "You saw how we spread the tales of the Bone War in just a few days—that's the reason the people of Cerre were primed to rise up against your army. We will spread the tale of how your family truly died, how the bone guild wronged you and then lied to cover up our evil, and how the council and grand master lied, even to us bone workers. We will tell them you were a martyr and would have been their savior."

Zera leaned against her. "Kreya . . ."

Kreya did not look at her. She kept her eyes on Eklor's as he drank in her words. "We will tell them how we were wrong, and you were right."

"Yes," he whispered.

"Stop the army," Kreya said. "And I will correct your legacy. You'll have the immortality you wanted. Not in flesh. But in memory."

"You will truly do this?" her enemy asked. And for a moment, she felt pity. She, perhaps more than anyone who had ever lived, understood him. She knew what had made him cross unforgivable lines. She knew why he felt what he felt and believed what he believed. She understood why he saw himself as the martyred hero, because she was not so different.

"I will," she lied.

Zera dug into her pockets for a talisman that would carry his words across the city. She activated it as Eklor called the command to stop: "Vron!"

Beyond the roof, she heard silence spread as every construct halted—their gears ceased, their cries and roars and screams fell quiet. But she did not go to the edge to look. She kept her eyes on Eklor as he drew another breath and, in a whisper, began the spell to steal Zera's life: "Iri—"

Kreya slammed her hand down on Zera's wrist, the one that held the knife hovering over Eklor's throat. The force of her hand plunged the blade down. Together, with Kreya's hand over Zera's, they silenced him for the final time.

CHAPTER THIRTY-TWO

They lit the pyre.

Kreya stood with her hands clasped behind her back as the flames coated Eklor. She kept her eyes on his face as his skin blackened and shriveled. She didn't intend to stop watching until it was finished.

In her ear, Zera murmured, "I am half expecting him to sit up."

"It's over this time."

"I'm not sure I believe in 'over' anymore. You remember that ballad about us from the Bone War, the one that ends with us watching the sunset together over the plains?"

Of all the ballads, that had been one of the least cringeworthy tunes. It had gotten about half the facts right, which was better than many others. "Sure. But I'm not going to sing it, if that's what you're asking."

Zera smirked. "I'd pay money to hear that. You have to do the alto part, though—remember, you're not a soprano. But my point is: the song ends when the sun sets. Really, though, you know what happens when the sun sets? It gets dark. Stars come out. The temperature drops. Eventually, you sleep. And then the sun rises again, and it's another day, and when you look back on your life, you don't know if you've made all the best choices or said all the right things, but it's not like it ends on the final ballad chord. It ends when it ends."

Kreya thought about that, as the burning man began to crumble in on himself. Soon, he'd be ash, and the wind would scatter the last speck of him across the city he'd nearly destroyed.

She had three more years of her story after the sun set today.

It would be enough.

OUT IN THE CITY, THE CONSTRUCTS LURCHED TO a halt.

Every inhuman soldier, every monstrosity cobbled together from flesh and metal, every nightmare that had crawled out of the mist-coated valley and poured up from the bowels of the mountain, stopped simultaneously.

Jentt let his knife fall to his side. He sagged against a broken lamppost. Around him, he heard ragged cheers, between the cries for help. He took one more breath, and then, limping, without the benefit of any talismans, just with what strength of will he had left inside him, he moved from construct to construct, yanking out the bones that powered them so that they could never come back and kill. He didn't stop until he had reached every single one in the street before him. Only then did he look toward the guild headquarters.

At the top of the headquarters, flames licked the sky as the pyre burned.

She did it, he thought.

We did it.

And maybe, just maybe, we all came out of this alive.

THERE WERE SO MANY DEAD.

As they left the guild headquarters, Kreya saw pyres lit in every square on every tier of the city. Gripping her by the elbow, Zera pulled her through the streets. "Move quickly, and don't make eye contact," Zera advised.

"Eklor intended to save them. We could do the same."

"By *killing* countless others. Even if you do it your way, taking life from the willing, it's a very bad plan. Don't even think about it. You'd be arrested and added to the pyres before you even finished explaining the cost."

But if she didn't try to save them, did that make her as bad as he was? On the other hand, did she have a choice? Zera was right—there was very little chance she'd be allowed to complete the spell. She'd be killed too.

Quickly and efficiently, Zera handled everything. Dropping gold in the right shop, she obtained a crawler. Slipping silver into the right hands, she located Jentt, Marso, Stran, and Amurra, and the relief she felt at seeing them was palpable. All of them piled into the crawler and left Cerre before the fires burned out.

Kreya worried silently as they traveled: Eklor had called the resurrection spell a "gift," and now she was the only one alive capable of giving it. But it was a gift that should never be given.

Yet I made an exception for Jentt. And for Amurra.

Was it morally wrong to deny that same choice to others? Or morally wrong to offer it? She'd always believed the knowledge of the spell should die with her . . . but after seeing the fires in Cerre, now she questioned that.

What if there was no right answer? That was a horrible thought. What if she never knew whether she was making the right decision *because there was no right decision?* She kept turning that over and over in her mind.

At nightfall, they halted and slept outside beneath the stars. Without talismans, it was a multiday journey, but none of them complained. Jentt hunted for rabbits, which Stran skinned and cooked. Zera insisted on bathing in a stream and returned happier and cleaner but with dampened silks. She didn't seem to mind the lost fashion.

They talked about minor things as they ate: tasks that Stran and Amurra would need to complete at the farm, whether or not the winter would be mild, how much better Stran was at cooking than he used to be. Eventually, they spread blankets out on the needles and moss.

Lying beside Jentt, Kreya stared up at the clouds drifting across the stars. The air had the crispness of coming winter to it. At last, she hinted at the question that had been haunting her since they slipped away: "Should we have stayed in Cerre?"

He knew what she was asking. Of course he did. He knew her. "Eventually you'd have been arrested and executed."

"Unless the laws were changed," Kreya said. "We could have tried—"

"Did you ever think that maybe this is *why* the law was written?" Jentt wrapped his arms around her, and she felt his warm breath on her neck. "Eklor may not have been the first to discover how to cheat death."

She considered that. It was one of the oldest laws in Vos. She'd no idea of its source or original purpose, but she did know it wouldn't be easy to overturn. The taboo ran deep, as she'd seen from her encounters with the villagers around her old tower. If people knew the cost of extra life, both to themselves and to others . . . *Some wouldn't care*, Kreya thought. But those with a conscience, who cared about others . . .

"Eklor's spell makes a lot of evil possible," Marso said. He was lying only a few yards away, closer to the fire. "You saw what he nearly did."

"Plus who will supply the bone?" Amurra said from the opposite side of the campfire. "Some would have to stay dead for others to live. Who makes that choice? Not that I'm not grateful for you bringing me back, but . . . I don't know that that's a choice anyone should be allowed to make."

Stran spoke up. "I am more than grateful. And I'd ask you to do it again in a heartbeat, and I think most people would. The temptation to save a loved one would be irresistible."

He was right—that was the problem, wasn't it? If the spell were known, it would be used. And abused. *Some lines shouldn't be crossed*, she thought. Eklor's books had been burned. So had Eklor himself. In three years, with her death, the knowledge would pass out of the world entirely.

And that was a good thing.

I can't tell, though, if this makes me the hero or the villain.

Maybe both. Maybe neither.

Maybe there were no perfect choices for anyone to make, hero or villain. Maybe there was only doing the best you could do with the time you had. That was an unsatisfying thought, but just because it was uncomfortable didn't mean it wasn't true.

"I wish I could have done more." She thought of Briel and the other bone workers who'd fallen. She thought of all the bodies in the street and pyres in the squares. If she'd been faster, smarter, less certain that she knew Eklor's plan . . .

Jentt cupped her face in his hands. In the amber glow of the campfire, she could see the seriousness in his eyes. "You can't save everyone. But you should know that you saved all of us. Gave us all second chances. And that's not nothing."

"But is it enough?" Kreya asked.

"I think . . . Yes," Jentt said.

Marso: "Yes."

Stran and Amurra: "Yes," and "Yes."

"Yes." Zera.

And Kreya let herself believe them.

CHAPTER THIRTY-THREE

They didn't speak of it again, or of much else. Quiet, they slept. At dawn, they packed their camp and continued on. The crawler lurched through forests and across cliffs, until it reached the old farmhouse.

Bathed in late afternoon light with the remnants of frost still clinging to the tips of the grasses, the farmhouse looked like a painting. Kreya climbed out of the crawler behind the others. Stran and Amurra both ran toward the door, their arms open.

Seeing them from the window, two children tumbled outside: Vivi and Jen. An elderly couple followed more slowly, the man holding little Nugget, soon to be called Evren. Stran and Amurra fell to the ground and were swarmed by their family. Following them came the bird construct and the other rag dolls. They flocked to Kreya.

She couldn't help smiling. This felt right.

The others held back, allowing Stran's family their moment, until Amurra beckoned them over, and they were all enfolded into the group embrace. Jen immediately climbed onto Jentt's back. Vivi tugged on Zera's arm. "You want to see me climb a tree?"

Zera laughed. "Absolutely."

"And you'll catch me when I fall?" she asked.

"Maybe we should save tree climbing for later," Zera said. "Climb on Jentt." Squealing, the little girl joined her brother in scrambling over Jentt. Stran was already holding the baby and breathing deeply as if he exuded an exquisite perfume, which Kreya was fairly certain no baby did.

Watching the children, Kreya picked up the bird construct and let it climb onto her shoulder. The rag dolls burrowed themselves into her coat pockets, chittering happily.

Amurra herded everyone inside, where they were greeted by the smell of freshly baked bread and simmering soup, made by Amurra's mother and father, who proceeded to serve everyone dinner. As she scooped the soup into bowls, Amurra's mother asked them, "Will you all be staying here for a while?"

"A few weeks," Kreya answered. "While we recover."

"Not so long for me," Zera said. "I'll have to get back. See what's left of my business. Rebuild my home. Make sure Guine and the others aren't permanently traumatized."

Kreya heard what she didn't say: *Or dead.*

They'd left before they could be sure of the full cost of Eklor's attack, before the bone makers could compare their stories and realize what Kreya knew. *We left to save me,* she thought. Everyone had fled the city for that one reason. She looked around the table and felt tears prick her eyes—she'd thought the bonds between them had faded over the many years, but as it turned out, they'd only strengthened with time.

We all saved each other.

"Marso, you'll stay as long as you want," Amurra said to him without even a question in her voice.

Kreya approved. This would be a good place for him. Far

better than where they'd found him, at least until he decided what he wanted to do with his life.

"I'd like that," Marso said, "if there's room." He smiled tentatively at them. "You'll have a full house, with four children."

Stran clapped him on the shoulder. "Always room for you, my friend." And then: "Four?" He shot a look at Amurra, who looked picturesquely confused. "You said that before, but . . ."

"Congratulations," Kreya said.

"But I'm not . . ." Amurra trailed off and then her face blossomed into a smile. "I will be? You read it in the bones, didn't you? You knew it when you first came here."

Chatter turned to new babies and the future, and Kreya let it all wash over her. She reached beneath the table and caught Jentt's hand in hers.

ZERA LINGERED AT THE FARMHOUSE FOR THREE weeks before returning to Cerre. She kept inventing excuses to stay: she'd leave once her cuts and bruises healed, she'd leave once Marso was settled in, she'd leave after Amurra confirmed she was expecting, she'd leave when the weather was clear . . .

At last, it was a perfect blue-sky day, a winter chill in the air, and she had no more excuses. She had responsibilities to both people and her business.

"Wear this," Amurra said, pushing a thick fuzzy coat on her.

"It isn't my style." In fact, it was hideous. She'd look like a sheep with arms. "But thanks."

"Better than freezing," Kreya said as she passed by, carrying an armful of wood for the fireplace. "Take the coat, Zera. Even if it makes you look stupid."

Zera scowled at Kreya's grin but took the coat.

She hugged each of them.

Last, she hugged Kreya. "I'll be back. That's a promise. You . . ." She didn't know what she wanted to make Kreya promise. Every time she thought about the future, she couldn't imagine it without Kreya in it. *We have time*, she thought. *I'll see her again.* She wouldn't have to say a final goodbye for almost three years. She repeated: "I'll be back. Don't you dare leave before then."

"I'll wait for you," Kreya said.

And that was as good as any promise.

Using a combination of speed and flight talismans—several dozen new ones that she'd made from chicken bones during her time at the farmhouse—Zera traveled home much faster than their journey in the crawler. It used up the weak, fragile bones quickly, but she had no intention of reselling such inferior talismans anyway. She'd only made them to occupy her hands while she'd been at the farmhouse.

Arriving at Cerre, she gave her name to the guards at the first gate and asked for their discretion, in exchange for silver coins, and she walked through the tiers with the hood of Amurra's fuzzy coat up.

In the coat, she wasn't recognized, and so she was free to stroll and note the damage. Every tier bore scars. At first, on the lowest tier, she thought it wasn't so bad. The poor district looked about the same as it always had: ramshackle houses smushed together. A few more were caved in than usual, and she thought she saw more people camped beneath makeshift tents of scrap metal and wood. It wasn't so bad, but it was clearly a problem in its own right.

Something to think on.

On the second tier, though, it was harder to pretend life was back to normal. People were trying. Markets were set up. But only a few houses were still standing. Most looked as if they'd been ripped apart—*Which they have,* she thought. Construction workers swarmed over many of them, but a few were clearly abandoned. She hoped their owners had fled, but she had the feeling that the reason was worse—no one who'd lived there was left alive to return. On the third tier, the sturdier halls were intact— the hospital and various guild headquarters—but Zera couldn't ignore the smashed buildings, the torn-up streets, or the way everyone walked a little too quickly, as if they were afraid they might have to break into a run at any moment. The fourth was equally scarred, despite all the gold being poured into rebuilding.

She at last reached the fifth tier and was pleasantly surprised to see that workers were reconstructing her home. Higher up on the tier, she could see other palaces were still in ruins, including Grand Master Lorn's. Pushing her hood back, Zera approached her house.

A construction worker stopped her at the gate to what had once been the statue garden. "Private construction zone, ma'am. The owner is not present, so no visitors—"

"Zera!"

She saw Guine, closer to fully clothed than she'd ever seen him, scramble over the tools and stacks of wood, skirt a pile of stone, and jog toward her. She felt a flood of relief. "Guine, you're alive!"

"*You're* alive! We didn't know!" He wrapped his arms around her hard, and she laughed at how enthusiastic his squeeze was. It was lovely to know he cared too.

"Yet you proceeded with reconstruction anyway."

"What can I say? I'm an optimist." He grabbed her hand. "Come! I'll show you everything we're doing. You're going to love it. I told them to double the size of your office. You're going to need it."

She let him pull her through the construction zone that was her house. He pointed out all the improvements he'd ordered: ordinary columns to support the foyer (so no helpful friends would be tempted to make her ceiling collapse again), extra bedrooms instead of the extraneous music and sitting rooms (for her friends who wanted to visit), and her new office. It wasn't complete yet—the workers were framing out a large window with a view of the valley and mountains. "It's all fantastic, Guine," she told him. "You've done an amazing job."

He preened. "I hoped . . . I *knew* you'd come back to us. The city needs you."

She squeezed his hand. "I . . . Thank you." She hesitated before asking the question she'd been dreading. "The others . . . Who is . . . Who didn't . . ."

He knew what she was asking. Soberly, he listed off those who had lived and those who had died. Many had lost family members. She realized as he went through the list that she only recognized about half the names. *They worked for me, they lived with me, and I didn't know them . . . I have to do better.*

She made a mental note to send them funds to help pay for whatever expenses they had. At least those who'd worked for her and befriended her shouldn't have to worry about where to live and how to eat while they pieced their lives back together. She'd visit them eventually, she promised herself, and make it clear they always would have a place with her, if they wanted it. This time, she promised herself she'd learn their names. Friends deserved that much. And more. "The hospitals will need more money," she said. "We'll send it to them, yes?"

"I've already set up my office," Guine said. "I'll run through your finances with you, after . . . When you passed through the gates, you used your name? People know you're here?"

"Yes, shouldn't I have?" Zera immediately thought of Kreya and the lines she'd crossed. *No, the lines we crossed together.* What did people know about what they'd done? And what would they be most unhappy about?

"The bone worker guild has been asking for you daily," Guine said. "Very insistent. If they know you're here, they'll be sending someone for you soon." He wrinkled his nose at her coat. "We have to get you into something more appropriate to wear."

She laughed to hide her concern and let him choose more elegant clothes for her. He frowned when she donned her once-exquisite bone worker's coat, however. Much of it was stained with blood, soot, and dirt. But he said nothing.

"Did they give any indication as to why they're so anxious to speak with me?" she asked.

He hesitated. "I . . . have my suspicions. But I think it's best if they tell you themselves."

Zera raised her eyebrows at him. He'd changed, perhaps because of the battle, perhaps because she'd left him to handle the aftermath. Before this, he never would have pushed back on any question or request. She liked this change in him. "You're in need of a promotion. How do you like the title 'manager'? Or perhaps 'director'?"

He grinned. "Ooh, director of bones? Senior manager of skeletons?"

"Your choice. But I want it official. You are my right-hand man."

That affected him. For an instant, she saw through all the artifice—he cared that she valued him. It made her all the more certain she was doing the right thing by promoting him. She should have recognized his worth long ago. Perhaps in a few years, she'd make him her business partner. "I won't let you down," he promised.

"You never do." She clapped a hand on his shoulder. "Now I'd better go see what Lorn and the council want." She could avoid them, stay and rebuild, until they forced the issue. Or she could return to the farmhouse, avoid them altogether, and leave the business exclusively to Guine. *Except that feels more like running,* Zera thought. And she had no reason to think the guild wanted to blame her for any of this.

They wouldn't care about the things she did bear the blame for: For not being certain Eklor was gone. For not staying closer to Kreya and Marso and Stran. For wasting those twenty-five years, harboring old pain. Squaring her shoulders, Zera left her palace and returned to the third tier.

This time, in her bone worker's coat, with her hood back, she was recognized. Men, women, and children drew closer to her. A few thanked her. A few merely touched the edge of her coat as if they were touching a relic. Most stared with expressions that were a mix of so many emotions that she couldn't read them: exhaustion, pain, hope. Even some anger. She understood it all.

She reached the Bone Workers Guild headquarters and climbed the familiar steps. The massive doors stood open—mostly because they'd been smashed down and still hadn't been fixed—and the guards greeted her with: "Oh thank the bones, you've returned! They've been waiting for you."

Zera wasn't certain that was a good sign.

Walking with purpose, she swept through the main hall to the guild masters' offices in the back. She wasn't stopped, though many called out a greeting. Later, she told herself, she'd ask for a list of who had survived. For now, though, she needed to know what the guild wanted of her. And whether she was able—and willing—to give it.

She pushed through the door to find three masters she knew moderately well clustered around the grand master's desk. It was overflowing with papers, as if it had erupted. All three of them jumped away from the desk as she approached.

"Masters Sirelle, Pudone, and Lamar." She inclined her head. All three were well-respected bone workers, each of them advanced in years. She noted that Master Sirelle had wrinkles that folded onto other wrinkles, and Master Pudone held a black cane with a white-as-bone head.

Politely, they bowed their heads at her. "Master Zera," Master Sirelle said. "We are so pleased you have returned. Reports were . . . unclear as to your whereabouts."

"I needed time for recovery," Zera said. She didn't owe them an explanation, but she felt it might go smoother if they had one. "I was told Grand Master Lorn wanted to see me?"

The three looked at one another. "Not precisely," Master Pudone said carefully. "Master Lorn has resigned from his position as grand master, to spend more time with his son, he said. The council suggested it would be wise."

Ahh . . . Sensible of everyone involved. Lorn had shown a stunning lack of good judgment, even beyond what one could blame on Eklor's persuasion talisman. She hoped his replacement would be less susceptible to blackmail and, equally important, uninterested in Kreya's forbidden knowledge. She prepared herself to deny any knowledge of her friend's whereabouts. "Who is the new grand master?"

Master Sirelle said, "We were hoping that you would be."

The other two nodded vigorously.

Zera laughed and then stopped. "Oh. You're serious."

All three of them assured her they were, piled compliments and guilt trips on her, and continued talking until she contemplated putting her hands over her ears like a toddler. She thought about the damage suffered by the city and the guild, wondered at the list of the dead, and then remembered that Guine had believed she'd need a bigger office.

"He knew," she murmured.

The three masters stopped. "Excuse me?" Master Pudone asked.

Guine had known what they'd offer her. *And he knew I'd say yes.* "This was never my dream," she informed them. "I never wanted this."

"But the guild, the city, *Vos itself* needs this," Master Sirelle said. "We need you. You have the bone knowledge, the business skills, the reputation, the brains, the charisma, and the compassion to be an excellent guild master."

"And I am partial to flattery, so thank you for that." She flashed a smile at them, but it faded quickly. Walking to the grand master's desk, she touched it. She remembered Kreya's coming to her all those weeks ago, reminding Zera that she'd always wanted to make the world a better place, and what had she done instead? Become rich? Become successful? Become someone who never left the fifth tier? *That was before,* she thought. *Who am I now? Who do I want to be?*

Unlike Kreya, she didn't know how many years she had left ahead of her. It could be three or it could be thirty. She could spend them as a working bone wizard, making more talismans and making more money and basking in the victories of the past. She could spend them in semiretirement with her friends at Stran and Amurra's farmhouse or build her own place nearby. She could travel, see the world like Kreya and Jentt planned. She could even accompany them. Or she could stay right here, become a philanthropist, and pour her gold into rebuilding the city, starting with the first tier. Or she could try to do a little of all of it: Make time for herself, make time for her friends, make time to help those who needed her help. And possibly fail. But at least try.

How do I want to use the time I have?

The life she used to have . . . she knew she couldn't go back to that. It wasn't enough anymore. Maybe she'd outgrown it. It was funny to think she could still outgrow anything at her age. But everything she'd done since Kreya had come back into her life—*Yeah, I don't want to relive a lot of that*—had meaning. What she'd done had mattered. *That* was what she wanted out of her life. Meaning, and the power to keep her friends safe.

"I'll be guild master," Zera said.

KREYA AND JENTT WERE READY AFTER TWO MORE weeks at the farmhouse, but they waited a full three for Zera to return, at Kreya's insistence. "I promised," she'd told him.

She refused to think about what she'd do if Zera didn't return.

She and Jentt had said they wouldn't stay long. At night, they'd whisper their plans to see the world, to taste foods they'd never tasted, to see wonders they'd never imagined, to breathe air far different from that of home. But she wasn't going to miss her chance to say goodbye to her oldest and best friend. Some things were worth any amount of time. Some were too precious to ever take for granted.

Kreya was outside sweeping a dusting of snow from the

front step when she saw a speed-enhanced horse trot across the sloping fields. Zera's multicolored hair and coat were unmistakable, even from a distance. Wrapping her own coat tighter around her, Kreya headed across the field to meet her halfway.

Dismounting, Zera hugged her tightly. "Yay! You're not dead!" She pulled back. "Yes, I'm going to greet you that way from now on. I think it should be how I greet everyone."

Kreya smiled. "Not dead and actually feeling well rested. You?"

"I am not exactly well rested." Zera unsaddled her horse and set him free to graze. She then hooked her arm through Kreya's, and they proceeded to the farmhouse. "I seem to have become guild master, which comes with an alarming amount of work. I am delegating as much as humanly possible, and I've promoted Guine at least six times in as many days. Grand Master Lorn has 'retired,' and I do wish he'd been a lot better at his job before leaving me with his messes." She went on to describe the heap of work, all the decisions, all the tests that had to be overseen for new bone makers, all the reviews of requests, all the meetings, all the paperwork.

Only when she paused for breath did Kreya call, "Zera's back!"

Everyone came tumbling out of whatever part of the farmhouse they were in. Marso was already in the kitchen, an apron wrapped around his waist and cinnamon dotting his cheeks. Zera pronounced him delicious after she greeted him, and she told Stran he needed a bath—he'd been hauling wood for the stove and had worked up a sweat. "I brought you all more talismans," Zera said. "Only a few. I haven't had much time for carving them lately, but I thought they could be useful around the farm." She dumped a handful of jeweled bones onto the table. "Unfortunately, I won't be able to stay long. But I will visit again. I'll visit often. And I hope you can make trips to the city, too."

They settled into talking, both reminiscing and sharing news. Marso served his cinnamon buns, which were drenched in sticky sugar—Amurra and Stran were teaching him how to bake. The two children managed to smear half the sugar on their cheeks and half on their chairs. Kreya wasn't sure if any of it made it into their mouths.

As her ragtag family talked and laughed, Kreya looked at Jentt across the table. He smiled back, and she knew he felt the same thing she was feeling: full of cinnamon rolls, full of life, and full of love.

It's time, she thought.

They spent the rest of the day and the evening all together, and then in the morning, shortly before dawn, Kreya gathered up all she'd need for journeying. Jentt packed his belongings as well, and he stuffed several extra cinnamon buns, wrapped in paper, into a side pocket of his bag. While he finished up, Kreya walked outside to check the weather. The sky was pale gray, with lemon predawn tinting the eastern mountains. Frost lay across the ground, but the wind was tame and she didn't taste any rain or snow in the air.

She saw a blur out of the corner of her eye, and suddenly Zera was in front of her. "So your plan is to disappear from our lives for three years and then die without us?"

"Less than three years now," Kreya pointed out.

Zera snorted to show what she thought of that statement.

"And I'm not leaving to die," Kreya said. She tried to find the words to explain. "I'm leaving to live. We have plenty of sunsets and sunrises left. We're going to see them from every part of the world we can."

"Will you come back?" Zera asked.

Kreya thought about saying she couldn't make any promises. She didn't know how far they'd travel or what they'd encounter on the way. Even a bone reader couldn't predict all the possibilities, so she couldn't make any guarantees. But she *could* make plans and have intentions. "Yes, of course I will."

"Fine." Zera sighed. "I suppose I couldn't have expected everything to stay the same and for you all to stay put here, for me to visit whenever I can. But I'll have Marso predict your return, and I'll ask Stran and Amurra to send word the second you two walk back into our lives."

"Excellent plan. I couldn't have come up with a better one myself," Kreya said. "No wonder they made you guild master."

"I can't tell if you're serious or mocking me, but I will be an excellent guild master."

"Of course you will." Kreya had no doubt about that.

Side by side, they looked out across the farm, toward the mountains. The mist rose off the valley to make clouds that ringed the peaks.

"Where will you go?" Zera asked.

"I think it's better if no one knows," Kreya said. "That way, no one will be tempted to find me and ask me to use the forbidden spell. But I want to see the Tririan Waterfall again. And we both want to sail on an ocean. Never done that before. I want to walk someplace where you can't see mountains in the distance. Meet people who have never heard of Eklor, who only know of the Bone War as a distant story from far away."

Zera wrapped an arm around Kreya's shoulder. "It sounds absolutely exhausting with far too much camping involved. But if it's what you want, then . . . I'm happy for you."

They spoke for a while more, trading promises and plans

and dreams, and then Kreya went inside to say farewell to the others: Marso, Stran, Amurra, and the kids. Hugging them all, Kreya and Jentt both promised to visit and to send word as often as they could.

While Jentt packed a few final meals, courtesy of Stran and Amurra, Kreya spoke with her remaining constructs and gave them a choice. They chittered among one another and then made clear their decision: some would stay and continue to watch over the farmhouse and the people they loved, and some—the bird construct and a handful of rag dolls—would come with the two of them into the unknown. The other rag dolls clustered around the children, prepared to protect them from whatever life threw their way.

At last, with all details settled and goodbyes complete, Kreya put on her coat with many pockets, and hand in hand, she and Jentt walked outside into the sunrise.

And they kept walking as the sun rose and set, and rose and set, again and again.

ACKNOWLEDGMENTS

We all know how the stories go:

Someone saves the day. The end.

Someone rides off into the sunset. The end.

Someone kisses the love of their life. The end.

But our stories—our real stories—don't end after a Great Moment. We keep living, day after day, until our last day. And sometimes our story doesn't go the way we thought it would, for better or for worse. Sometimes it's terrifying how much of our future is unknown and out of our control. We never know how much time we will have or if we've made the right choices on the way. That's why I wrote *The Bone Maker*.

This book is about life after "the end." It's about second chances.

It's me saying to you, "Keep living your story."

This story wouldn't exist without the efforts of many incredible people. I'd like to thank my wonderful editor, David Pomerico, who always sees exactly what a book needs and whose brilliant insights helped shape Kreya's tale, and my amazing agent, Andrea Somberg, who is unfailingly supportive and encouraging. I'd also like to thank Jennifer Brehl, Mireya Chiriboga, Chris Connolly, Liza Cortright, Kara Coughlin, Angela

Craft, Michael Flynn, Pam Jaffee, Ronnie Kutys, Lainey Mays, Debbie Mercer, Aja Pollock, Virginia Stanley, Evangelos Vasilakis, Kayleigh Webb, and all the other phenomenal people at HarperCollins who brought this book to life!

And thank you with all my heart to my husband, my children, my family, and my friends. I will treasure you beyond the end of all our stories.

ABOUT THE AUTHOR

Sarah Beth Durst is the award-winning author of over twenty fantasy books for adults, teens, and kids, including the Queens of Renthia series, *Drink Slay Love*, and *Spark*. She won an American Library Association Alex Award and a Mythopoeic Fantasy Award and has been a finalist for the Science Fiction and Fantasy Writers of America's Andre Norton Award three times. She is a graduate of Princeton University and lives in Stony Brook, New York, with her husband, her children, and her ill-mannered cat.

More titles from Sarah Beth Durst

The Queen of Blood
Book One of The Queens of Renthia
The spirits that reside within this land want to rid it of all humans. One woman stands between these malevolent spirits and the end of humankind: the queen. She alone has the magical power to prevent the spirits from destroying every man, woman, and child. But queens are still only human, and no matter how strong or good they are, the threat of danger always looms.

The Reluctant Queen
Book Two of The Queens of Renthia
In *The Queen of Blood*, Daleina used her strength and skill to survive the malevolent nature spirits of Renthia and claim the crown. But now she is hiding a terrible secret: she is dying. If she leaves the world before a new heir is ready, the spirits that inhabit her realm will once again run wild, destroying her cities and slaughtering her people.

The Queen of Sorrow
Book Three of the Queens of Renthia
The battle between vicious spirits and strong-willed queens that started in the award-winning *The Queen of Blood* and continued in the stunning *The Reluctant Queen* comes to a gripping conclusion in the final volume of Sarah Beth Durst's Queens of Renthia trilogy . . .

The Deepest Blue
Tales of Renthia
The natural magic of the classic *The Island of the Blue Dolphins* meets the danger and courage of *The Hunger Games* in this dazzling, intricate stand-alone fantasy novel set in award-winning author Sarah Beth Durst's beloved world of Renthia.

Race the Sands
A Novel
In this epic stand-alone fantasy, the acclaimed author of the Queens of Renthia series introduces an imaginative new world in which a pair of strong and determined women risk their lives battling injustice, corruption, and deadly enemies in their quest to become monster-racing champions.